MAKE ME, SIR

MASTERS OF THE SHADOWLANDS: 5

CHERISE SINCLAIR

VanScoy Publishing Group

ABOUT MAKE ME, SIR

> *I don't think there is any other option for me than 5 stars. I'd give it a whole lot more if I could. I loved Marcus and Gabi's story. It held me entranced and made me laugh, cry, and scream...but all the while I was awed at how Cherise Sinclair has written such an amazing and original story...AGAIN!* **Top Pick!** - Romance Reviews

Her job is to make his life miserable. His job is to make her submit. Whose heart will surrender first?

Across the country, rebellious BDSM submissives are being systematically kidnapped, one from each club. When her friend falls prey to the slavers, FBI victim specialist Gabrielle volunteers to be bait in a club not yet hit: the Shadowlands.

She finds that being a bratty sub comes naturally, especially when she gets to twit the appallingly conservative Master of the trainees. But she soon discovers he's not as stuffy as she'd thought. Or as mean. She'd expected punishment, even humiliation, but she sure never expected to fall in love with a damned lawyer.

Courtesy of a prima donna ex-wife, Marcus loathes disobedient submissives. When the club owner insists he admit an incredibly bratty trainee, he's furious. But as he comes to know Gabrielle and sees the alluring sweetness beneath the sass, he starts to fall for her.

Unfortunately, Marcus isn't the only one who believes the feisty redhead is a prize worth capturing. And in the world of the slaver, such treasure is worth a hefty fee.

> *If I had to pick one book to take with me to a desert island, this would be the one. It has a strong, but vulnerable heroine, an overprotective, dominant hero and an outstanding story line.* - Guilty Pleasures

Make Me, Sir

ISBN 978-0-9861195-0-7
Published by VanScoy Publishing Group
Cover Artist: April Martinez

TO MY READERS

The books I write are fiction, not reality, and as in most romantic fiction, the romance is compressed into a very, very short time period.

You, my darlings, live in the real world, and I want you to take a little more time in your relationships. Good Doms don't grow on trees, and there are some strange people out there. So while you're looking for that special Dom, please, be careful.

When you find him, realize he can't read your mind. Yes, frightening as it might be, you're going to have to open up and talk to him. And you listen to him, in return. Share your hopes and fears, what you want from him, what scares you spitless. Okay, he may try to push your boundaries a little—he's a Dom, after all—but you will have your safe word. You will have a safe word, am I clear? Use protection. Have a back-up person. Communicate.

Remember: safe, sane, and consensual.

Know that I'm hoping you find that special, loving person who will understand your needs and hold you close.

And while you're looking or even if you have already found

your dearheart, come and hang out with the Masters of the Shadowlands.

Love,

Cherise

CHAPTER ONE

Her eyes puffy from crying, mouth set with determination, Gabrielle Renard walked down the hallway of the FBI's Tampa field division, hunting for the correct office. There it was. She stopped and took a careful breath—*I can do this*—then straightened her shoulders and shoved the door open.

It was a typically bland room with coffee-stained, brown carpeting and off-white walls, and the scent of sweat, coffee, and overly musky cologne sure didn't help her stomach. A metal desk with a computer occupied the right side. On the left, two men sat at a small conference table, papers strewn across the surface.

One had his back to her, and with dismay, she realized why the cologne smelled familiar. Agent Preston Rhodes. Only three or four inches over her five feet five, the pale, brown-haired creep had the whiny personality—and the morals—of the hyenas in *The Lion King*. During her one-month stint in Tampa last year, he'd even tried to coerce a victim's sister into bed.

The other man had black hair and eyes, an olive complexion, and deeply carved lines bracketing his mouth. He frowned at her and asked, "Can I help you?" in a clipped New England accent.

Rhodes turned in his chair and scowled at her. "What are you doing here, Renard?" He glanced at the other man. "She's a victim specialist with the Miami field office."

Ignoring him, Gabi spoke to the dark-haired agent. "Are you in charge of the investigation of the women kidnapped in Atlanta?"

Rhodes glared. "What the—"

The man silenced Rhodes with a look. "I'm Special Agent Galen Kouros. Why?"

"I want to be one of the decoys." *And you're going to let me.*

"Do you now? Just how did you happen to hear about them?" His icy voice sent an answering chill up her spine. She let her own anger wash through her.

"One of the kidnapped women is a friend, and her mother called me after your visit." Weeping hysterically, begging for help from Kim's FBI friend. Gabi had driven to Atlanta for information from Kim's mom and also the local FBI office. None of it had been good. Gabi looked away, blinking back tears. "I found out another young woman had been kidnapped and shot."

"The only details released to the news were that a woman had died of a gunshot wound on the freeway. How did you get more?" The agent leaned back in his chair, studying her.

"There are rumors here and there." Especially in the seething Atlanta field office. Not so easy here. But during her brief stay in Tampa, she'd discovered that one of the secretaries loved to gossip. She'd also told Gabi that Rhodes's very appropriate nickname was Dickhead.

Kouros pointed to a chair across from Rhodes. "Sit."

New Englanders could be so brusque. He needed to meet a southern gentleman and learn some civility. But she obediently took a seat.

"Tell me what you know. All of it."

"A total of four women, including Kim, were kidnapped in Atlanta. All members of BDSM clubs. The last one escaped on a freeway by running out into oncoming traffic. She died of a gunshot wound before the ambulance arrived. But she managed to tell a trucker a few things." She must have been in agony. Terrified. Gabi swallowed.

"Go on," Kouros snapped.

"Apparently the kidnapper said more women were to be kidnapped in Tampa." She frowned. "Um, the last delivery of women is August twenty-ninth, and then they'll hold a slave auction." *They'll sell Kim.* She gathered her thoughts. "You're putting female agents as decoys in four Tampa fetish clubs, hoping the kidnapper will target one." It seemed a little far-fetched. Why would he go after them and not another woman in the club?

"You're remarkably well-informed." He hadn't moved as she talked, his stillness a contrast to Rhodes's fidgeting. "I can see there are some loose tongues in this office."

Dickhead stiffened.

Ignoring him, Kouros eyed Gabi. "What qualifications do you have for playing a decoy, Ms. Renard? I'll admit you're motivated—and because of that I doubt you can be objective. You're the right age. You're pretty enough, probably smart enough. But you're not an agent; you're support staff—a social worker. Why should I use you instead of an agent?"

At first she hadn't seen any way to help. She was a counselor, not a field agent. Then she'd checked the agents they planned to use. "It doesn't matter if I'm objective or not. I'm not going to work the case, just play decoy. Second, you only have three agents for decoys, not four. As far as I know, none have visited BDSM clubs before."

His face hardened at the further evidence of how much information she'd obtained, and she continued hurriedly, "I have experience." *A little and long ago, but who's counting?*

He sat forward like a cat scenting a mouse. "You're submissive?"

She nodded.

"You're not seriously considering using her," Rhodes burst out. "She'd blow the whole operation."

As Kouros studied her, his gaze drifted over her face, lingered on her cheek. "How'd you get the scar?"

The ugly memory sliced her as easily as the knife had sliced her flesh. Her hands fisted. "Wrong place during a gang war." And she'd promised herself she'd never willingly get near violence again. *How plans do change.*

"You're braver than you appear." Kouros actually smiled. "You might just do, Ms. Renard. As it happens, I need a decoy for the Shadowlands."

Rhodes stared at him. "You think you could get that asshole owner to admit *her*? She's not an agent."

"Zachary Grayson had a good point. An inexperienced, nonsubmissive woman might manage to pass in a busy public place, but the members of his club wouldn't be fooled." Kouros turned to her again. "The Shadowlands is a private, very exclusive BDSM club outside Tampa. Assuming we can talk him into it, the owner will set you up as a trainee sub."

She opened her mouth to agree, but he held up his hand.

"You're missing one vital piece of information the victim gave us—and we confirmed. I want you to think twice before we go any further. You see, the kidnapper is targeting only blatantly rebellious submissives. Noisy ones. The buyers want the pleasure of breaking their spirits."

"No. That can't—" *No, not Kim.* Her stomach twisted.

Kouros's face softened. "You're not getting the point, Gabrielle. I'm talking about *your* involvement. The decoys will have to demonstrate disobedient, insolent behavior. If you're familiar with the lifestyle, you know how a dom will react."

Gabi stiffened. Doms wouldn't tolerate rudeness. They might just stop the scene and let the sub go—or might discipline her.

"Ah. I see you know." A corner of Kouros's mouth rose. "Grayson says only a few Shadowlands doms like brats, so either you'd end up sitting alone with no chance to attract attention or he'd need to get you into the trainee program...which forces the trainer to deal with you, whether he wants to or not."

She nodded. To be dealt with. Her hands had gone clammy.

"Another fact. Despite their protests, the club owners are sworn to secrecy, so aside from the owner and Rhodes, no one else there will know you're playing a part. That includes the dom in charge of the trainees, who, according to Grayson, is a hard-ass when it comes to disrespectful submissives. Are you sure, Gabrielle?"

She clasped her hands together, hoping to hide her trembling. Knowing she'd be setting herself up as a target for a murderer had terrified her so much she'd thrown up before leaving the motel.

Now this. To beg for punishment from a dom who didn't know she was playing a part? *Oh God.*

But for Kim? All through college, Kim had shaken her awake from nightmares of the past, listened to her, comforted her. Now Kim was *living* in a nightmare.

Gabi raised her chin. "I'm sure."

Marcus Atherton walked into the Shadowlands entry and nodded at the domme and security guard across the small room. Down the center, his five trainee submissives knelt nicely in a line. He strolled around them, checking that clothing was neat, appropriate, and seductive. "Y'all look very nice tonight," he said. "I'm proud of you."

Vivacious Sally, Goth Dara, and sweet, gay Austin had been there before he'd taken over the program last spring. After he and the owner, Z, had talked at length, they'd added Uzuri, with her gorgeous, chocolate-colored skin and the soul of a prankster, and a newer bisexual, Tanner, who wanted a mistress or a couple.

"I will not be in charge of you this evening." Z's voice-mail message had requested that he free himself up tonight, but hadn't said why. "So Mistress Olivia has kindly agreed to supervise y'all."

Their unhappy expressions warmed his dom's heart. They'd become as attached to him as he was to them. When he saw mischief rising in Sally's eyes, he added, "You best be nice to Mistress Olivia, or next time I'll ask Mistress Anne to watch over you."

They actually paled.

He had a mind to tell Anne—the sadistic mistress would enjoy their response immensely. "I'll have an eye on all of you. Don't let me down now."

They murmured, "No, Sir" and "We won't, Master Marcus." He nodded and stepped back to let Olivia take his place.

The hefty domme smiled at the trainees. "First, let me run through my rules." She slapped a switch against her tight latex pants, and the movement drew every gaze.

Chuckling, Marcus stepped into the main club room and waited for his eyes to adjust to the dim lighting from the chandeliers and wall sconces. This early, no one played on the equipment against the walls; no murmur of conversation came from the sitting areas. The lingering scent of cleansers mingled with the fragrance of leather.

Within an hour, the Shadowlands would rumble to life. Odd how much he'd come to love this club.

He looked around and spotted Z. Dressed in his usual black silk shirt and tailored slacks, the owner of the Shadowlands sat at the circular bar in the center of the room, talking to the bartender and his submissive.

As Marcus walked over, Cullen grinned. "Hey, buddy, I met your new trainee. Great hair." The bartender's voice echoed in the huge, silent room.

"What new trainee?" Marcus gave Z a quizzical glance.

Z frowned. "I'd hoped you'd arrive earlier, Marcus. I certainly didn't intend to spring this on you."

"The trial ran late." And had been satisfying as hell. By the time he finished his closing argument, the jury had been of one mind, and the bastard who'd preyed on young boys hadn't had a chance. Guilty. The sense of satisfaction in knowing he'd taken one more monster off the streets made all the late nights worthwhile. "What's going on?"

"I'm sorry about the lack of discussion, but I have another trainee for you." Z nodded toward the back. "I told her to wait for you by the chain station."

Marcus stared at him. They always talked over any addition to the trainee program. And now a new one, just like that?

Z took a sip of his drink. "I appreciate your taking Gabrielle on, Marcus. She's rather misbehaved, and she's going to need a firm hand. Please keep her for a month—say the end of August—before you give up on her."

Anger started a sullen glow in his gut. Z hadn't asked a favor; he'd given an order. *What kind of bullshit is this?* From the set of Z's jaw, there would be no discussion about refusing this trainee. Marcus could either take on the submissive or step aside as trainer.

But he liked supervising the trainees, helping them broaden their education as submissives, helping them find a dom to match their needs. And the volunteer position filled his need to give back to the community. He tapped his fingers on the bar and considered his options. Perhaps he should meet the new trainee before burning his bridges behind him. As he'd slowly come to know the other Masters, he realized he'd never found a club that suited him so well.

"I'll work with her." *For now.* Then he gave Z a steady look and drew his line in the sand. "You are the owner, sir, but they're my trainees. I would be most grateful if you could remember that." *Don't do it again.*

Gray eyes level, Z tilted his head in acknowledgement and slid the trainee's paperwork down the bar top.

With a grin, the bartender set a drink on the bar. "You know, Marcus, you say *fuck you* almost as politely as the boss."

Marcus huffed a laugh. No one stayed riled up around Cullen very long. He scanned the papers, giving Cullen the high points. A short summary would go on the bulletin board for the other Shadowlands Masters since they all participated in sub training. "No medical disease or problems. No phobias she's willing to admit to. She doesn't want any serious pain, piercing, scarring. Bondage and sex are okayed." Fairly normal for a trainee's choices. "Would you please give me a set of trainee cuffs and ribbons?"

The bartender rummaged in the shelves below the bar top, then handed over a pair of gold-colored leather wrist cuffs and a box of colored ribbons.

Marcus added the appropriate ribbons to the cuffs, the colors indicating what the trainee would permit: yellow for mild pain, blue for bondage, green for sex. No red ribbons for severe pain. "Many of the choices have question marks. The information about her past experience is sketchy." He glanced at Z, hoping for an explanation.

"I don't know much. I'm simply doing someone a favor." Z gave Cullen a faint smile. "Does that sound familiar?"

"It does." Cullen's laugh boomed out as he glanced at his submissive, a tall, golden-haired sub tough enough to handle the giant dom. He waggled his eyebrows. "Sometimes it's even worth the effort."

Andrea wrinkled her nose at her dom and said, "Thanks, Señor."

Marcus remembered that Cullen had taken her on as a favor when he had charge of the trainees. Well, maybe this new trainee would prove as delightful. "Did Gabrielle herself request that you let her into the program?"

"She wanted in, but a friend—Galen—did the asking for her. He hopes that as a trainee she can find what she needs. He says she's quite badly behaved, and he recommends you not go easy on her." Z frowned. "She might prove a challenge even for you, Marcus."

A difficult submissive. Wonderful. "I'll do what I can. In fact, I'd best go make her acquaintance and get started." He clipped the cuffs to the back of his belt, nodded to the two men, and smiled at Andrea, remembering what a run she'd given Cullen before he'd reeled her in. Way too much work. Maybe Z was wrong, and this new trainee would be quiet and sweet and obedient.

She wasn't by the chain station.

Marcus frowned and looked around, finally spotting her in the hallway for the theme rooms, staring in at the medical room setup. She appeared mesmerized by the gyn table, enema bags, and shelves filled with speculums, dilators, and other fun toys. After walking over silently, he leaned a shoulder against the wall and crossed his arms, taking the time to study her.

Not ugly, but not particularly beautiful either, at least from what he could see. Medium height, nicely padded. A long blue skirt hid her ass and legs. He approved of the black bustier, which pushed up a fine set of breasts. Her shaggy-styled hair barely reached her shoulders. She was a redhead like Nolan's sub, but more of a strawberry blonde, and her coloring was so pale that she almost glowed. Not a freckle in sight. A light sunburn had pinkened her shoulders and breasts, and he smiled. How far down did the burn go?

His gaze dropped. Submissives went barefoot in the club, and she had pretty feet, but she'd painted her toenails a vibrant blue. *Blue?*

"Did you get yourself lost?" he asked.

She jumped and spun so quickly her skirt wrapped around her legs. Apparently she'd dyed one fluffy lock of hair on the left to match her toenails. A long scar, a shade lighter than her skin, ran from her left cheekbone to the corner of her mouth. Despite the whiteness indicating it was an old injury, the sight bothered him on a visceral level, that a sub coming into his care had been hurt.

"Oh, hey. Hi." She shook out her skirt and grinned at him. "I'm just poking around. New place and all that."

"I see." Interesting face, he thought. Not a model's face with jutting cheekbones and sharp chin, hers was all soft curves. Not beautiful, but...friendly. When she smiled, dimples flashed in her cheeks.

But what was she doing by the theme rooms? He asked gently, "Were you instructed to wait here?"

"Ah." The grin disappeared, and a wary expression shaded her wide brown eyes. "Master Z said the trainer would come back to fetch me."

"And did he say, 'Wait here,' or did he give you permission to wander around?"

When she blushed, her ivory complexion turned a delightful pink. If nothing else, he could look forward to enjoying that.

"He said, 'Wait here.'" She waved her hand toward the chain station. "Guess I shouldn't have moved, huh?"

Had she no idea of how to address a dom? How to obey? "I do believe that might have been a mistake." And so might this trainee Z had dumped on him.

CHAPTER TWO

The model-gorgeous guy in the suit didn't like her. Gabrielle saw that already, but no real problem. The only one she had to impress was Master Marcus, and hopefully the suit wouldn't tell on her. The man positively oozed rich and powerful, so he must be a big shot in the club. "I guess I'd better get back there before my boss arrives."

"Who?"

"Master Marcus. I'm waiting for him."

"You most certainly possess a poor idea of how to wait." He stared at her for another minute, disapproval radiating from him. "I have a notion that introductions are in order before you work your way further into trouble. I am Master Marcus."

She choked. *Oh, no. This day is so not going well.* "Ah." She cleared her throat and tried again. "Nice to meet you. Um—"

"And might I ask your name?" he asked politely. Too politely.

She took a second look at him, at his fancy tailored suit. Dark gray with pinstripes. Oh please, like she'd really believe he was a dom at all? "Gabrielle Anderson. Are you sure you're Master Marcus?"

He cocked his head. The guy was way too good-looking. Tall,

broad-shouldered, lean. His hair, a rich brown shading to gold on the ends, was flawlessly styled. Definitely a perfect person like her parents. *Gag.* Even his tan wasn't leathery, but just dark enough to set off incredibly blue eyes. Very sharp blue eyes, in fact, and turning colder by the second.

"Why would you think I'm not Master Marcus?" he asked.

Well, good grief. She waved a hand at him and kept the *duh* from slipping out. Just in case he really was Master Marcus. Maybe he hadn't changed yet or something. "The suit? Where are your leathers or latex or...biker jacket or vest? And black? Did you forget to wear black?"

He stared for a second, as if she'd turned into a drooling idiot, and then simply roared. Deep, full laughter—amazing coming from someone who looked like he should have a stick up his ass.

She felt heat flooding her face and decided she really didn't like him. Maybe he was the club accountant or administrator or something. Shifting her weight, she looked past him. Hopefully the Marcus guy would arrive soon. She needed to get all established before the arrival of the kidnapper—the *unsub*, as a real agent would call him. She frowned. *Unsub* sounded too much like *fake submissive. That would be me*. Maybe she'd call him a *perp* instead.

"Best you tell me about your previous experience in BDSM," the suit said, and damn but he appeared totally different when he smiled. How many women had he destroyed with that devastating dimple in his left cheek and crease in the right? "Was it mostly in downtown clubs? Perhaps of the Goth variety?"

"Well, yeees. Why?" Several years ago too, but that's not what she'd written on her application.

He motioned for her to precede him down the hall, and when she stepped in front of him, his hand closed on her nape. Firmly, as if she were a stray dog. "I do believe you'll find a private club a mite different. A wider age range, diverse incomes, assorted tastes. Many doms here wear leathers and black; some prefer other attire."

Her stomach sank with the authoritative way he'd gripped her neck. No accountant from the back would act like this—she'd run into a dom. In a suit. Who called himself...? "You really are Master Marcus?"

"I'm afraid so, darlin'." He stopped at the place where chains hung from the low rafter and released her, only to walk around her slowly as if she stood on a display stand. "Is all your experience in public clubs?"

"Uh-huh." In her college days, she'd pop into a club, have some fun, and maybe take someone home. But she hadn't indulged since then. She'd set her sights on the FBI from day one and wasn't about to mess up her chances by doing anything less than respectable.

"I see." He tapped the ribbing on her bustier. "Remove that, please."

She stared at him. Just like that? *I only met you, dammit.* She hesitated, but the merciless look in those blue eyes kicked her into gear. After undoing the hooks, she tossed the bustier onto a chair outside the ropes that fenced off the scene area. She forced her arms to stay at her sides and tried to ignore the air-conditioned draft on her bare breasts.

"Very pretty." When he brushed sure fingers over her shoulder, into the hollow below her collarbone, and over the upper curve of one breast, her body woke up from her breasts all the way to her pussy—and that was damn disconcerting considering she didn't even like the guy. But he had that ruthless attitude going for him—the dominant edge that put butterflies into her stomach as if she'd actually swallowed the fluffy bugs.

"And did you play somewhere else?" he asked. "Privately?"

Her cheeks warmed. "Not...really. I might have gone home with a man after, but for kinky stuff, I stayed in the clubs. More public or something."

"I see. You didn't trust any dom enough to let him restrain you without other people around."

"Ah." She'd never thought of it like that but—okay. He was right. She nodded.

"I prefer to have verbal answers," he said ever so softly. "'Yes, Sir' will serve for now."

She couldn't keep the shiver from running down her spine. The guy wielded a razor-sharp voice, no matter how soft it was. "Yes, Sir."

"That sounds very pretty, sugar," he said, and the caress in his voice turned all her bones into a seriously mushy state. Until he added, "Remove the skirt, please."

She looked up, and his eyes could be just as lethal as his tone. Why did he bother to say 'please'? She stepped out of the skirt, wishing she'd done more time in the gym. Done any time in the gym. Maybe walked a little at least. Nothing like a fat ass to impress a man.

But hey, this wasn't about impressing the fussy dom. She'd come here to lure a kidnapper—a killer—into a trap. She shivered.

His eyes narrowed. "Do you have a problem with being unclothed?"

Hell. *Keep your mind on business, Gabi*. "No, Sir. Just cold, Sir."

"Um-hmm." He walked around her again, inspecting her as if she were the star at a dog show. Totally insulting—and yet she felt her nipples contracting to dagger points and a disconcerting wetness between her thighs. She shifted to put her legs closer together.

"Master Z requested I take you on. Did you read the rules for the trainees?"

"Um. Yes." She caught the hint of ice in his eyes and added a hasty, "Sir."

He unhooked a set of golden-colored leather cuffs from the back of his belt. After buckling them on her wrists, he carefully checked the fit and then attached her left cuff to a chain dangling from the rafter. "The safe word for the trainees is red," he said as he reached for another chain and did her right arm. He kept the chains long enough so that her arms could remain at waist level. "I want for you to use it if you become overwhelmed in any way, from fear, pain...whatever. It will bring the dungeon monitors a-running."

"If I use a safe word, does that mean everything is off?" She couldn't afford to blow this.

His face softened. "No, sugar. It means I stop whatever we're doing and we sit down and chat for a bit."

"Oh. Okay. Good. Um, Sir." *Can I really see this through?* This lethal dom wasn't anything like the ones she'd played with in the downtown clubs. Fear wavered inside her, and she shoved it away. Mostly.

She saw his gaze on her and realized her fingers were tracing the scar on her cheek. He pulled her hand down and enfolded it in his warm one. "Gabrielle, do you have a problem with bondage you didn't mention on the application?" he asked.

"No, Sir." When he didn't move, she added, "Really. I'm just a little nervous, Sir."

"All right then." He walked to the wall, and the chains attached to her wrist cuffs began to tighten, pulling her arms over her head. He stopped before she had to go up on tiptoe.

She tried to be grateful for the small concession, but suddenly she felt...naked. Really naked, much more than when she'd taken off her clothes. Then she'd worried about how she looked. Now... now she felt the intensity of his gaze as he strolled around her again.

"What...what are you going to do?"

"I'm fixin' to acquaint myself with my new trainee's body as we have a chat." His fingers ran over her sunburned shoulders, and he murmured, "Sunscreen, darlin'—you best use more of it."

A pause. He shot one of those stabbing blue looks at her.

"Yes, Sir."

"There you go. That does sound nice." He played with her hair, fingered the blue streak and shook his head, then ran his finger over her lips.

As her mouth tingled, she couldn't help but wonder what he'd taste like. Could he kiss? Would he?

He caught the direction of her stare, and his lips quirked. Don't react, she told herself, yet when he stroked his hand down her neck, her breasts seemed to swell in anticipation.

"Our trainees are long-standing submissives. The membership knows that," he said and frowned at her. "Your application didn't contain much information on your previous experience in the lifestyle, and I'm wondering if you're ready to jump into something like this."

"I have experience." *A little bit*. "I'll be fine."

"There is no easing-in period for trainees, you know."

"That's okay," she said quickly. "Don't treat me special or go slow or anything. I want to jump right in."

His eyes narrowed, and then he shook his head and let it go. "Tell me why you want to be a trainee?"

His hand cupped her breast, and she shivered at the gentleness of his touch and the slight abrasion of his skin. His fingers weren't soft and pampered like she'd expected. Hadn't Master Z said the trainer was an attorney? "Why don't you talk like a lawyer?"

He blinked and smiled. "I grew up in a small town in Georgia. But I can sound quite lawyerly in court." He caressed her breasts for a minute. "Gabrielle, I do believe I asked you a question."

Oh. How was she supposed to remember a cover story when he was...groping her? Hell of an interrogation technique—she'd have to recommend it to the field agents. "Um, I want to learn more about the lifestyle and myself." Master Z had mentioned some of the right reasons. "I want to hook up with a nice dom, but in the clubs, they seemed mostly interested in one-night stands, and I was never sure who to trust."

He watched her intently as his thumb rubbed over her nipple. She could feel it bunching and wanted to squirm. "What type of dom? Are you hoping to be a slave?"

Do I look insane? Then again she stood here in the middle of a BDSM club. Maybe she *was* nuts. "No. But I'd like to find someone who is more than a weekend dom," she said, and the statement might have been true if she participated in the lifestyle. But she'd left her kinky side behind with college. *Respectable"R"Me.*

His hands curved around her waist, and the fact that he was working his way...down...created all sorts of funny feelings in her. Would he actually touch her...?

"You marked yes to sex on the trainee form," he said.

God, talk about getting right to the point. She hadn't thought it through until Master Z had bluntly explained what she could expect if she checked yes for that option. And she'd decided absolutely not. But during the briefing talks, Special Agent Rhodes, the asshole, had carefully avoided the subject of *her* having sex, but repeatedly mentioned that all the kidnapped submissives had had public sex in the clubs. She couldn't afford prudish behavior.

Besides, she'd done incredibly stupid things in her teens and in college, including one-night stands just for a thrill. She could damn well manage to have sex with a few strangers now if it meant she might save Kim.

It still made her feel a little...dirty. *I'm not that kind of girl anymore*. "Sex is okay. Sure."

His eyes narrowed. "You've just run smack-dab into one of my rules: don't lie to your dom. If you're feeling uncertain, say so." He stroked his fingers down and across her hips. "Try again, Gabrielle."

"Oh." She swallowed, trying not to get distracted as his hand massaged her butt. *Sex*. Right now her body yelled for it. But her head... Dammit, she couldn't let her squeamish behavior derail this operation. "It's only nerves, Sir. I want sex."

"Mmmhmm." He avoided her pussy and knelt to slide his hands down her legs, hopefully not seeing the dimples and bulges in her thighs. At least she had good calves and ankles. He touched her blue toenails and snorted softly.

A stiff, conservative lawyer. Just like her father.

As he rose and his firm hands ran back up, he ordered, "Tell me about your experience with oral, vaginal, and anal."

Why couldn't he show some conservatism with his questions? Whatever happened to modesty? Privacy? With a sinking sensation, she knew the man wouldn't allow any, either physically or emotionally. *Pull up your big-girl panties, Gabi*. "Yes to the first two. I've... One guy wanted to do the other, and I wouldn't."

He nodded. "So you have had some experience. We'll discuss anal sex some other time." He stroked a finger over the tender crease between her hip and thigh and then patted her pussy. "I will require you to keep yourself bare with no stubble. Is that clear?"

Her life was changing faster than she found comfortable. Would the Internet have instructions on how to shave down there without slicing off something essential? "Yes, Sir."

"To continue: how about other doms touching you? Or taking you? Or women? Members can request a trainee for a scene, which might involve anything from light sensation play to bondage, pain, and/or sex."

"I think—"

He touched her pussy, and she gasped as the low heat inside her turned to flames. He gave her a devastating smile that creased his right cheek. "You're wet, Gabrielle. I do like that." He drew his finger up slowly, stopping on the very top of her clit, and she could almost feel it pulsing against his touch. She swayed, grateful for the support of the chains.

He'd only touched her. Hell, she'd had *sex* with guys and not gotten this turned on.

"Answer me," he said.

"Damn you, how am I supposed to remember what you asked?"

His chuckle sounded as low and smooth as his voice. "You might not, but here's your next rule: a submissive is always, always respectful to a dom. Any dom, but especially her trainer...if she knows what's good for her."

His damn finger remained right there, making her world spin. "Yes, Sir."

He caught her gaze. Held it. "I will punish you if you rile me up by being disrespectful, Gabrielle. Am I clear?"

"Yes, Sir." If she moved, just a little, pushed her hips toward his hand, would he notice? Would it make—

"Stay still."

She closed her eyes, trying not to whine like a baby. Mean bastard to get her worked up and not finish the job.

"Now answer my question."

What the hell had he asked? Oh, other doms, touching, taking, women. "The thought of doing anything with a woman squicks me out. Didn't I mark that?"

"I like to double-check what subs write," he said. He straightened, moving closer until she could feel the heat of his body, until his eyes filled her world. "You'll scene with different doms, you realize. How about more than one man?"

"I expected the variety of doms." Master Z had warned her, again and again. "But I've never had two at the same time." *Except once.* The horrible memory shriveled everything up inside her. Could she tolerate more than one man touching her? And yet, what if she liked the men? A tiny bit of excitement slid through her, and she couldn't tell if her shiver came from disgust or anticipation.

His keen eyes didn't miss her reaction. "If I put you between two doms, what will you do, Gabrielle?"

Hell. She bit her lip. "I'm not sure... I guess I'll try?"

His smile warmed her right to the bone. "Good answer." He tugged on her hair, still smiling. "You had any experience with flogging? Canes? Spankings?"

She swallowed hard. "Spanking. A really soft flogger. Not...the rest."

"All right. You had question marks beside most of the impact play. When I see question marks on a limit list, I take it as a request to explore further."

Her hands went damp. She'd seen a lot of scary stuff on the application, and yet, as he watched her with utter self-confidence, she figured—maybe—she might manage okay. Somehow he made her feel as if she could trust him not to go too far.

But she hadn't seen him angry yet. How would he react when she disobeyed him? She had to behave like a bratty submissive; that was the whole point.

"Spread your legs," he said.

Wanting to get a hint of how he'd respond, she scowled and said, "I thought you told me not to move."

Although he slapped her thigh lightly, the sting ran right to her clit. "Best apologize, and do as I asked. I do not like and I will not tolerate bratty behavior."

Oh God, he wasn't going to give her much leeway at all for acting as a decoy. Her worries ratcheted up another notch. "I'm sorry, Master Marcus."

Her thigh burned, and despite her anxiety, excitement fizzed through her veins, even more than when he'd touched her clit. More? Because he'd swatted her? *Please tell me I didn't like getting whacked.*

As if he had all day for her to think about things, he waited with his arms crossed. When she finally opened her thighs, he gave her an approving smile. Curving his fingers over her hip, he got a firm grip. His other hand touched her pussy, and she tensed as her anticipation ratcheted up a notch. His fingertips grazed over her lightly, spreading licks of flame that converged on her clit.

He slid his finger between her labia, opening her more, and pushed firmly inside her. She gasped as pleasure zinged across her nerves, sending her up on tiptoe. She tried to jerk away. Too intimate. Too much.

His grip only tightened as he thrust farther, in and out, side to side, each movement increasing the seething tension growing in her body.

Dammit, he was studying her again, like a specimen, and she shook with the feeling of being just some object. *Can I do this?*

"Easy, sugar," he said and released his grip on her hip to cup her cheek instead. With his hand cupping her pussy, his finger still inside her, he brushed his lips over her mouth, and she sighed at the gentleness. How could he act so...ruthless and yet comforting at the same time.

"I'm only checking your size, your response." His lips curved, creating a dimple in his left cheek. "I do hate to get the wrong size toys."

Toys? Her vagina clamped down around his finger, and he laughed.

"Took a shine to the idea, did you?" After pulling his finger out, he pushed in two, stretching her. Then three.

Too much. She squirmed, unsure if the fullness felt erotic or just uncomfortable. He set a hand on her bottom, holding her there for a minute as her pussy throbbed around him.

"You have a snug little pussy, sugar," he murmured and withdrew. After licking his fingers as if tasting a new kind of ice cream, he smiled. "And you taste very nice."

Something inside her relaxed. He liked her taste. And wasn't that another one of those stupid female fears? Why didn't guys ever worry about things like that?

At least his touch lessened some of her concerns, not only about sex with strangers, but about sex, period. It hadn't interested her in quite a while. But if Master Marcus wanted to take her now—and the tailoring of his pants couldn't disguise his huge erection—she was completely ready.

To her surprise—and dismay—he released her from the chains without doing anything else. She wanted sex, and he didn't? "But..."

Ah, the expression on the little submissive's face was priceless. She'd just encountered the first of the lessons she'd have to embrace.

As she stared up at him with beautiful brown eyes, Marcus pressed his palm between her legs again, enjoying the telltale wetness. "You will arrive dressed appropriately for a fetish club, but I may remove some or all of your clothing. Your body is mine to play with as I please—unless I give another dom permission."

He paused then continued. "You are not to touch yourself. You are not to climax without my permission. That includes both here at the club and any other time, including when you're at home. I'll put a limit on it though—for the next two weeks, all pleasure for you will come at my command or not at all."

She shivered, and he felt the involuntary clenching of her pussy. "Yes, Sir," she whispered.

He picked up her clothing from the floor and handed it to her. She wasn't a long-standing member of the club, so he'd start from scratch with protocol instructions. He quickly ran through what she'd need to know for tonight: respectful behavior, appropriate ways to address a dom, kneeling, the meaning of her ribbons, and how much touching other doms could do. Seeing the mixture of dismay and arousal on her face, he wondered again at her request for training. She didn't seem as...wholehearted...as most subs who begged to be trainees. "Do you have any questions?"

"You really do sound like a lawyer sometimes," she said under her breath, and before he could react, she asked, "Will I do any scenes tonight or—"

"That's up to me. Entirely."

She glanced at the clothing in her hands and back up with a pleading look in her eyes. Big, appealing puppy-dog eyes.

He shook his head no.

The little sigh she gave made his lips quirk. Truly she was rather cute, bless her heart. She had her work cut out for her though. Protocols, an attitude of service, holding back orgasms, various types of play and toys. Preparing for anal play. Instruction in oral if needed. He eyed the blue streak in her hair. People who followed the rules rarely put blue in their hair. She'd already earned a swat on the leg at a time most subs would try their utmost to appear sweet and obedient. He understood Z's concern over her attitude.

His mouth tightened. His ex-wife had loved to indulge in full-blown bratty behavior, not because she was inherently ornery, but for the show. She wanted the attention—not his, but everyone else's. Of all the subs, he particularly disliked the insolent and ill-disciplined ones.

At the bar, Andrea smiled at him. "Master Marcus."

"Please tuck away Gabrielle's clothes until later." He nodded at Gabrielle to hand her clothing over. She did with another little sigh. Just to check her reaction to being touched in public, he clasped her breast. His arm behind her back prevented her retreat as he caressed and teased her nipple to a stiff point. Her hands had fisted. They'd have to work on that, but she hadn't moved. She flushed with embarrassment, but after a minute, her body relaxed and she unconsciously leaned into his touch.

"Good job, little subbie," he said in an undertone for her ears.

She looked up at him, desire and surrender in her eyes, and then stiffened as if surprised at her response—as if displeased with it.

Thanks for the challenge, Z.

CHAPTER THREE

For a good part of the evening, Gabi served drinks as Marcus had explained each trainee did for part of the night. She still wasn't sure exactly why. He never gave her clothing back, so she stayed naked and all too conscious of how her breasts and butt jiggled and drew attention from the men...and sometimes the women too. The doms did more than look. As they gave their drink orders, they'd touch her. Never on her breasts or pussy, but running a hand up and down her arm or massaging her butt lightly. One had stroked his fingers up her inner thigh, stopping an inch short of the V between her legs.

It left her in a state of constant excitement. As she walked through the club, the air would brush over her skin and call her attention to the dampness of her pussy.

Every now and then, she'd catch sight of Agent Rhodes as he wandered around, pretending to watch the scenes and trying to appear as if he belonged there. He'd probably never set foot in a BDSM club before, and he was so not a dom.

Had he spotted anyone suspicious? Rhodes and Kouros had told her not to look for the perp, but she'd tried anyway. Unfortunately she couldn't figure out how she'd differentiate him from any other man. All the doms intimidated her—hell, the whole place did. She'd never seen a club like this. The dark Goth clubs she'd visited in college compared to the Shadowlands like SpongeBob cartoons to a Hitchcock movie.

Ominous atmosphere? The Shadowlands did it with style.

Leather everywhere: the heavy couches and chairs, the floggers and whips and tawse hanging on the walls, the bondage tables and spanking benches. Black iron chandeliers and wall sconces sent flickering light over members who wore everything from nipple clamps to skintight, head-to-toe latex and stiletto boots. Master Marcus had sure told the truth about the range of styles. He wasn't the only dom in a suit, and a couple of dommes dressed that way too. Not every dom wore black, but she'd noticed the ones who didn't still had an aura of sheer self-confidence and command.

The roped-off scene areas stayed busy, giving her a fast education in the lifestyle. Floggings she'd witnessed before, but this place had a special, extra-large area for whip play. Talk about scary. She'd never seen nasty-looking electrical things pushed inside vulnerable places and turned on. Or needles stuck into nipples for fun. *Fun*? Or sex in every way, shape, and form.

As she headed away from the bar with her drink orders, she saw a woman lying on a sawhorse bench. And...dear heavens, two guys, one man thrusting into her pussy, the other getting a blowjob. The sub's arms were strapped down—she couldn't prevent them from doing anything they wanted. Gabi totally forgot to serve drinks, gawking like a virgin at a strip joint.

Why did watching this seem so erotic? She tried to imagine herself there, and a flash of terror ran through her and was burned away by the heat. Boy, talk about confusion...

She caught Marcus's masculine scent of amber and musk a second before he stopped behind her. Looking over her shoulder at his stern jaw, she tensed, expecting he would berate her for taking a break. Instead he wrapped an arm around her waist and touched her—intimately—right out there with all the spectators.

Oh God. She squirmed as his fingers slid through the wetness of her pussy, and realized she'd grown even damper while watching the scene.

"Well, sugar," he murmured in her ear, "obviously a ménage is one I'll add to your list to try."

His touch zinged across her nerves, increasing her arousal like fanning a flame. She squeezed her drink tray as she tried to hold it steady, and she couldn't figure out if she wanted to push him away—or grab his hand and move it up an inch to reach her clit, and that was just wrong. *I'm here to do a job, to act like a bratty sub. Get to work, Gabi.* "Try two men? No way, Jose. Ain't gonna happen," she said loudly, expecting another swat on her thigh for rudeness.

He smacked her *mound.* The light stinging slap sent fire and pain ripping through her. She almost dropped the tray as she tried to jerk away. He hauled her back against his chest with frightening ease.

He said in a level voice, "Be respectful, trainee." He released her and walked away, leaving her much, much hotter than a minute before. Her abused clit burned, her labia stung, and the glasses on the tray she held rattled.

She not only felt hotter, but inadequate too. Marcus sounded like her father—cold and controlled. Her shoulders hunched at the memories. *Never good enough for him or Mother*. Not good enough for here either. Marcus already thought he'd gotten a loser of a trainee, yet she hadn't attracted a kidnapper. Had she? She glanced around uneasily, wondering if the perp watched her.

No matter. *I can only do my best.*

After a slow breath, she forced herself back into action and served drinks, although her pussy was so swollen, she probably appeared bowlegged.

When she finished, she set her empty tray on the bar with a

sigh of relief. Maybe she'd make a quick trip to the restroom and give her nerves a chance to calm down.

"Gabrielle." Master Cullen waved her closer, then finished drawing a beer. He nodded to two drinks on the bar top. "Pet, be a good girl and run these over to the couple sitting by the suspension area."

He gave her an easygoing grin that had her smiling back. "Yes, Sir." A few steps from the bar, she realized she should have smarted off to him. *Duh, Gabi.*

At the suspension area, two doms had trussed a submissive in an elegant array of ropes, and she dangled in midair. Nearby a muscular, black-haired dom in black leathers observed the scene. His sub sat beside him, very pregnant and very cute, looking rather like a fat poodle next to a wolf.

Gabi steeled her nerve. "Here go, dude." She slapped the two drinks down on the coffee table hard enough to send liquid sloshing over the sides. "Oops. My bad."

His gaze stopped on her gold-colored wrist cuffs, and his face hardened into solid rock. "Here go, dude?" he repeated softly; then his voice turned cold. "What is your name, trainee?"

Oh crap. "I'm Gabrielle"—*don't say Sir, don't say Sir*—"Sir." The respectful term slipped out; she just couldn't hold it in under his ruthless stare. Damn, he and Master Marcus had this intimidating stuff down to a science. *Don't let him psych you out.* She tsk-tsked at him. "My grandmother said you shouldn't frown like that because your face might stay that way."

"She's got a death wish," he said under his breath. Rising—and *oh, joy*—the guy was as tall as Marcus. He gripped her arm and glanced at his sub. "Wait here, Kari. I'll return in a second."

"Yes, Sir," his sub said and gave Gabrielle an appalled look.

After glancing around, the dom dragged Gabi across the room to a station where a domme caned a potbellied, older man. Gabi winced as the man's gag-muffled groan followed each whacking noise. The nasty dom didn't plan to borrow that cane, did he?

He pulled Gabi farther, heading straight toward...Master Marcus. Hell.

Marcus's smile faded when he saw Gabi. "Is there a problem with the trainee, Master Dan?"

Oh, this is not good.

"Damn right." The dom stared down at Gabi. She hadn't realized brown eyes could look so pitiless. "Either incredibly poorly trained or simply insolent. I think insolent, myself."

"I see." Master Marcus's gaze dropped to her. "That would be a downright pity, wouldn't it?"

Okay, blue eyes could definitely turn colder than brown ones. A tremor shook her body as the dom passed her off, and Master Marcus's equally merciless grip closed around her upper arm. "I do thank you for bringing her to me, Master Dan. I'll take care of it."

One corner of Master Dan's mouth curled up. "Good enough." He gave her a dismissive look as if she were a puppy that had peed on his kitchen floor, and walked away.

She shifted her weight and peeked up from under her eyelashes at the suit.

Arms folded over his chest, he studied her with disapproval. "Well, you got yourself in a heap of trouble. Did you not understand my instructions as to the behavior of a trainee?"

Why did she feel as if she'd let him down? Making him happy wasn't her job. The cheerleading team in her brain started chanting *brat, brat, brat*, and she said in an irritating whine, "I've served drinks all night, and my feet are tired, and I just wanted to have a little fun. He didn't have to be such a jerk about it."

"Your feet are tired, and you want to have fun. I see." His lips curved slightly. "Then we might should get you off your feet."

His hand closed on the back of her neck again as he headed over to a small sitting area where a younger dom and one with silvery gray hair sat talking. The older one glanced up. "Marcus, how are you doing?"

"Quite well, thank you, sir." The warm reply was a vast contrast to how he'd sounded a second ago. "Master Sam, I would like to offer y'all a coffee table for your comfort. She complained her feet are tired, so I have a notion that resting on hands and knees would suit her better."

Coffee table? When Gabi tried to pull away, Master Marcus slid her legs right out from under her so quickly she'd have belly flopped if he hadn't caught her. "Hands and knees, please, Gabrielle," he said and set her on the floor.

This was...just wrong. Avoiding the legs beside her, she sidled around far enough her butt was toward the wall at least.

He sighed and picked her up, setting her back down with her ass toward the center of the room, then shoved a foot between her knees, forcing her legs apart. Exposing her more fully. "You stay right there now."

"Thanks a lot, boss," she snapped.

Stinging pain slashed across her bottom, and she yelped.

"Silence, sub," the old guy said, motioning with the switch he held. *A switch*. Hell, no wonder it'd hurt. His pale blue eyes examined her without any compassion at all. "I dislike noisy coffee tables."

Marcus ran his hand over the burning spot. When she winced, he chuckled. "Gabrielle, you will serve as a coffee table until I return. I would recommend you hold very still—anyone whose drink you spill can have a blowjob from you."

A blowjob? She stared up at him in disbelief, a solid knot forming in her stomach. *I don't want to do that. I don't want to be here.*

He paused, and his voice took on a deeper, cutting edge. "Am I clear?"

She really, really didn't have the guts to challenge him—not when he used that tone. Tears blurred her vision. "Y-yes, Sir."

He bent and stroked his hand over her hair. "Much better. I'm sorry you won't find this a comfortable time, sugar." The sympathy in his voice made her want to lean into him. To beg him not to leave her.

But he did. He walked away. She dropped her head, not willing to look at anything or anyone. Naked, on hands and knees, her butt exposed. A second later, the old man set his beer on her back. The cold, damp bottle made her jump, and thank God, he'd kept hold of the drink or she'd have knocked it right off. The younger man put his can of beer on her too. They must keep the refrigerator here at subzero temperatures, she thought as goose bumps rose on her skin.

She stayed in place, not moving a muscle, and realized after a few minutes that having her legs spread helped her balance. Not that she'd ever forgive Mr. Perfect anyway.

The two men talked, arguing over Tampa's baseball team, over a recent suicide off the Skyway Bridge, over Master Z's mouthy sub and her latest infraction. They picked their drinks up, set them down, paying as much attention to her as if she really were a coffee table.

Then she realized Master Sam had set his drink right on the edge of her shoulder blade. Feeling the bottle teeter, she stopped breathing. It settled. *Tiny little breaths. Don't move.*

"I do think she makes a fine piece of furniture." Marcus's voice came from behind her, and she startled, just a tiny bit, caught herself...and the bottle tipped. The glass hit her back, and cold beer drizzled off her ribs and downward to pool at the base of her spine. Horror ran through her, and her fingernails dug into the hardwood floor. *No no no*. At least the other man had already picked his can up or she'd have spilled them both. She pushed herself up to a kneeling position, and the cold beer trickled down between her butt cheeks, making her anus pucker.

"Hell, I hadn't finished yet," came the gruff tones of the older man.

"Truly a shame." Marcus shook his head at her. "Well, she'll do better next time, I assume."

This isn't fair. You guys set me up, you bastards. Gabrielle saw the older guy unfasten his leather pants, and she closed her eyes. *Oh no. They wouldn't...*

"She any good at this?" Sam asked Marcus.

"First night here. I don't know," Marcus said. "Do you prefer me to direct her, or will you?"

I don't need any stinking directions. But she sure wouldn't smart off to Marcus right now—giving a stranger a blowjob was bad enough. *I don't want to do this.*

"Feel free." Sam sheathed himself with a condom, glanced at her. "I prefer being covered. Get up here, girl." He leaned back and closed his eyes, his cock rising from his leathers like a flagpole.

She blinked up at Marcus, wanting to break down and beg.

He simply waved his hand toward Sam in a "get on with it" motion.

She crawled over and knelt between Sam's legs. *Biting it off would probably come across as a little too defiant. Satisfying...but stupid.* Her heart pounded, and her hands had gone clammy. She combed her hair back. *I've done oral sex before. I'm actually pretty fair at it.* After wetting her lips, she took a firm hold and started to put his cock into her mouth.

"Slower, sugar," Marcus murmured.

She glanced over her shoulder.

He'd taken the empty armchair next to Sam. Leaning back, he crossed his legs at the ankles, as if he'd settled in for a Sunday football game. "Lick him like an ice cream cone. Tease him a smidgen before you get down to business."

Tease him? She'd planned to get him off as quickly as possible. But from the implacable set of Marcus's jaw, the dom figured to draw this out. Or maybe he considered it part of instructing a trainee. Her heart sank—she had told him she wanted to jump right in. With a silent sigh, she licked up Master Sam's cock.

He'd used an orange-flavored condom. A giggle escaped her.

He opened his pale blue eyes and winked before closing them again.

After that, somehow, it wasn't difficult to do a good job. Marcus supervised the entire time, murmuring soft instructions. "Circle the tip." "Suck hard." "Massage his balls with one hand." "Grip the base tightly."

She hadn't felt excited about doing this, but somehow having Marcus watch set her pulse racing. Her breasts tingled where they rubbed against Sam's pants, and she flushed. How could she get excited by this...this humiliation?

Her mouth had started to tire when Sam stiffened and came.

"Very nicely done, sugar," Marcus said. "Don't stop yet. Ease him down gently."

When Sam's cock softened, Marcus pointed to a small stand discreetly camouflaged by the ferns in the planter. "Fetch some wipes. Clean him up and dispose of the condom." She started to rise, and he added, "Your response is what?"

"Yes, Sir," she snapped before thinking. She came to attention, saluted, and included a glare for good measure.

As she stalked away, she heard Sam's gravelly voice. "You're going to have a fun time with this one, Marcus."

Probably just as well she didn't hear Marcus's reply. When she'd finished cleaning Master Sam, he ruffled her hair. "Good job, girl." After tucking himself back into his faded leathers, he rose and headed for the bar.

Gabrielle hesitated. *What now?*

Before she could stand, Marcus leaned forward, grasped her around the waist, and pulled her between his knees, her back to him. With firm hands, he adjusted her position until she knelt, bare bottom resting on her heels, knees widely spread, and her palms on her thighs. As his hands covered hers, she saw white scars and thickened skin over his knuckles. A lawyer that got in fights?

Leaning forward, he squeezed her shoulders, and his cheek

brushed against her hair as he spoke softly in her ear. "When I say kneel, this is the posture I wish you to take. Concentrate on getting here quickly for now. We'll work on gracefulness later."

"Yes, Sir," she said, not wanting to fight. His legs enclosing her felt...good, as did his warm hands on her chilled skin and his cheek against her ear. Safe. And maybe he even liked her a little bit.

He reached around her to caress her breast. She bit her lip, wanting to push into his touch, and that just didn't make any sense. Why did it feel as if he had the right to fondle her? With anyone else, she'd feel as if she were being groped.

When he slipped his other hand between her open legs, she stiffened. He simply continued, sliding his fingers in her wetness, and pleasure flooded her senses.

"Well, sugar," he whispered, one finger tracing circles around her clit. "You might act like you didn't enjoy making Sam happy, but you seem a tad aroused. Might that be true?"

A mortified flush scalded her cheeks. True, she hadn't wanted to start, but sucking on Sam's cock, hearing Marcus's firm instructions—and imagining *his* cock instead—had sizzled her veins.

"Answer me, sugar." He pinched her nipple, a small admonishment, and dammit, she was hot enough the tiny pain sent a shot of electricity straight to her pussy. It sure didn't help her focus that his finger kept sliding up and over her clit.

"You know it's true," she said sullenly.

The lack of a *Sir* earned her another pinch, on her clit this time, and she yelped. "Sir. Yes, Sir."

"Gabrielle, you seem to have difficulty following the rules. Are you sure you want to be here? I do think a trainee position is demanding too much of you."

"I can handle it." *Maybe*. However, physical punishment might be easier than him turning her on as easily as if he'd flipped a switch. And her emotions were...off. She wanted to stay right here with his arms around her. But that wasn't the job. *Decoy. I'm a decoy.*

"You are a stubborn little thing." He released her. "Stand on up now."

Already missing the safety and the warmth of his embrace, she rose to her feet. Off to one side, a group of both submissives and doms were observing and laughing. She'd acquired an audience. Time for bratty sub to emerge.

But...oh God, she didn't want another one of his punishments. She wrapped her arms around herself, feeling cold. Alone. Wanting him to hold her again. Stupid her, for wishing he'd like her.

Stupid her for thinking about anything but the task at hand.

As Marcus stood, Gabi motioned to the audience and said loudly, "Everyone else in this place has on clothes. This isn't fair, S —" She barely kept herself from saying *Sir*. What the hell was wrong with her?

His mouth thinned. "Well now, I reckon we can find you something to wear." As she stared at him in surprise—*he'd caved in*? —he led her back to the bar.

The giant bartender wandered over. "What can I get you, Marcus?"

"I do believe I could use some thick nylon rope and upper decorations, paper and a marker."

The bartender rummaged under the bar. As he set out a coil of rope and the rest of Marcus's requests, he shook his head at her. "Have you been a bad sub, pet?"

"He's just being pissy," she said and got a snort of laughter from the bartender. She frowned at the items on the bar. *Rope*? "But...but I wanted clothes..."

"You want to be here? Then show me." Master Marcus's cold voice shriveled her willpower to nothing.

Under his pitiless blue gaze, she couldn't find...anything...to say. Staring up at him, she realized that despite Z's assurance that

Marcus would keep her for a month, this dom might refuse to work with her. And he was the only trainer. "I do want to be here."

The corner of his mouth turned up, as if he saw her uncertainty. "Then wear your... clothing... politely for the remainder of the night." Marcus wound the rope around her, his sure hands twining it under and between her breasts, pulling it until the pressure caused her breasts to stick out and the skin to tauten.

It felt...strange. Snug as if the ropes held her in an embrace. And as he touched her, as his intent eyes studied her, she tingled and her nipples bunched into little points.

Once finished, he nodded in satisfaction and opened the small plastic envelope on the bar top. Two beaded pieces of jewelry fell into his hand.

She frowned, recognizing them a second before he bent and put his mouth over her left nipple. He set a hand behind her butt and prevented her from stepping back. *Oh my God.*

He sucked forcefully, his tongue swirling around the crest. As her breast swelled, the ropes seemed to compress even more, and the feeling of his mouth...pulling...sent pleasure spiraling to her pussy. He straightened and rubbed her nipple, keeping it erect as the skin dried. By the time he stopped, she was ready to moan.

Until he put a clamp on the very swollen, sensitive peak.

She squeaked, tried to grab her breast to yank the damned thing off, and he caught her hands.

"It'll settle in a minute, but as contrary as you are, I got a notion you won't leave these in place," he said, his eyes on her face. "Let's just remove the temptation." He forced her hands behind her back, and one snick later, he'd locked her handcuffs together. And oh, God, the position squeezed the clamp until it felt like fingernails were biting into her nipple.

Under the feel of the cuffs, the control he took over her, she couldn't hold back her whine. "Please, Sir."

His head tilted and he studied her. "Please release you? Or give you more?"

The accuracy of his question stabbed right through her. The clamp hurt and yet... *More. I want more. Push me, control me...* "Release."

He didn't free her, either from the restraints, or his gaze for a long, long minute. "No. You're not being truthful with me...and you've also proven you have no discipline whatsoever." He bent and sucked on her other breast, squeezing the areola between his teeth. Fire shot down into her pussy. Again he teased her with his fingers until her nipple dried.

The second clamp went on, and she hissed at the stinging, burning pain. She twisted and yanked on her cuffs to get free. "Dammit!"

He studied her face. "You have a safe word, Gabrielle. You could use it about now."

He'd like that, wouldn't he? "No," she gritted out.

His eyes hardened, and he tugged on one clamp. "No, what?"

"No, Sir." *Damn you to hell and back.* She glared at him.

"I can smell your arousal, sugar," he said softly. "Do not continue to sass me, or I will bend you over a bar stool and take you right now so everyone else can see how excited you are."

She took a step back. *He wouldn't.*

But from the unyielding look in his eyes, she knew he would. And the image, the thought of how it would feel to be taken here by him made liquid pool in her lower half. How could this merciless *lawyer* be the first man to excite her in...forever?

Even knowing she should keep poking at him, she bit her lip and kept silent. *I really, really don't want to play the brat anymore.* Besides, she had the people around the bar avidly watching, so maybe she'd done enough for now. She'd definitely annoyed Mr. Lawyer, after all.

He wrote on the paper and tucked it under the rope. She tried to see, but her breasts blocked her view of the writing.

"You don't have to serve drinks any longer tonight. Go and walk ten laps around the bar. Since you appear to enjoy attention, you can let the doms admire your...clothing."

He waited. With a sigh, he tugged on a clamp strongly enough her response broke right out of her. "Yes, Sir!"

"Take yourself off then."

Agent Rhodes was sitting off to one side, sipping his drink and watching. As Dickhead's gaze traveled over her roped and clamped breasts and his mouth twisted into a sneer, she felt cheap. Dirty.

She firmed her lips and continued on, trudging toward the back of the bar, wishing she could leave. But she couldn't. *This is for you, Kim. And when you're home, we'll go out and laugh about what I did to get you back. We will.*

She glanced over her shoulder and realized Master Marcus hadn't moved. As he talked with Cullen and another dom, he watched her as if wondering what she'd do next. Yet his expression didn't make her feel dirty—just powerless, which somehow melted her insides.

A second later, a young dom stepped into her path. "Cool jewelry," he said.

"Leave me alone." She tried to detour around him.

"You're a rude one." He grasped one dangling nipple clamp in one hand, using it like a painful leash as he cupped her other breast.

Owwww. Hands clenched, she held still, knowing Marcus watched. Had given permission. Somehow that made this stranger's touch feel right, even disconcertingly exciting. The dom fondled her breasts until they burned, and let her go.

Two more doms did the same. What had Marcus written on the paper?

It didn't stop. Her snapping and insults simply resulted in the clamps getting tugged until her breasts cried for relief. She tried walking faster, but doms still slipped off the bar stools to stop her.

Two laps. Three. And all the time she walked, she felt Master Marcus studying her.

Eight laps...

Ten laps. Oh thank God, she'd made her ten. She looked around. With the club almost empty, she didn't need to play decoy any longer. Her night was over, and she wanted to go home so badly she shook like an addict needing a fix.

Marcus still sat on the bar stool, sipping a drink, his face unreadable.

She stopped in front of him, saw no one stood close enough to hear. "Please, Sir. Can I get these off? May I go home now?" If he said no, she'd probably cry.

The fine lines at the corners of his eyes crinkled. "Sugar, since you asked so prettily, I'm happy to do that little favor for you."

She'd expected him to free her wrists first. Instead he pinned her between his knees. He set one hand on her left clamp and said, "Brace yourself, sweetheart."

"What?"

He removed the clamp.

"Aaaaah!" She couldn't keep the wail from escaping as blood rushed into her abused nipple. Locked securely behind her back, her arms jerked futilely. Her breast burned as if he'd covered it with acid.

"Shhh." He bent and licked lightly over the sore peak, easing the burn slightly, and soon each circle of his wet tongue sent erotic pulses to her pussy.

As the ache receded and the heat inside her increased, she realized she was panting. She tried to retreat.

He chuckled. "No, stay here, sugar." He tucked an arm around her waist, an iron bar imprisoning her.

Before she had a chance to get ready, he detached the other clamp—the sadistic bastard—and gently touched her breast with his tongue. The sensations roiling inside her were too much: pain and need and confusion. Like an earthquake, a shaking started in her stomach and worked its way out until even her knees trembled.

He straightened, his hands on her waist keeping her from falling. After studying her for a moment, he unclamped her cuffs and pulled her into his arms. She laid her head in the hollow of his shoulder and felt as if the world around her were crumpling. What was wrong with her?

His arms tightened, his rock-hard body a place of stability. "It's all right, darlin'. Shhh."

The pain eased to a low throbbing, and her trembling diminished as she rested against him.

"You've never had on nipple clamps before, have you?" he murmured. "Never done a public blowjob, never had rope work, never really submitted. Was anything on your application honest?"

He knew. Closing her eyes against the sense of failure, she swallowed. "Some."

"Why the lies?" His voice was level, and his arms firm around her. His chest rose and fell slowly and evenly with each breath.

"I wanted to make sure you'd take me as a trainee." At least that was honest.

As if he could tell, he sighed. "Means that much to you, sugar?"

"Yes, Sir," she whispered into his shoulder.

"Why?"

Anxiety ripped at her. Must he keep asking questions? "I-I can't explain really. It's just something I want—I need." *For Kim.*

"Well." He didn't move for a minute. Two. "All right, darlin'. If Master Z is willing to give you a chance, I'll do the same."

Oh thank God, he wasn't going to make her leave. Relief brought tears to her eyes, and her voice thickened. "Thank you, Sir."

"Don't lie to me again, Gabrielle."

She'd have to lie to him her entire time here. She had a

moment to get her expression under control before he set her back, holding her for a second to ensure she could stand. She kept her gaze lowered so he wouldn't read the guilt in her eyes. Let him think her embarrassed or ready to cry or whatever.

After removing the paper from under one rope, he set it on the bar. He unwound everything quickly, making the throbbing in her breasts increase again. When she tried to touch them, he brushed her hands aside, and smiling slightly, he massaged them, ignoring her moan of pain, giving her a level look when she clasped his wrists to make him stop.

She let her arms fall to her sides, although her hands fisted. Pain mingled with pleasure as each brush of his fingers on her nipples sent need shooting to her clit. She bit her lip, feeling the heat rising within her. When she chanced a peek at him, he was studying her—her face, her hands, her shoulders. A slight smile curved his lips.

"So, Gabrielle." His thumbs circled her distended, very sensitive nipples, somehow making her clit throb as well. "What did you learn from this lesson?"

That I've never known I could be so turned on. No. Bad answer.

She glanced at the writing on the paper he'd tucked under the ropes: ENJOY THE PRETTY BREASTS. ENJOY THEM LONGER IF SHE ISN'T RESPECTFUL. MASTER MARCUS. No wonder the doms had manhandled her. *I've learned how really mean you can be* didn't seem like a good answer either. "Not to demand clothing."

His mouth thinned slightly. "Try again."

"Not to demand anything and to show respect, Sir." Thank God the place had emptied. Even Agent Dickhead had left. He'd wait in the parking lot to tail her discreetly to her apartment, undoubtedly hoping the kidnapper would act during his watch.

"That's right." His lips curved up. "Give me a kiss and thank me for your lesson in manners."

Gee, boss, thanks for torturing me?

His hands closed around her arms, and he pulled her forward.

She winced when her nipples mashed against his suit—thank God the material wasn't rough, she thought, before his lips closed over hers. Velvety and firm. Competent and gentle.

And then he took her deeper, so hard and fast her head spun. His grip on her arm kept her in place; his other hand cupped her jaw as he plundered, finishing off his lesson of just who was in charge.

CHAPTER FOUR

The lion's deep-throated roar sent a chill down Gabi's spine. Holy hell, she hadn't been here in a while, and she'd forgotten what they sounded like up so close. The sweat under her arms wasn't totally from the heat. A voice in her head scrambled around like a mouse, screaming, *Run run run! He'll chomp me down in one bite*. She hauled in a breath, smelling the ammonia of cat urine mixed with the tropical flowers and the moist morning air. After checking the lush undergrowth and moss-covered trees for any stalking felines, she hurried to catch up to her group.

While the mix of men and women listened attentively to the guide, Gabi trailed behind, not paying attention. After all, she'd taken Big Cat Rescue tours before. Today she just wanted to enjoy the cats and not think about last night.

One out of two wasn't bad.

In the next cage, a panther relaxed on a thick tree limb and regarded the group with a poise that reminded Gabi of Master Marcus. And that was the problem. Instead of taking her mind off Marcus, the tawny-colored cats kept reminding her of him. Sleek and smooth and self-confident. Marcus even had the same stalking gait and measuring gaze.

In contrast she felt like a dog. A round cocker-spaniel puppy tripping over her fat, fluffy feet. Licking everything in sight. She grinned, remembering how she'd licked Master Sam's orange-flavored cock.

Yeah, she was doing a fine job of thinking of something else. With a resigned sigh, she stretched, trying to get her body to wake up. She'd gotten back last night hours past her usual bedtime.

And today she felt just plain tired...and sore too. Even her silkiest bra rubbed painfully on her sensitive, swollen nipples. One more thing to remind her of that damned dom...and how his touch had been so sure and a little rough.

She'd dreamed about him.

Why couldn't Z have given her to a different dom? One who wasn't so cold...and then so warm. One minute Marcus had instructed her as if she hadn't left grade school, and the next he'd kissed her... His lips had been firm, and he'd held her as if he had a right to take what he wanted. She closed her eyes as a full-fledged hot flash turned the air to a sauna's temperature.

Dammit. This was not the time to get excited over a guy. As a decoy, she'd fully expected to get swatted or be embarrassed for misbehaving, even to get groped and have sex with people she didn't know, but she'd never conceived of *wanting* someone. Of course Marcus was gorgeous, yet she'd never found all that chiseled handsome stuff so hot before. But Mr. Stuffy Lawyer somehow turned her on just by looking at her.

Maybe due to her lack of recent activity. After Andrew, she'd lost interest in dating, since when she'd broken up with him, she'd realized she'd once again picked a man her parents would approve of. You'd think she'd learn. That kind of man liked her in the beginning, then started getting more and more critical. She never lived up to their expectations—never lived up to her parents' expectations either. She'd never be perfect.

Marcus is...and dammit, I don't like perfect people. Well, it didn't matter. After another night or so of her insolence, Marcus would hate the sight of her.

That just made her feel even more miserable.

Behind her, from the parking area, the peacocks screamed, recalling her to reality. A bad reality. Grumpily, she trailed after the group, scuffing her sneakers on the dirt path. In a nearby pen, a panther chirped, the sound an octave lower than her cats' voices.

Her poor kitties. When she'd moved into the cheap apartment the FBI had obtained for her, her two boys had sulked, displeased at leaving all their well-marked furniture behind. She understood totally. This job made her feel like an animal in a zoo—stuck in a tiny, ugly enclosure under all sorts of rules, with someone watching all the time. It was probably why she'd thought of visiting here this morning, to sympathize with the other trapped beasties.

She shared another bond with the big cats here. They knew all about hunting.

Despite the scorching sun, Gabi shivered. *I'm prey*. Hopefully the kidnapper had taken the bait and was stalking Gabi right now. If not, or if he didn't try for the other decoys, the investigation would stall until he made a move—undoubtedly in some other city. Part of her wanted to be his chosen one, the hapless victim who'd lure him into a cage of FBI agents. Another part, scared shitless, begged to go home and curl up with her cats.

How many women had he ripped from their lives and sold? Kouros said the guy could have been doing this for a while. She felt her fingers rubbing the scar on her face and pulled her hand away. *I don't want to be his target*. But she had no better way to help her friend. What would happen to Kim—to all the other women—if he wasn't caught? *Stay the course, Gabi.*

The tour had stopped as the guide talked about a tiger rescued from a zoo. While they watched, an attendant threw a watermelon into a pond. Gabi giggled as the huge cat sprang down a slope and launched himself after it. Water sprayed everywhere.

As she walked to the parking lot, still grinning, she turned her cell phone back on. Two missed calls from Rhodes. Before she'd made it to her car, he called again. *Oh joy.*

"Hello," she said.

"You aren't cutting it, Renard..." He continued on in full Dickhead mode. She hadn't done a good job or been noticeable enough... "Two other women made more of a splash than you did last night, Renard. A blonde and a little brunette. Better looking than you too, so tell me why the kidnapper would choose you if he could grab one of them?"

Well, that hurt. Maybe it shouldn't, since she knew she wasn't especially pretty, but still... She bit back her first response. As a social worker, she'd learned that calling someone a sorry-ass loser tended to screw up any chance of cooperation. A shame the scum-sucking dipwad couldn't grasp the concept. "I understand," she said sweetly. "But bear in mind if I'm too badly behaved, they'll wonder why Z doesn't boot me out of the trainees. But I'll try to be louder tonight."

"You will damn well be louder."

Or what? You'll take me off this job and get a person with no clue of how to behave in a club? She changed the subject. "Do I have someone watching me during the day?"

"Of course. There's always one agent somewhere near you. Just go about your business and leave the work to us."

Her hand clamped on the phone. Work, huh? She'd far rather serve as the backup. Maybe she should stick clamps on his dick and let him discover the joys of decoy duty...if anyone could find what was probably an itty-bitty dick. She grinned. "Will do."

She snapped the phone shut. He sure hadn't changed since last year. She grimaced. After a school shooting in Tampa, the authorities had called in victim specialists from other areas, including her Miami office. Dickhead had headed up the investigation, and they'd butted heads over his crass behavior toward women, like the sisters of the shooters—ones who felt they couldn't say anything. Due to his high connections, her complaints got ignored. He was such a bastard.

But right now, the bastard had a point. She needed to ramp up her bratty act.

She rolled her eyes. To think she had competition for the brattiest in the club. Unfortunately the most disobedient sub wouldn't receive a trophy, but slavery instead. Her amusement died.

She had agents watching her back, but the other two submissives in the Shadowlands didn't. If the kidnapper took those women because Gabi hadn't made a good enough effort... How could she live with that?

So...must be louder, nastier. She flipped the phone open and shut, trying to think of showy ways to demonstrate she was a badass submissive. Rude attitude, check. Insults? Hmm.

She smiled. The teenage victims she counseled sure had good ones. Maybe make a list and memorize some.

What else could she do to show her brattiness? She slid into her car, then giggled, remembering one of Marcus's orders.

She hadn't wanted to shave down there anyway.

After lifting weights for an hour, Marcus walked into the locker room of the fitness club. He nodded at the lanky college student changing into a karate uniform. "Tim, how are you doing?"

"Good, man, good." Tim finished knotting his brown belt. "Sensei asked if you'd arrived yet. He wants you to mentor a couple of new boys."

"Ah." Marcus frowned. He'd cleared some of his cases, had a closing argument to prepare, another court date after that. As a prosecuting attorney, he never lacked for things to do, but he'd much prefer to guide the next generation in the right direction rather than skewering them in court. He'd find the time. "Please tell him I would be happy to help out."

"Good deal. Their mama brought them in—sounds like they're sliding into a gang."

"Got it." As the young man headed out, Marcus shook his head. *Damn gangs*. Well, he'd give the sensei a hand with getting the boys onto a better track.

Pulling on his gi, Marcus glanced at the wall clock. After class, he'd have just enough time to shower and change before heading to the Shadowlands.

He smiled, looking forward to the evening. He enjoyed working with the trainees and doing scenes with the various subs in the club, but Gabrielle had added a sense of challenge he hadn't felt in a long time. Hadn't realized he missed.

And yet he didn't like misbehaving submissives. As he tied his black belt, he pondered on his anticipation. The new trainee had an appealing little body, soft and curvy. Her face had character, which he believed more attractive than mere beauty, although she was pretty too, with those rich brown eyes and the pale skin warmed by her red hair. So yes, her appearance attracted him.

Her personality? She had a quirky sense of humor and a soft, sultry giggle that made him laugh. Definitely smart. And she had an easygoing charm—at least when she wasn't trying to be obnoxious.

She'd tested him all evening. But the few times he'd seen her submit had been heady. He'd wanted more. Wanted her in bondage, with willing surrender in her eyes.

What would she be like in bed? When she'd kissed him, she'd focused her entire attention on him. Not worrying about other people, her clothes, her hair—just giving her all. That kind of concentration was as sexy as it was compelling.

A man had to wonder if she'd concentrate on fucking as completely.

He started to harden and gave an exasperated snort. Having a woody in a karate class? Bad idea. Besides, it was too early to think about taking the little sub. Too soon to even make solid plans on how to train her. As unpredictable as she was, he'd need to play it by ear. Hopefully he'd figure out why she had such a rebellious attitude, and then he could center some scenes around the problem.

Smiling, he slammed his locker shut and snapped on the padlock. Any way he looked at it, he doubted he'd be bored tonight.

Boot camp, Shadowlands-style. The wood floor hurt Gabi's knees as she knelt in the entryway with the other trainees for Master Marcus's inspection before the evening began. As he strolled down the line, she kept expecting him to bark out, *Is your rifle clean, Private*? She stared at the floor. *Don't giggle, dummy*.

Shoes appeared, nice charcoal gray slacks, a suit coat, and... When she met Marcus's intent gaze, her amusement disappeared —along with the rest of her mind. He held her, frozen in place, with only the power in his eyes.

Then he smiled. "Welcome back to the Shadowlands, Gabrielle. Stand yourself up now."

Feeling gawky after the smooth grace of the others, she scrambled to her feet and imitated the stance they'd taken. Feet shoulder-width apart, hands clasped behind her back, straight posture, chin up. *Sir, yes, Sir*. But as his razor-sharp gaze scrutinized her body, she flushed and her nipples contracted into peaks, thankfully concealed by her vest. *Surely that wasn't supposed to happen in boot camp*.

"You look very nice," he said in his deep, molasses-slow voice, and his approval made her feel as if she'd gotten a gold star on her spelling paper. Of course, she deserved a gold star for her attire.

She'd gone for a barbaric appearance with a laced-up leather vest and matching short leather skirt. Knowing she'd be barefoot, she'd painted her toenails a garish red. Temporary tattoos of swords and thorns circled her upper arms.

He ran his hand over one tattoo, and his eyebrows quirked. As his callused palm continued down her arm, her knees weakened. How could a man's touch—just his damned touch—mess with her like this?

His gaze intent on her face, he lifted her hand and nibbled her fingers.

When her toes curled, he smiled slowly. "Tonight you'll waitress on the dance side of the room. Remember, you may not play with anyone without my permission, but you're encouraged to stop and talk." His bourbon-smooth voice spiraled around the top of her spine and slid straight down to her groin like a sip of hundred-proof sex. "With all the instructions you had last night, I'm not sure I explained this well. Master Z could easily hire waiters, but serving drinks means you meet the doms without the pressure of finding something to say. Make sense, sugar?"

He paused. Unfortunately she wasn't here to meet doms, except for one kidnapper. "Yes, Sir."

"Then off you go."

Midway through the night, Gabi's skin had started feeling too small for her body. Serving drinks should have bored her. But the doms flirted with her. Touched her in a way that would get them tossed out of a normal bar, often caressing the bare strip of skin between her vest and skirt. One even wrapped a big hand around her thigh as he talked to her. Always polite, yet making it clear they might someday ask permission for her...company.

As she wandered across the Shadowlands with another set of drinks, the music from the corner dance area throbbed against her with an almost sexual rhythm, punctuated by shrieks and moans from the scenes around the room's perimeter. A lot of the screams came from where Master Sam of the orange-flavored condom was whipping a submissive at the chain station. His nasty-looking, short black whip left long red marks on the woman's tanned skin.

Gabi edged closer and cringed at how each pause between strokes seemed calculated to cause the most pain.

The sub screamed again, the sound higher than before. Sam stopped and talked to her, stroked her hair, and checked the chains and cuffs holding her arms over her head. When the sub mumbled something and smiled, Sam chuckled, kissed her lightly, walked back to his place...and resumed.

Resumed. God, it was terrifying to watch. *I so don't like pain.* Yet the bond between Master Sam and his sub grew as he continued until it was almost visible. He focused on her response to each blow so thoroughly the building could have fallen down without his noticing. That kind of attention was...compelling. Exciting.

Nonetheless, each crack of the whip made her flinch. *No whippings for me, thank you very much.* In fact, she really, really hoped to play the brat without getting any painful punishments.

At the bar, Master Cullen took her tray, a smile on his craggy face. "You've done well, pet, and your serving duties are over. You're to join Master Marcus now."

"Oh. Okay." She saw his raised eyebrows and amended, "Yes, Sir." *Join Marcus.* As she remembered her dream from last night and where Marcus's hands...and mouth...had been, heat ran through her. She licked her lips. What would he do today? Would he play with her in a scene? Her insides melted like ice cream on a summer afternoon.

A second later, the excitement faded away, leaving her cold inside. She wasn't here to have fun. On the contrary, she was here to get noticed...somehow...and she hadn't succeeded very well so far. Although she'd sassed the members, a bratty waitress didn't get much notice. She needed to be obnoxious in a dom-sub scene, which meant she'd have to defy *Marcus.* She pressed a hand over the nauseating knot forming in her stomach.

The huge bartender leaned a thick forearm on the bar top. "Little sub, you look worried about something. Is your problem with Master Marcus?"

"No, Sir." *But I'm going to be his problem shortly*. "Not at all."

Master Cullen studied her face for a second. "Then talk to him about it, love. That's what he's here for."

"Yes, Sir." She hurried away, unable to insult him after his concern for her. Only she should have been rude anyway. *Get over being a nice person, Gabi.*

As she searched the room for Marcus, she stayed alert for anyone who acted too interested in her—although the kidnapper probably didn't wear a sign saying BAD GUY, and as a new trainee, she attracted attention from everyone.

She eventually found Marcus watching a scene at the stocks. A male submissive was bent forward with his hands and head secured. His domme wore a strap-on cock and thrust it into his ass as vigorously as any man Gabi had ever seen. Gabi gulped and took a step back. That looked just strange. Fascinating but strange.

Although the sub's moans sounded as if he were dying, his eyes glowed bright with excitement, and his jutting cock seemed ready to burst. "Please, Mistress," he begged. "Please let me come."

Poor guy.

Gabi turned her attention to Marcus. He stood so relaxed, yet had an aura of owning the space around him. Somehow he never seemed off balance, and she never seemed to find hers. With a sigh, she joined him.

He smiled down at her and ran a finger along her jawline, sending every nerve into "gimme more" entreaties. "You're doing well, sugar. Although I hear you're a tad sassy, the members think you're a wonderful addition to the trainees."

Great, how was she supposed to be a hard-ass when that ass wanted to melt right into a puddle? "Thank you, Sir." Then the meaning of what he'd said registered—all her work and they only considered her *sassy*? Not disobedient? Not disrespectful? *Hell.*

"Now rest here a spell and give me your impressions of the scenes you witnessed this evening."

"Um. Okay." She nodded to the strap-on scene. "I can see he's enjoying himself, but a guy begging doesn't do anything for me."

A corner of Marcus's mouth tipped up. "No," he murmured, "I reckon you're definitely a submissive."

Submissive. The way he said the word sounded like a caress, but somehow in this place, it was a lot more frightening to admit to. In bondage games before, she'd never given up anything except mobility. Here...just the look in Master Marcus's eyes made her breath stop—the look that said he'd demand more of her than just her physical freedom. The thought was exciting...and terrifying.

When she instinctively edged away, he curled his hand around her nape and moved her back. The warmth of his palm spread outward until her skin burned. "Continue, Gabrielle."

She wet her dry lips and forged ahead. "Well, watching Master Sam whipping someone bothered me. The whip, the pain made me want to crawl under a table and hide."

Marcus chuckled. "Good to know. Sounds like there was something that attracted you?"

The dom could give lessons in observation. "I... The interaction between them? I can't describe it." She'd felt that kind of encompassing... communication... just once. Her first time in a club, an older dom, and a short scene. And she'd never found anything close again. Until now.

Marcus's eyes softened. "That's the heart of a scene. Very good. Go on."

"Um. The two girls and one guy... I'd have enjoyed it better without the extra girl."

He laughed. And waited.

She tried to retreat again, but his hand still held her in place.

This sharing of...private feelings...the more she did, the more uncomfortable it was. She'd told him about the scenes that hadn't affected her much, but now...

His thumb stroked the hollow at the base of her skull, giving her goose bumps. "What's wrong, sugar?"

"I...I don't know you. And talking about this stuff is too personal. Answering your questions yesterday was bad enough." But now he wanted to dig into her *fantasies*, dammit.

His hand still curled around her neck, he turned her to face him more fully. The crinkle of the sun lines said he understood, but the set of his jaw said he wouldn't relent. "You're correct. This isn't a normal dom-sub relationship, and someday I hope you will have a real one. For now, I am responsible not only to watch over you, to teach you, to help you find a good dom...but also to see to your needs."

Her mouth dropped open. "You... I don't have needs. I mean, I'm just here—"

"Everyone has needs, darlin'. That you think you don't means we'll just have to explore longer."

This time the goose bumps came totally from his words and the implacable look in his eyes. *Oh God.*

"Tell me about other scenes." He regarded her as if he could see right into her heart and soul, and that was just scary. He was demanding more from her than she wanted to give...to anyone.

No choice. She drew herself up, pretending he wasn't touching her and that his masculine scent didn't turn her brain to mush. *Think*. "The man locked in the cage creeped me out." That was safe enough to say. "The wax play was..." She choked, trying to figure out what to call it. *Definitely don't say interesting and scary erotic*. Acting rude when strapped down to a table with wax dripping onto her skin sounded past masochistic. "Frightening."

He raised an eyebrow. "Was it now?" Why didn't he appear convinced?

"And the sub seemed out of it, like she'd had too much to drink or something."

"That's called subspace, sugar. You could call it drunk on endorphins, maybe. It's a good thing—a kind of euphoria."

"Oh. Huh." She considered the picture again. The sub had been smiling, obviously close to coming, and higher than a kite. A happy kite. "Okay."

"More."

"That's all." *Better stop while I'm ahead.*

"Did you happen on the scene with the dom taking his sub in the ass?" he asked softly.

She swallowed. Oh, had she. The woman had come so violently, she'd screamed louder than the submissive Master Sam had whipped.

"I see you did." He put a finger under her chin, forcing her to meet his gaze. "Are you interested in trying anal sex, darlin'?"

God yes. No. "Um. Maybe? No." She rubbed damp hands on her skirt. The thought of him behind her, pushing... "No."

His right cheek creased. "Well then, we not only need to work on your honesty, but we'll need to get that pretty asshole of yours prepared."

What? Her "*pretty asshole*" puckered in terror. And her breasts tightened with arousal. Why did she have so much trouble remembering this was just a job? *I'm so confused.*

"And speaking of preparation, you'd best show me your pussy. I forgot to check your work during inspection."

Lift her skirt up so he could look at her down there? She flushed, and then the rest of his sentence registered. "*Check your work.*" *Oh God.* Her breath caught, and her stomach dropped right out of her body. She hadn't shaved. She *deliberately* hadn't shaved, but now she really, really wished she had. He'd be so unhappy with her. Disapproving. Like her father, who acted as if she never did anything right.

I'm not supposed to care about Marcus's reactions. Bratty sub, bratty sub, bratty sub. She dragged up her inner diva and tossed her head. "What work?"

His eyes narrowed as if he saw how much effort it took to put on the rebellious act. "Lift your skirt, Gabrielle. Now."

The power of his voice swept through her, and she wanted to —needed to—melt into a puddle at his feet. She realized her hands had already gripped the bottom of her skirt and started to lift. *No no no*. She forced her fingers open, let the skirt drop. *What I do must attract attention. Be rude. Blatant.* Hauling in a quick breath, she blew a raspberry. "Lift it yourself, big boy."

A moment of silence from him. Then he shook his head. "I believe I will do just that." He gripped her arm, dropped down into the chair behind him, and yanked her facedown over his knees.

"Hey!" The realization of what he planned to do hit her. Spank her? As if she were a kid? Humiliation scraped her insides like sandpaper, increasing as she remembered how many people stood nearby. They'd see... The shame and horror and fury tangled into a foaming brew. She kicked frantically and tried to push back to her feet.

He shifted her until she had no leverage, and hooked his right leg over her ankles. She felt her leather skirt lifted, a brief wash of air, and then he slapped her bottom. Hard.

"Ow!" Fury won, and she yelled it. Make a scene? If he wanted to spank her, he'd just see what kind of a nightmare a poorly disciplined sub could create. Spank her? "You fucking dipwad!"

His voice remained perfectly controlled, but she could feel his anger simmering. "I'm getting downright weary of your ornery behavior. Yesterday, being as you were new, I didn't take you much to task. But you're trying to rile me up on purpose, and I do believe you've bitten off more than you can chew."

He paused as if to let her speak, but she had nothing she could say.

"You best count for me. If you show me you're sorry, I'll stop at ten. Otherwise I'll spank you until the cows come home."

"That's a dumb-ass idea." She was too angry to curb her mouth. "You're a dumb-ass." She tried to kick and got nowhere. "Even *Jesus* thinks you're a dumb-ass."

She heard a snort of laughter. Then his *way-too-hard* hand slapped her left butt cheek.

Burning pain. "Ow!" *He can't do this to me, dammit.* "You dick-weed! Are you always stupid, or is today a special occasion?"

"Gabrielle, I got a notion I might enjoy walloping you. Let me know when you're fixin' to start counting, subbie." Then the blows rained onto her bottom like all hell crashed down on her. And each slap hurt—really, really hurt.

She kicked and screamed. She needed to make him stop, to do something to hurt him back—she bit his leg.

He stopped and grabbed her hair before she got a good grip, then yanked her head away from his calf. *Ow ow ow.* "No, Gabrielle," he said firmly as if to a child, and a flash of shame raced through her. She'd tried to bite him?

He held her head up long enough for her to get the point, then released her hair and spanked her again. Even more harshly. When everything around her seemed to pulse with red-streaked pain, he stopped for a second. "You want to count, Gabrielle?"

"One!" She sucked in a breath, mad enough the words slid right out. "You asshole, one!"

Marcus clenched his teeth together to keep a bellow of laughter from escaping. Nolan and Dan had stopped to watch, and their shoulders shook with the same effort. Damn, how could he want to beat her curvy ass and still think she was so cute?

He waited until his voice steadied. "Bad-mouthing your dom isn't respectful, subbie. I do believe your count is at zero." As she squirmed, he caught flashes of her curly pubic hair. He sighed and gave her three more swats, this time on the tender undercurve of her cheeks.

She let out half a growl, half a shriek. "I'm sorry. One! One, okay? One, Sir."

He paused. "That does sound better, Gabrielle. One, then."

Anger gone, she pressed her face against his leg and began to cry.

His gut twisted. He enjoyed giving erotic spankings. And although fighting with a screaming little subbie was fun, hurting a crying one was entirely different. This felt too much like kicking a puppy. But backing off would be the wrong choice. She had to learn at gut level that her behavior had consequences.

Still, he lightened his blows and slowed enough so she could count: "Two, Sir. Three, Sir..."

When the count reached ten, he looked at her poor bottom and shook his head. He hadn't struck her nearly as forcefully as he did masochists and spanking addicts, but her fair, fair skin glowed a fiery red. She might even have a bruise or two just because her soft ass wasn't accustomed to punishment. He sighed and stroked her back, giving them both a second.

He noticed Nolan's sub when she trotted up and handed her dom a tube of lotion. Nolan caught Marcus's eye and wiggled the tube, then ran his knuckles over Beth's freckled cheek, her skin almost as pale as Gabrielle's. The dom had obviously run into the problem before.

Marcus nodded.

Nolan came over, flipped open the lid, and squeezed some lotion on Marcus's palm.

Wintergreen and the milder sunflower-like scent of arnica drifted in the air. Very nice. "Thank you, Nolan."

The dom's rough face held sympathy. "It really does help," he said quietly, then led his sub away.

"Don't move, sugar," Marcus warned Gabrielle. Dammit, this would hurt almost as much as the spanking. He set one hand on her lower back to hold her and started to massage the ointment into her reddened skin.

Her soft sobs broke into a thin scream, obviously from between gritted teeth.

Marcus winced. "This will help the bruising, sweetheart," he said, and despite her squirming, he did a thorough job.

Done. Marcus closed his eyes and exhaled. Damn Z for putting him in this position. This little sub should *not* be in the trainees. He waited another minute, stroking her gently.

"It's over, darlin'," he said finally and helped her stand. Her face was tear streaked and red from crying, and his heart squeezed.

He pulled her down to sit on his lap, leaning back so she could get most of her weight off her tender bottom. She still gave little hiccuping sobs, and he cuddled her close. Damn, he hated having to punish a sub, no matter how well deserved, and this time seemed worse than normal. Despite all her insolent behavior, she was a very likable woman.

He stroked her hair. *Why are you here, little sub?* "You could use your safe word, Gabrielle. You don't need to stay."

A pause. Her chin firmed despite her quivering lips. "No."

He sighed and rubbed his cheek on her silky hair, inhaling a feminine fragrance of rose and amber. "All right, Li'l Miss Stubborn." In that case, he needed to reinforce the lesson she'd just learned. Hopefully learned. "Respect, Gabrielle. A submissive must be polite and respectful. Do you understand?"

She sighed like a weary child and whispered against his neck, "Yes, Sir."

"I'm very glad. I don't think either of us wants a repeat of this." He held her as she settled and relaxed into him, accepting his comfort, which helped them both feel better. As a submissive needed the security of a dominant's arms, the dominant needed to provide it.

For some reason, with Gabrielle, his instincts cried out for him to hold her, to shield her, to protect her. Did she seem more vulnerable than most, despite the smart mouth, or was he pulled to her cheerful warmth like a winter fire? He tipped his head back and stared at the dark ceiling rafters. Damned if she wasn't getting to him. *God help me.*

She felt so soft in his arms. Her breathing evened out, and her slender fingers unclenched; one hand rested on his shirt over his heart. His shoulders relaxed as he realized she was snuggling. How long since he had held a woman who snuggled against him?

With a silent sigh, he pressed a kiss to the top of her head. "Up you go, darlin'." When she rose, he steadied her on her feet. "Now show me your pussy."

This time she not only didn't smart off but looked downright frightened. Slowly she lifted her skirt and showed him the red curls still adorning the mound he'd ordered her to shave.

When Master Marcus shook his head in disapproval, Gabi took a step back and tried to blink away the tears filling her eyes. Her butt hurt so bad, she wasn't sure she'd survive more punishment.

"I'm not fixin' to spank you again, Gabrielle," he said and rose, "although I am disappointed." Without further words, he hooked her cuffs together behind her, guided her to the submissives' sitting area, waited for her to kneel, and attached a chain from the floor to her cuffs.

"You just set here awhile. I'll send for you in a bit."

She hadn't realized how much she loved the molasses-thick warmth in his voice until it had turned cold. She lowered her head, unable to summon any ambition to act like a brat.

CHAPTER FIVE

Well, that had been amusing. The spotter for the Harvest Association sipped his bourbon as Marcus dragged the redhead to the area for chaining up submissives when their masters had duties elsewhere. Delightful show she'd put on, but now she appeared rather subdued. If one good spanking knocked the defiance out of her, she wouldn't do at all.

Fairly pretty, although a shame about the scar. Marred goods brought a lower selling price. But she was a decent age. Young enough to appeal, old enough to have some reserves. The ones inexperienced in life tended to shatter like glass. The Harvest Association prided itself on offering quality stock, and for the upcoming auction, they were selling an attitude, essentially promising that a master would have a good amount of fun before he finally broke his new slave.

Well, no hurry to make a decision. He'd already targeted two subs from the Shadowlands. They could pick this one up in the next harvest if she proved satisfactory.

He smiled. He did have a fondness for red hair.

Marcus would take requests from doms to scene with her. Might be fun to sample the goods beforehand.

Gabi's knees hurt. Her butt hurt. Her eyes felt swollen from crying, and her running mascara undoubtedly made her look like a raccoon. But inside she felt...content. Warm like when the kitties lay on her stomach.

He'd spanked her.

Damn him, she told herself, trying to find a spark of true anger. None there. She'd pushed him. Mostly as her bratty decoy dictated, but...part of her had wanted to see how far she could go. How far he'd *let* her go.

Not far at all, and he'd corrected her instantly. Painfully. He sure hadn't done the constant, silent disapproval like her parents. And then he'd held her as if the spanking had wiped her slate clean.

Had she hoped he wouldn't put up with her crap? Would take charge and punish her?

After fifteen minutes or so, she still hadn't discovered any explanation for her weird emotions. Out of the corner of her eye, she caught a flash of red.

In a short red vinyl skirt and bustier, the brunette trainee who always seemed so energetic trotted over. "Hi, Gabrielle. I'm Sally, if you don't remember."

Gabi straightened and pulled herself together. "You can call me Gabi. It's a little easier."

"Okay, Gabi." The brunette leaned against a chair and massaged her foot. "Damn Master Z's rules that subs either go barefoot or wear übersexy stilettos that would leave us crippled. More crippled."

Gabi managed a smile. "My feet haven't hurt like this since I waitressed in college."

"Oh, girlfriend, if your feet are the only things hurting at the end of an evening, you're in good shape."

"Yeah. So I've found."

"He really pounded on you good." Sally gave her a sympathetic look. "When he took us from Master Cullen, I thought he'd be a pushover. He's such a gentleman, you know. So polite and he never raises his voice, but damn, he's strict."

Gabi grimaced. "No kidding."

"He's death on bratty behavior. I heard him tell Nolan that his ex-wife acted out a lot, and we've noticed he chooses only the super-obedient ones for himself. Like his girlfriend—she makes you want to gag, she's so sweet."

He wanted his subs obedient and sweet. The information sent a pang through Gabi. *He'll never like me then.* Even if she wasn't acting defiant for the FBI, she'd still never be considered amenable. That just wasn't part of her makeup.

"Anyway, he wants you in the medical room. Do you know where it is?"

"At the back, down a hallway on the right?"

"That's it." Sally unhooked the chain and unclipped Gabi's cuffs, freeing her hands.

"Thanks." Trying to imagine what Marcus planned, Gabi threaded her way across the room, around a knot of arguing doms, past a crying sub with a domme whispering, "There, there." She dodged a gay couple working out their upcoming scene. Every man got a quick look to see if the perp might somehow give himself away. No such luck.

She passed the Goth-looking trainee and received a disapproving stare...as if her insolent behavior reflected badly on the other trainees. Gabi hadn't thought about how the other subs would view her actions, and a stab of guilt made her wince. *Sorry.*

In the hallway, she approached the medical room with increasing apprehension. Last night she'd seen all the nasty-looking equipment...and Marcus was angry at her. She stopped in the doorway, absently rubbing clammy fingers over the scar on her cheek.

The gynecological table took up the center of the room. A

sink and cupboards occupied the left, shelves at the rear, and a rolling stand with an enema bag hanging from it stood in one corner.

By the sink, Master Marcus was removing his coat. He tossed it over the back of a chair and rolled up the sleeves of his white shirt, baring disconcertingly muscled forearms. Spotting Gabi, he patted the exam table. "Up here, sugar. On your back."

Her feet stuck to the floor as if someone had covered the hardwood with adhesive. Last night she'd been appalled to see a woman getting an enema. It hadn't looked like fun at all. Surely he wouldn't...would he? She didn't even have to fake her defiance this time. "Whatever you're planning, I don't want to do."

He raised an eyebrow. "I believe I instructed you in the proper response to a command?"

The authoritative look in his eyes killed her rebellion dead. "Yes, Sir." She moved toward the table so slowly he huffed a laugh and grasped her by the nape again as if she were a cringing cur. Yet the feel of his warm, firm hand settled some of her nerves, making it easier to jump up onto the table. Her sore bottom met the cool leather, and she squeaked.

He chuckled. Then with his hand behind her back and another between her breasts, he firmly pushed her flat. Her heart jammed itself up in her throat, and she couldn't help glancing at the pole with the enema bag.

A crease appeared in his cheek, and he ran his hands up and down her upper arms. "Relax, darlin'. I'm not going to put long tubes up your pussy or ass."

"Thank you, Sir," she said fervently. He laughed, and damn, he seemed so different when he smiled that she wanted to say something, anything to keep the curve on his lips. He had a tiny crease off the corner of his—

"However, I am going to strap you down fairly tightly."

Her gaze shot up.

"And then, I'm fixin' to shave that little pussy of yours."

Oh God. No way. "I would rather do it myself. Really."

He ignored her and pushed the metal tray table toward her feet.

"Listen, I appreciate the offer, but I'm not interested in your help." He'd touch her, look at her down there, and the lighting here was way too bright. Her insides curled right up into a tiny little ball.

"I didn't ask your opinion." His steady gaze pierced her. Then his lips quirked up. "You're acting as nervous as a long-tailed cat in a roomful of rocking chairs."

With good reason, dammit.

At the foot of the table, he set her feet into the stirrups. When he strapped her ankles in, her eyes widened. Her gynecologist never did that. *Oh, this isn't good.*

After pushing her skirt up to expose her lower half, he slid her down the smooth leather until her butt rested on the edge of the table. A wide strap across her body just below her breasts pinned her arms to her sides. Then he secured another one across her waist and nodded. "That looks just fine."

Just fine? She wiggled, and as the full realization of her helplessness zinged through her, a thin sweat broke out on her body. She couldn't lift her arms, and her dread rose with each thwarted movement.

Arms folded, he watched her struggle. "Gabrielle." He spoke just the one word, his voice deep, breaking her out of the panic.

She looked into his steady eyes. He was utterly self-confident. Controlled. *Dominant*. A weird, glowy feeling lit inside her like a candle, melting her fears.

And heating her instead. She tried to close her legs, testing the restraints without success. Her pussy was completely exposed, and he'd be putting those lean, powerful hands on her most private parts. Oh God. More heat poured into her as if the candle had set something aflame.

He smiled and said softly, "There we go."

A metal stand held a bowl of water, razors, and bottles. After pushing it to the foot of the table, Marcus sat on a rolling stool and stationed himself between her legs. With a tsking sound, he pushed the stirrups father apart, opening her completely.

She stiffened, unnerved at the way he'd repositioned her. Not asking, just doing. He'd do to her just as he pleased. Excitement tingled across her skin, and she felt her nipples bunching so tightly they hurt.

The hum of conversation drew her attention to where people stood in the hallway, looking through the huge windows. At her. At her exposed pussy. She moaned and closed her eyes.

A warm hand stroked over her calf, a soothing, petting gesture. "Trainees are often on display, sugar. Can you handle that?"

His concern made her breath catch. How long since anyone had worried about her feelings? She tried to push the thought away. *Don't get caught up in this sub stuff, girl. You're here as a decoy, nothing else.*

And aside from the craving to run screaming out of the place, she was handling it just fine. *Handle it better.* What if the kidnapper stood out in the hallway with the other people? The thought chilled her and spurred her into action. She rattled the stirrups and snapped, "Doesn't look like I have much choice, now does it? Do you tie up all your girlfriends?"

Silence. The stool squeaked as he rose. He walked slowly to her side and looked at her for a long minute, and then the sternness in his gaze faded into such understanding that her eyes burned. He cupped her cheek, his thumb stroking over her lips. She had to firm her chin to keep it from quivering.

"Do you get more mouthy when you're scared, darlin'?"

She couldn't think of a thing to say.

"Gabrielle, trainees have a lot more experience in the lifestyle, and they want what the Shadowlands offers. You, however..."

She stiffened, jolted into awareness that she might have

pushed him too far. She hadn't even made it through two nights, and he wanted to boot her out. But Z said he couldn't if she refused to go. "I do, Sir. I want it."

He studied her. "I don't believe you. You know, if anyone but Master Z had admitted you..." He sighed. "If I asked you to leave right now, would you?"

She set her lips and shook her head.

"I think you're biting off more than you can chew, but so be it." He looked at her a minute longer, then touched his finger to her nose. "Stubborn."

She inhaled in relief as he returned to his stool. A second later, a warm washcloth landed on her pussy, making her jump.

Marcus frowned through the entire shaving process. He could usually get inside the head of a sub and figure out what made them tick, what they wanted and what they needed as well. But this little one...

Not used to being handled intimately. Not comfortable with public display although he believed her when she said she'd played in clubs before. The Shadowlands, however, was more personal than a horde of strangers.

He finished shaving the top of her mound, then inserted two fingers into her vagina, ignoring her gasp. Hot and silky. Very nice. Again he noted her tightness—as if she hadn't had a man in a long time. He doubted her hiatus from sex came from a low sex drive since she was definitely aroused right now.

Thrusting unhurriedly in and out of her soft cunt, he felt her muscles constrict around his intrusion. His cock hardened, demanding he intrude farther, but he couldn't do that. Although he'd arrange scenes for her with other doms, he'd wait for a while before taking her himself. She needed to know she could trust her trainer.

Eventually though...he looked forward to playing with her. Her sassiness didn't annoy him, not in the way he'd thought it would. It was more of a challenge. And in between her idiotic rebellions, her cheerful personality drew him like a fire on a cold mountain morning. A few burns from sparks might prove worth the chance to get warm.

After withdrawing his fingers from her vagina, he pulled the skin taut on her outer labia. She had pretty curls, the same golden red as on her head. A natural redhead. The fiery color was well suited to her personality. The razor scraped her clean, exposing skin the color of rich cream. Plump pink inner folds peeked out from the center.

He drew her buttocks apart, smiling at her instinctive stiffening, and removed the scant hair closer to her anus. The puckered bud would obviously need some preparation before she accepted a cock there.

After rinsing off the shaving cream, he massaged in gel to decrease the irritation and considered his problem. Unlike the other trainees, Gabrielle hadn't been a part of the Shadowlands for months. To make the situation worse, her previous club play had been light. And because of her constant defiance, they'd gotten off to a bad start.

No wonder Z's friend considered her a problem. No dom would put up with such excessive insolence for long. Or one might consider it an excuse to whip the hell out of her. The thought turned his stomach, yet he had few choices here. She needed to want to please him more than she wanted to defy him, but until she did or he figured out what would motivate her, he'd have to discipline her.

It seemed like punishing her was all he'd accomplished tonight. He stroked her thigh and felt the faint quiver. Her eyes were closed, her breathing a little fast, nipples in taut peaks. Needy. Already restrained. Marcus smiled. He'd very much like to give her as much pleasure as he had pain, and nothing made a woman more vulnerable or created a bond faster than giving her an orgasm.

Leaning forward, he framed her pussy with his hands and ran his tongue up and over her clit.

She'd known he'd finished when he rubbed in a cool gel and stroked her thigh comfortingly. Gabi relaxed. She'd worried for a minute when he'd pushed his fingers into her pussy, but then he'd simply resumed shaving her. He'd let her up now, and maybe she could leave. She really, really wanted to go home and try to get her emotions back under control.

She saw him lean forward, felt his hands pull her labia apart, and...something hot and wet slid right over her *clit*. She jerked so hard the straps pinched her skin. *Oh my God*! He was licking —*licking*—her. The blast of heat ran through her like a forest fire.

His tongue worked inward, stroking newly bare areas never before touched like this, then playing with her clit, teasing the hood and grazing over the very top. Her entire body hit complete need as if she'd turned into a sports car, zero to a hundred in eight seconds.

She gasped when he pushed two fingers inside her, ruthlessly stretching her open, sending pleasure deep into her core. He pulled back slowly, circled her entrance, then thrust his fingers in and out, setting up a fast, driving rhythm. Dear God, this wasn't sex play, this was a total you-will-come-now, done by someone who knew just how to make it happen. Her hips kept trying to rise, defeated by the strap across her waist. Pressure formed low in her belly and coiled tight...tighter. She hovered on the peak for just a second.

And then he pulled her clit into his mouth and sucked, sliding his tongue over the most sensitive spot.

Everything inside her exploded, shooting pleasure outward so strong and fast that her head should have shattered. More waves of heat burst through her until her fingers tingled.

His tongue lapped her gently, making her vagina clench again and again, each time meeting the solid fingers inside her. God, she couldn't move, couldn't escape, and every time she tried and failed, another wave would sweep over her.

When the roller coaster finally stopped, he removed his fingers, and she shuddered at the feeling of loss. For a minute, he stroked her thigh, easing her down, and then walked around the table.

"You come quite nicely, darlin'," he said softly. He put an arm on each side of her shoulders, and she had a moment to see those thick forearms before he bent to nuzzle her neck. His wonderful scent, a subtle amber and musk, surrounded her. When his beard shadow scraped the hollow under her ear, goose bumps bloomed across her body. He kissed her gently, nibbled her lips, and plunged in.

She could taste herself and then only him as he took her mouth, demanding a response in the same way he had her orgasm. She melted inside under the heady knowledge that he could take what he wanted from her—and she'd give him whatever he wanted.

When he pulled back, his eyes were heavy-lidded. "You kiss as nicely as you come, Gabrielle. Next week we'll have more time together, but I didn't want to leave you uncomfortable until then."

The sound of a high voice drew her notice, and she realized people still stood in the hallway, watching. Audience. She had a job to do, even though she'd rather lie here and soak up his attention—his approving attention that made her feel as if he liked her. Damned if she didn't really want him to like her.

No, Gabi. Think, think. Must act like a brat for the audience. A little difficult to do, considering how she was tied down. And she'd just come. Then again, she could attack the man where it would hurt the most—on his performance. "You think I got off? That was a hiccup from too much lunch," she said loudly and heard a few gasps as well as a titter of laughter.

His eyes narrowed. "An ornery one, aren't you? Trainee, I

believe you'd best have no confusion over what you're feeling. Perhaps a lesson is in order." The expression on his face wasn't angry, quite, or annoyed, quite. Not even determined. He acted as if she'd merely confirmed his expectations. Without explanation, he turned and took gloves and lube from the shelves beside the sink.

Glove? Lube? *Wait*. "Sir?"

"Shhh, sugar, I think it's time for another hiccup." Still standing, he grasped the table's stirrups and ratcheted them upward until her feet were not only widely spread, but as high as his shoulders. The position lifted her butt an inch, but the strap around her waist kept the rest of her body flat on the table. "That's just right."

She raised her head to see what he was doing, but he held his hands below the level of the table. Giving up, she laid her head down, wanting to take back her words, yet oddly excited at not knowing what he'd do next. Nothing about him was predictable; she had a feeling he never would be. He was...smart. Maybe too smart for her, and that was an uncomfortable thought.

After resuming his seat on the stool, he glided his tongue and lips over her pussy, slower this time. Her head started to spin. When he licked over her clit, she clenched her hands at the sudden return of need. He bit her labia, and the strange, stinging pain somehow made everything else more intense. He kept teasing her, and she realized he planned to make her climax again. If she thought to prevent it... Well, she couldn't, she realized, as her clit hardened under the firm attention of his tongue. No matter what she wanted, he would have her coming again in front of all these people.

Then something slick and round circled her anus. "Wait—I didn't agree to this. Hey!"

"No, I planned to explore anal sex in your training later," he said and pressed his finger against the puckered circle of muscle, making her squirm. "But things change. You have a tight little asshole, sugar. Push back against me now, and you'll find it easier."

She pulled in an unhappy breath and, realizing she had no choice, did as he asked. A merciless gloved finger penetrated where no lover had ever gone before. A tremor shook her at the way he'd relentlessly done as he wanted.

"Gabrielle. Look at me."

She lifted her gaze.

He watched her face as his finger eased farther in. Not quite pain. The cool lubricant made him very slick, yet even the slightly increased girth of his knuckle stretched and burned. As he took possession of a place that was so very private, her insides felt funny—as if he'd taken possession of her inner self as well. She tried to squirm away and failed. "No...please."

"Shhh. You don't have the reins, sugar." The controlled power in his low voice slid into her; his steady eyes pinned hers, forcing her to focus on him...and yet his finger didn't stop moving, the lesson inescapable. He could touch her anywhere.

I don't like this. It was too intimate, left her feeling exposed and—

His eyes released her. He smiled and lowered his head. *Oh God, he wouldn't...*

A whine escaped her when he licked her clit again, so hot, so wet. Before she could adjust to that added stimulation, he slid two fingers inside her vagina, ruthlessly creating a counterpoint of thrusts with the finger in her bottom. His tongue rubbed its demand on one side of her clit, then the other, then the top.

Sensations blasted through her from too many places, and her arousal grew, building high and hard. Somehow, as if a switch flipped, the uncomfortable sensations in her anus changed into a dark pleasure, merging with the slick sliding in her vagina until her whole pussy—her whole lower half—felt like one giant clit about to explode.

Every muscle in her body contracted. Her hips lifted futilely against the strap, trying to get closer. Her breath froze, waiting for just a little more, anything more...

His low chuckle vibrated against her labia, and then he licked insistently right over her clit, his tongue staying on it, wiggling right...there...and everything inside her spasmed in a giant tsunami of sensation, sweeping her away. The sensations from her anus added a whole new dimension until even her skin seemed to expand, billowing outward. *God God God.*

As the waves subsided, and her brain clicked back on, she could still hear her yelping screams echoing around the room.

Laughter and some applause came from the hallway. She opened her eyes, blearily realizing that people had definitely watched her. Oh hell.

"Nice hiccups, Gabrielle." Master Marcus's final tonguing sent a shudder up her center.

She bit her lip. *I am totally not going to taunt him right now.*

With baby wipes from the tray, he proceeded to clean her so thoroughly, front and back, that a mortified flush heated her face.

When he finally helped her off the table, her head spun as if she'd ridden a merry-go-round for an hour, and he caught her with a powerful grip before she did a face-plant. Chuckling, he wrapped a blanket around her and sat her in a chair to one side while he cleaned the room.

He pulled on his suit jacket and stood in front of her for a second, then shook his head and scooped her into his arms.

"Jesus, wait, you can't carry me," she gasped. What if lifting her strained his back? What if he dropped her?

He only laughed. Hell, he wasn't even watching where he walked.

She struggled to get out of the confining blanket, and he said in a firm voice, "Lie still, li'l subbie, or you'll have a different type of lesson."

Oh, that definitely sounded like a threat. She stilled. As he carried her out of the hallway and into the club, she stared at the distant floor, cringed, and looked up at his face instead. He had a stern jawline. His white shirt was opened a couple of buttons, displaying his corded neck. Against her shoulder, his rock-hard bicep bunched, yet he didn't act as if he carried anything heavier than a...a poodle or something.

She tried to relax, unsure if she liked the sensation of being cared for—whether she wanted to be or not.

At a small sitting area hidden from the main room by a row of plants, he settled into an oversize leather chair. She glanced around. Completely private...she wouldn't have to perform right now.

He tipped her against his chest, settling her head into the hollow of his shoulder. "There we go," he murmured. "Are you comfortable, sweetheart?"

"Yes, Sir," she whispered. He was being so nice. Unexpected and unwelcome tears prickled her eyes. "Why are you doing this?"

He pushed her hair back behind her ear, then put a finger under her chin, lifting her face. "What do you mean by 'this'? Holding you?"

"Yes. And...and getting me off when you didn't...and shaving me...and—"

"You are very inexperienced in true dom-sub relationships, aren't you?" With her head against him, she could hear the laugh rumbling in his chest. "Many reasons, sugar. First, I'm holding you now because you needed to be held." He kissed her lips softly. "As your trainer and dom, it's my job to see that you get what you need."

"But I wanted down."

His mouth turned up in a faint smile. "What you need, sugar, not what you want."

Why did that send a tremor through her yet make her snuggle closer? Why did an iron-hard arm behind her back feel like safety?

But as her parents complained, a more argumentative person

than Gabrielle had never lived. "I didn't need to get off." Hadn't even thought about it.

"You need to learn that pleasure as well as pain comes from your dom's hands." His eyes met her, level and confident. "And you need to know, right down to the bone, that I have access to every part of your body."

He'd shaved her, such an intimate task, and touched her, controlled her, forced an orgasm from her. He'd put his finger into her bottom and made her come again. Even now, his arms held her so firmly that she realized she remained under his control.

Her whole body started to shake as if she'd been sitting in the snow, and her breath thickened, forcing her to work for air. This wasn't what she'd signed on for. He kept taking...more, like with a Monopoly game, seeing her hotels and land disappear piece by piece until the banker owned her. *I don't want him to own me.*

I don't...

She tried to get up. His arms caged her.

He rubbed his chin on the top of her head, enjoying the light feminine scent. He'd discovered the lingering fragrance in the crease of her hip and in the hollow of her neck. Her lotion matched her shampoo. Her clothing today was coordinated, and yesterday her toenails had been the same blue as her hair. She liked pushing against rules, but in her own life, she liked...consistency? Order?

So maybe her need to rebel wasn't to reject rules entirely, but just those imposed by another.

Her reaction to his control—the way she trembled now—worried him. So new to domination. She shouldn't be a trainee. *What the hell are you doing, Z?* Her fetish club visits had probably given her a few thrills. A sub's first time under command, no matter how lightweight, could be a revelation for her. But she had no experience with surrendering not only her body but her emotions as well.

Is that why she kept defying everyone? She wanted to submit, yet it frightened her? *No. Maybe.* He frowned. Sometimes she appeared uncomfortable with her own behavior, as if she didn't want to disobey. Other times her sassiness seemed true to her personality.

And right about the time he wanted to write her off, she'd respond so sweetly she'd rouse every dominant instinct in him.

He tightened his arms around her for both control and comfort and simply held her. Because that's what she needed now —and so did he. The memory of spanking her didn't sit well with him.

A man didn't hurt a woman, not where he came from. In BDSM, he'd learned many submissives loved being given pain to heighten their pleasure. It had taken him longer to understand that pain dispensed for punishment could often fill a submissive's emotional needs.

Other aspects of BDSM had proven easier to accept. Domination. Bondage... He definitely enjoyed bondage, watching a little sub squirm, then give him...everything.

How long before Gabrielle reached that point?

Probably a while. She was quite the piece of work.

At the sound of soft footsteps, he looked up to see Celine mosey past the sitting area. Although he'd dated the lovely blonde a few times and occasionally topped her here, he hadn't called her in a month or so. Not since he'd realized his income and his status in the club interested her more than his personality.

She glanced over, pretended surprise at seeing him, and came to kneel at his feet. "Can I get you a drink, Master?"

Dammit, her use of *master* grated on him. The title, used without his name, implied he was *her* master, a relationship encompassing far more than a few scenes.

Gabrielle stirred. She stared at Celine, then squirmed, trying to rise.

"Stop, Gabrielle," Marcus said. He frowned at Celine and jerked his head in a way that left no chance for her to misunderstand. An experienced sub, she knew better than to interrupt obvious aftercare.

Pouting, she rose and moved away.

Gabrielle had stilled, but her uncomfortable expression said the quiet moment had passed. And it was indeed time for him to return to check on the other trainees. He ignored his reluctance to let her go and set her on her feet. Her balance stayed good. Her eyes were clear and alert, although her tear-streaked mascara tugged at his heart.

But she was back to normal. He had no excuse to sit and hold her longer, no matter how much he'd enjoyed it. How content he'd been.

She started to adjust her skirt from where he'd tucked it under the waistband.

"Leave it as it is, Gabrielle. People should get a chance to admire my handiwork." When she glared, he smothered his laugh. Definitely back to normal. "Follow one step behind me and speak only when addressed. Do you understand?"

"Yes, Sir."

CHAPTER SIX

As Gabi followed Marcus around the room like a pet, she tried to summon up her bratty sub, but it felt as if he had an invisible leash hooked deep within her. And each time he gave her an order, instead of getting angry, she melted inside.

He wandered through the room, checking on his other trainees, stopping to chat with members in his quiet drawl. He liked people, she could see, and got along well with everyone. A charmer, always knowing the right words to use. Like her father.

"Stay here for a second, sugar," he said.

She scrubbed her hands over her face, trying to figure out where her spine had gone. *In a puddle on the floor* wasn't an answer she wanted to hear.

Marcus stepped away to speak to the blonde who'd offered to get him a drink.

Obediently Gabi waited. *Come. Stay. Nice dog.* She amused herself with lifting her lip in a snarl and silently growling at the blonde who'd moved close enough to rub her breasts over Marcus's arm.

When he returned, he touched Gabi's cheek. "Thank you for your patience, sugar. Now I need to find Sally and—"

"Marcus."

The deep, rich voice made her spin. *Master Z. Oh, hell.* Heat rushed into her face as the owner's gaze ran over her. He didn't react to her skirt tucked in her waistband, baring her pussy. Why did her exposure feel more embarrassing with someone who knew who she really was?

Speaking of who she was, she needed to pull herself together. No matter how many warm fuzzies she got when Master Marcus complimented her, she mustn't follow his orders.

"Z, how are you tonight, sir?" Master Marcus said, his slow drawl making his voice even smoother than Master Z's.

"I'm fine. How is your new submissive?"

"After a few bumps in the road, I believe she's learning." Master Marcus's tone chilled. "I fear she has less experience than you implied."

"Indeed." Master Z frowned. "May I speak with her?"

Marcus hesitated and then nodded.

Master Z stepped closer, tipped her chin up, and studied her face. "It sounds as if you're having a rough time, little one," he said for her ears only. "Are you all right?"

His sympathy made her eyes burn, and she took a second to steady her voice. "Yes, Sir. I'm fine." Involuntarily she glanced at Master Marcus and saw his brows had drawn together.

A short blonde standing slightly behind Master Z had the same displeased expression.

Jessica Randall stared at Z in shock. He acted so concerned and had touched that new sub so protectively. *I've never seen him do that before*. Not like that. A knot in her chest hurt as if she'd swallowed something—like jealousy—that kept growing.

"If you're sure," Z said to the redhead. He squeezed her shoulder and stepped back.

The arm he put around Jessica didn't warm her as it usually did. "Jessica, this is Gabrielle, our new trainee."

A trainee? Not a new sub of Marcus's? Surprised, Jessica turned to Marcus and hesitated a second. She didn't really know him that well. Nonetheless... "You brought in a new trainee? She's not even a member."

"Master Z is doing someone a favor," Marcus said, his drawl more clipped than usual.

Jessica pulled away from Z and scowled at him. "But Rainie is at the top of the list. She's supposed to get the next trainee position."

"This isn't your concern, Jessica," Z said, his voice dangerously low.

"That isn't fair." Jessica set her hands on her hips. Rainie had whooped and screamed in delight over the chance to be a trainee. "Why is Rainie getting passed over for someone who never—"

"Silence." The snap in his voice not only shut Jessica up but everyone else in the immediate area.

She took a step back, knowing she'd gone too far. And with Z that was never a good thing.

He pulled a leather gag from his pocket. "You've exceeded my patience, Jessica."

A gag? She glared at him and shook her head. He'd had it in his pocket—like he'd planned to gag her all along.

His eyes turned from gray to almost black, and her resolve crumbled into mush. When he crooked his finger—*come*—she obeyed.

After work on Monday, Jessica drove down the tiny country road toward the Shadowlands. The spatters of rain against the windshield matched her mood perfectly—the mood she'd suffered since Saturday night. How dare he have gagged her? He knew how much she hated that, dammit. She moved her jaw side to side, feeling as if the stupid thing still filled her mouth. She should have punched him.

Instead she'd melted. Like always. The touch of his sure hands firmly tying the gag, the overpowering way he looked at her, the unyielding grip on her shoulder as he kept her right beside him—she'd probably never get enough of that, even if they lived to a hundred.

If we're still together. The disheartening thought pulled her down like quicksand. Sinking. Inescapable.

After slowing her car, she drove through the iron gates and up the palm-lined driveway. Under the rain, the flowers turned their bright blooms toward the ground, muting the landscape.

Z rarely gagged her, so why had he last Saturday? Because of that woman, Gabrielle? Her eyes narrowed. A new trainee brought in without any warning seemed strange. He and the trainers—first Cullen and now Marcus—usually discussed potential trainees to the point of nausea, wanting just the right person. Aside from Andrea, they'd always chosen them from longtime members.

Why the change? The unease inside her grew. The way Z had looked at Gabrielle had been...different. Of course, he always acted as if all the subs in the club were his responsibility to protect. Jessica loved that...mostly. She did hate the way submissives came on to him, even though he made it clear Jessica was his sub. She couldn't blame the other subs—who wouldn't want Z?—but so many were drop-dead gorgeous. She couldn't help wondering when he'd find one he liked better than her.

But this new trainee wasn't beautiful. She wasn't as overly round as Jessica, but still a little on the heavier side. Friendly-looking, with a wide smile and big eyes. And yet, Z had squeezed her shoulder and smiled at her as if she was more than a new trainee. Like they had a secret or something.

Why hadn't he said anything about doing a favor for someone?

Then again, all this week, Z had acted reticent. She'd even asked if something at work had bothered him. His patients were all children, and sometimes their problems, their pasts, ripped him up inside, but he'd said no.

And then she'd wondered if he was unhappy that her doctor had taken her off the pill last month, forcing them to return to condoms. But he hadn't seemed upset at the time. She pulled the car into the side parking lot and turned off the engine. The gusting wind rocked the car as she watched clouds blacken the sky.

Maybe she'd blown everything out of proportion. She had to admit she felt insecure right now...with good reason. Z's sons had arrived yesterday to spend a few days with him before they returned to the University of Florida, and Z wanted her to meet them. Avoiding his children for—oh, a lifetime—seemed a much better plan, but he'd refused to listen to her protests.

"You've stalled long enough, pet," he'd said yesterday morning as she prepared to leave, and she'd seen the amusement in his dark gray eyes. "You might as well get it over with."

He could be such a jerk sometimes.

Okay. Here goes nothing. She slid out of the car and went through the side gate to the back, hoping to find them on the covered veranda where she could easily escape. No such luck. Great. Her hands grew clammy as she climbed to the third floor. The sprinkling rain and the wind turned her hair into a tangled mass. She sighed. So much for the time she'd spent making herself pretty. Could life get any better?

She reached the third floor and knocked.

Z opened the door a minute later, dressed in his usual black slacks and black shirt. "Did you lose your key?"

"Uh. No. But I didn't want to..."

He chuckled and put his hand on her lower back to direct her into the house. "You didn't want my sons to discover their father has a life beyond being a parent?"

"Well. Yes."

Z turned her to face him, setting his hands on her shoulders. “Kitten, my boys know who you are.”

“Oh.” What had he told them? Why hadn’t she asked more questions yesterday like, *What exactly do the boys know about us?*

He led her into the living room, where the two young men sat in the dark leather chairs. Z stopped beside the couch and said, “Jessica, this is Eric. He’s a senior this year”—he pointed to a tall, lanky blond—“and Richard, a junior.” Richard had black hair and brown eyes. Muscular. Both wore jeans. Richard’s T-shirt displayed a country-western band; Eric’s a metal chick band.

“It’s nice to meet you both,” she said, taking a seat on the couch. She leaned against the end, idly tracing a dent in the leather left from Sunday morning when Z had bent her over the arm, then... She jerked her hand away and straightened, feeling herself turn red.

Z chuckled and said, “I’ll get you a drink, Jessica.” The way his eyes danced with laughter, he knew exactly what she’d remembered. The jerk.

As he left the room with his silent gait, she turned her attention to the two young men. They were studying her closely.

Although Eric frowned at her, Richard grinned in obvious approval. “You’ve been seeing Dad for a year?”

“A bit more.” And nothing had changed in that year.

“How’d you meet?” Eric asked. His cold gaze assessed her, and his mouth twisted as if he thought her a whore who’d wandered off her street corner. She tried not to take it personally. He probably acted that way toward any of his father’s women.

“It was a dark and stormy night,” she started, winning a snort of laughter from Richard. “An armadillo lay in the center of the road, and when I braked, I skidded right into a ditch filled with water.”

“Did you miss the armadillo?” Richard’s brown eyes held concern.

He sounded as protective as his father. She gave him a warm

smile. "I did. Then I walked here to see if I could call a tow truck."

Z handed her a drink. He joined her on the couch and rested his arm across the back. "She bore a distinct resemblance to a drowned cat."

The two boys laughed.

"Thanks a lot." Jessica frowned at Z, but when her eyes met his, she remembered the rest of that night. How he'd taken charge, forcing her to take a shower, drying her off himself... everywhere... despite her protestations. He'd overwhelmed her—he still did, dammit.

The laugh lines beside his eyes crinkled as if he remembered as well.

"Yeah, well, Mom says hi," Eric said, drawing their attention back to him. "She's getting a divorce from that loser. Finally."

"Finally," Richard echoed. "She's sure got screwed-up taste in men...aside from you, of course."

Z inclined his head. "Of course."

"I've noticed with divorced people that after the first marriage, the next choice is always crappy," Eric said, aiming the cut right at her.

She tried not to wince, but even knowing how a son might resent his father seeing anyone new, the insult still hurt. She knew she hadn't concealed her reaction well when Z squeezed her shoulder.

"Eric." Z's firm voice had the same effect on the young man as on the subs in the club.

Eric flushed. "Sorry." He shoved to his feet and crossed the room, not quite stomping. "It's just... Fuck, Dad, look at her. She's *our* age. She could be your daughter, for Christ's sake."

Z sighed. "Only if I'd started making babies at eleven."

She'd known meeting his children would turn into a disaster. Jessica forced a smile. "I appreciate the compliment, Eric. Especially since turning thirty this year really sucked."

He didn't look like he believed either of them.

Richard grinned at his brother. "Put your foot into it, dumbass."

Eric scowled at him, then her. "Yeah, well. Sorry."

No, you aren't. She looked down at her hands as her stomach twisted around the lump that had formed. Maybe he had a point.

Hopefully the personnel office wouldn't waste their time trying to hire her, Gabi thought as she walked out of the Tampa department store. The muggy air filmed her skin with damp until her inexpensive tan slacks and button-down shirt felt pasted on. With a disgusted sigh, she pulled the newspaper from her bag and checked the next stop on her job-hunting excursion. Oh joy—an auto repair shop needed a receptionist.

The job-hunting directive had come from the two agents leading the investigation. Kouros and his partner wanted her to appear unemployed so the kidnapper'd think no one would notice if she disappeared. But, *please*, she hadn't liked looking for work even when she'd really needed a job.

She'd have to play this game for three more weeks. Unless the perp tried for her. The thought sent a shiver through her. Sure she had backup, but she knew too well arrests often went bad. She could get kidnapped like Kim.

I could die. Her life could end. Just...stop. She looked around. To never walk on sun-scorched sidewalks again, never see a limitless, blue sky, or hear a little girl giggle over an ice cream cone. She worked with the survivors of aggression every day, knew the devastation that accompanied senseless death.

Now she'd purposely put herself squarely in the path, like lying down in front of a train. She swallowed. At least this time, the violence would only be directed at her. If everything fell apart, no one she cared about would get hurt.

Because people did get hurt when bad things happened. Despite the heat of the afternoon, her skin chilled as she heard again the sharp blast of a pistol in a small room, heard Danny's low grunt and the gut-twisting sound of a bullet punching through cloth and flesh. Red splattering out across everything. The way he'd hit the floor, limbs flopping—her scream wiping out the thud. The shock on his face made it all so much more horrifying. He hadn't thought he'd die that day.

As her chest tightened and sickness welled inside her, she shook her head. *Stop, just stop*. She forced a long inhalation. Another. Rubbing her hand against the brick wall behind her, she let the abrasive pain anchor her in the present. In the here and now, where cars flowed down the street. Most were white. Then a yellow sports car. A red pickup. A horn beeped, and brakes squealed. Two teenagers, hair in dreadlocks, argued as they sauntered past. Then one threw back his head and laughed. *Life goes on.*

Shaking inside, she watched the noisy, energetic world around her. She'd gone a year without any flashbacks and had hoped they'd left completely. After all, Danny and Rock had died ten years ago. That day had been one of those life-defining moments, the day she'd discovered that horrible things really can happen and people you love can die. Suddenly. Violently.

After scrubbing her face with her hands, she strode down the sidewalk as if to outrun her memories. Not possible, but sometimes she could fast-forward to the end. How she'd cowered in a corner, unable to run, blood pouring down her cheek, more between her legs. A man had entered the tiny apartment. Silver-haired, deep lines beside his mouth, his face open and honest. His long-sleeved shirt clean and white, with no terrifying red splotches.

She'd whimpered like a hurt animal, unable to stop the pitiful sounds. When he had come closer, she pushed back against the wall, making herself smaller, tugging at her torn clothing as if it could shield her. He'd snapped something, and someone handed him a blanket. He'd stepped forward. She shook her head, *no no no*, but he had simply opened the blanket and dropped it onto her lap. And then he'd backed up and knelt a few feet away. Far enough that she had managed to breathe again. Could look at him. "*My name is Abe, and I'm with the FBI, sweetie*." He'd waited a moment for her to understand, then said, "*I'm here just for you. To help you. Let me take you someplace safe*."

There is good in this world to balance the bad.

She'd been given a gift—a person who understood, who listened, who helped put her life back together. And using him as a model, she'd become an FBI victim specialist—someone who could reach past the terror. Could listen. Could help.

Speaking of which...

A bench at a bus stop provided a seat, and a tall maple lent some shade against the burning sun. With the ugly disposable cell phone Agent Kouros had provided—*did she look like a person who'd carry a gray phone?*—she checked the status of a victim's compensation process and called her temporary replacement, Zella, to remind her of Josh's court date and that the teen would need hand-holding.

As Gabi answered Zella's questions on the other cases, guilt stabbed deep inside her. People depended on her, and she'd run off to Tampa to serve as a decoy. When they'd finished reviewing, Zella said, "The boss says you're off on medical leave." A pause. "I heard a rumor from the Tampa office you're there doing something exciting."

Gabi's mouth dropped open. Then anger bit. Someone should muffle that gossipy secretary. She watched the traffic—black car, taxi, white car—and said truthfully, "I'm seeing no excitement here. I'll be back and raring to go within three weeks or so."

"Good to hear. I've heard a lot of whining about your absence, especially from the kids."

The warmth that spread through her outfaced the sun. *It's nice to be missed*. "Thanks. See you soon."

After disconnecting, Gabi dialed Rhodes. He didn't answer. Of course. Dickhead wouldn't take calls if he wasn't on duty. Yet someone needed to deal with this quickly. Scowling, she dialed the backup number.

"Galen Kouros." She'd have known him from the New England accent.

"This is Gabrielle Renard."

"Gabrielle. What can I help you with?"

She bit her lip. Ratting on someone. Maybe she should have—

"Is there a problem, Gabrielle?"

"Well, I hear there're rumors I might not be on medical leave, that I'm doing something exciting in Tampa. Perhaps it's not that bad, but—"

"And how did you hear this?" His voice took on a grim tone.

Oh hell, she wasn't supposed to contact her office. "Ah. I called to check that my replacement is doing all right and answer questions about my caseload."

Silence and a sigh. "Victim specialists. I suppose I should have expected that. Bighearted social workers." He made the term sound more like an insult than a compliment. "I'll deal with the leak and speak with your replacement. You concentrate on your current job."

Considering the way he made Gabi feel like an idiot, the poor secretary was in for a rough time. "Yes, sir."

"I spoke with Z by the way; you did a fine job at the club last weekend. Your prior experience is making a difference—the other three decoys aren't doing nearly as well."

After he'd clicked off, she stared at the phone for a moment. A compliment? Well. How nice after hearing all of Rhodes's complaints.

And enduring Marcus's disapproval. Her throat tightened at the memory. How could the disappointed look in the dom's eyes be more difficult to bear than a physical punishment?

Not relevant, Gabi. Get back to work. She scowled as she uncrumpled the page of ads. On to the next token job application. Only a block away. She slung her purse over her shoulders and headed down the sidewalk. She felt sorry for the poor agent trailing her, waiting in the hot street while she filled out fake applications in air-conditioned offices.

But he'd get the weekend off, while she'd have to continue her act at the Shadowlands.

And she'd see Master Marcus again. Her heart gave an extra beat. What was it about that man—that dom? How could she want another perfect suit-person like her last boyfriend? The last few dates with Andrew, he'd never stopped criticizing her: her attire, her manners, her attitude, even the way she made love. When she'd realized he sounded like her parents and that she'd permitted him to make her feel inadequate, she'd called it quits.

Mr. Perfect Marcus was just one more like Andrew—even a lawyer, for God's sake. *Do not get attracted to another conservative prig, Gabi.*

At the intersection, the light changed, and she followed the cluster of pedestrians across the street. Two men beside her razzed each other about a failed weekend date. Having fun.

Unlike her reserved father, Marcus did seem to have fun. He had a big, open laugh, and he joked with his friends. She sighed. And when he wasn't unhappy with her, he'd been so warm she'd wanted to curl up at his feet.

Even after she'd taunted him, he hadn't lost his temper. Instead he'd tried to figure out what would reach her. As a social worker, she recognized how he searched for a susceptible place where he could push her in the direction he wanted her to go. He might well find it. She had vulnerabilities, everyone did, and maybe she had a few more than some.

He's gotten to me, hasn't he? She already wanted to please him and felt bad when she sassed him...and she really wanted to see him again.

The realization worried her. How could she possibly look

forward to being under his control? God, that spanking had hurt. She hadn't cried like that in years. But afterward he'd held her, pressing her head against his strong shoulder, murmuring comfort in that rich drawl. Had anyone ever cared for her so sweetly?

Or aroused her so thoroughly? She'd sure never come so hard. Ever. The memories had given her lushly erotic dreams every single damned night, and she'd wake up hurting from needing to come.

But she hadn't gotten herself off. *Gold star for me*. He'd told her not to come without permission, and she wanted to please him, even though her entire purpose in the Shadowlands was to defy him. Yes, the devious, perfect dom had snuck under her defenses. She set her jaw. Too bad for her...and him.

Straightening her shoulders, she walked a little faster. Next Friday and Saturday, Master Marcus could deal with her defiance, and she could deal with his response...somehow. That's just the way it had to be.

CHAPTER SEVEN

Carrying a tray full of drinks, Gabi paused as the members watching a noisy ménage session blocked her path. She shook her head. The whole place was filled. How wonderful. More people to laugh at her getting in trouble.

She had a feeling tonight wouldn't be nearly as pleasant as last night.

On Friday, she'd pushed herself to extreme brattiness, but aside from one swarthy dom and the bartender, who'd both punished her, no one seemed to care. Marcus had arrived late, then done a scene with that blonde, so he hadn't had a chance to give her hell.

Marcus is here tonight. The knowledge sent excitement skittering along her nerves.

When the submissive in the ménage scene groaned, one of her doms laughed. Curious, Gabi edged her way forward. Unfortunately she got too close to the dom in black leathers who'd called her insolent, the one named Master Dan.

He frowned at her and jerked his head, a silent *get back to work*. He sure wasn't very nice. Why did some of the doms act like they owned her and others didn't?

When he turned his back, she stuck out her tongue and crossed her eyes. Laughter rippled around her, and the pregnant sub tucked under his arm giggled. Grinning, Gabi returned to the bar. That had felt good.

As she walked out of the crowd, she glanced over her shoulder and noticed the golden armband circling Master Dan's bicep. Interesting. Sam and Cullen both wore those gold bands. So did Master Marcus. Once safely out of Dan's sight, she stopped to scan the room. Apparently only a few doms wore armbands: the swarthy, muscular dom she'd met—to her misfortune—a domme with a male sub, another domme with a female sub.

When the brunette trainee walked past, Gabi stopped her. "I know dungeon monitors wear gold-trimmed vests, but what's with the armbands?" She nodded at the two dommes. "Do those gold bands mean anything?"

"Oooh, girlfriend, did we forget to warn you about them?" Sally rolled her eyes and grinned. "Those identify the Shadowlands Masters."

"And that's different from a dom how?"

Sally rested her tray on her hip and thought for a second. "Okay, you know how some doms are just a little dominating like maybe a one-scoop ice cream, and others have a lot more—maybe two scoops of domination?"

Gabi nodded.

"Well, with the Masters, think supersized hot fudge sundae." Sally giggled. "And that's only the domination part. Add in beaucoup experience and control and all that. They're voted Master status by the members, and it's sure not a popularity contest."

"Oh. Got it."

"Masters are the best to play with, but..." Sally wrinkled her nose. "Although the regular doms can boss us a little, they have to ask Marcus for permission to do anything else. But the Masters are *supposed* to help with the trainees, so they can pull you into a scene or use you for a demonstration. And if you're bratty and Marcus isn't around, they'll punish you themselves."

"Now you tell me." Gabi scowled. "That Hispanic one with all the muscles? Last night, he came down on me like a load of bricks —put me in the stocks and allowed anybody who thought I'd insulted them to whack me with a paddle."

"Ouch. I wondered how you ended up there. Master Raoul's usually more forgiving than Marcus. You must have been even naughtier than me." Laughing, Sally tsk-tsked at Gabi before responding to a dom's wave for service.

Gabi slowly headed for the bar. So that's why the regular doms hadn't done anything about her behavior. Looks like she'd need to concentrate on upsetting the Masters. *Oh doesn't that just sound like fun?*

As she neared the bar, she spotted Master Marcus. God, he was gorgeous...and dangerous. Despite his deceptively lazy stance, power seemed to radiate from him, and when his sharp blue gaze landed on Gabi, electricity sizzled like a cut power cord, throwing sparks everywhere.

Next to Marcus stood a rough-looking man wearing a black, sleeveless T-shirt and a gold band on his arm. Scars on the man's face and hands created white lines over his dark red-brown skin. As his unwavering, black eyes watched her approach, Gabi seriously considered detouring around both him and Marcus. But as she hesitated, she spotted Agent Rhodes at the end of the bar, reminding her of the stakes involved.

Okay, Kim—this is for you, honey. Jaw tensed, she headed straight for Marcus and the other guy. She forced a cocky grin and greeted Marcus. "Hey, hot stuff."

His smile died. "Gabrielle, you don't want to do this."

Ignoring the way his voice made her insides tap-dance, she turned to his tough friend. "Hey, buddy, how's it hanging?"

Marcus's lips pressed into a straight line.

A flash of amusement flickered in his friend's eyes before disappearing into darkness. "Your new trainee, Marcus?"

"I'm afraid so. Gabrielle, this is Master Nolan." Marcus tilted his head at her quizzically. "How long did it take before you could sit comfortably after last Saturday?"

Two whole days. She took an involuntary step back, then made herself walk around them to set her tray down. Leaning an elbow on the bar top, she said breezily, "Oh, not that long."

Master Marcus's intent gaze moved over her face, her body, lingering on her hands.

She felt her hand rubbing the scar on her cheek. *Oops*. After tucking her hair behind an ear, she plastered on a nonchalant grin.

Marcus saw his puzzlement duplicated in Nolan's eyes. Gabrielle wasn't as confident as she tried to sound. His mention of spanking had tensed every muscle in that pretty little body and paled her face. Now her fingers traced the long scar on her cheek, which he'd learned meant she'd jumped past anxiety into fear.

Why did she keep pushing to get punished?

Some submissives craved pain, but she wasn't one of them. Some wanted attention, and he still wasn't convinced she didn't... but she seemed genuinely mortified by spectators. Some subs' only method of relating to people was to behave like brats, but Gabrielle was a naturally friendly person. She had an infectious laugh, chatted easily, and charmed everyone. In fact, almost every single dom in the place had requested to do a scene with her.

He found most of her sassy behavior downright cute. Except for the times like now when she deliberately antagonized a dom.

As Marcus studied her, she swallowed and shifted her weight, her eyes darting away. Definitely scared.

Dammit. Spanking her hadn't worked, and he doubted he could stomach hitting her harder. But his responsibility as a trainer demanded he teach her the consequences of insolence.

"*Hot stuff*," she'd called him? "Master Nolan, could I request that you please keep her here for me?"

"You got it." Nolan curled his hand around her upper arm, not even appearing to notice her instinctive attempt to retreat.

"Let me go!" She slapped at him. "You're not my boss."

Her loud protests continued as Marcus retrieved his toy bag from behind the bar, and amusement mingled with his concern. He'd spent a lot of time thinking about her, wondering what to do with her...and trying to remember he was her trainer and nothing more. Damned if he wanted to be attracted to the little nuisance.

After planning out some possible scenes for her, he'd added a few extras to the bag. Odd how apropos one happened to be.

When he returned, she was still struggling and cursing Nolan. "You dumb-ass ape, get your hand off me. What—are you the first in your family to be born without a tail?"

The dom stared at her as if he couldn't believe the show, and Marcus almost grinned. When he'd discussed Gabrielle in the Master's meeting before the club opened, Nolan hadn't believed she could prove much trouble. Well, now he knew.

After setting his toy bag on the bar, Marcus gripped her hair. "Be silent."

For about thirty seconds, her natural submissiveness shut her up as if he'd corked her mouth. Then she started again. "Listen, I don't like manhandling, and this—"

Marcus took her wrists, pulled them behind her back, and clipped the cuffs together. When she opened her mouth for another yell, he shoved a leather gag between her teeth. He tied it firmly, smiling at the muffled shriek.

Then her inability to talk or move registered. Her body stiffened, and her eyes dilated with fear.

Before she panicked, he put his hand under her chin to force her to meet his gaze. "Gabrielle." He held a pink squeaky toy and shook it so the bells inside rattled. A squeeze made it squeak. "Anytime I gag you, you will hold this. The toy is the substitute for your safe word, sugar. If you drop it or make it squeak, everything stops."

Her brown eyes were huge, and she trembled like a terrified mouse. Why did she do this to herself? He slid his hand up to cup her face, and the unconscious way she rubbed her cheek on his palm told him she trusted him—would willingly submit. Only she didn't.

With a sigh, he stayed on the path he'd set out. He put the toy in her hand. "Do you understand, sugar? Use it if something is too much for you. Make it squeak now so I know you can."

As she made the toy sound several times, her breathing slowed.

"All right then." He stripped off her stretchy, bright yellow hot pants with regret—she'd looked damn fine in them—lingering for a second over the soft, bare skin of her ass. Seductive, mouthy little sub. Then he gripped her waist and laid her, stomach down, on the bar, with her legs dangling off the edge.

Her teeth clamped on the gag, and she pulled uselessly at her cuffs, then tried to squirm off the bar. Seductive, mouthy, *stubborn* little sub. Marcus glanced at Nolan. "If you would please?"

Nolan nodded and leaned on her legs, pinning her against the bar and preventing her from kicking in the process. After gripping her cuffs, the dom had her well immobilized, although she continued to struggle like a fish tossed on dry land.

Marcus glanced at Cullen, who drew a beer as he observed the show. "Loan me a knife, please." Before Gabrielle could react with more than widened eyes, he patted her bottom. "I'm not going to cut on you, darlin'."

She stared at him for a second, then gave up and lay limp under Nolan's grip. Apparently the mention of a knife had scared the sass right out of her.

Cullen set the drink on the bar and tossed a knife at Marcus.

Marcus caught it out of the air. He took a piece of knobby, palm-sized ginger from his toy bag and cut off one of the finger-like parts. "This is ginger, Gabrielle, like what is used in Asian cooking." He shaved off the brown coating and carved the long piece into the shape of an anal plug with a thick thumb-sized part, a narrower section, and a wide end to keep the plug in place.

When he held it up, Gabrielle inhaled sharply, obviously recognizing the shape.

Marcus smiled into her eyes. "The fun we'll have tonight is called figging."

When Nolan chuckled, she stiffened as if she'd forgotten his presence.

"I can't use regular lubricant or it'll block the effect. Can you lube her with her own juices?" Marcus asked, glancing at his hands. "If I get the oils near her pussy, she's going to screech like a steam engine."

Nolan snorted. "No shit. Guess I can help out this once, *hot stuff*." The dom pushed her legs apart and slid his fingers over her pussy. He chuckled. "She's nicely wet, Marcus." Ignoring her muffled yells, Nolan lubed up her asshole.

Cheeks pink with outrage, Gabrielle glared as Marcus picked up the ginger. He nodded at Nolan. "Best you try to relax yourself, Gabrielle."

As Nolan held her buttocks apart, Marcus slowly pushed the knob into her ass. Her tight ring of muscle fought against the intrusion—just as it would offer up a token protest against a cock before closing like a vise around the base. He hardened at the thought.

The ginger slipped into place, and she moaned.

"There you go, sugar. Now you'll learn what hot stuff really means. I do want you to know ginger doesn't cause any harm at all...no matter what it feels like."

Leaning an arm on the bar, he kissed Gabrielle's cheek and her forehead. "Such a pretty face to glare so much. Wouldn't you rather be polite and not have to be unhappy all the time?"

His blue gaze was soft, his resonant voice almost a croon, and Gabi had to close her eyes to keep him from seeing just how devastating his question was. *I would. I hate when you're mad at me.*

"Ah, darlin'," he said gently, "we'll get there. It'll happen."

She kept her eyes closed until she heard him move away. He'd gone behind the bar to wash his hands, leaving the heartless dom still leaning against her legs. She could hear the laughter and conversations about her, and her cheeks flushed. She'd done well in attracting attention, hadn't she?

When Marcus came back, Nolan stepped away and asked in his gravelly voice, "If you don't need any more help, I'm going to round up my sub."

"I appreciate your assistance," Marcus said.

"My pleasure." Nolan gave Gabi's bottom a light, stinging slap, and she gritted her teeth on the gag to keep from yelping. "Would you like her caned tonight? I'm getting out of practice."

Gabi tensed. *Say no, say no.*

"Hmm." Marcus grazed his fingers over the stinging area. "If she doesn't learn some manners soon, I believe she might benefit from your expertise."

As Nolan headed away, Marcus gripped Gabi around the waist. With an easy swing, he set her on her feet. As the thing in her butt shifted, she shivered and wiggled, trying to get more comfortable.

"I hoped you'd leave her up there," the bartender said, leaning on one hefty arm and looking at her appreciatively. "I haven't had a pretty bar ornament in a while."

"Not this time." Marcus ran his warm hands up and down her arms. His eyes held laughter as he smiled at her. "I don't think she's going to be holding still without some help."

Cullen frowned. "What did you want the knife for anyway?"

"Ginger root. She called me 'hot stuff.'"

The giant dom stared at Marcus for a second, then roared with laughter.

What's so funny?

Marcus removed her cuffs and her yellow vinyl top, and finally her gag.

Thank you, God. She rubbed her cheeks and swallowed, trying to eradicate the taste of the gag. A gag, anal plug, bar top. *Oh man.* She'd expected a spanking, maybe even a whipping. Not this kind of thing. As Marcus put the restraints into his bag, she realized everyone still watched her, probably hoping for another show. Damn them anyway.

She scowled at Marcus and Cullen. It didn't take any effort to want to annoy them. *A bar ornament, my ass.* "So am I supposed to wait tables with this thing up my butt?"

Elbow on the bar, Cullen propped his chin in his hand and watched her as if she were an amusing bug.

"No, Gabrielle," Marcus said in a level voice. "You are going to sit with me and practice self-control. Don't make me regret removing your gag."

"Wouldn't dream of it, hot stuff." She pursed her lips in a kiss, hearing the people around the bar laugh.

His expression didn't change. As he studied her with those blue, blue eyes, she felt herself flush and something quiver inside her, a mingling of shame and desire. Unable to meet his eyes anymore, she dropped her gaze.

"C'mere, sugar," he said softly. He sat down, back to the bar, and lifted her onto his lap.

When her weight landed on the thing in her butt, she winced, and her temper shifted as well—with good reason. After all, some *asshole* had shoved something in her *asshole.*

His callused fingers curled around hers, and he positioned her hands palm down on her bare thighs. "I want your hands to stay just like that."

"Fine," she muttered, then growled as he forced her knees apart and draped her legs on the outside of his, spreading her open. *No. I am not going to sit here with my pussy wide open for everyone walking past to stare at. This is too much.* Without saying a word, she tried to slide off his lap.

He chuckled. “I don’t think so.” He cupped one hand over her left breast, and his other over her mound, holding her in place.

She stilled, her heart rate increasing at the thrill of his strong hands on her most vulnerable areas. His palm, hard and callused, pressed against her bare labia. She quivered in his grasp as he fondled her breasts, rolling her nipples until need clawed through her.

“Nicely quiet. I like that, Gabrielle,” he murmured into her ear, his breath warm against her cheek. “Say, ‘Thank you, Sir, for providing me with a seat.’”

Her hesitation earned her a quick pinch on her nipple, and the tiny pain streamed like a lightning bolt to her pussy. How could she possibly find this exciting? But his fingers rested on each side of her clit, and if he started touching her there, she’d have a climax on a damned bar stool. She breathed through her nose until the heat passed. “Thank you, Sir, for providing me with a seat.”

“Very nice.” Despite the fact he’d forced her to comply, his voice was warm with approval, the approval that she’d discovered she really, really wanted.

She tried to think of something atrocious to do next, and suddenly the hand between her legs started to move. He touched her wet, wet labia, making another approving sound. “Do you realize how your body betrays you, Gabrielle?” he said in her ear as his finger circled her entrance. “You make all these defiant noises, but your body says, ‘Take me. Please.’”

He rubbed her clit, and then moved his legs farther apart, spreading her even more. “I do like having you open so I can play with you as I please,” he murmured, his sexy drawl thicker than normal.

Over by a sitting area, two trainees frowned at her. In the locker room, they’d complained about how much time Marcus had to spend with her because of her behavior.

Other members wandered past, staring and laughing at the

naked sub getting tormented on her dom's lap, and she flushed. *Don't pay attention to what Marcus is doing. Watch for the kidnapper.*

But he kept teasing her with erratic touches, and her focus started to erode. He knew just how to touch her, dammit. Arousal and embarrassment coursed through her, and her fingernails dug into her thighs as she tried to stay still. As her clit swelled, she became aware of the thing in her butt. It had...warmed. That didn't make sense. She'd seen him cut it up; it didn't have any batteries or wires; it was just a root of ginger. Sure ginger was a spice, but a fairly mild one. Wasn't it?

It heated more, and she squirmed, realizing he'd placed her so her buttocks rested solidly on his lap with no way to get the thing out. Her anus started to burn—like the plug was flaming inside her. It needed to come out. Now. She struggled to get off his lap.

He tightened his grip on her breast, his palm flattened on her pussy, holding her in place. "Stay put, Gabrielle. You do not have permission to move," he said, but the ice in his voice was no match for the fire in her bottom.

"It burns." She pushed at his arms, but he had a hell of a grip for a lawyer. She didn't care if she got in trouble. It felt as if someone had stuck a burning stick up her bottom. "There's something wrong. That thing—"

"Does it feel like hot stuff?" From the amusement in his voice, he'd known exactly what would happen. Her gasp of outrage made him laugh, and she wanted to scream at him. It was burning her.

"Please, please, take it out." Her body broke out in a sweat as the fire increased.

"No." Ignoring her struggles, he played with her, rolling her left nipple, then the right between his callused fingers, slowly, each time increasing the pressure to the edge of pain. Her breasts felt full. Heavy. Her nipples throbbed. And then he moved the hand over her pussy, sliding a lean finger into her wetness and up and around her clit. In and around. Her clit swelled as if imitating her breasts, each tortuous circle waking her to a frightening need.

"Don't. I don't want this." She grabbed his wrist and tried to push his hand away from her pussy.

"Put your hand back on your thigh, Gabrielle." The steel in his voice cut through her resistance. A tremor shook her deep inside as she obeyed.

"That's the way," he murmured. "You will stay in place whatever I do, whatever I take from you."

Her spine seemed to melt into his chest as if his removal of her choices had taken her with it.

"Such a pretty little sub," he whispered. He kissed her hot cheek. "Just stay quiet as I play."

She somehow held still as he teased her clit, ever so slowly, arousing her pussy to a different fire, one that vied with the burning pain in her bottom. When he pinched her nipples, pain and pleasure seemed to zing like electricity between her bottom and her pussy and her breasts, drawing her closer and closer to coming. She moaned, drowning in sensation.

He ruthlessly brought her right to the brink, until she couldn't remain quiet, until she squirmed uncontrollably against his hold, needing to come so badly that she whimpered. She burned... everywhere. Each merciless stroke shoved her closer until the world receded to only the feeling of his hands and the fire of the ginger. Every time she got close to the edge, he lightened his touch, keeping her on a throbbing, burning precipice.

Marcus nuzzled the cheek of the little sub squirming in his lap. She hovered right at the peak of both pain and pleasure, and one firm touch would send her screaming over the edge. Her breathy whimpers were a joy to listen to, as was her inability to put two words together into one of her insults. Master Z walked by, studied her for a second, and nodded at Marcus.

That had been a very unreadable expression from the club owner, Marcus thought. Almost concerned...pitying. Putting the thought aside, he returned his attention to his sub. Her responses delighted him. He might have to force her to let down her defenses, but once gone, she openly gave him everything. He nibbled on the lovely curve between her neck and shoulder to add to her sensations, and another low groan broke from her.

"Beg me, Gabrielle," he said, making it an order. "Beg me to let you come."

Ah now, he'd obviously pushed too far, for she tried to growl her defiance.

"You'll give it all, sugar," he whispered and slid his finger up her engorged clit, too lightly to get her off but hard enough to increase the quivering of her thighs. The scent of her arousal blended with the light fragrance of her skin and hair. "Beg me."

Her lips tightened, and he laughed. Stubborn little sub. So honest in her defiance. How long since he'd had such a challenge? He set his hands on the outside of her bottom and pushed her ass cheeks together. Pressure on the ginger root would increase the burn.

She stiffened and gave a husky moan. "Please. Oh, God, please, Marcus."

Almost. "Who?"

"Sir. Pleeeease."

"All right. You were polite, Gabrielle, so I will reward you," he murmured. He swirled a finger in her juices, then started high over her clit, up past the hood, and worked his way down in tiny slick rubs. Her entire body stiffened as he came closer to the goal. Finally he reached the sweet, swollen nub and slid over it once.

Her back arched; her head thumped into his shoulder as she screamed, a satisfying, high sound that made him even harder than before. He gritted his teeth. If he had her soft, little ass squirming on top of his cock much longer, he'd bend her over the bar stool and take her.

He tightened the arm he'd put around her waist to keep her in place and circled her clit a few more times to draw out the after-waves. A few seconds of that and she sagged against him like a balloon that had lost its air. Little shivers shook her body at intervals.

To please himself, he moved his hand up to cup a soft, swollen breast. He kissed her moist cheek. "Say thank you, Gabrielle."

Her eyes were half-lidded. Her lips curved slightly. Absolutely beautiful. "Thank you."

He turned her and took her mouth. She yielded completely, wonderfully.

Eventually he drew back, despite his roaring need to take more. Her wet lips were swollen and red from his kiss. She'd closed her eyes, and her thick red-gold lashes clashed endearingly with her pink cheeks.

Lesson. This is a lesson, Atherton. Recalling his mind to the task, he brushed his cheek over hers. "I do enjoy giving pleasure to polite submissives, sugar." He left the second part unstated—that rudeness would receive pain.

Her eyes lifted and met his. The vulnerable look pulled at his heart. Then he watched as, like a prison guard, she locked her emotions away.

The bitch was running late. Cesar Maganti glanced at his watch: 1:30 a.m. In the shadows beside his target's apartment building, he leaned against the wall. Sweat trickled slowly down his back. His coverall, showing him as an appliance company employee, felt like an overcoat in the humid night.

Not long ago, Jang had reported that Candi'd left the downtown BDSM club, so she should arrive any time now. With luck, he'd have her boxed, called in, and ready for pickup the minute the docks opened in the morning. She'd be the second woman of the four ordered.

He watched as a car entered the parking lot. A red Jeep—

nope. A drunken couple got out and staggered into a ground-floor apartment. He doubted they'd seen anything but each other. Weekend nights were definitely the safest time to snatch someone. Two years ago, when the Overseer had e-mailed him a how-to-kidnap guide, he'd laughed his ass off. But the bastard's suggestions had been dead-on.

The *Overseer*. Fancy name for a fucking pimp. But the patronizing asshole paid good money for each batch of girls. Last time the profit on the order had kept his PI agency afloat. This year it'd pay off his gambling debts and keep him from ending up in the Gulf as an example.

This girlie and then two more and home free.

And there she was. *C'mere, chickie*. She parked and locked her battered, white compact sedan, then walked toward the stairs on the end of the building. Healthy women—the types he kidnapped—rarely used the elevators. He checked the area. A car headed out on the far side of the lot, its lights dancing over the shrubbery. All clear.

Maganti smiled as the brunette approached. Nice rack. When she reached the stairs, he stepped out of the shadows. "Hey, Candi," he said, grinning. "Haven't seen you in a while."

He'd used her name deliberately. Instead of screaming and running, she hesitated. With an alcohol-sogged brain, she took a moment to realize she didn't know him. Her eyes widened and—

He nailed her with the Taser.

She dropped in a nice heap. After yanking the prongs from her stomach, he gave her a tranq injection to keep her out for a couple of hours at least. Long enough to get to the docks, pass her off to the guys doing the pickup, and get his money.

Maganti fetched the heavy washing machine box from behind the building, hefted her in, and sealed the top. Using a hand trolley, he rolled the box to his cargo van and up the ramp. After closing the door, he dumped her out and cuffed her wrists and ankles. No point in growing careless. As he drove out of the parking lot, he knew what anyone watching would see—an appliance truck leaving after making a delivery. Another idea off the Overseer's list. No one questioned repair guys. *Had an emergency call, ma'am. The machine flooded the laundry room.*

Once out on the road, he tossed his clear-lensed glasses onto the passenger seat and removed the baseball cap.

Two little birdies left to go. Whistling a tune, he thought about the woman cuffed in the back of the van. Long hair. Nice ass. Big tits. He hardened. If he hurried, he and Jang could have some fun with her before the boat arrived.

CHAPTER EIGHT

Later that evening, Marcus wandered through the club, checking on his trainees. Two of the newer doms had requested Sally. Marcus had hoped two doms might intimidate her a tad, but she was topping from the bottom as always, telling them what to do, what they messed up. Damn.

A young dom-sub couple had Tanner for a flogging scene, and the young man not only looked fit to burst but grinned between each stroke. Having already done scenes, Dara, Austin, and Uzuri now served drinks. Dara's session had lasted awhile, and Marcus smiled at the pink stripes running up the back of her thighs.

He headed toward the stocks to check on Gabrielle. Marcus had wanted to see how she handled a new dom and mild erotic pain, so he'd agreed to let Holt, a dom in his late twenties, switch her.

After that, he might nab one of the free subs for a playtime of his own. The battle with Gabrielle earlier and her climax under his hands had left him hard as a rock—but fucking her during this constant defiance stage of hers wouldn't be wise.

At the stocks, the blond dom wore a black jacket and leather pants. After her introduction to Holt, Gabrielle had eyed his biker jacket, which apparently matched her conception of a dom's proper attire, and smirked at Marcus. Marcus chuckled. She might drive him crazy, but the little redhead certainly didn't bore him.

He chose a seat at an angle to the play area. Holt had secured her well, with her head and hands restrained in the wooden bar and her yellow hot pants pulled down to bare her ass.

The little sub was quite a colorful sight. Pale, pale skin. A yellow top that barely contained her pretty breasts. The three yellow earrings in her right ear matched her clothing, two blue ones in the left to match her dyed locks, and a curling vine tattoo on her arm duplicated the colors. In the brighter light of the scene area, her hair glinted in a myriad of reds and golds—and blue. Odd how he'd only thought her pretty at first, but she truly was a lovely sub.

As Holt walked in a slow circle around her, Gabrielle's face flushed, her hands clenching. Her weight shifted from leg to leg as if she realized how vulnerable her ass was in that position. Nervous. Excited. Very nice.

Taking his time, Holt played with her pussy and breasts to increase her arousal. Marcus had watched the dom work before. He did a fine job, although Marcus wanted to be the one with his hands running over her soft ass and teasing her pale pink nipples to stand erect.

Holt started to switch her lightly, watching her reactions.

After a few gentle swats, Gabrielle fisted her hands, and her mouth tightened—not in pain, but as if she struggled with herself. Here we go, Marcus thought, not sure whether to laugh or curse.

"Is this all you got?" she asked loudly. "Hey, even that stuffy trainer hits harder."

Stuffy trainer. *Well, damn.*

In a tuneful voice, she sang, "Anything you can do, he can do better..."

Marcus smothered a smile.

Holt tapped the switch on his palm, then tossed it aside, obviously deciding to see why she deliberately provoked him. He sauntered around the stocks and fisted his hand in her hair. The music from the dance floor drowned out whatever he said to her. Then he walked back and picked up the switch. Marcus assessed him—still in control. No anger. Good enough.

Turning his attention to Gabrielle, Marcus stiffened. Her face had turned dead white and expressionless, her eyes blank. What the hell had Holt said to her? Even as Marcus rose, Holt swung, caught her abnormally still body language, and pulled the blow. He tossed the switch aside again and reached her head just as Marcus got to the ropes.

"Marcus, help me get her loose. She's frozen up." With one hand, Holt rubbed Gabrielle's back; with the other, he unlatched the bar. He crooned, "It's all right, sweetheart. You're safe." He flipped back the upper bar that trapped her neck and wrists. "Gabrielle. Look at me, Gabrielle." He shook his head at Marcus. "She's out of it, dammit."

But her legs hadn't buckled, Marcus realized as he pulled her shorts up and helped move her out of the stocks. His gut tightened. This wasn't a normal reaction at all. Holt wrapped an arm around her, holding her up, still in charge of the scene. When her legs buckled, Marcus forced himself not to reach for her, but God, he wanted to—to snatch her away, to hold her, to see what was wrong.

Holt looked up. "I'm still a stranger to her, and I'm not going to play pissing games with a terrified sub. Take her."

Marcus gave him a grateful nod and swung her into his arms. "Sugar, you're safe. Relax now. You're safe." He stepped out of the roped-off area.

Olivia in a dungeon monitor vest waited nearby to see if they needed help.

"We got it," he murmured to her and settled onto a couch, Holt dropping down beside them. With an arm behind her back,

Marcus leaned Gabrielle against his chest, then cupped her cheek. "Gabrielle, I need for you to look at me now," he said gently.

Her eyes were wide, unfocused, much like a sub in endorphin overload, but her stiff body, pale face, and clammy skin indicated something else. Worry deepened and sharpened his voice. "Gabrielle. Look. At. Me."

She jerked as if he'd slapped her. Some of the blankness receded from her gaze. She blinked and stared at him, then around, obviously not remembering how she'd ended up on his lap. When she shivered, he wrapped his arms around her.

Holt fetched a fluffy subbie blanket and tucked it over the girl.

"Thank you," she whispered and frowned at the young dom. "I was with you, wasn't I? The stocks?"

"You were, Gabrielle." Holt took her hand and watched her reaction carefully. She didn't jerk away. "Can you tell me what happened? What scared you?"

She shook her head, her brows together.

"Did I hurt you?"

"No." Her smile wavered a little. "I don't..." Her muscles tightened.

"Easy, sugar," Marcus murmured.

She glanced up at him. "Marcus?" Her body relaxed, melting into him.

He kissed the top of her head. She trusted him, and the knowledge warmed him. Relieved him. To see the feisty little sub reduced to frozen fear had worried the hell out of him.

"You smarted off to Holt," Marcus said. "Do you remember?"

She nodded, glanced under her lashes at the dom. "Um. Yeah. Sorry."

"You tried to get a rise out of me," Holt said. "Did you really want me to switch you harder?"

Tensing again, she shook her head. "Uh-uh."

Marcus frowned. One more time where her insolent behavior

didn't make sense. She didn't like pain. Sometimes a sub wanted a dom's attention, but Gabrielle already had that.

He shook his head. *Analyze later, Atherton*. Right now, he needed to know what had caused her response, and since she didn't remember, they'd go through it step-by-step. "Holt grabbed your hair," Marcus said. Moving slowly, he curled his fingers into her hair and pulled.

If anything, she softened against him.

Holt grinned. "Well, that certainly wasn't it."

"Then Holt said something to you. Do you remember what, darlin'?"

"He did?" She bit her lip and frowned at the younger dom. "You grabbed my hair, and you bent over and—" Her muscles started to tense.

"Gabrielle," Marcus snapped.

She jerked and looked up.

"There we go. Stay with me, darlin'." He stroked her shaggy hair, and she eased back with a tired sigh. "Holt, can you give it to her piece by piece?"

Holt's mouth flattened, and he squeezed Gabrielle's hand. "I don't want to scare you again, sweetheart, but we need to find out what did this. Do you understand?"

She nodded, but her body stilled. She might not consciously remember the cause, but something inside her did.

"You little brat," Holt said.

Gabrielle's exhalation was almost a laugh.

Smiling, Marcus rubbed his chin across her head. Nothing kept this spitfire down long, did it? The knot in his stomach loosened.

"Guess it wasn't that." Holt smiled and fed her the next part: "You obviously want to be beaten hard..."

A tiny flinch from her, but no fear.

Holt nodded. "...or maybe you're a dirty slut who—"

Gabrielle's body turned rigid. Her eyes went blank.

"That's it." Marcus lifted her chin again. "Gabrielle, look at me. Now!" he snapped.

The bond he'd established with her reached deep, and she shuddered. Her eyes focused on his.

"Good girl," he murmured. "You're a very good girl. Stay with me, darlin'." *Because you're scaring the hell out of me when you don't.*

She sighed and leaned into him again.

Marcus glanced at Holt. The dom's face tightened with unhappiness and guilt. "I wanted to find out if she liked being called names."

Quite a few subs got off on a dom calling them *slut* or *whore* or *dirty*. "You weren't out of line, Holt. I've never seen such an extreme reaction to verbal humiliation. This is something from the past."

"Yeah, well." The dom ran a hand through his hair. "You going to work on this with her?"

"Definitely."

"All right then." His expression turned harsh. "If you discover who taught her that kind of fear...I'd enjoy giving him a lesson in manners."

Marcus nodded. *So would I.* As the other dom walked away, Marcus stroked Gabrielle's pale cheek and studied on the matter.

"*Dirty slut.*" Some women might be disgusted, some affronted, some turned on. But Gabrielle's reaction seemed closer to a catatonic flashback. What could have happened in her past to set such a trigger? The most likely cause would be...

His arms felt so good, and he shed heat like the sun on a summer day. Gabi pressed her cheek against the smooth shirt covering his muscular chest. She should get back to playing decoy, but her body didn't want to move. She stared at the stocks. They'd released her, carried her here, and she didn't remember. How could she have blanked out? As fear spiraled up her spine, she took a death grip on Marcus's suit. *Don't let go.*

At her movement, he ran his knuckles over her cheek and

used his thumb under her chin to turn her face up. His intense scrutiny felt as if he could see through her clothing, even her body, all the way into her inner self. She couldn't look away.

"You ever played out a rape scenario, sugar?" he asked in a rough voice, as if the ugly word had abraded away the smoothness.

As her skin turned cold, nausea wrung her stomach like a dirty washcloth. She dug her fingers into his forearm and encountered only rocklike muscles. "No." *No no no*. "No, please, Sir."

"I see." He released her face and curled his strong fingers around hers, anchoring her in the present. "When were you raped?"

Her air disappeared as if he'd hit her in the solar plexus, and her next inhalation struggled against the constriction in her chest. "How...how did you know?"

His eyes stayed steady on hers. "I didn't, darlin'. But now I do. When?"

She swallowed. "Ten years ago. I got caught in a gang war."

"Mmm." The unemotional acknowledgement somehow let her breathe. She looked down, watching how his thumb traced small circles on the back of her hand. Slowly her muscles unknotted.

"Does a man taking control bother you?"

"No. It all happened in the past, and I deal with it okay. That's why I didn't put anything down on the questionnaire as a problem."

He made a disgusted noise in the back of his throat. "Don't lie to me, darlin'. Look at me now."

She tried not to flinch from the intensity of his blue gaze. *I don't want to talk about this; I just want you to hold me.*

"*When* does being dominated cause problems?" And as if she couldn't understand the question, he nodded toward the stocks.

Okay, so maybe sometimes she didn't do so well. "I never thought about it." *And I never want to.*

Even as he kept her gaze trapped, he stroked her cheek gently, and as always when he mixed all that power with gentleness, everything in her melted. His eyes softened, and he murmured, "Little sub." He kissed her forehead. "Think about what you felt in the stocks...and tell me about the last time you froze."

She said lightly, "Well, seems like once—"

"Don't be acting up, Gabrielle." His fingers took her chin in an all-too-effective control. "I want to hear about the last time something made you sick and scared."

No sidestepping would evade his insistence on answers. "I dated a guy for a while. He'd pull my hair and fuck rough, and I liked it. A lot. But he called me names once..." Her hands turned clammy, and she tried to look away.

His hand tightened on her face. "Stay with me here, Gabrielle." His sharp eyes cut through her fear like a knife. "Tell me the words he used."

"Slut." The word reverberated in her skull, and her pulse filled her ears like breaking waves in a storm. She swallowed, forcing nausea back. "Whore. Cunt. Stuff like that."

"Ah, there we go. It's all tied to the words." He was silent a minute, thinking, then frowned at her. "You're still shaking, darlin'. We're going to sit a piece while you take a bit of rest." His hand slid to her nape and pressed her head against his shoulder. As the noise in her brain diminished, she could hear the slow beat of his heart, and each thud somehow settled her world.

She heard him speaking off and on... Coaxing the rough-voiced dom to give a construction job to a teen with a bad rep. Someone with a light Hispanic accent talked him into joining a poker night the following week. The techno music changed to classical—Rachmaninoff.

He held her firmly, his arms never loosening. Sometimes he'd drop a kiss on top of her head as if to let her know he hadn't forgotten her. And she felt more content right there, right then, than in just about forever.

Eventually he sat her up, laughter in his voice. "You falling asleep there, sugar?"

She shook her head and remembered to answer. "No, Sir." A second's pause and she risked looking up. "Thank you."

"You're very welcome, but we're not quite finished, darlin'."

Oh dear.

"First, and I mean for you to remember this: verbal humiliation is a hard limit for you. You tell any dom that before you start a scene. Do you understand me?"

A hard limit meant a *definitely won't do that*. "Yes, Sir."

"Good enough. Now I want to use a few of those words and see how you react." As he waited for her nod, he took her hand.

To brace herself, she gripped his wrist. "Okay."

"Slut," he said softly, his eyes watching her closely.

She winced, then took a breath.

"Dirty slut."

Same reaction.

"Cunt. Fuckhole."

She'd heard them before, could hear the nasty voice as—she pushed the memory aside. "I'm fine."

"You're brave, darlin', not fine. There's a difference." He kissed her forehead. "So rough sex or force doesn't bother you—only the words?"

That didn't make sense, did it? Staring at the scars on his knuckles, she tried to think. "I... When...it...happened, other stuff had happened first"—*Danny and Rock dying. The slicing pain down her face, blood everywhere, and*—"and I was numb, I guess. Not feeling anything at all, but...I couldn't shut out the voices."

"Voices." He rasped the word, emphasizing the *s* that made it plural. Under her fingers, his wrist muscles flexed to iron.

If he had directed that icy fury toward her, her heart would have stopped—instead his anger made her feel as if she wasn't alone in an unpredictably violent world. She stroked her hand over his forearm, ruffling the golden hair.

After a few seconds, he took a long, slow breath and kissed the top of her head. "All right. Just the words. I do like knowing you wouldn't freeze if someone attacked you"—he smiled slightly —"so long as they didn't call you names."

Her laugh sounded like a hiccup, but better than nothing. "I can guarantee that." A guy had jumped her three years ago, and she hadn't frozen at all. Apparently a man's knees only bent one way.

"Good girl." His brows drew together. "I do *not* like that a few words can paralyze you so badly. You didn't even think about a safe word. What if you weren't here but playing somewhere in private?"

"I..." She'd known from her date's reaction that she'd scared him. The thought of blanking out like this terrified her. And all because of a few nasty words. "I didn't lose it with you."

"Little trainee, if you didn't trust me with your body and with your emotions to some degree, you wouldn't have returned after the first night."

"Oh." She'd have tried to return for Kim's sake but might have failed if he'd truly scared her. Even now her body seemed to sing, *safe, safe, safe*. "Good point."

"From your reaction to Holt, having someone else say the words is too risky." He lifted her hand and kissed her fingers absentmindedly. "But you don't react enough if it's me. Of course, you knew I'd say them. Maybe I should surprise you."

She huffed a laugh. "I don't think the other doms would like you ruining their scenes."

"No. But we might could find a different method." He frowned. "Still, you should get some professional help, Gabrielle. Talking through this with someone—"

"I did have counseling afterward," she interrupted. "This didn't come to light then." Or during job evals. *Of course, I didn't want to believe I had a problem*. "But now... Well, if I can't fix it myself, I'll get help, but there's no way I can do that at this time."

Sorry, Agent Rhodes, but I need to visit a psychologist. I'll go back to playing decoy later. Tempting. Nonetheless, she'd stay. For Kim.

But God, what if someone—a killer—called her names? Her skin chilled. She needed to get over this now. "You said 'a different method.' What do you have in mind?"

He hesitated. "This might be too realistic, might raise more demons than we want to deal with right now."

His use of *we* wiped away the chill. She wouldn't have to face her fear alone. "Go on."

"The Shadowlands has a yard for people who want to play outside. Sometimes Master Z closes it down and sets up"—she saw him reject the *r* word and choose another—"capture games. Submissives are given a head start and then chased by their doms. They might get punished for their escape or fucked or both."

Marcus grabbing her. Pushing her to the ground. Holding her hair and... Heat slid through her, hot enough to liquefy her lower half. Until she imagined a man—any man—forcing her, and she chilled.

"I will be damned," Marcus said slowly. "I wouldn't have thought the idea would excite you, but it did. For a moment. Tell me what turned you off after that."

The sharing came easier this time, maybe because he listened so carefully. "A stranger grabbing me and holding me down."

His brows drew together. "What excited you?"

She looked away, a flush of embarrassment heating her face. *Yeah, tell the nice dom that he turns you on.*

His warm hand cupping her cheek, he forced her to look at him. "Talk to me, sugar."

"You," she whispered. "You grabbing me."

"I see." He stroked the underside of her jaw with his thumb. "Most women want to choose the man who stars in their fantasy, darlin'. Especially ones with a history like yours. But acting out a capture fantasy wasn't what I had in mind."

"Then what?"

"A game of hide-and-seek. And when I catch you, I'll call you nasty names."

"Get real."

"I am. The gardens feel dangerous, especially with others acting out their chase games. If you are sufficiently nervous...I think it might work. For tonight, all I want is for you to say a safe word rather than freeze. That will, at least, make you safer if you're in a BDSM scene."

Not a rape fantasy, just a children's game. Her mouth still felt too dry, her heart too fast. "But only you?"

His eyes held complete understanding. "Me. I am the only one who will chase you. No one else."

She nodded, feeling like a bobblehead doll she'd won at a carnival years before. "Yes."

CHAPTER NINE

Marcus tucked Gabrielle behind the bar where Cullen could keep an eye on her and went to change out of his suit.

When he returned, he stood off to one side for few minutes, amusement trickling through him. Apparently she'd recovered enough to sass Cullen; he'd gagged her with a ball gag, which not only silenced her but added the humiliation of making her drool around the rubber ball.

Cullen occasionally stopped mixing drinks to wipe her chin and—from the way her color came and went—give her hell. New submissives often misread the sociable bartender, figuring him easygoing. They rarely made the mistake twice.

Marcus strolled over, pausing to exchange greetings with the various members around the bar.

Cullen glanced at Marcus's black jeans and sleeveless T-shirt. "Nice to see you in real clothes for a change. By the way, I found your trainee too mouthy to tolerate."

Marcus looked at Gabrielle.

She stared at his clothing as if she'd never seen a dom in jeans.

Suppressing his amusement, he waited until her gaze rose to

meet his, then looked at the gag in her mouth and let his disappointment in her behavior show.

To his surprise, her eyes reddened with tears before she turned her head away.

Something twisted inside him. The bond between them continued to develop. She not only trusted him, but she wanted—needed—to please him. So there was hope for her after all. But the connection went two ways, being balanced by his need to protect and nurture. And possess. He found he didn't like seeing her under someone else's restraints. "Release her, please, sir," he said to Cullen.

Cullen unsnapped her arms and handed her a cloth before undoing the ball gag. She wiped her face, scrubbed the spit away, and glared at Cullen.

When the bartender looked at her in disbelief, Marcus clenched his jaw to keep from laughing.

"Here I thought Andrea was bad." Cullen grasped her hair in his big fist and growled at her, "Apologize, sub, and thank me for the lesson." The sheer power he put into the words had her stammering out an apology and thank-you before she could get her sassy attitude back.

The people seated at the bar laughed.

Marcus regarded her carefully. Although flushed, she displayed no pleasure at acquiring an audience with her behavior. Whatever reason she had to misbehave, it wasn't to attract attention the way his ex-wife had done. Thank God. "Come, Gabrielle, before you get in more trouble than you can survive," he ordered.

When Cullen turned his back, she stuck out her tongue. As laughter rippled around the bar, she hurried to Marcus's side, her eyes dancing with mischief.

In the dim bar, her smooth, pale skin almost glowed. He ran his knuckles over the sweet curve of her cheek and tucked a silky curl behind her ear. "Little brat," he murmured.

She grinned at him.

Unable to resist, he bent to take her soft lips, pinning her between him and the bar so her body plastered against his. High breasts, lush ass. And when her arms circled his neck, he simply let everything go and savored kissing a yielding sub. This sub—Gabrielle—who made every other submissive seem bland. He nipped her bottom lip to tease her mouth open, then swept inside her mouth. She kissed him back with a hungry urgency. His arms tightened as he lost himself, plunging deeply and taking everything she offered so generously. When he hardened, she moaned and rubbed against him.

He stepped back reluctantly, pleased at the pink flush in her cheeks, the heat in her eyes. Slowly he ran a finger over her damp lips, wishing he could justify taking her upstairs to one of the private rooms.

But no. You're her trainer, Atherton. She needs help, not a good fucking, although she might enjoy... No. He stepped back.

Cullen shook his head. "Another one bites the dust. You want your toy bag, Marcus?"

"No, thank you." He set a hand in the hollow of her back, guiding her across the room to the side door and into the prep area for the Capture Gardens.

The potential participants stood in a line for Z's mandatory check. A psychologist, the Shadowlands owner spoke with any couple or group wanting to play the games, and occasionally denied admittance for reasons no one else could see. The other Masters insisted Z read minds. Delusional idiots.

Gabrielle had turned quiet when they entered, her muscles tightening. He pulled her closer, wanting to reassure her it would be all right. But she needed to be nervous to make this work. And it might not be all right. Her nestling against his side gave him perhaps as much comfort as it did her.

When they reached the head of the line, Master Z touched Gabrielle's cheek with his fingertips, and his dark brows drew together. "Are you certain you want to participate, little one?"

he asked, sounding more like an overprotective father than a dom.

"Yes, Sir," she whispered.

"All right." He stepped aside to let her pass, then frowned at Marcus. "You realize she's as scared as she is excited? There's something in—" He paused and smiled slightly. "Indeed, you're on top of it. Have a nice game, Marcus."

"Thank you, sir." After Marcus moved past, he glanced back over his shoulder. That was...odd.

The hum of excited conversation echoed off the dark-paneled walls. Heart pounding, Gabi scraped her toes on the cool roughness of the stone floor and watched the club members waiting to enter the garden. To play scary games.

She'd almost backed out when Master Z had questioned her. *No I'm not certain.* Still...she couldn't leave herself with such an idiotic vulnerability. And how would she ever find someone she'd trust as she did Master Marcus? But she was scared. Oh yeah.

The line filed forward, with submissives going out to the gardens while their doms gathered on one side of the room. Eventually she and Marcus stood a few feet from the outside door. Beside a table piled with unlit glow sticks, Master Sam wished the preceding couple a good time, then turned to Master Marcus.

"Marcus, I didn't know you planned to play tonight." The silver-haired dom smiled. His pale blue eyes examined Gabi. "That's a pretty yellow outfit. Might as well match it." He picked up three yellow plastic sticks and flexed them until they glowed. "Give me your arm, girl."

She held her hand out. He fastened one around her wrist, one on her ankle, and the last on Marcus's wrist. "The colors are a safeguard so the dungeon monitors can check that a dom grabs the right sub. In other words, only Master Marcus may claim you, Gabrielle. Clear so far?"

"Yes, Sir." *Only Marcus. I can do this.*

Marcus put his arm around her. "Remember the club safe

word is red, sugar. Dungeon monitors will be in the gardens to make sure people follow the rules."

She answered the concern in his eyes with a firm nod and smiled at Master Sam. "Thank you, Sir."

He winked at her and turned to the next group, three men—two subs, one dom. Did the poor dom have to chase them both down?

Marcus guided her to where a Hispanic Master stood beside the door. Gabi winced. He'd been the dom who'd had her paddled for mouthing off.

He grinned at Marcus. "Do you want her prepared?"

Marcus regarded her. "No, I believe this is enough excitement for one little subbie. Thank you, Raoul."

Whatever prepared meant, Gabi thought she was glad to have avoided it.

"However, Gabrielle, I do want you in a slave dress," Marcus said.

"A what?" She followed his gaze to a bunch of faded, raggedy dresses hanging on hooks.

"Hang your clothing up and put on one of those, please."

His polite words didn't cover up the steely tone. She automatically took a step and then heard a man laughing behind her. *People. Audience*. How could she have forgotten her task here? Guilt washed through her as well as a chill at thinking the perp might be in the room. She couldn't relax, mustn't relax, must do her job. "I'd rather wear my own clothing, thank you very much," she said insolently.

"You're starting this again?" Marcus asked gently. "Now?" He contemplated her as if she posed a perplexing chess puzzle.

"Hey, it's not much to ask." She set her hands on her hips. "Those rags are ugly."

"They are indeed, but I thought you'd prefer them to the alternative." He glanced at the other man. "Master Raoul, a full prep please. I would ask that you be verbally polite."

Master Raoul looked as affronted as if Marcus had hit him. "Have I ever—"

"No, I'm sorry, my friend. I said that poorly," Marcus apologized in his rich southern drawl. He caressed Gabi's cheek. "We recently found that verbal abuse brings back a traumatic experience, so I'm making that a hard limit for her."

"I see." Dark brown eyes studied her for a minute. Then Master Raoul smiled slightly. "Well as long as I can abuse her physically, I'm sure we'll get along fine. Gabrielle, strip completely, including your cuffs, hang your clothing on a hook, and return to me here."

"But..." What the hell was a full prep?

"Do you need help, *chiquita*?" the dom asked softly.

The leather vest he wore didn't come close to hiding his muscular build, and his forearms were the size of her calves. Power lifter, she'd bet. He could probably rip her clothes off without bothering to undo them first. "No, Sir."

Although Master Marcus had pressed his lips together, the corners of his mouth turned up. The bastard.

She stalked over to where two other subs were changing into slave rags. Gabi pulled off her clothing and hung it up. She tried to pretend she remained fully clothed, but the air brushing against her bare skin and the amusement of the doms waiting to one side destroyed the illusion. She unbuckled her cuffs and hesitated. Was she supposed to hang them up too?

"I'll take them, Gabrielle." Master Raoul took the cuffs out of her hands.

Startled at his sudden appearance, she flushed and started to cover herself.

He snorted. "You have a modest sub, Marcus?"

Shaking his head in disapproval, Marcus joined them. With a firm grip, he moved her arms to bare her body. "After your first night, I'm surprised you'd need reminding, darlin'."

He stepped back, and his gaze ran over her slowly, lingering on her breasts, her pussy. The air itself seemed to heat. "You have a lovely body, sugar, and I do like seeing you without clothing."

His open enjoyment warmed her almost as much as the heat in his eyes, and she stared up at him, feeling the earth slide sideways.

After a moment or an hour, he ran a finger down her cheek, and the simple touch made her shake inside. "Go with Master Raoul to get prepared for the gardens."

Before she could answer, the muscular dom grasped her upper arm and guided her to the door.

Feet dragging, she looked over her shoulder, hoping for a reprieve. Marcus jerked his head in an unmistakable *go on now.*

Fine. "Whatever," she muttered and rolled her eyes.

Unfortunately that meant she saw Master Raoul's expression, like one more peep would get her butt blistered. Dropping her gaze, she kept her mouth shut as he escorted her across the soft grass next to the building.

A lanky man in leathers waited with what appeared to be a pressure sprayer. "I always get this job," he complained. "Why don't I get—"

"Because Heather would chop your hands off at the wrists." Raoul turned to Gabi. "Hold your hair up for me."

"Why?"

Master Raoul shook his head. "Don't keep pushing, little sub. Jake, toss me the switch."

A long, thin stick flew through the air. Raoul caught it and slapped it on his leather pants.

She took a hasty step back, trying not to cringe. *I'm really getting to hate pain, and I don't much like you either.*

"Do I need to repeat myself?"

"No, Sir." She gathered her hair off her shoulders and held it up with one hand.

"Good enough. Now hold still." He nodded to Jake.

The brown-haired dom pumped the sprayer and turned the

nozzle toward her. Warm liquid, lightly scented with lemon, sprayed across her front and, as he walked around her, her back and legs. "Done," he said.

Gabi let out a sigh. Well, that wasn't too bad. She'd expected worse. As she slid a finger down her stomach, she realized the liquid was oil and giggled. They'd oiled her like she'd star in a greased-pig contest.

Raoul's grin flashed white in his tanned face, and even in the dim light she saw how his dark eyes softened. He looked entirely different. Like a nice person. "You have a pretty laugh, Gabrielle," he said. "You can let go of your hair now." After sliding the switch under his belt, he held his palms out to Jake and received a squirt of oil. With blunt-fingered, callused hands, he oiled her unsprayed arm.

Just about the time she started to relax, he moved to her shoulders, the other arm, her back, rubbing the oil into her skin. She stiffened. Hadn't Marcus said it would be only him? But she'd screwed that up, hadn't she?

He was unhappy with her. Again.

Seemed as if she always did something wrong. Either she wasn't loud and rebellious and nasty enough for Agent Rhodes's idea of a brat, or her behavior disappointed Master Marcus. And disappointing him...hurt.

"What's making you so sad, chiquita?"

She blinked and focused on Master Raoul. He'd stopped to study her face, his expression so kind she wanted to spill everything out. She shook her head instead. "Nothing you can help me with."

"And Master Marcus? Could he help?" Raoul asked softly.

The burning in her eyes was unexpected and totally unwelcome. What was this place doing to her? "No." She gave him a crooked smile. "It's my problem."

His dark gaze didn't leave hers for a long moment. "I think you'd find he would listen, *querida*." He squeezed her shoulder, then knelt to rub the oil into her legs, up her calves, her thighs. It felt good, strange, even a little exciting until he neared her pussy. Her muscles tightened. To her relief, he rose to his feet.

She relaxed...and then he put his big hands on her breasts. She squeaked, stepped back, and bumped into Jake.

"You're not done yet, subbie," the younger dom said. He held her upper arms firmly despite her struggles as Raoul massaged in the oil. When he stopped, her breasts felt achingly swollen.

He wasn't done. She stared over his shoulder, and yet she could feel his keen gaze on her face, as he teased and pinched her nipples, wakening them with slow circles, gentle friction, and little jolts of pain until they stood in rigid peaks. To her horror, she felt herself dampening.

As if he could tell, his eyes crinkled with his smile. "I think you're ready for Master Marcus now." He brushed a kiss over her lips. "You're a sweet little sub, for all your mouthiness."

Jake released her arms, saying, "Have a great run, Gabrielle."

Raoul walked her back to the door, but rather than going inside, he pointed to the huge yard and a wide grassy path between tall bushes. "Run that way, Gabrielle, and then wherever you want. Give Master Marcus a good hunt."

Staring around her, she walked in the direction he'd pointed.

With a loud sigh, he pulled the switch from his belt and gave her a stinging swat right across her bottom. As she yelped in shock, he growled, "I said run, sub. Run!"

She sprang away, hearing the swish of the switch. Her bottom stung like hell—he'd got her good. Bastard dom, acting all sweet and then nailing her like that.

Her breasts bounced painfully as she ran, and she slowed quickly. As the plush golf-course-length grass tickled her feet, a sultry night breeze wafted against her bare skin. It felt strange—wrong—to walk around outside with no clothes on.

Rubbing her arms, she continued on. Hedges loomed on each side, opening into secluded areas with menacing shadows. "*Give*

Master Marcus a good hunt," Master Raoul had said, so she turned down a smaller path, working her way deeper in. Other glow lights twinkled here and there, reminding her she wasn't the only submissive in the game.

What a beautiful place though. The moonlight paled the curving flower gardens. Fountains splashed and gurgled everywhere, and lights under the water glowed. White fog drifted through the humid air and swirled around her ankles. *Fog?* She glanced up at the cloudless night sky and frowned, then realized the fog came from the fountains, spilling like thick mist over the sides.

They created fake fog, just for fun? She shook her head, trying to be amused, except the stuff made the place really eerie.

A man's voice broke the quiet. "Lords and ladies, the hunt is on. Find your slaves and do what you will."

Oh my God.

Multicolored glow sticks danced like fireflies through the darkness. People ran here and there. Some of them. Other lights moved slower, more deliberately. The doms. Stalking their slaves.

And the sounds... A scream from the right. The slap of flesh on flesh and whimpering—someone getting spanked. Gabi turned her head and heard wet sounds and simultaneous grunts from the left—someone getting taken. Hard.

She had a quick image of Marcus grabbing her, forcing her to her knees, and driving into her. She sucked in a breath. He wouldn't. That wasn't what she wanted. Yet her nipples peaked, and her body dampened again.

He'd be out there somewhere, searching for her yellow glow stick. Hunting her. The air seemed to heat, wafting over her skin like a hot breath.

She walked, taking one path after another, veering around the tiny nooks, averting her gaze from the people in them: a black woman chained to a tree trunk getting flogged. A skinny, naked man kneeling, his dom's cock in his mouth. A hefty domme in a shiny latex corset riding a man on all fours, steering him toward a secluded area. She'd bridled the guy, Gabi realized. *Yeehaw.*

Still looking over her shoulder at the couple, she ran into a solid body and squeaked.

The man grasped her arms in a firm grip. "Easy, subbie."

She looked up. Pale eyes and silvery gray hair glinted in the moonlight. "Master Sam."

"I'm one of the dungeon monitors this evening. Remember the safe word, girl?"

"Red." They stood on a bigger path where others could see them...maybe the perp even, so Gabi added, "Oh lord and master. High muckety-muck."

His thin lips curved into a pleased smile, and his hands tightened.

Uh-oh. She tried to retreat.

Despite her struggles, he turned her easily and then swatted her bottom really, really hard, right on top of where the switch had hit.

The burning pain swamped the stinging left from the switch. "Damn you, that hurt!"

He pulled her back against his chest to murmur in her ear, "I'm a sadist, girl, and I enjoy the sound of pain. If you don't want to scream, watch carefully how you behave around me."

A tremor of true fear ran up her spine before he chuckled and let her go. This time she ran like hell.

A few minutes later, she slowed and bent over to brace her hands on her knees to catch her breath. *Note to self—must exercise more*. When she straightened, she saw a solid wood fence blocked her way. She'd reached the far end of the gardens. How many acres was this place? She turned to head back, choosing a path that led past a pure white flower garden glowing in the moonlight.

A dark shape stepped out of the nearby bushes. "Come here, dirty slut."

She froze, her breath gone, unable to move as the man stalked closer.

"Gabrielle." He grasped her shoulders and shook her gently. "Gabrielle. Look. At. Me. Use the safe word. Say it."

Marcus. It's Marcus. She stared up at his strong face. His masculine scent blended with that of the tropical flowers, and she could breathe again. "Red," she whispered.

He smiled and pulled her into his arms for a hug. "Very, very good, darlin'."

When he started to release her, she clung, and without objecting, he held her as her pounding heart rate slowed, as her muscles unknotted. Eventually he pulled back. "Ready for more?"

No. But she firmed her lips. Turn into a brainless vegetable because of some words? Nothing Marcus might do to her could be scarier than that. "Yes."

"More it is. I'm proud of you, sugar." He leaned down to kiss her, lightly nibbling at first, then taking her mouth with such a fierce, possessive hunger that her world filled with his touch and taste.

God, the man could kiss.

He whispered, "Stay brave, little sub." He took two panther-quiet steps. Then the shadows swallowed him.

She frowned at how well he'd disappeared and realized she saw no yellow light. He'd taken off his glow stick, probably hidden it in his jeans pocket. Sneaky bastard.

After a few steps, she broke into a run. Let him try to keep up —why should he have this too easy? After rounding a corner, she turned. No sight of him.

Callused hands grabbed her and jerked her back against a hard body. "Filthy fuckhole."

She froze.

"Safe word. Say it, Gabrielle."

"Red."

Four more times, he sent her into the darkness and found her again. At the last interception, reeling with exhaustion, she spat the word at him without even a pause. "Red, you bastard."

He laughed, and then his hand fisted in her hair as he held her and took possession of her mouth. He kissed her as she'd always dreamed of being kissed, hard and deep.

When he pulled back, he had to drag her arms from where she'd wrapped them around his neck. "Let's head back, sugar," he said in a slightly hoarse voice.

She gave a small sigh. His kiss had energized her, and right now she wished he'd chase her for...fun...instead of to spout dumb words at her. "I s'pose."

"You suppose?" Instead of moving away, he stepped closer. His hard hand cupped her breast. Held it. Weighed it in his palm.

She gasped at the sudden streak of fire through her.

"You don't seem all that tired, darlin'," he said with the slow drawl thick in his voice, the one he got when he was angry or considering doing something interesting, like really playing the game.

Her mouth went dry as her skin seemed to tighten. If he chased her for real, would she get scared? She saw the same question in his eyes. She considered and decided within a bare second. Maybe he'd frighten her, but the idea of having him catch her... take her...sent heat rolling low in her pelvis. A tremor shook her as she threw caution away. "I'm not tired at all, Sir. In fact, I might run back to the house and get a less ...wimpy...partner."

He gave a deep laugh. "Might you indeed." He pulled his glow stick out of his pocket and fastened it on his wrist, then tilted her chin up. "You think you'll make it there before I catch you?"

Her breath caught, and it sure wasn't from fear. She snorted derisively. "Piece of cake."

He stepped back. "I'll count to one hundred."

Counting in her head, she poured on the speed for seventy-five seconds, veering right and left, then left again, picking directions that led away from the house. Yeah, he'd never find her. Of course, he always did. Trying to catch her breath silently, she walked, keeping her wrist in front of her. As she peered through the darkness and white seething fog, she realized few of the glow sticks moved quickly anymore. Most were in groups of three, showing the dom had caught his sub. A few matched colors hovered low to the ground, and she giggled, knowing exactly what that meant.

She reached the back fence again, and no Marcus. Turning, she took a path leading toward the house, a little disappointed. The idea that Marcus would want—really want—to make love to her had set her blood on fire.

The other subs always sighed when they talked about him.

She grimaced. Most of the trainees—except for Sally—didn't like her because of her bratty behavior. Her steps slowed as the excitement trickled out of her. Aside from her parents, people liked her; here almost no one did. Her shoulders sagged.

A couple of trainees said she took up too much of Master Marcus's time. She sighed. He probably felt the same way. She sure wouldn't be a very satisfactory trainee. He never acted disgusted—she'd had a lifetime of handling that, after all—but she hated disappointing him over and over. She massaged the aching place under her ribs. "I am so looking forward to when this is over," she muttered.

Somewhere near the middle of the gardens, a woman screamed out her climax, and Gabi stopped at the jolt of envy.

Yet the game had lost its appeal. *I'm not here to play*. When this ended, she'd never see any of these people again. Even if she could, no one would welcome her, not after the way she'd acted. She swallowed against the lump in her throat, and her eyes blurred.

Speaking of games, she needed to get back and resume her act. Returning without Marcus would be a good defiant action. Lifting her head, she searched for a path to take. Her gaze snagged on a bright yellow glow a few feet away. Not moving.

"I do believe you're the only sub I've seen reduced to tears before her dom caught her," Marcus's soft drawl came from the shadows. He'd been standing there, watching her wallow in unhappiness.

She gulped, wanting to bury her face against his chest and cry. *Not going to happen, wussy girl.* She straightened her shoulders and lifted her chin, realizing she stood in the open, illumined by the moonlight. "I felt sorry for myself since my wimpy dom can't catch a snail crossing the sidewalk."

A snort of laughter. "I do enjoy your way with words, trainee." A pause and his voice lowered, the threat as obvious as a cat's unsheathed claws. "Run."

Oh God. Fear ripped across her nerves, and she bolted toward the thicker bushes. If she got around those—and she did—he'd have a more difficult time spotting her bracelet. But she lost track of him.

Panting, she stopped and spun in a circle—and spotted a yellow glow stick. A few feet away. Perfectly still.

"Run."

Her heart hammered even before she sprinted across the path. He—What was he going to do when he caught her? He really was a cat, toying with his prey. She veered around a hedge and ran straight into him, a solid wall of muscle. "Oooph!"

He chuckled and set her on her feet. "The next time, sugar, I'm taking you down." He stepped back a pace. "Run."

CHAPTER TEN

The low-voiced threat sent excitement churning through her, making her aware of the cool fog against her ankles, the way bushes scraped on her naked body when she got too close, the way her breasts jostled as she ran. A corner. Another. She popped into a secluded spot to catch her breath, and back out and—

He grabbed her from behind.

"No!" Instinctive terror blasted her. She twisted and shoved at him frantically.

Marcus... It was Marcus, not a stranger. *Okay. Okay*. Using her head now, she pulled and sidestepped, and his hands slipped off her oily body.

"Li'l brat." He made another grab for her.

I'm a greased pig, all right. Giggling, she dashed for the far side of the clearing, gaining only a few yards before his hand closed on her arm—and she yanked out off his grasp. No hitting or scratching, she reminded herself.

"You are a slippery little thing, aren't you?" he said, his southern accent markedly increased. The bastard grabbed her hair.

"Ow!" She turned to hit him—rules be damned—and he moved faster than she'd thought possible. Setting an arm behind her shoulders, the other up between her legs, he yanked her hips forward, tipping her backward, then dropped down on his knees with her in his arms. Before she got her balance, he rolled her onto her stomach.

No way. She got her feet under her and lunged forward.

With a low laugh, he caught her ankle and yanked her back, then set a knee on her butt. His weight pinned her, making her feel...odd. Excited.

Yet the second his powerful hands closed on her shoulders, terror engulfed her in a cold, mindless fog. She froze.

He stilled. Waited. She caught a whiff of his musky amber scent, and warmth dissipated her fear. It was Marcus touching her. Knowing *his* knee rested on her bare bottom, *his* weight trapped her, made all the difference. She wiggled and couldn't resist taunting him. "You rat-bastard dipwad, let me go."

Chuckling, he tightened his grip. "Mouthy little sub." The wrist cuffs snicked off his belt. "I am going to enjoy what I do to you."

Oh God. Under the growing tension, unable to help herself, she squirmed, and he simply put more weight on her. Controlling her.

Despite her thrashing, he firmly buckled one wrist cuff on and the other, then clipped them together behind her back. When he removed his weight, she thought he'd pull her to her feet. Instead his knee pushed between her thighs, keeping her legs apart.

His jeans scraped against the sensitive skin of her inner thighs. For a minute, he didn't move. And then he stroked her legs, traced the crack between her butt checks, squeezed her waist. He ruthlessly touched her how and where he pleased, and her skin burned under his callused hands until it seemed she might set the grass beneath her on fire.

He set his palm between her legs to cup her heat and gave a satisfied, "Mmmmh. You're nice and wet, darlin'."

His touch roused her, yet...she felt too naked, too restrained, too vulnerable. Needing to escape, she wiggled. Helplessly.

"No, Gabrielle." His voice deepened, a smooth threat as his hand pressed on her ass cheeks, holding her in place. "Stay put, sugar. I want to examine my prize."

The commanding voice, the knowledge he wouldn't let her move, melted her inside. This was what she wanted, needed. Someone to take the control from her. She turned her head and rested her cheek. The cool grass scraped and tantalized her bunching nipples, an erotic contrast to his warm hand on her bottom.

"Good girl." His unyielding hand held her down as with his other, he touched her intimately, caressing her folds and sending heat lancing up her center. When he slowly pressed a finger through her puffy tissues and up inside her, pleasure boiled up so violently that her eyes almost crossed.

His finger slid out, then pushed in deeper. He made another pleased sound. "Yes, Li'l Sassy, I'm going to tie you down, spread you open, and see how much of me you can take."

Oh God, yes. Her pussy clenched around him.

With a low laugh, he rose and lifted her easily to her feet. Holding her wrist cuffs, he reached around her and teased her breasts, pulling on her nipples, until her breasts burned with the same need as her pussy. As he pushed her toward the darkest section of the tiny area, he said in a low voice, "I intend to take my time later, but right now, little escaped slave girl, I'm going to fuck you hard." The rude word in Marcus's smooth voice was jarring. And so hot her knees wobbled.

Something glinted in the pale moonlight, and she saw that a heavy chain ran down from a thick tree branch and intersected four chains that opened to hold up...a tire swing. Rather than a standing-up position, the tractor-sized tire lay horizontally. "A swing?"

"You'll know why in a minute." Marcus unclipped her wrists,

grabbing her quickly before she could escape, and tossed her onto her back between the two sets of chains. The tire had canvas attached over the hole, providing support in the center. Her neck rested on the tire rim. *I don't want to make love on a damned swing.* She sat up.

Marcus laughed and shoved her down, then clipped her wrist cuffs to the chains beside her shoulders. The tire rocked wildly as she struggled, yet her excitement increased with each unsuccessful yank against the chains. When he walked to the bottom of the swing, she kicked at him. "I don't want to have sex here."

"I didn't ask what you wanted." He caught one leg in his merciless grip, and now she'd seen him without the suit, she knew just how muscular he was. "And I'm going to enjoy tying you up, sugar." He tried to bend her leg up, but she kept it straight—that was the whole point of the game, right?

She almost giggled. So maybe not all her insolent behavior was playacting. And every time he made her obey, it seemed to fan the flames in her roaring furnace.

With an amused sound, he held her leg in one hand and poked her in the ribs with a knuckle. She squeaked, and suddenly he had her leg bent and had her ankle in a strap hanging from the chain. He did the same on the other side, and there she was, naked and outside in a garden, faceup on a tire swing, wrists hooked to the chains, straps holding her legs up and apart.

God, this was so wrong. Kinky. Insane.

Yet heat seared her skin as he ran his hands over the backs of her thighs, leaving tingles in their wake. "I want that little pussy all the way down here where I can get to everything," he said and pulled her hips until her bottom hung out over the end of the tire and her legs angled toward her shoulders. He secured a strap up and over her pelvis to keep her hips from moving. At all.

Her pussy was open and exposed, and the slight movement of the swing wafted air over her wet folds. He studied her for a minute and smiled. "There you go, all ready for anything I want to do to you. You look beautiful, Gabrielle," he murmured.

She couldn't take it anymore, not from him. "Gabi."

"Excuse me?" His fingers slid between her folds, circling her clit.

Her breathing increased as her clit seemed to engorge. "My friends call me Gabi."

"Well, now, I do believe we might be considered friends," he said, amusement obvious, as he teased her, rubbing one side of her clit, circling her entrance, then repeating. He was too damned good at using his fingers, dammit. Her need grew, her pussy craving to be filled almost as much as her aching nub of nerves needed more of his touch. She squirmed, trying to get more.

"Stay still, sugar." He slapped her bottom, and the sting burned right into her clit.

She moaned.

His fingers paused. "I asked Holt to see if you enjoyed a little pain. Looks like you do."

Her eyes shot open. "No. I don't like pain."

"Mmmhmm." He slid a finger into her, so fast and deep she choked. A burn ignited from the inside out. Her words tangled on her tongue as pleasure rocketed through her.

He slapped her bottom harder.

Aaaah! The pain set her pussy on fire, and she almost came right then.

He laughed, low and deep, running his hand over the stinging area. "I'll be adding a tad more variety to your trainee scenes so we can explore this side of your nature."

Her tongue felt thick, and all she could think about was the way his fingers moved slowly in and out of her, occasionally moving out to slide over her clit until her whole pussy seemed to swell. "What?"

"Sugar, you like a little pain with your sex." He illustrated by swatting her butt forcefully enough to make her cry out, then pumping his fingers in and out of her vagina. Another swat. Thrusting. The burning on her bottom merged with the sizzling heat surrounding his fingers, and everything in her tightened, waiting... She gripped the chains as her hips tried to lift.

When he withdrew, she whimpered.

At the sound of a condom wrapper being ripped open, her eyes widened. Her pussy pulsed, so swollen and wet, and the thought of him—of Marcus—actually inside her made it all worse. She needed him to take her, to possess her all the way.

At the silence, she looked up and saw him studying her. A corner of his mouth turned up. "You're ready for me, little slave girl," he said softly. She felt him swirling the head of his cock in her wetness and shuddered in anticipation. He brushed it over her clit and sent a tremor up her spine. She was so close.

A second later, his thick shaft slid into her, and she groaned at the astounding feeling. Then firmly, inexorably, he pressed deeper, filling her, stretching her. *Too much.*

"No. No, stop." She pulled on the chains and tried to slide up and away.

His hands tightened on her hips. "You can take it, sugar."

She gasped for air, and her legs rattled the chains uncontrollably. As she strained helplessly against the hip strap and his powerful hands, the knowledge he could do anything he wanted shot through her until she almost came right then.

Oh God.

"You're hot and wet, li'l Gabi," he said slowly, as if he savored each word, as if he knew the way his dark, sexy voice melted her insides. His hands slid under her bottom and squeezed. "And I intend to hammer into you until you scream for me." But he still moved slowly, his size almost painful, until he had sheathed himself completely inside her and his balls brushed against her buttocks. He pulled back, then eased in.

Within a few strokes, her body adjusted and the movement of his cock turned into a slick slide of thrilling, wonderful friction.

She moaned.

"There we go." Without warning, he slammed into her. The starburst of sensation blazed upward, arching her back. He plunged deeper—the hammering he'd promised—and her need grew. God, she wanted even more. Her hips tried to move again, jerking uselessly. She groaned.

"Let me show you why swings are fun, li'l sub," Marcus said softly. His cock slid out as he pushed on the chains, and then he yanked the tire back, slamming her pussy back onto him like a pile driver. Smiling, he played the swing, back and forth, turning it slightly so his shaft pressed against one side of her vagina and the other.

So much, too much, and yet she couldn't make it over the top. Everything coiled so tightly inside her that each exquisitely wonderful movement almost hurt.

Lovely, Marcus thought, rocking the swing enough to keep her right on top of the pinnacle. Every muscle in her body was tight, her hands clamped around the chains. And her little moans had turned to a continuous soft song of need.

He knew the feeling. His balls felt as if they were being squeezed by some ball-crushing domme as he forced his climax back. He slowed the rocking and changed his grip to the strap over her hips so one hand could keep the swing going. So should he play with her clit to send her over?

No, he wanted to take her hard, have her come hard, shock her a little. Since he'd started with erotic pain, it would be fitting to finish with it. He got a good grip on the strap crossing her hips and let the tire rock away. As his cock slid partway out of her pussy, he slapped her ass, then yanked the swing back to impale her. To engulf his rigid shaft in her hot, wet silk. Again and again. The way she clenched with each slap almost destroyed his own control.

Faster. More. A handful of strong swats and her voice rose. Her stomach muscles under his knuckles turned to rock. Another swat and yank and she broke into a violent climax. Her shrieks corresponded to the forceful clenches of her vagina around his cock like a giant sucking device. Hearing her come, feeling her pussy try to milk him, he couldn't fight it any longer. He released his control and gave the tire a series of short, hard yanks. His climax roared through him, ripping from his balls into his cock and out in hot blasts of pure sensation.

With a groan, he rocked the swing gently, giving her a last few spasms—and when the hot walls of her vagina rippled around him, he wanted to take her all over again.

He ran his hands over her body, pleased at the soft, moist curves. The fragrance of her light feminine sweat mingled with the heavier scent of sex. He leaned forward, letting his weight down on her. Her soft breasts flattened against his chest, and he could feel her heart hammering. She blinked up at him, looking dazed, and he took her mouth. Even dazed, she kissed with the same wholehearted focus and response that she brought to having sex. That she used when talking to someone, he realized.

He could have happily stayed there all night with the swing rocking slightly and his little sub under him. Gabi, not Gabrielle. Fitting. She was as sweet and spicy as he'd thought...and worried she'd be.

She's not yours, Atherton. Regretfully he kissed her one last time. He pulled out slowly and walked over to dispose of the condom.

When he undid the straps, she lay limp, eyes closed, still not recovered. Not surprising—she'd had a rough night, emotionally and physically, then come like a dream. He lifted her from the swing and settled onto the ground, leaning on a tree and nestling her against him. Amazing how nicely she fit into his arms. He rested his chin on the top of her head, enjoying the scent of her fresh, spicy shampoo and the lemon fragrance from the oil. Her flushed cheek lay against his shoulder, and her breath, still fast, puffed warmly against his neck.

He'd actually planned to take her slower, drive her a little mad first, but her spirited fight had left him with a primitive urge to conquer and mark her in the most basic of ways. As a lawyer, he liked to believe in civilization; as a dom, he'd learned how easily the animal instincts could surface.

He nuzzled the tiny damp curls at her hairline—sometimes those animal instincts were purely fun.

He'd barely gotten settled when three chimes broke through the night, stilling everyone to silence except a woman who climaxed in high yips. Laughter spilled through the gardens, and then the sounds of movement. "Wake up, sugar. We have to head in."

"Mmmmh." She rubbed her cheek on his chest and went still again.

He frowned. The energetic little sub wasn't rebounding in her usual speedy fashion. Then again, how many times tonight had he terrified her, making her blank out? Although the desensitization was for her good, it would have an impact. He'd topped the night off with a chase, rough sex, bondage, and pain. No matter how much she'd enjoyed the capture game, it had undoubtedly shaken up her emotional equilibrium. No, even if she bounced back now, he wouldn't—couldn't—let her go home alone to experience whatever aftermath or nightmares might come at this point. "Gabi."

"Mmmhmm."

"You will be spending the night with me tonight, Gabrielle. You have the choice of where. My place, your place, or one of the upstairs private rooms."

She stirred in his arms. "But—I need... I mustn't..."

He saw the effort she made to think. "Do you trust me, Gabrielle?"

Her head dropped back onto his chest, her breathing slowing again. "Mmmhmm."

Good enough.

At the front St. Andrew's cross, Z held his cell phone to his ear and listened to the FBI agent rant about Gabrielle's irresponsibility. With a huff of disgust, he snapped the phone shut and shoved it in his pocket. *Idiot agent.*

Turning, he took a moment to study Jessica. He'd restrained her on the cross only a few minutes before. Color good, breathing easily, her gaze on him. Very nice. It wouldn't hurt her to wait on his pleasure. Especially since she knew she'd incurred his wrath for trying to interfere between a dom and sub...again. Little Miss Protect the Other Subs.

He turned to watch Marcus half carry Gabrielle out of the Shadowlands. Whatever had happened in the gardens had sent the brave little decoy into a place where she wasn't safe to drive, and Marcus was taking her home with him.

Guilt weighed heavy on Zachary's shoulders. He'd wanted to tell Marcus the truth for Gabrielle's sake, but he'd given his word, and so Marcus had pushed her—as a dom should. He was undoubtedly picking up on the discrepancies in her behavior. He wouldn't go easy on her, not once he realized she'd kept secrets from him.

Z frowned, wishing he knew the dom better. Friendly but reserved, Marcus was taking his time in becoming friends with the other Masters. Nonetheless, he was a fine dom with a profound sense of honor and protectiveness.

Yes, little Gabrielle would be safe with him.

However, he'd better give Galen and Vance a heads-up. Unlike the idiotic Rhodes, the two FBI agents in charge of the investigation were experienced and careful doms, and they'd understand what had happened to the trainee.

Zachary massaged his neck as he looked around the club. Less than half the members remained this late at night. Although he'd changed the music to Enigma's quieter chants, his head still throbbed like an overstretched balloon. He'd spent the evening talking with the members, leaving himself open to every emotional nuance, trying to find a hint of a predator in his club. Now his brain felt as if it might explode. At this point, he couldn't read anyone, no matter how close he got.

He couldn't even tell what Jessica was thinking—but from her body language, she'd take a cane to him if he let her loose at this point. He'd gagged her again before strapping her to the cross. He shook his head at the fury in her eyes. Normally he found her impertinent attitude delightful; he had never wanted a meek submissive.

But with a kidnapper targeting rebellious subs, every time she smarted off, his anxiety rose another notch. The thought of someone hurting Jessica... His jaw tightened. The man would die. Painfully.

He'd tried to talk her into taking a vacation right now, without him, and she'd laughed at him.

But Jessica wasn't the only sub in the club in danger. He could damn well at least remove one target.

He spotted Sally a minute later and motioned her over, then checked Jessica again. Arms and legs in an X position, nicely open and exposed, her lush breasts begging for use. She caught his eye, and despite the gag, her growl came through clearly. He snorted a laugh and stepped out of the scene area as Sally trotted up.

The vivacious trainee grinned at him. "Master Z, can I do something?"

Keeping an eye on Jessica, Zachary studied Sally. As mischievous as a basketful of kittens, the trainee was as sassy as she was sweet. She topped from the bottom whenever given a chance, which happened all too often. Although the Masters could control her and did scenes with her occasionally, she had both more experience and more intelligence than far too many of the other doms. Too clever and too stubborn for her own good. He'd begun to wonder if she'd ever meet the right dom. "I have a favor to ask of you, Sally."

"Sure. What can I do?" She'd gone for her favorite schoolgirl costume in a tied-up white shirt and short plaid skirt. Her braids swung, and she bounced on her toes as if he'd offered her a candy instead of wanting her help.

"I want you out of Tampa for a couple of weeks." Zachary held up his hand to keep her from speaking. "I can't explain except to say you haven't done anything wrong. Not in the least. I'm dealing with an internal club matter."

"But it'll leave the trainees short."

Typical of her to worry about the others. "I'll work it out with Marcus." He smiled, knowing the perfect bribe. "There's an airline ticket for Des Moines waiting for you at the United counter. Eleven tomorrow morning. Go visit your family before school starts. Deal?"

Her eyes widened. "Really? Hell, yes." She caught his frown and swallowed. "I mean, thank you, Sir."

"Much better." He tugged on a braid, then hesitated. She lived alone. "One more thing, pet. Please call here when you get to Des Moines. Just leave a message on the machine that you arrived safely. And if you're worried about...anything...let me know."

She gave him a suspicious look. "Something's wrong. What's going on?"

The sociable imp always knew all the gossip. He lifted her chin. "You will not discuss this, or that I asked you to take time off. Nothing. Am I clear?"

From the way she shrank, he'd scared her. Excellent.

"Yes, Sir. Get ticket, leave Tampa, check in, and don't talk about it at all."

"Very good. Off you go now." He returned to the club's other contender for brattiest sub. Jessica. Earlier he'd felt her emotions, a hodgepodge quite unlike his straightforward sub. Sadness definitely, uncertainty also. Her behavior had been worse than normal, especially in the Shadowlands, and damned if he knew why. Perhaps something to do with his boys' visit. He studied her for a minute.

Damn, he loved her—loved her more every day they remained together. She returned it, but could he keep her happy? He was older, as his sons had so tactlessly pointed out, and love didn't overcome everything. Over the last year, he'd carefully avoided any commitment so that she could back out of their relationship if she wanted.

Did she want to? Was her behavior a prelude to calling it quits? Or a reflection of his own moods?

They needed to have a long, long talk, but not now, not when he couldn't share the information about the kidnappings and investigation. Damn the FBI bastards for insisting on secrecy.

Rubbing his neck, he strolled back to his feisty kitten. Her green eyes shot sparks at him as he took advantage of her helpless condition to enjoy her breasts, using his mouth and fingers until her nipples stood out in hard, dark red peaks. He moved down to her soft thighs, spread so invitingly open—her pussy, already wet and slick. He teased her, waiting for when her growling turned to panting and her face flushed with arousal.

And then he removed her gag and took her mouth, stroking his tongue against hers, working his fingers over her clit. No matter what might happen, for the moment, she was his. As her clit engorged under his touch, she whimpered and squirmed.

When he stepped back, her body strained toward him, needing more. As she remembered where she was, she turned adorably red. "You manipulative jerk."

"Am I now?"

His cold tone snapped her attention to his face, and she winced. He held her gaze and unzipped his slacks. Being taken in public embarrassed her, but it also excited her. He smiled slowly. How many climaxes would it take before she'd lose her voice? Until exhaustion overwhelmed any urge for disobedience?

"Z. Master. Wait."

"No," he said softly. "I will not."

Well, he'd certainly been wrong about the redheaded sub. The spotter leaned back against the bar, smiling. A few minutes ago, Marcus had dragged the submissive from the Shadowlands. Not a peep out of her.

Looking broken—but that's what he'd thought before. Apparently a dom could subdue her for a time, as with the spanking last week, but she came right back, snapping and biting. He'd laughed when she'd noisily objected to the slave clothing.

And because of her spirit, the figging scene had been most entertaining. Yes, he'd definitely include her in his report this week. Delightful.

A shame Marcus hadn't paddled her when she had the ginger up her ass. A submissive anticipating the next blow would clench her buttocks, but the increased pressure heightened the burn from the fig, so she'd relax only to receive a hard swat on the ass.

Well, when they harvested her, he'd suggest it. Perhaps as part of the auction to keep the buyers amused. He might even volunteer to wield the paddle.

Grinning, he nodded at Cullen, then glanced over to the submissive area. Still an adequate variety and he had a craving for a soft one. He considered. There was a younger woman, and he did enjoy youth, but no. He'd utilize the plump, older sub. Tears came too easily on a young one. Older ones resisted better, giving more satisfaction when they screamed and begged.

CHAPTER ELEVEN

This is totally insane. Stupid. Gabi scowled as she let Marcus help her out of his sedan. "I feel fine," she said. "I don't need—"

"Yes, you do, darlin'." He put his arm around her as if he thought she'd fall down without his help. "You can act as ornery as you want, but you're not going to stay alone tonight." He nuzzled the top of her head.

"Oh honestly." She might have had a chance to protest at the club...if she could have managed, but for some bizarre reason, her synapses hadn't all been firing. After talking with Z, he'd had Sally fetch her purse and clothes and stuffed Gabi in his car before she could pull it together.

On the ride to his house, she'd thought about Agent Rhodes and had almost panicked until she remembered that Master Z had hugged her and murmured he'd notify her friend. Dickhead would have a fit, and wasn't she a bad person to enjoy that he'd yell at Master Z rather than her?

But in all reality, Marcus was right. She shouldn't drive right now, no matter how much her conscience objected.

That settled, she felt her excitement rise. Master Marcus had brought her to his home. She'd stay with him...all night. And she wanted to. To sleep in his arms, maybe have sex again. Find out more about him and... Damn, don't be stupid. *This is a temporary assignment, Gabi, not a date.*

Motion detector-regulated lights came on as they walked up to the front and through a black iron gate into a tiny entranceway filled with sweetly fragrant gardenias. Inside, Marcus let go of her to turn and punch numbers into a security pad. After the humidity of the night, the dry, cool air made Gabi shiver. She wore her yellow top and hot pants Marcus had helped her put on. Hell, he'd practically dressed her. Now, standing here in fetish wear in this nice house, she felt like a slut.

She took a step back, reaching for the handle of the door.

Turning from the keypad, Marcus frowned and stepped closer. His warm hand cupped her cheek. "What's wrong, darlin'?"

"I just..." He wanted honesty, and her brain was still moving too slow to come up with some excuse. She gestured to her clothes. "I feel sleazy."

"Then take it off." The corners of his eyes crinkled as he smiled. "On the rare occasions I bring a submissive home, I generally make her spend the weekend naked."

"You—" When she gave him an appalled stare, his laugh filled the room, sending quivers through her stomach.

"Yes, I really do." His thumb traced her lips as he studied her. "I'm not a twenty-four-hour dom, but I consider nights and weekends to be open season on little subs in my house."

All weekend? "But—"

"But you've had enough tonight, lucky little sub, so don't get flustered on me."

When she sighed in relief, he laughed again. "Let me show you around." He walked ahead of her to turn on lights, and she couldn't help but notice how his jeans and T-shirt clung to his hard body.

The entry opened into a great room where one side held an

intimate seating area, the other side a man's favorite toy—a giant HDTV. She grinned. The decor appeared very Marcus. Creamy white walls, light marble tile floors, rich brown leather chairs and couches. Everything balanced, the colors clean but warm, although the lack of brightness struck her as sad.

A decorative glass-fronted black iron woodstove separated the living area from the dining area. How fun. Tampa did—occasionally—get chilly enough to warrant a fire. Did he sometimes throw a blanket on the floor and make love to a woman in front of it? The stab of longing to be that woman struck her without warning. "You have a lovely home," she said, turning away from the room and the emotion.

"Thank you. Now come along, darlin'." He cuffed his fingers around her wrist, making her stomach quake, and led her down the hallway to the master bedroom. Beige carpet, creamy white drapes, a massive bed covered with a dark blue satin quilt. The carved wood dresser and bedside stands matched the dark wood of the four-poster bed. Curiously she ran her fingers over a scratched section of one of the spindles. Everything else seemed in perfect condition.

Even though she hadn't spoken, his dazzling smile appeared. "From restraints."

Oh. She stepped away quickly, abruptly aware of her isolation with a man, someone she'd only known two weeks. A dominant.

His eyes narrowed. Then he pulled her into his arms. "Gabi, no matter where we are or what we do, your safe word still works. And as it happens, I'm not fixin' to throw you on the bed and tie you up. You're done for tonight." His hand moved down her back in a slow stroke of comfort.

Why did she feel so safe whenever he held her? She pressed her forehead against his chest. *I'm an idiot.* "I'm sorry. This just feels so strange. It's not like I haven't gone home with a man before—Well, maybe not for bondage, but—You know." *For sex.*

He smiled faintly. "I doubt you were perfectly sober those times."

"Ah." She blinked and scowled. That sounded a little...bad. "I guess." No wonder this felt different. Not only home with a dom, but without any nice inhibition relievers.

"We can fix that, at least. You go take yourself a shower while I open some wine."

Covered in oil, sweat from running, dirt on her hands and knees. Major sticky *ew*. "I'd love a shower."

He reached into the closet and pulled out a long, dark blue silk robe, then showed her the bathroom. "Use anything you like. There're spare toothbrushes and combs in the bottom drawer."

Well. She shook her head. The man obviously enjoyed...entertaining. Then again—well-off, charming, gorgeous? Women probably had hairpulling wars over him.

In the huge walk-in shower, she let the hot water beat some sense into her brain. *He's not for you. Remember that, Gabi.* After scrubbing her body and wincing at the various bruises, she ran her fingers through her hair. Twigs. Leaves. *Ew.*

The built-in shelf held shampoo that smelled like Marcus, as well as a handful of hotel samples undoubtedly provided for his guests. Sheesh, her love life should be so lively. She tried to ignore the unhappy twinge. *I'm just one of many*. Actually, her status was even lower. She was merely a trainee he'd rescued because she'd wussed out on him and couldn't get herself home. *Remember that, Gabi. You're not here as his date.*

She picked a shampoo that smelled like citrus and spice, washed her hair, then stepped out into the steamy room. The fogged-up mirror gave a blurry image of a woman with wet hair, no makeup. Good thing Master Marcus had big balls, or he'd scream and run out of the house at the sight of her. She grinned. Poor man. After she'd cried all over him last week, he'd had to look at her raccoonlike, streaky makeup all night. Domination—not for the faint of heart.

After pulling on the borrowed robe, she walked into the living room. Empty. The lilting, soft voice of Sarah McLachlan came from the speakers. Glass clinked in the kitchen. A few seconds later, Marcus appeared, handed her a glass of wine, and brushed a kiss over her lips.

"You look better." He glanced down at himself and smiled ruefully. "I need a shower too. You led me on quite the chase, subbie."

She giggled.

He laughed and tugged a lock of her hair. "So pleased with yourself." He nodded toward the living room. "Make yourself at home, and I'll be right out."

The tile floor felt smooth and cold under her feet, and the robe slid silkily against her bare skin as she walked across the room. She took a sip of her red wine. A lovely pinot noir. Just what the doctor ordered.

She wandered over to one wall to check out the pictures. Family shots with a sweet-faced woman, and a gray-haired man who had Marcus's chin and eyes. One with a myriad of relatives. Many photos of teenagers of all ethnicities on basketball courts, in karate tournaments, building a house. A picture with Marcus at the center of a bunch of teens. She smiled at the way they'd crowded around him, obviously trying to get closer. Marcus with his arm across the shoulders of a teen wearing gang tattoos. The boy grinned from ear to ear.

She studied the karate photos for a moment, realizing that like the teens, Marcus wore a white gi, only his belt color was... *Oh wow. Don't start a fight with the nice black belt, Gabi.*

The bookcase contained a variety of subjects: law, ethics, best sellers, horror with Stephen King predominating. Huh. Hers held social services books, psych books, sociology, Shakespeare, romances, and fantasy. They probably wouldn't get along at all in real life. Then again—she studied the pictures of him with the boys—he might have a few more facets than she'd thought. God knew her father wouldn't be caught dead on a basketball court, let alone one in the slums.

At the sound of footsteps, she turned.

Marcus walked into the room, pulling on a silky robe like hers, and as he tied it shut, she saw how the hard, contoured muscles of his chest tapered down to a taut, flat abdomen. She'd never seen him without a shirt, and her fingers tingled with the need to touch. The alcohol had definitely given her a buzz, dammit. She rubbed her hands on the robe—*bad Gabi*—and smiled at him. "Now what?"

He motioned toward the couch. "Let's sit, and I'll grill you about your life."

Her feet froze to the floor. Questions? She couldn't answer questions about her life. "Um. I'm a little tired. Maybe I could bed down somewhere out of the way?"

"Don't be fibbing to me, darlin'. You were tired before. Not now." He regarded her with eyes sharp enough to cut. "I take it there are parts of your life you'd find uncomfortable discussing?"

Sometimes it was majorly disconcerting how he went from down-home Southern to lawyer-speak. "I really do need to get home. Would you mind letting me have enough money for a taxi. I'll pay you back on Friday. Sir."

Very interesting, Marcus thought. He sipped his wine and studied her, watching her fidget at his silence. The little sub had plummeted from relaxed and laughing to stiff and uncomfortable.

On the drive here, after she'd roused up, she'd chatted about politics, society, a big cat rescue place that his nana also loved, and then argued with him about crime in the cities and how to address it. He'd enjoyed every minute of the ride. The woman was cheerful and compassionate and very, very smart. Hell, she not only debated as well as he did, but derailed him with off-the-wall comments about the scenery, then jumped back on the train without a problem—leaving him in the dust.

But apparently the thought of talking about herself made her want to flee. When he met her eyes, she dropped her gaze with the instinctive submission she'd shown a few times before. For whatever reason, she'd left her bratty sub shield behind at the club. *I like the woman she is without it.* Warm, energetic, bright. Dammit, she *fit* in his home. No, more than that—she *enhanced* it.

When he walked around her slowly, she shivered. No makeup, pink from the shower, hair shaggy as a drowned poodle's, the robe swathing her in fabric—and she tugged at his heart like a magnet. He wanted to cuddle her against him...then drag her under him and take her again. Affection and protectiveness and lust: he might find himself in serious trouble here.

He stopped in front of her, deliberately invading her space. "No, you're not running away home, Gabrielle."

Her chocolate brown eyes held wariness. What made her so skittish?

"We are going to sit down and enjoy our drinks and some conversation. If I ask you a question you don't care to answer, tell me so. I do ask that you not lie to me."

She'd managed to keep her gaze level on his, but the tiny muscles around her eyes tensed. Apparently she'd already lied to him about something.

Well, he'd deal with that another time. For now, they'd discuss her experiences at the club and where to go from here. He took a step back, releasing her from his control. "Holt looked like he enjoyed having you as a submissive."

Her sigh of relief made him smile.

When Master Marcus pushed her toward the couch, Gabi gave up the fight and complied. She sat down at one end, hoping he'd choose a chair or at least—

He took a seat in the middle, then put both their drinks on the coffee table. After lifting her legs onto his lap, he kept pulling, forcing her to slide down until her back rested against the arm of the couch. To her dismay, the tie of her damn silky robe loosened, letting the front gape open and exposing her breasts.

When she started to fix it, he gave her a stern look. "Leave it open. I enjoy looking at you."

Her fingers went limp. Thank God they'd left the club, since she wasn't sure she could defy him. Somehow the time in the Capture Gardens had wiped away her resistance, and here in his house, his commands and the implacable look in his eyes sent quivers all the way to her bones.

His chin tilted up slightly. "Your answer is...?"

"Yes, Sir." She picked up her drink, needing to have something to hold.

"Very nice, sugar." He grasped her left foot and firmly massaged the aching muscles. God, that felt good. When his thumbs pressed deep into the sole, her eyes almost rolled up in her head.

He smiled slightly, selected another spot, and did it again. Seduced into talking by a foot rub. Sneaky dom. "I'd like to know how you happened to get in a gang war, Gabi. Will it bother you to tell me?"

"Um." When she tried to pull her foot back, he didn't let her. Just waited. She recognized his technique, had used it herself, yet even knowing that, the silence pressured her with the need to fill it. But this... Her chest tightened. *I don't want to.* Yet he'd tried to help her this evening. Maybe he needed to know what kind of a wreck she was.

He waited, his hands even warmer against her skin—or maybe the room had grown colder. She'd grown colder. She took a fortifying sip of her drink. "Okay, if you really want to know... I'd run away from home and was living on the streets in Miami with a couple of men. I was pretty naive. They taught me a lot." Amusement tickled her throat as she realized how his stuffy lawyer soul would react. "Although I never mastered hot-wiring cars, I got good at picking pockets." *And pleasing Danny and Rock in bed.*

Like she'd figured, his facial muscles tightened until his cheekbones stood out. "How old were you?"

"Sixteen."

"They should be horse whipped."

"Too late. They're dead." Amusement died as sorrow swept through her, a cold wind that left an ache deep inside her chest.

"Tell me, sugar." He released her gaze and massaged her other foot. The strength of his hands felt like stability in a wavering world.

"I lived there around a year or so. The streets got rougher. Money got harder to find, so Rock started dealing even though two gangs were fighting for the territory already. One gang showed up at the apartment. They killed Rock and Danny and..." She shrugged, trying to act nonchalant, despite the way her stomach had turned over. Everything in her curled up into a tiny ball of pain. She swallowed. "I didn't die—just got cut up a little." *And raped.*

His gaze traced the scar down her face. "So you were there when they killed your friends?" he asked softly.

Finish the story; get it over with. She jerked her head in a nod and stared at the red wine in her glass. "Danny opened the door, and they shot him." *The pistol blasted, the sound shocking, terrible, filling the room, drowning out the shouts, her screams. Danny seemed to fly back. He hit the floor, his eyes wide, mouth open, blood everywhere. She hadn't even managed to stand up. He'd made love to her early that morning, told her she was his special girl.* "Rock had a gun on the kitchen table. He shot once and... They had a machine pistol." *Bullets splintering the wood, ringing against metal...against flesh. His body jerked like he was having a seizure, and everything turned red as he hit the wall.*

Marcus pulled her onto his lap and wrapped his arms around her. He did that a lot, didn't he?

"You know, he'd buy me romance novels. We were broke, but somehow he'd still find me books," she whispered, heart aching.

His gaze didn't leave her face, a lifeline to keep her from drowning in the past. "Go on. Tell me the rest."

"I grabbed a knife and tried—"

"You attacked them with a knife?" Marcus interrupted in a strangled voice.

"They shot my Danny and Rock. I was so mad, and I wanted to hurt them. I got the one with the gun, actually." Her hand closed in a fist as if the wooden handle fit there. She felt the nauseating horror when the blade had slid in to the bone. His scream still brought her out of sleep sometimes.

Marcus uncurled her fingers and clasped her hand instead.

"I didn't kill him," she said, unsure even now whether she was relieved or disappointed.

"Sugar, you might have found that hard to live with...and they'd have killed you in turn."

"Probably. They cut me instead." *Their cursing, the knife flashing, the odd splitting down her cheek. Warm liquid on her face and neck, turning the white flowers on the couch a garish red. The pain—God, the pain. Their laughter changing. Calling her horrible names. Hands pushing her down, holding her, tearing her...* She heard herself whimper.

"Shhh, darlin', shhh. It's over." Marcus's voice. His wonderful, masculine scent.

She found a bit of air, used it, and found a bit more. Her fingernails had dug trenches into his palm. She forced her hand open and tried to laugh. It sounded ghastly. "When the cops busted in, I was... Well, at least they didn't shoot me. And then one man"—*Thank you, God, for giving me Abe*—"one man talked me out of the corner I was hiding in."

His arms tightened as if he could protect her. Far too late for that. Yet when he sighed and rested his cheek on top of her head, his concern washed her fear away like waves rolling over a sandy beach. "I'm sorry, Gabi," he murmured. "For you and for your friends."

"They were only in their early twenties. Younger than I am now." *Too young to have everything stop.* The bitter sorrow never quite left her. "Well, that's the story."

He stayed silent for a minute, and she didn't mind at all. He could hold her all night if he wanted.

"You've obviously been with other men since then," he said.

"Mmm-hmm." Her cheek against his chest, she could feel the springy hair beneath his silky robe. "I had trouble the first couple of times." Kim had encouraged her, held her when she had nightmares afterward. She'd been the one to drag Gabi to a BDSM club the next year. Nothing scared Kim; no conventions slowed her down. Gabi buried her face against Marcus and pulled in a slow breath. *We'll save you, Kim. Hang on.*

"But you got to the point you could go home with a man... with a little liquid incentive?" Marcus said lightly, helping her return to stable ground. His hand massaged the tensed muscles in her shoulders.

"Yes."

"Your first night, we talked briefly about more than one man. And when you watched a ménage, it excited you." He paused. "Gabi, is a threesome something you really want or will it give you nightmares?"

"I...I'm not sure." She blew out a breath, torn between the push and pull. "I think I might like to try it. Having sex actually quieted some of my fears." She swallowed and added, "Sometimes, even with one man, I feel too many hands, and it scares me. Maybe I could get past that."

"I see." He rubbed his chin over her head. "I'll mull over how to set it up."

"Thanks." *I think.*

"Did you go home eventually?"

"Yeah." Not that she'd wanted to. Her parents' disapproval had hung like a miasma in the air: *You brought it all on yourself.* "I went back to school and everything."

"What do you do now?"

"I'm—" "*I do ask that you not lie to me.*" She realized she'd hesitated too long, way too long for an experienced dom.

"I take it this is one of the things you prefer not to discuss?" he said, his voice as gentle as the hand rubbing her arm.

"Yes, please, Sir."

He sighed and shifted her to lean more comfortably in his arms—and to where he could watch her face, she realized. "Then let's talk about why you're so defiant a submissive. Why you're insolent even when you don't want to be."

Oh hell. *Tell the truth...without getting into the real truth*. "Uh. I'm just like that. Even as a kid. My parents are...rather rigid, and I've never been much for following rules."

His chuckle rumbled inside his chest. "I can believe it."

"I guess I never got out of the habit."

His perceptive gaze pinned her. "You were a rebellious child, and you have a sassy nature, but sometimes there's more, darlin'. I think something drives you to cause a fuss. Any idea why?"

She averted her eyes and shut her mouth.

Silence. He cupped her cheek, turning her face back. "I want to help you, but I need to know what's causing all this. Don't you trust me enough to share it with me?"

Guilt sent dark streaks through her, but she couldn't. Her throat clogged. She managed to shake her head. *No.*

"I see."

He let her bury her face against him so she could force the tears back. Could pull herself together. When she finally pushed upright, he smiled at her and put her glass of wine into her hand. "Let's watch a movie."

He acted as if nothing had happened, as if she hadn't disappointed him. The relief was immense. "I'd love to."

"I don't have any chick flicks, and I doubt you'd enjoy horror right now. But I keep some DVDs for my sister's children. How about *Shrek* or *The Lion King*?"

"Tough choice." She often watched movies with her young clients. *The Lion King* was her favorite, but a guy would probably prefer: "*Shrek*."

She fell asleep listening to an ogre talking about the layers of an onion.

She awoke the next morning feeling wonderful. Well, aside from the various aches screaming at her when she moved. Scraped knees. And a tender butt. She grinned, remembering Master Raoul's switch.

During the night, she'd woken from a horrible nightmare with Marcus's deep, slow voice pulling her to safety and comfort. Ignoring her apologies, he'd turned her so her back rested against his chest. Since he'd refused to let her wear anything to bed, his hot, hard erection had rubbed on her bare bottom. And then he'd cupped her breast in one lean hand, kissed her shoulder, and told her to go back to sleep.

She'd drifted off unsure if she regretted his control or not.

She slid out of bed. No sounds from the house. After brushing her teeth, she futilely wished for real clothes. After pulling on her robe, she stepped through the bedroom's sliding glass doors. He had a swimming pool big enough to swim laps. A giant inflated swan floated in the clear blue water.

Clad only in loose cotton pants, Marcus stood in the grassy backyard outside of the pool's screen cage. After a minute, she recognized the controlled movements of tai chi. One movement slid into another, infinitely slow and perfect. Panther graceful. She'd taken self-defense in college and never looked like that.

When he finished, he stood for a bit, then headed toward the pool. He spotted her and smiled...and her heart did a twitchy thing, as if it had wiggled in happiness.

"I saw your pictures in the living room," she said, striving for casual. "You do a lot of this karate stuff?"

"Some." He walked across the grass. "I was a skinny hairless wimp at thirteen, and I wanted to impress a sweet young thing, so

I signed up for karate. A month later, Marybeth abandoned me for a football player, but by then I was hooked on martial arts."

A wimp? His strong shoulders were twice the width of hers. Crisp golden hair covered the muscular planes of his chest. His biceps rippled under taut skin; tendons stood out on his forearms.

She wanted to touch him so badly she shook inside.

After stepping into the caged pool area, Marcus stopped in front of her. "You look much better, darlin'. How do you feel?"

"Good." She clasped her hands together. *You're not a girlfriend, Gabi; you're just a messed-up trainee he took pity on.* "Uh, I'm ready to leave whenever you are."

He tilted his head and gave her a quizzical look. In the morning light, his blue eyes appeared clearer than the cloudless sky above. "Are you now?"

When he ran his fingers down her jaw, her skin heated as if he were the sun. Unthinking, she rubbed her cheek against his palm and then flushed at acting like a starstruck teenager. "Don't." She took a step back. God, he was probably laughing at her.

The corners of his eyes definitely crinkled, but his gaze held heat, not laughter. "Does a sub get to say 'don't'?" How could a quiet voice sound so threatening?

Her mouth turned dry, and her heart skipped a beat. "No. No, Sir."

"I thought not," he said softly. "Hold your robe open for me, Gabrielle."

The muggy heat of a Florida morning hadn't changed, but with his command, the air itself thickened. Her fingers shook as she untied the belt and grasped the front, parting it. Exposing herself to his gaze.

"You have a beautiful body, little sub." He cupped her breasts, weighing them in his palms, running his thumbs around tightening nipples.

She closed her eyes over the heady wash of sensation. His nearness, the warmth of his sure hands, the slight scrape of rougher skin over her nipples. Above all, more than anything, knowing it was *his* touch.

When his fingers stilled, she opened her eyes and saw him watching her carefully. "You look a little flushed, sugar. Maybe we should—"

If he said he wanted to eat breakfast now, she'd kill him. With a huff of exasperation, she abandoned the robe and grasped his hands, pressing them harder against her breasts. "More."

His eyes cooled, and he pulled his hands out from under hers.

Her heart shrank. Couldn't she do anything right? "I'm sorry, Sir." Lowering her arms, she bowed her head, wishing she could sink down into the concrete.

To her surprise, he chuckled and put his arms around her. "It's all right, darlin'. I do sometimes forget you're still new to this. And we're new to each other."

The wave of relief shook her. After a second, she clasped her arms around his waist and burrowed a little closer. "I didn't know how to tell you I...I wasn't flushed because of the heat. I wanted to continue—but not if you don't want to," she added hastily.

He kissed the top of her head. "As it happens, I do know the difference between an overheated sub and an aroused one," he said mildly. "As for me wanting to..." His hands curved under her bottom and slid her pussy up and down a very hard erection.

Oh. Well. She didn't get time to feel stupid. As his hands massaged her butt, he tilted her hips so her clit contacted the base of his cock. Her breasts flattened against his bare chest, and the heat inside her flared to life. "Um."

His laugh ruffled her hair. "I think you're flushed again, Gabi. Go get in the pool." He pinched her bottom.

She stared at him in disbelief. "You want me to cool off?"

His chin raised, and the stern look he gave her knocked all the air from her lungs. She flung her robe over a lounge chair and hurried to the shallow end.

She walked down the wide steps in the corner of the pool. The water was only slightly cool...until it reached her groin, and then it felt like ice water against her burning pussy. She squeaked and looked to see if he'd noticed. Her mouth dropped open.

He'd stripped his pants off. Long, powerful thighs, narrow hips, and tight buttocks. *Oh my*. As her insides melted, she checked the water around her to see if it had started to boil.

Near the deep end, he picked up a pole and herded the swan toward her. Gabi snickered. Who'd have thought Mr. Stuffy would keep a blow-up swan in his pool, let alone one a good four feet or so across the back.

After setting the pole and something else on the edge of the pool, he came down the steps. Without speaking, he picked her up and laid her on the winged back.

Plastic warm from the sun scraped her breasts, teasing them to hard points. Giggling, Gabi tried to crawl up farther. She hadn't played on one of these for a—

His hard hands yanked her back until her legs dangled into the water, forcing her to grab the wing on the opposite side. She glanced over her shoulder. His erection jutted upward out of the water, wonderfully thick and long. Veins bulged down the length. The head looked like velvet, and her mouth watered.

Holding her legs, he moved backward and up one corner step, raising his cock to the level of the swan.

"Marcus, what are you doing?"

"Enjoying my little sub before breakfast." He spread her thighs open and slid his fingers in her wetness and over her clit. The rush of pleasure ignited a fire inside her, one he worked into a hard blaze as he mercilessly stroked her clit to hardness.

He released her for a moment, took a step toward the edge, and she heard a condom wrapper being torn open.

"Brace yourself, sweetheart." Without further warning, he thrust inside her, burying himself to the hilt. Impossibly large, stretching her to the point of pain, yet the pleasure so intense her back arched. *God*. Her vagina strained to accommodate him, throbbing around the intrusion. His hands held her hips, keeping her immobile. His groin pushed against her pussy, and as the swan rocked under her, the crisp hairs teased her swollen, puffy labia. She moaned.

"Now that there's a nice sound," he murmured. His fingers curled tighter around her hips, and he slid his cock out slowly. Too slowly. She wanted to push back, move him faster, but her legs dangled uselessly above the pool floor. He controlled the movements of the swan and of her body, and she could do nothing but hang on.

He took her hard. Mercilessly.

Right there in the pool, before breakfast, without asking first.

Took her so thoroughly that she came twice before he finished.

CHAPTER TWELVE

After several more days of the bogus job hunting, Gabi wanted to scream. It wouldn't seem so bad if she needed a job, but she didn't. Her feet ached as if someone had pounded on them with a mallet. She swung her legs up to rest on the back of her couch.

Where's a nice foot-rubbing dom when you needed one?

She sighed, remembering last weekend and the careful power of Marcus's hands. On her feet. Her breasts. Her pussy. In the pool, he'd slid those strong fingers under her and stroked just hard enough, pinched... She sighed, and her clit throbbed as if the memory had woken it up.

The memory of how he'd tossed her on the swan and simply taken what he pleased still made her quiver inside. That morning, she'd done anything he'd wanted, as if their time in the Capture Gardens had set a pattern of her giving in. Submitting.

And I loved it. Loved seeing his smile of pleasure when she did as he commanded, loved basking in his approval instead of causing him disappointment. He hadn't played lord and commander all the time. After the pool—and the shower—they'd cooked omelets and biscuits for breakfast, arguing about the ingredients, about who'd wash up, about anything. If anyone had kept count—and Mr. Lawyer had—she'd won more arguments than she lost. He hadn't acted like she was his slave. Well, not until they'd put the dishes away, and she'd said something about it being time to leave.

He'd gotten that dominating look in his eyes, and his drawl had turned to rich velvet. "No, darlin', you're not leavin' yet. You haven't gotten to...enjoy...my bed yet."

Oh Lord, she was getting all needy just thinking about it. Damn him.

She heard a thud. A thump. What sounded like a herd of horses stampeded through the room, and her two black cats tangled into a rolling ball under the tiny kitchen table. Gabi snorted a laugh. Whoever said cats were quiet pets needed his head examined. They might stalk silently, but the rest of the time...?

With a mutual hiss, the boys gave up the fight, and first Hamlet, then Horatio landed on her stomach.

"Oomph. Dammit, guys." Smiling, she stroked them. Horatio with long, fluffy fur, Hamlet with short, sleek fur, they'd been a birthday present last year from her grandmother. Little fur babies to love from someone she loved. "You know, boys, your mama must have entertained the neighborhood, 'cause you sure don't look like brothers." She added wistfully, "I wish I had a brother or sister." But her parents disliked how much a child interfered with their lives and had never considered having another after Gabi.

Hamlet pushed against her hand, demanding a head scratching.

"That's me, guys. A handicap to a career." She'd tried to be the perfect daughter at first. When that didn't gain her any increased affection or attention, she'd gone the other way. Perhaps not the best thought-out scheme, but at least when she'd misbehaved, they noticed her.

As if to commiserate, Horatio rubbed his cheek against her chin.

She rubbed back. "Maybe they'd have done better with cats." *Or not.* At ten, she'd begged for a pet and received a list of reasons for their refusal. *Scratched furniture, pet dander, noisy*... "They'd only like you two if you were silent and hairless. Without claws."

Hamlet stared at her with appalled green eyes; he'd always been more conservative than Horatio.

After a glance at the clock, she groaned. "Guys, I need to get moving. I'm meeting our dear, sweet buddy, Dickhead—and the other two agents—at some Clearwater beach hotel." Rhodes would probably spend the entire time tearing her apart. Dammit.

She'd asked Agent Galen to assign her a different agent, but Rhodes had specifically requested the Shadowlands. Of course, he'd prefer the ritzy private club to the others. Because of his seniority in the Tampa office, they couldn't arbitrarily remove him.

Horatio flicked his ears forward as if to ask why she didn't just disembowel the obnoxious agent. What else were claws for?

"Don't tempt me." She swung her legs down and sat up. "What bothers me about this assignment is Marcus. After all my years of smarting off to the parental units, who'd imagine I'd want to behave? Well...behave most of the time."

She grinned, remembering how she'd stepped out of the shower before Marcus, then reached back to push the lever to cold. The man had a remarkable command of the profaner elements of the King's English.

And a hard hand.

And amazing stamina.

She sighed. He wasn't quite as conservative as she'd thought.

Then again, his decor seemed pretty dull. And his clothing. And the way he talked sometimes—Mr. Lawyer. She shook her head. No, they weren't really alike at all.

And he doesn't like brats, so she sure wasn't his type. He'd only taken her home because she'd been a mess, and the master of the trainees was a walking, talking example of overprotectiveness. Well, if she'd been his pity fuck for the weekend, she'd enjoyed it. Even if the thought did hurt.

She picked up Hamlet, kissed the top of his furry head, and set him on the floor, then did the same with Horatio. Slinging her purse over her shoulder, she glanced around the apartment. Beige on bland on insipid. Very creative decorator.

Hamlet and Horatio sat side by side, disgust at her abandonment plain in their postures.

"We can do this, guys. Only two weeks and we go home." Back to her cozy, colorful apartment, back to their cat condos and window perches.

Back to a life without a stuffy, domineering lawyer who sometimes seemed like something more.

Once in the fancy Clearwater hotel, she checked to make sure no one had followed her. She grinned, remembering Dickhead's cursory lesson that she'd titled "How to Be an Agent in Five Easy Steps." Nonetheless, she dutifully got off the elevator two floors early and climbed the stairs to the proper floor. How did they manage to do this covert stuff without feeling like idiots?

Winded, she stopped in front of the door to the hotel room and watched the elevator and stairway for a minute. Just in case. The silence in the hallway grew heavier as she stood there. Her amusement died as she remembered why she was here. Because someone wanted to sell her, to break her like an animal, to use her until she died. *Oh, Kim.* She pounded on the door.

It opened, and Agent Rhodes stepped back to let her in. "About time you got here, Renard."

Her relief at being inside faded. She glanced at her watch. Two minutes late. She turned away to look around at the room decorated in warm colors of sand and brown, highlighted with tropical oranges and reds. Still a little winded, Gabi dropped onto the L-shaped, sectional sofa without waiting for an invitation. Next time, she'd stop the elevator two flights *above* the hotel floor and walk down. And the minute she returned home to Miami, she'd join a gym. She meant it this time. Really.

"What happened to the meeting?" she asked, glancing around the empty room.

"A conference call in Buchanan's room. Kouros said they'd return shortly." Rhodes took a seat at the other end of the sofa and smoothed down his black suit, adjusted the cuffs of his white shirt. He wore J. Edgar-approved conservative clothing, undoubtedly chosen to facilitate his way up the ladder.

He picked up the coffee cup on the table and took a sip. "You're not a trained agent, Renard, but the stunt you pulled last night jeopardized the investigation. I don't know why you have your head up your ass—or maybe I do." His lip raised in a sneer. "I've seen how much you like your evenings."

Gabi set her hands on her thighs, keeping her fingers open, her palms down. A victim specialist had to keep her temper, to counsel, to talk through, to negotiate. He did have a point, she thought guiltily. She shouldn't have tried to work on her own personal problems at the Shadowlands. But she was glad she had. How could she allow herself to stay so vulnerable to a simple word or two?

But no need to worry about it now. "Rhodes," she said, giving him a level look. "Your comment is inappropriate. Please confine yourself to a discussion about the investigation."

His face flushed. Had he forgotten how often she'd called him on his behavior last year? Amusement tickled her throat. Maybe he thought that because she was a submissive in the club, her whole personality had changed. *Not.*

He glared at her. "Then, sticking to the discussion, I want you to know if you pull another stupid trick like going off with one of your fuck buddies, I'll have you fired. You got that?"

She sighed. Narrow-minded asshole. "Bear in mind I don't work for you, Rhodes. I volunteered for this, and I can unvolunteer at any time and you can try to whistle up a new submissive to take my place." She smiled at him sweetly. "Good luck with that."

He opened his mouth and then closed it. Good choice. Considering her teenagelike bratty behavior in the Shadowlands, he'd probably forgotten she wasn't someone he could push around. But as a child of an English professor and a corporate lawyer, she could not only out-pompous him, but could probably rip him to pieces verbally. And that wouldn't achieve anything except a moment of—very nice—satisfaction.

Unfortunately, complaining about him wouldn't get her far. Others had tried, but he had too many high-level buddies. And he'd undoubtedly do his best to destroy her reputation in turn.

She sat back slowly as a nasty realization surfaced. If Rhodes put his twisted slant on what she had to do in the club, this job could well kill her career. Her chest tightened as she thought of everything she'd worked for falling to pieces.

Before she could decide what to do, two men walked into the room. One was Galen Kouros, classically tall, dark, and handsome with a very unclassical limp. She hadn't seen him walk before, but from the way he leaned on a black cane, he no longer chased after criminals on foot. The lines in his face might come from pain, not a bad temper.

Despite the contemporary tan slacks and a white shirt, the other man looked like a medieval Scottish Highlander: a fair-skinned face with hard, flat planes; tied-back, light brown hair; tall and wide-shouldered. Both unshaven guys had the drawn appearance of people who hadn't seen a bed in recent history.

Interesting contrast though, a team of light and dark—did the light one play the good guy during interrogations?

"Ms. Renard, it's nice to meet you in person. I'm Vance Buchanan." The brown-haired warrior had an easy smile. He reached over the coffee table to shake. His hand was the size of a boxing glove. "And I believe you've met Galen."

"Agent Kouros," she said politely to the other agent.

Buchanan snorted. "You can make it Galen and Vance. Would you care for a soda or coffee?"

"Sure. A soda would be great," she said.

As Galen took the chair opposite Dickhead, Vance got her a can from a small fridge, handed it over, then sat across from her. "We asked you to join us today for a couple of reasons, but mostly to bring you up-to-date."

The grimness of his expression made Gabi's insides tighten. "What's happened?"

"You're very perceptive." He rubbed his face and sighed. "We've determined who are the most notably rebellious submissives in the various Tampa clubs, and one of the women appears to have disappeared last Saturday. Another hasn't been seen since the week before. Just like in Atlanta, the subs belonged to different clubs. Our decoys haven't been touched."

"Oh. Damn," Gabi whispered.

"The good news is this confirms the kidnapper is taking insolent submissives. The bad news is that both decoys in those two clubs did a fair job appearing rebellious. Maybe the kidnapped women seemed feistier or more appealing, or our agents are too new to BDSM or gave themselves away in some manner. And, much as I hate to add it, public sex might play a part. One decoy has sex at the club, but restricts it to another agent who's pretending to be her dom—and happens to be her husband. The other decoy sticks strictly to nonsexual activities."

"We just don't know enough," Galen broke in with a grunt of disgust.

"Still no clues?" Gabi asked.

They shook their heads. "If we hadn't checked, these two subs might have gone missing for quite a while before anyone noticed," Vance said. "The kidnapper apparently chooses single women who don't speak with relatives or friends every day. And he covers his tracks. In Atlanta, he sent one victim's employer an e-mail saying she had a death in the family and needed time off."

Rhodes had leaned back in his chair, looking frustrated but lacking the sheer unhappiness the other two showed. He undoubtedly cared more about the success of the investigation than the victims.

"We're leaving all the decoys in place in case the kidnapper strikes a club twice," Galen said. "But, Gabrielle, the chances are increasingly high he'll take someone from the Shadowlands."

The chill rattled her bones like an icy wind. What if something went wrong? *I'm not a brave person, dammit.* When the can she held started to crumple, she gently set it on the coffee table and took a calming breath.

Galen set his cane against his leg and leaned back. With a look that seemed all too familiar, his keen gaze went from her hands to her face. Reading her. An experienced agent...or an experienced dom? She narrowed her eyes at him, and a hint of a crease appeared in his cheek.

She looked away. *Honestly, Gabi, it's just your imagination.* After so much time in the Shadowlands, of course she saw doms crawling out of the corners like cockroaches.

Vance said, "We're keeping the news of the missing women quiet for now in hopes of not alerting the unsub. Since we don't know where the delivery will take place, our only chance is to follow once a decoy is kidnapped. It's vital you do your utmost to attract his attention."

With his words, the fear she'd dammed broke over her like a tidal wave. She dropped her eyes, putting her hands between her knees to hide the trembling. A swallow cleared the tightness in her throat. "Yes, I know." Her chin lifted. "I'll do my best."

The sympathy in Galen's eyes almost did her in. "I'm sorry, Gabrielle. It's not fair to you at all."

"What do you mean not fair?" Rhodes said, his higher voice like a rasp against her nerves. "We're guarding her." He added under his breath, "She's not risking anything except a chill from lack of clothing."

Gabi saw the furious stare the big agent gave Rhodes.

Galen shook his head at his partner and responded to Dickhead in a soft voice almost as bladelike as Marcus's. "You show her the respect you would for any volunteer—and you'd better guard her very, very well, Rhodes. Am I clear?"

Rhodes's face turned pale.

Yeah, you idiot, not easy being on the other side of a pissed-off dom, is it? Gabi sighed. And that's where she'd remain for the next two weekends. Even worse, after the night they had spent together, Marcus wouldn't understand. At all.

CHAPTER THIRTEEN

On Saturday, Marcus halfheartedly watched Cullen lightly flog Andrea in the nearby scene area and tapped his fingers on the arm of the chair. After looking forward to seeing Gabi all week, her attitude on Friday night and this evening had come as an unwelcome surprise. Last Sunday at his house, she'd been enthusiastic and loving, and he'd found her sassiness as cute as it was fun. She'd brought his home to life with her husky little giggle. He'd wanted more.

And he'd thought—hell, he'd known—she'd felt the same. But on Sunday, when he'd returned her to the Shadowlands, she'd jumped in her car and... Well, he'd pretty much have to say it looked like an escape. Fleeing.

Marcus shook his head. Last night, she'd treated him as if nothing had happened between them, and had returned to her bratty, inconsistent behavior with a vengeance. *Why?* She'd loved surrendering to him at his house. He'd been a dom long enough to know she hadn't faked her submission there and that much of the crap she pulled here was forced. But he sure hadn't figured out what to do about it.

A scream from the scene area drew his attention, and he

smiled as Cullen tossed his flogger aside. The big bartender undid his leathers and first took Andrea's mouth, then her ass, employing a couple of interesting toys to ensure they both had a good time.

A very good time considering the pretty sub couldn't stand when Cullen unstrapped her from the sawhorse.

As Cullen cared for his sub and cleaned the equipment, Marcus did a mental check of his trainees. He'd given permission for Dara to go upstairs with a newer dom who appeared mesmerized by her piercings.

Austin had lusted after an older dom for months and finally got up enough nerve to flirt. Quite successfully. The dom had checked with Marcus, then dragged an enthusiastic Austin off to the dungeon. Marcus smiled. There might be a relationship starting.

Uzuri had left early, and since Tanner had already played with a couple who'd wanted a third, he'd finish the evening by serving drinks in the theme rooms. Apparently Sally had gone home to visit her family before school began. Surprising that the little minx hadn't mentioned her plan to leave; sassy as she was, Sally took her responsibilities seriously.

Gabi was serving drinks and causing trouble. After dumping a soda in a dom's lap, she'd asked if he wanted ice with his drink. She'd blown up a condom and popped it behind two doms having a discussion. And then she'd told a dom who was buckling ankle cuffs on his sub that he looked good on his knees. *Well.* Marcus had barely gotten out of hearing before he'd burst out laughing.

He sobered. The practical jokes could be tolerated, but she'd also grown increasingly insolent, deliberately trying to incite a reaction.

He'd made no progress at all. *Dammit.* His jaw tightening with frustration, he turned his gaze to watch Cullen finish stowing cleaning supplies.

The bartender scooped Andrea off the floor, where she'd

waited with a blanket around her. In the sitting area, he dropped into a leather chair hard enough to earn an *oomph* from the sub. She glared at him. "I can't believe the way you haul me around like I'm some doll."

Rumbling a laugh, Cullen slid a hand under her blanket. "You're my doll, love, and you're not going to forget it."

She melted at his touch and the tender look he gave her and snuggled closer.

Envy rolled through Marcus, and he set it aside. He knew full well the pain of loving the wrong woman was worse than the benefits. Before he and Patricia had divorced, she'd either frozen him out, pretended to love him to get her own way, or had temper tantrums. He'd actually preferred her rages—at least when angry, she'd shared her emotions honestly.

He thought of Gabi and the night she'd spent with him. How she'd snuggled closer to him in bed, how the rebellious spark in her eyes had changed to surrender, how she'd touched him... Those emotions had been honest. Or had they? Could he have misread her completely?

"You okay there, Marcus?" Cullen asked.

This wasn't the time to indulge in unhappy woolgathering. He dredged up Gramps's favorite saying. "Fine as frog's hair, thank you."

"How's your brat?"

"*My* brat seems to have a button she pushes at intervals to switch on a demon inside her."

Cullen barked a laugh.

"Seriously, she's like a whipped dog, licking your hand one moment and attacking the next." Marcus frowned. "I think she knows why, but she won't tell me."

Marcus spotted the sub. In a neon blue halter top and vinyl skirt, Gabi had a dragon tattoo running up her shoulder, and earrings resembling golden claws decorating the curve of her ears.

His little dragon sub was still sassing the members. "You ever met her, Andrea?"

"Only to fill her drink orders at the bar."

Marcus studied her. Andrea was a sub, had been a trainee, and was a compassionate woman. "Maybe she'd be more forthcoming with you."

"Introduce us," Andrea said after a second's thought. "I won't break a confidence, but I'll talk to her if I can get her alone."

"Good enough." As Gabi neared the group, Marcus beckoned for her to join them.

Her eyes lit at the sight of him, but then her lips firmed. When she stiffened her shoulders and raised her chin, he knew she'd decided to smart off. Yes, he could read her, even if he couldn't figure out her motivation.

She stood in front of him, setting her hands on her hips. "You guys are sure lazy bastards. Don't you have scenes to do, subs to beat?"

"Kneel. Now." Marcus pointed to his feet, putting enough snap into the command to get her to obey before her mind could react.

She dropped to her knees and, a second later, glared at him.

He smiled and pulled her between his legs, facing outward. Defiance or not, her sweet body felt just fine under his hands. He squeezed her shoulders, tracing the muscles beneath the soft feminine padding, enjoying the lovely curve of her neck. Wouldn't she look beautiful in a strapless gown—perhaps a pretty blue to match the streak in her hair. "Gabi, you've met Master Cullen. His sub is Andrea. She was a trainee back when he had charge of them."

Interest brightened Gabi's face. "Nice to meet you, Andrea."

Andrea glanced at Cullen and got a headshake—*no talking*—that made her glower.

Marcus smothered a chuckle and informed Cullen, "From the expression on your sub's face, she is still not adequately trained."

"Apparently not." Cullen's lips twitched before he frowned darkly at Andrea.

"I'm sorry, Señor." She buried her head against him and added in a placating, sweet voice, "I love you."

Cullen snorted. "Nice try, pet. I should still beat you."

Her whispered "You just did, *cabrón*" carried as clearly as Cullen's responding bark of laughter.

The wistful expression on Gabi's face squeezed Marcus's heart. She wanted what Andrea had with Cullen; he could see her longing. So why did she behave in a way so as to ensure she'd never have such a relationship?

"Although Andrea didn't live on the streets like you," Marcus told Gabi, "she grew up in the slums. And she caught grief from the other trainees."

"But the trainees are nice..." Gabi said, but he heard unhappiness in her voice. Were they giving her trouble?

After getting Cullen's permission to speak, Andrea said, "Only one sub was obnoxious, and she not only hated my background, but also that the most gorgeous man in the place was interested in me."

"I wasn't that interested in you, darlin'," Marcus protested, earning a snicker from her before she clarified by patting Cullen's arm.

"*This* gorgeous man."

"Which trainee?" Gabi asked.

"She isn't here anymore." Andrea's mouth thinned. "She planted money in my locker so everyone thought I'd stolen from her. Master Marcus and Dan grilled me like a criminal and threw me out of the club."

Marcus winced. He still felt guilty over the way they'd treated her.

Shocked, Gabi twisted to stare up at the trainer. "*You* were rude?" She'd thought Mr. Southern Lawyer always acted like a gentleman.

Andrea snorted. "Dan was rude; Master Marcus just backed him up. Of course after I got past wanting to kill them, I realized I did look guilty. And they were so furious thinking I'd betrayed Cullen's trust, they weren't seeing clearly. They made a mistake."

Snickering, Gabi widened her eyes at Marcus. "You mean you're *not* God? Nooo, say it isn't so!"

He leaned forward, cupped her breasts in his powerful hands, and whispered in a slow drawl, "While you are here, li'l sub, I am *your* god."

The sound of his deep voice, the feel of his palms as his thumbs grazed over her nipples, turned her insides liquid and melted her bones. Even a god couldn't turn her on as quickly. She closed her eyes for a second, just to savor being close to him, being touched, then sighed and let it go. *Get back in the game, Gabi.* "Did the trainee get in trouble at least?"

Andrea laughed. "After the guys finished questioning Vanessa, they left her to Z. By the time he got through with her, she was crying so hard he had to call her a taxi. Then he got her banned from every club—well, pretty much in Florida. I had no idea how well-known he is.

"Anyway, Master Z apologized to me here. Then Master Dan and Master Marcus apologized too, in front of everyone, even though they'd already talked to me before, and I'd forgiven them and everything." She frowned at Marcus. "You guys almost made me cry."

"Turning into a regular watering can, aren't you, love?" Cullen stroked her cheek gently with his huge hand.

"You wish," Andrea growled and nipped at his fingers. She wrinkled her nose at Marcus. "It was when you two gave me that humongous gift certificate to the best fetish-wear place in Tampa that I got teary-eyed." She said to Gabi, "My budget didn't go far, and I always looked like a poor relation in here, so I had a great time buying new clothes. I still haven't spent it all."

"I've enjoyed the benefits," Cullen rumbled, running his hand across the low bodice of Andrea's skintight vinyl dress. "So why don't you let me admire this new dress from the rear. I'd enjoy a beer."

"Yes, Sir." Andrea slid off his lap.

Marcus squeezed Gabi's shoulder and murmured in her ear. "Grey Goose, please."

As she shoved to her feet, the "Yes, Sir" came out before she thought. *Do better*. She sucked in a breath, stuck her hand out, and shouted, "*Heil* Hitler," then goose-stepped toward the bar. And tried really hard not to think about the disappointment that had darkened Marcus's eyes.

Dammit. I hate, hate, hate this.

Master Raoul had been talking to Andrea, but when Gabi reached the bar, he moved away.

Andrea grinned at her. "You're driving Master Marcus nuts, you know."

"Yeah. I know." And making them both unhappy. The lump in her throat made it difficult to talk.

"You doing it on purpose?"

The straightforward question coming from another sub left Gabi at a loss. The doms were the enemy, so to speak, but other submissives belonged on her team, and the habit of confiding in friends almost overcame her brains. "In a—" She shook her head, trying to get back on balance. "Maybe. Kind of."

Andrea snorted. "There's an answer. How come?"

"It always seems like a good idea at the time." Gabi shifted uneasily. "Is Master Raoul ignoring us?"

"Nah. He just likes to talk to the newer doms and subs." Andrea drew her finger through a wet spot on the bar. "So what did you do on the streets?"

Very blunt person, wasn't she? Gabi grinned, realizing she could like her a lot. "I broke into houses, shoplifted, picked pockets." Andrea's dress had a pocket on one side. Leaning forward,

Gabi reached for a stack of napkins farther down the bar, bumped into her...and lifted her car keys.

"Here," Andrea said, pushing the pile of napkins closer.

"Here," Gabi mimicked, setting Andrea's key chain on top of the napkins.

Andrea broke into laughter. "You're good! My cousins tried to learn, but they're too ham-handed." She caught Gabi's frown and added, "They're all reformed and respectable now."

"Oh. I'm glad."

"No kidding. All our indiscretions happened in the past, but it was still awkward, since Cullen's a fire inspector and Dan's a cop."

Dan, the hard-faced one. "He's a cop? That figures." Gabi massaged her arm, remembering the way he'd dragged her across the room to Marcus.

"Oh, I know that grip. He's a cop to the bones. Kari—the pregnant one—is a schoolteacher, and everyone says Dan's mellowed a lot since meeting her."

"Uh-huh, I can tell he's a real pushover now." Gabi leaned an elbow on the bar. Raoul hadn't budged, so she could indulge her curiosity about the other Masters. "Who's the dark-haired Master, the one with black eyes who looks so mean?"

"Master Nolan. Building contractor. And his sub, Beth, owns a landscaping business—she redesigned the gardens here."

"Well, that's a relief."

"Huh?"

"I mean I'm glad Nolan and Dan are taken. Scary dudes. I wouldn't want to do a scene with one of them. Of course, when Marcus gets angry..." *That's even worse*. Gabi mocked a shiver, ignoring the dull ache in her belly from making him unhappy again.

"You're scared, and you still sass them?" Andrea frowned. "That's not very smart."

Gabi shrugged. "My father insists my shoe size is bigger than my IQ."

As Andrea sputtered with laughter, Master Raoul walked over to get their drink orders. Finally.

Late Saturday night, Jessica sat upstairs in Z's private third-story rooms and fumed. She hadn't gone to the Shadowlands yesterday because of a late client appointment—estimated tax payments could screw up the best schedules—and had looked forward to tonight. But Z had said he didn't want her in the club. And the jerk wouldn't tell her why, just claimed he had internal club problems.

Sure he did. She paced across the living room. Galahad watched, the end of his tail flicking as he contemplated chasing her feet. At least *he* wanted to chase her.

In the quiet room, she could hear the sounds of the Shadowlands, the low pulse of the music, mostly the bass. Occasionally a high cry. Very little, really. Z had said he'd put in an excessive amount of soundproofing when he set up the club.

What would he do if she went down there? Jessica tried to rub the chill from her arms. He'd left no room for misunderstanding. Stay out of the club tonight and next weekend too. He'd smiled and said that was all he'd ask, just tonight and next weekend.

Her mouth thinned. When she'd worked on the Shadowlands accounts, she'd noticed the new trainee's membership lasted only a month—after next weekend, Gabrielle would be gone.

Well, maybe I'll be gone too.

The thought pierced her heart like a sharp blade. She shook her head. Z's withdrawal had something to do with that...that *person*. What if he wanted to play with her without Jessica around to get her feelings hurt?

She stared at the wall. In the beginning, Z had let Cullen join a scene and touch Jessica. Did Z figure she should share him with others?

Anger sliced into her brain so sharply it took her breath away. *I won't, damn him.* Her hands fisted, and if he'd been present, she'd have hit him. *Man, I need to get out of here before I make a scene like a child.*

She trotted down the inside stairs and stopped in the ground-floor hallway. *No car.* Z'd picked her up, saying she could join the guys' poker game after closing. She was stuck here until Z left the club. Dammit.

At the bottom of the stairs in the empty hall, she paced up and down, and if she kicked the wall a few times, well, tough.

An unknowable amount of time later, she heard the sound of a key, and Z stepped through from the club. God, he looked tired. Under the unforgiving hall light, harsh lines bracketed his mouth; another line carved between his eyebrows. How could he make her heart leap, make her worry about him, and make her hate him all at the same time?

He saw her and inclined his head. "Jessica. Is there a problem?"

"No." *Yes.* She stomped on the urge—the need—to hold him, to let him comfort her and to give him comfort in return. He looked like he badly needed a hug.

No. He could just take himself off and get soothed by someone else.

Maybe he'd gotten tired of having a short, fat sub. "I need a ride back to my place. Can you ask one of the guys to give me a lift?"

"Hadn't we planned you would spend the night?"

"I changed my mind." She sounded like a kid having a temper tantrum and couldn't summon up the energy to care. He'd left her alone all evening. He didn't want her there. His sons hated her and thought her too young for him—and maybe she was. "Either find someone to take me home or do it yourself."

He studied her face for a long moment and then sighed. "All

right, kitten. Perhaps that would prove best for tonight." He held out his hand. "I'll drive you home."

She didn't take his hand. Everything inside her hurt. She'd expected him to argue, to push her into talking about her fears, to...to show it mattered to him whether she stayed or left. "Thank you." She turned and headed toward the door to the garage. They'd have a long, long, silent drive home.

Right now her only goal was to make it there without crying.

In the parking area near the Clearwater Downtown Docks, Cesar Maganti drank his coffee and watched the boat lights bob up and down in the darkness. The wharf never stayed totally quiet, even this late, but no one paid any attention to his big appliance truck.

Muffled screams of pain came from the back of the truck as Jang toyed with the female they'd taken earlier. She'd barely awakened from the sedative before Jang had started. He was a brutal bastard but reliable, and discreet help was difficult to find. The Overseer didn't care if the girls were roughed up some as long as they'd heal up in two to three weeks' time. That left a lot of leeway for someone like Jang.

The girl started to cry, and Maganti heard the wet sounds of sex.

On the seat beside him, his phone vibrated. Maganti checked the number. The Overseer. "Yes?" No identification, no trace. Both of them used disposable cell phones that would get tossed after the last pickup.

"I received your message about a problem with the order."

Maganti sat up as anxiety burned off his relaxed mood. "Yes. I'm sorry, but—"

"What happened?"

"The lighter-colored piece is more trouble than it's worth."

The Overseer's list included a sassy blonde and a brunette from the Shadowlands. Maganti was to take whoever proved safer.

But his investigation showed the blonde had a relationship with her dom and saw him during the week as well as on BDSM nights. Often a woman who only played at a club could disappear without making waves. Hell, half the time a dom wouldn't even know a sub's real name. But a husband or lover would search forever and create all sorts of stink.

"I see. And the other?"

"Unavailable." The fucking brunette had disappeared into thin air.

"That's disappointing. Let me check if I received an update." The clicking of a keyboard broke the silence on the phone. "Ah yes. There's a very fine piece that fits our specifications. I'll send you the new parts number."

Maganti grinned. Score! When the brunette cunt had disappeared last Sunday, he'd worried he'd lose a fucking quarter of his potential fee. "Good enough. I'll watch for it." He didn't know where the dude got the names of the females; he didn't need or want to know.

"Any trouble securing the rest of the order?"

"Nope. I'm waiting for the pickup now, in fact." He'd grabbed this bitch easily enough. Even better, the only people who might miss her were at her job. On Monday, he'd send her boss an e-mail explaining she'd had a death in the family.

"Very good. Will the new part be ready before next Sunday? After that would be too late."

"If the new piece checks out, I'll package the last order for shipping on Friday or Saturday."

"Good." Silence indicated the Overseer had hung up.

Maganti heard retching noises coming from the back and turned to yell at Jang, "Get that fucking gag off before she chokes." He spotted a boat pulling up to the dock. "Her ride's here. Let's move."

CHAPTER FOURTEEN

The Shadowlands had closed. Holding his little trainee's wrist, Marcus led her down the private hallway, then outside. After the dry air-conditioned atmosphere of the club, the sultry air wrapped around him like a sweaty fist.

Gabi stopped. Her eyes were big and frightened, making him want to pull her into a hug and reassure her. "I need to go home now," she said.

"You live alone and don't have a job at present. Is there a reason you can't stay a couple of hours longer?"

Her mouth opened, then closed. She'd decided not to lie to him. This time.

"That's what I thought." He took her around the corner to Z's private yard at the rear of the Shadowlands. The other three doms had already congregated on the veranda. Z wasn't in sight.

Gabi stopped again, obviously seeing everyone present was a Shadowlands Master. "But—"

"Kneel right here, sugar."

She did so silently, which told him how terrified she must be. She stared at the men.

Many doms, one sub. Of course she was worried. He caressed

her cheek. "Gabrielle, I am planning to do a scene with you, but it will be only me and you."

Her shoulders relaxed.

Better. "Stay here for now, darlin'." He strolled over to the other Masters, who stood across the veranda by the small refrigerator.

"'Bout time you decided to join us for a poker night, buddy." Cullen grinned. "Can I hope your reluctance means you don't know how to play?"

"Poker? I thought Raoul said bridge."

Laughing, Cullen handed him a beer.

Still in his black leathers and T-shirt, Nolan gestured toward Gabi with his drink. "Did you bring her to play poker, or is there a problem?"

"Problem." Marcus looked at him, then Cullen and Raoul. "I'm not getting what is going on in her head. She's submissive and at times beautifully so. And out of the blue, she'll turn defiant, even past the point of self-preservation."

"I've seen that." Cullen scratched his jaw. "Damned if I've figured out her motivation either."

"What can we do, my friend?" Raoul asked.

"I'd like to do a scene with her, get her into subspace, and find some answers. But I usually have an idea of where I'm going. This time—"

Cullen nodded. "You want backup if needed, and other eyes in case we can spot a clue."

"Exactly. I realize it will delay the game."

"Comes with the territory," Nolan said. "Besides, Z called a bit ago. Said he had to take Jessica home and he'd be late. You want to wait?"

Marcus hesitated and then shook his head. "He's deliberately keeping something back about her. I'll do this without him."

"You need help setting up?" Raoul asked.

"No setup. I'll use the posts out here." Marcus turned to

check on Gabi. She knelt, watching him, her nervousness apparent in her wide brown eyes and clenched hands. So quiet. Why so submissive now? "Come here, please."

She rose quite gracefully, he noticed. She'd obviously practiced a bit.

Nolan grunted in approval, and Cullen murmured, "She's a pretty sub, Marcus."

When she stood in front of him, she asked, "Yes, Sir?"

"You're beautiful like this," he said, seeing the need to please shining in her eyes.

She flushed.

He tucked a lock of hair behind her ear. "I'm going to flog you, sugar."

Gabi inhaled sharply and took a step back. Was he insane? "You kept me here to—"

"I'm not a sadist, Gabi, and we both know you enjoy a bit of pain. This is just a different type." Without giving her time to think it over, he guided her between two patio posts that had bolts embedded up high.

"Here you go," the rough dom—Nolan—called and tossed Marcus two short chains.

Marcus used them to restrain her between the posts so that she faced the veranda with her arms lifted like in a victory cheer V.

Her breath caught as she pulled on the chains. Could she let him do this? "I—Why now? Not before in the club?"

"You do better with less people around, darlin'."

Oh, damn, he'd noticed. Even as she tried to figure out what to do, excitement speared through her, rapidly turning to heat when he removed her halter top with sure fingers. He unzipped her short vinyl skirt and pulled that off as well, leaving her naked.

Oh God. Her heart started to race, and she could feel her nipples peaking, her skin tingling with anticipation.

His gaze ran over her, face to hands to breasts, and he gave her a slow smile. "All excited before we even start."

She flushed, and her eyes strayed toward the other doms. What must they think? Why was she the only submissive here?

He noticed the direction of her gaze. "Sugar, I'm going to blindfold you."

Be blind? Gabi shook her head, her fear rising like the mercury in a thermometer on a hot day. "Sir, no."

He cupped her chin, meeting her eyes with his steady ones. "Gabrielle, you'll concentrate better on the sensations and not on who's present. I will not do anything that you don't know about, and I will not leave you alone, not even for a second."

She saw the question in his face: *Do you trust me*? And she couldn't hold out. All evening she'd hated how she had to keep disappointing him time after time. Masters Nolan, Raoul, and Cullen had been members of the club for years; surely none of them were the kidnapper. With relief, she realized she didn't need to act like a brat. She could do what Marcus wanted this time.

Excitement started in the hollow of her back and tingled up her spine. *Flogging*. "Okay."

"That's my girl," he said, making her heart leap with longing. He tied the padded blindfold on snugly.

As the blackness enfolded her, she tensed, and yet her skin tingled as if someone was running a Fourth of July sparkler over it.

"You have a safe word to use if you need to." He didn't move but stayed close enough that the heat of his body warmed hers as he stroked her hair gently.

As her breathing eased, she heard the other men talking quietly. Cullen's louder laugh. The fragrance of the sea and tropical flowers and Marcus's own masculine scent. She raked her toes against the concrete to remind herself of where she was.

He abandoned her hair and ran his fingertips down her body. She jumped.

"Easy, sugar." His hand grazed across her skin as he moved to stand behind her. He braced his chest against her back and curved his fingers lightly around her throat, the most subtle of reminders of how vulnerable she was. He murmured in her ear, "There's nothing you can do wrong, because all the control belongs to me. You don't have any say in what happens."

The concrete seemed to soften under her feet.

His breath brushed her ear. "You can scream or sass or cry. It doesn't matter. I will still do what I want to do." He turned her head far enough to take her mouth, roughly, possessively, reinforcing that she could do nothing to stop him.

Even as she shifted her weight anxiously, heat pooled low in her belly. This was her desire—to yield. To surrender.

He ran his hard hands over her, his touch almost painful; then cuffs closed snugly around her ankles. Unbreakable. Chains clanked as he secured her legs widely apart.

Air wafted over the bare, wet skin of her pussy and inner thighs, cool against the heat.

"Now you're open to me, and I will do whatever I want. All you can do is take it, li'l subbie."

The words sounded like a threat, and yet given in his soft drawl, they made her shiver with anticipation. *Touch me, please.*

He must have knelt behind her, for his hands grazed up the backs of her thighs and moved between her legs. He stroked through her folds. She could feel she was awfully wet despite her fear—or maybe because of it. Flogging. He would hit her—

"Stay with me here, sugar," he murmured. His finger slid directly over the top of her rapidly hardening clit, and her mind went blank as the sensation sizzled across her nerves. She groaned and pushed her hips forward.

"That's right." His finger circled, melting her insides. Even as he played with her clit, he kissed the right cheek of her bottom and then bit the soft flesh hard enough to send a shock of pain up her spine and shoot her arousal higher.

She'd never felt like this. He was playing with her as her cats toyed with their prey. Her hips squirmed; she couldn't tell how to move to increase his touch on her clit. As the chains clanked, she remembered the other doms and froze. A flush scalded her face.

Marcus laughed, low and deep. "Yes, they're watching, Gabi. They see how you've surrendered to me, and how you're going to give me everything I ask tonight." The pleasure in his voice surged over her like an ocean wave.

Abandoning her throbbing pussy, he rose and set his solid chest against her back. When he cupped her breasts, heat moved through her, up and down, electricity lost in the maze of her body. He teased her nipples, rolling them gently between his fingers, increasing the pressure slowly into pain.

Caught in his trap, she'd pull away from the hurt and then push forward, needing the pleasure. He sucked on her earlobe, his breath riffling her hair. Encircled by him, unable to escape, she whimpered.

"You're such a good girl," he murmured and stepped back.

A second later, velvety fingers ran up and down her back—not his hands. A flogger, he was teasing her with a flogger.

He hit her lightly. And again. Soon the tiny, thuddy sensations went up her thighs, her butt, her back, the rhythm never faltering, the impact slowly increasing. Her bottom, her thighs began to sting, and gradually the blows hurt as a burning pain lingered behind each slapping blow.

Before it reached too much, Marcus slowed and eased off.

Realizing she was using the chains for support, feeling a little dizzy, she straightened, thinking he was done.

Instead she felt his breath on her mound.

She inhaled sharply as her pussy suddenly woke. When he slid his hands between her legs, her knees shook. His fingers curled upward over her lower buttocks, and his thumbs drew her labia slightly apart, completely exposing her clit.

She shuddered at the sensation of being touched as if he had the right.

He ruthlessly opened her farther. “Very pretty, darlin’, all swollen and pink.” His tongue, hot and wet, slid directly over it, and lightning ran straight up her spine with an almost audible hiss.

His merciless fingers held her still as he closed his lips around her clit. He ran his tongue over the swollen nub of nerves, rubbing one side, then the other, as his top lip pressed down on the hood.

Her body went stiff; her legs quivered. Unrelenting, he continued as her insides coiled, tightened, her breathing stopped. Hot stroke after hot stroke. The pressure grew until nothing could hold it back. Her body exploded, a tsunami of pleasure engulfing her. Her hips tried to buck against him, and he held her still, controlling her even through her orgasm.

Before she finished shuddering, he started flogging her again. Gentle caresses and tiny *thumps* from the multiple strands of the flogger. The rhythm never faltered as the strokes grew harder and harder, stinging against her skin, yet somehow the burn increased the throbbing between her legs.

The blows began to hurt.

He eased up, slowed, stopped. And then he knelt in front of her and ran his hands up her legs.

Again? Oh God.

She shook as he stroked her with hard hands, pulling her pussy against his mouth. He didn’t tease her—no, his lips demanded that she respond.

As his tongue slid over her, her clit hardened, swelled, and her insides coiled under his touch. She moaned, losing track of everything, as the stinging on her skin blended with the fire drawn in circles by his hot tongue. The pressure inside her tightened, and then he closed his lips around her and sucked, flickering his tongue over her clit at the same time.

"Oooh God." The wail escaped her as everything inside burst outward in waves of pleasure.

"That's my girl," he murmured. "Let it go."

He flogged her again, harder yet. And made her come again. The pain on her skin grew, yet so did the pleasure until each blow of the flogger excited her more and tightened her clit, until his breath on her mound pulled the stinging into her clit, transforming it into excitement. Until the pain itself squeezed through her as tightly as his lips around her.

When the blows started again, she couldn't tell. Somehow the ground had disappeared from under her feet. She couldn't hear the whip anymore, just the rush of her breath and thud of her heart. Her arms and legs were gone; nothing was there except the clouds around her. White puffs that billowed and bumped against her back in soft little jostlings.

"Gabi." So insistent a sound. "Gabi." The demanding, deep voice pulled at something inside her as if it could tug her heart out.

"Uh-huh." Her tongue didn't move right, and she tried again. The clouds around her lightened until the sky showed through them. So blue. Clear blue. Intense...eyes.

"Tell me why you're so disobedient."

It took a minute to get through. *Diso...what? Disobedient.*

"Why, Gabi."

Her lips felt numb. His eyes were so blue. "I have to. Noisy sub. They said."

"Said what, sugar?"

"Get attention. Noticed."

Marcus frowned at his little sub. Eyes glazed, breathing slowly. The pain and pleasure had overwhelmed her until she rode a wave of endorphins and submission. She was deep into subspace, and the most beautiful woman he'd ever seen.

And he'd hit topspace, his senses overly acute, her every breath and movement pulling him further in, binding them into one. But "they said"? Was she hearing voices? "Who said, Gabi? Who told you to get noticed?"

Her brows drew together, and she blinked. "Kouros. Agent Kouros."

What the hell? At his house, she'd dodged his question about a job... "Where do you work, Gabi?"

"FBI."

It took a second, and then the word hit him like a bullet in the chest and he grunted at the impact. Chairs creaked behind him as the other doms rose, probably as stunned as he was. *She's been playing me?* "You're an FBI agent?"

Her brows drew together. "Yes. No."

"You're undercover."

"Yes." Her head sagged.

He needed to get her down. Glancing at the other doms, he jerked his head for help. Raoul and Cullen unbuckled her wrists and Nolan her ankles. Marcus supported her weight and then scooped her into his arms. She'd lied to him. But no matter what happened, a dom didn't abandon a sub after a scene.

He settled onto a wide porch swing with Gabi on his lap. When Nolan offered a sheet, he nodded. The evening felt too warm for blankets, but she'd need the comfort of something over her nakedness. Nolan tucked it around her body, and she shivered.

"Easy, sugar," Marcus said. "You're just fine. I've got you, darlin'."

As the endorphins wore off, her euphoria would disappear and the pain from the flogging would start to register. He hadn't flogged her hard, but she'd taken a while to get deep enough into subspace.

She stirred again, probably feeling her skin stinging. Blinking up at him, she offered a lopsided smile. "Hey."

Despite his anger, his heart tugged. She looked so sweet, nestled against him like a milk-fed puppy, her eyes open and honest.

No hidden reserve. He hadn't realized its existence until it had disappeared. Secrets. Dammit. He hauled in slow breath.

"Hey," he answered gently. His anger and his need to demand explanations would have to wait until they returned to even footing. She was too vulnerable right now.

"Rest, sugar. I have you," he repeated. Her unique scent of rose and sandalwood and feminine musk slid into him.

Her fingers stroked his chest lightly as she snuggled. Her trust sent fury surging through him, because he'd trusted her in turn and she'd lied. As he rocked, he considered how Z had insisted Marcus take on a trainee they hadn't discussed and insisted he keep her for a month. An unyielding fist squeezed his guts, and he lifted his head.

The others had pulled up chairs around him. Cullen, ever the bartender, handed Marcus an opened can of soda.

He took a long drink, but the cold bite of carbonation didn't remove the bitterness of betrayal. "Z knew. That sorry bastard knew."

Nolan's black eyes studied the little sub as he drank his beer. "Seems likely." Anger ran through the calm words.

At a sound from the house, Marcus glanced up at the third story. Z stepped out onto the landing and came down the steps to the veranda.

"Gentlemen," Z said as he neared the group. "I'm sorry to be so late." As every Master on the patio turned their attention to him, Z took a step back, one hand massaging his forehead as if someone had punched him—something Marcus really wanted to do. "What's wrong?"

"We've discovered a few interesting facts about the new trainee," Cullen said in a level voice. He nodded toward Gabi.

Z's face went still. "What happened?"

"She's okay. Just in subspace," Cullen said quickly.

"I see." Mouth thinned, Z asked Marcus, "You questioned her?"

A twang of guilt hit, and Marcus pushed it aside, recalling the nights he'd lain awake, trying to figure out the trainee Z had insisted he take. His voice came out hard. "She's not a disobedient submissive—she's an FBI agent. What else have you lied about, Z?"

Just then, Gabi squirmed on his lap. Using his arm as an aid, she pulled herself to a sitting position and rubbed her face. She smiled at Marcus. "I've never felt anything like that before."

"Probably not." He tried but couldn't damp the anger soon enough.

Her smile wavered and died. She looked at the others. At Z. Back at Marcus. Her face paled to the color of Marcus's white shirt, and she wrung her hands. "It's all funny in my head, but I remember...I told—"

"Yes," he interrupted. "You did." Fury at her deception made his words clipped. Cold.

Her brow furrowed. "You questioned me—like a criminal. You wanted me to trust you just so you could do that to me." She shoved to her feet, staggering back on shaky legs.

Marcus rose hastily to put an arm around her.

"Don't touch me, you bastard." She shoved at his arm. "Get away from me. I'm out of here. Never—"

"You're not driving in this condition, Gabrielle," Marcus said even as Z did. He glared at Z. "Stay out of this."

Without answering, Z moved closer to cup Gabi's cheek. "Are you all right, little one?"

Marcus's anger flared higher as he fought the need to pull his sub out of Z's reach.

She made such an effort to smile at Z that Marcus's heart twisted. "I'm fine."

And they could both feel her tremble. Dammit, he needed to stay with her; she couldn't be left alone. He tightened his grip. "I'm taking her home, Z, and then we'll talk."

"No," Gabi snapped and jerked away from him.

"Gabrielle," Marcus warned.

"You have no—nothing to do with me." The look of betrayal on her face matched his own, and he felt as if he'd kicked a defenseless child. "I don't want you near me. You bastard." Her voice broke, and she turned away.

Marcus considered. He could overrule her and take her home, but his presence right now would be more damaging than someone else's. Especially since he still didn't understand what was going on. "Raoul?"

"Yes," Raoul said, understanding immediately. "I'll drive her car—and her—to her place." He pulled Gabi into his arms, ignoring her protests. "This isn't up for discussion, chiquita. You don't have a choice."

When she sagged, too tired to put up a fight, Raoul said, "Nolan, can you follow and bring me back after? It might take a while, since I want to make sure she doesn't drop. Further."

"Can do. No problem." Nolan shot Z an icy stare. "But you and I will talk."

"Understood." As the two doms escorted Gabi through the side gate, Z pulled out his cell and told someone Gabi was being driven home. He shut the phone on the sound of a man cursing and kneaded his brow. "What a night."

"No shit." Cullen handed Z a drink, getting a surprised look. "Yes, I'm pissed off, but you rarely do anything without a reason, so I'll wait until I hear it."

Marcus wasn't feeling that charitable. Guilty as hell was his judgment.

Cullen took a chair, stretching his long legs out, deliberately lowering the sense of an impending fight. Z and Marcus remained standing.

Marcus braced his feet. The other Masters had known Z for years. Marcus hadn't, and the bastard had damned well destroyed any chance of that. Marcus planned to have his say, tear up his membership card, and never look back. Right now his only question was whether to use a fist to punctuate his statement.

Z's gaze met his. "Marcus." He sighed. "Let's talk. I have decisions to make, and since the secret is out, you all can help." The bastard pulled two chairs over and shoved one to Marcus before sitting across from him and Cullen. Deliberately taking the hot-seat position.

Despite his anger, Marcus had to admire the man's self-possession. Dropping into the chair, Marcus set his elbows on the arms. Waiting silently.

"The FBI came to me two weeks ago," Z started. "The previous month, a submissive had been kidnapped and then escaped. Before she died of a gunshot wound, she said someone was kidnapping rebellious subs for a slave auction—for men who want the pleasure of breaking them. More slaves are scheduled to be taken from Tampa, and the final pickup of victims is next Sunday."

"Son of a bitch," Cullen muttered.

"Three subs from different BDSM clubs are missing in Atlanta. The FBI has no leads, so they placed decoy submissives in Tampa/St. Pete clubs. Gabrielle was assigned to the Shadowlands. I had to give my word not to tell anyone, even you, Marcus, although I did protest the secrecy. Both sides had valid arguments, and unfortunately the FBI is in control of the decision."

Z looked at Marcus, no expression on his face. "I gave her to you because I could ask you to keep her when any other dom would have dumped her after the first night. Or abused her. I knew you wouldn't let your anger rule you." Z leaned back and took a drink of the beer Cullen had given him, obviously giving them time to absorb everything.

His word. Marcus scrubbed his face, feeling the rough stubble. An honest man didn't break his word.

Cullen snorted. "Dan would call this a clusterfuck."

Marcus stared out at the palm trees. The black shapes blotted out the stars. Cullen had it right; this was a clusterfuck with no path that didn't involve betrayal or damage. Knowing Z's protectiveness toward submissives, Marcus understood his need to help. With a sigh, Marcus gave up. "It must have got you all riled up to see her punished for doing her job."

Z's shoulders sagged, the only sign he'd worried over Marcus's opinion. "Nothing about this has been easy for anyone." His eyes met Marcus's. "Marcus, I am sorry."

"Appears to me you didn't have a choice. And Gabrielle knew what she was getting into."

"I doubt that. Although I insisted she fill out the questionnaire honestly, I daresay she pushed her own comfort zone—she didn't want to take a chance she'd fail to attract attention. Unfortunately, I believe her experience was limited and lightweight and several years ago."

"Fuck." Cullen's face turned to granite. "I ball gagged her. How could I not have—"

Z nodded. "And that reaction justifies the reasoning for secrecy. How can you punish misbehavior appropriately if you know the sub is acting? The two agents in charge of the investigation are both experienced doms; they knew how we'd react."

"Brave little sub," Cullen said. "I know FBI agents are tough cookies, but..."

Z winced. "Not to add to your guilt, Marcus, though I doubt it can exceed mine, but she's not an agent."

"Excuse me?" Marcus said, keeping his voice as polite as he could manage.

"I didn't find out until this week when her backup sniped about her lack of training." Z rubbed his forehead again. "She's a victim specialist—a social worker who helps the victims of crime."

"Why the hell is a social worker here?" Marcus asked. His jaw felt so tight it might shatter.

"One of the women kidnapped in Atlanta is her friend. Gabrielle volunteered—demanded—to help. I daresay BDSM-experienced submissives are in short supply among FBI agents, so they took her up on it." Z shifted in his chair. "Marcus, she's one of the bravest people I know. She is completely terrified and doing this anyway."

Terrified. He'd seen her fear. Every single night. He set his drink down carefully. He'd made her fear worse. He'd spanked her. Mercilessly. He'd hurt an innocent, vulnerable woman and made her cry.

CHAPTER FIFTEEN

Gabi's brain slowly thawed from an icy ball into something functional. Her fingers clenched her crocheted throw to her breasts like a security blanket. Her eyes opened to focus on her bland apartment.

She tried to move. Failed. She frowned down at the thickly muscled arm around her waist, holding her against a hard chest. *I don't know that arm.* Marcus's arms were powerful but leaner. She looked up, past the corded neck, the strong jaw, and into chocolate brown eyes. Not blue. "Master Raoul."

He smiled at her. "Back with me again? How do you feel?"

What was he doing in her apartment? As her memories flooded in, her breath strangled in her throat. Flogging. Marcus. Questions. The other doms. Her jaw clenched. This dom had stood and watched while Marcus turned her into jelly and interrogated her.

She shoved his arm away and rose, ignoring the weakness in her legs. "I want you to leave now." Pulling her blanket more tightly around her bare shoulders, she tried to conceal her shivering. Her apartment felt as if someone had set the air-conditioning to thirty degrees, and the chill had gone bone-deep. She might never be warm again.

"Chiquita..."

"Go away." In her head, she could see her mother's disapproval at her rudeness. *I don't care.*

"You're still shaking, Gabrielle," he said.

Raoul had been kind to her. He'd stayed silent on the drive home, not trying to make excuses for Marcus or blaming her for lying to them. Instead he'd held her hand in his big warm one as if to remind her she wasn't alone. He'd escorted her to her apartment. Once inside, he'd ignored her protests and held her as she had a meltdown.

But her shaking was his fault. Marcus's fault. The back of her thighs and her bottom stung as if she'd acquired a horrible sunburn and made her even angrier. She lifted her chin. "I'm fine. You did your job, and I thank you."

But for what he'd helped with, she might never forgive him.

As if he heard her thought, he winced. "Gabrielle, you realize Marcus only wanted—"

"If you don't leave right now, I'm calling the cops." She managed to pick up the phone without dropping it.

He set a business card on an end table, smart enough not to hand it to her. "Gabrielle, if you need someone—a friend—please call me." His dark brown eyes held only concern when he added, "Just to talk or for a shoulder to cry on. You don't have to be the strong one all the time."

Oh, yes, I do. "Thanks for the offer." She nodded toward the door.

He left quietly. She locked the door behind him and leaned against it.

What have I done? Brought back, escorted into the apartment, no chance for the kidnapper to get her. *Oh, Kim, I'm sorry...*

She'd blown her cover. Rhodes would never understand why she'd blurted it all out.

I don't understand either.

But Marcus had known exactly what he was doing. He'd deliberately worked her into such a wreck she couldn't control her thoughts, let alone her words. And questioned her. In front of others. His betrayal felt like a gash in her soul, spilling blood with every beat of her heart.

Her knees buckled, and she dropped down onto the thin carpet. Horatio and Hamlet crept out from behind the couch to rub against her legs. "I trusted him," she told them. Horatio broke into a low purr and set a paw on Gabi's knee.

Her eyes prickled with tears. "I did. I trusted him. God, I'm stupid." Even though she'd pretended not to care, inside she'd been sliding deeper and deeper under his spell.

Well, the spell had broken. *Wake up, Cinderella. Your glass slippers have shattered and cut your feet.* She rose and staggered a few steps. How could a damn flogging turn her muscles into limp noodles? Her legs felt as if they belonged to someone else. Could she even stand up long enough to shower? But she had to. Had to wash away the sticky sweat and arousal, to eradicate his touch and scent.

But hot water and soaping after soaping couldn't remove her memories of his strong hands, the scrape of his shadowed jaw, his warm breath. As her back and butt and legs burned, she felt again the rhythm of the blows, the slow increase in pain...and need.

Oh God.

After toweling dry, she wiped off a clear spot on the steamed-up mirror, then turned. Pink lines remained from the flogger. Light along her back, darker on her bottom and the backs of her thighs. Nothing was welted or raised. The redness would probably disappear by tomorrow.

Yet it seemed like Marcus had marked her...had somehow branded her as his own.

Anger sliced through her, the pain sharper than her stinging skin. Yet beneath it was a terrifying sense of satisfaction—an internal voice that said *yes* to his marks of possession.

A clusterfuck. Marcus leaned back in his home office chair and stared at the white ceiling. Interesting term. What a shame he couldn't use it in court. *The accused stole an M16 and then... Yes, ladies and gentlemen, it was a real clusterfuck.*

The evening had definitely been a clusterfuck.

Before he and Cullen had left the Shadowlands, Z said he'd explain to the Masters and ask them to keep the investigation secret. With a stab of pity, Marcus had agreed. Z had looked exhausted.

Apparently Marcus wasn't the only one feeling like he'd kicked a helpless puppy.

Raoul's report hadn't helped. The little sub hadn't cried or fully recovered, but threatened to call the cops if Raoul didn't leave. Everything in Marcus wanted to go to her, to make sure she was all right. A dom didn't put a sub in that kind of shape and abandon her.

Guilt weighed like a heavy hand on his shoulders. Despite the fact that he'd done his best with good intentions, he'd screwed up, damaging where he'd only wanted to help.

Damn Z anyway.

Marcus rubbed his eyes and glanced at the clock. Four a.m. But he couldn't sleep. Instead he booted up his computer.

Realizing Gabi probably used a fake name, he'd demanded her correct name from Z. *Renard.* He typed *Gabrielle Renard* into the search engine.

The results appeared on the screen. She worked in the FBI field office in Miami. A victim specialist. A social worker, just as Z had said.

After reading for a while, he leaned back in his chair and

stared at the ceiling. She helped the victims of violence and seemed to mostly work with children and teens. When she'd talked about her murdered friends and her rape, she'd mentioned a man who had—how had she put it?—talked her out of the corner she'd hidden in. Had he been a victim specialist perchance, the one who started her on this path?

"Get a kindness, pass it on." That was his mother's motto. Apparently Gabi lived by it. Mama would like her.

After shutting the computer down, he poured himself a brandy. In his backyard, he took a chair and propped his feet up on another. Above the city lights, the stars shone brightly in the black sky, a comforting assurance that the universe continued on, despite the disasters on one tiny planet. As he watched, a meteor streaked across the sky and fell.

Well, he knew some of the little sub's past now, and from the articles, she exemplified both dedication and compassion. A soft-hearted woman. Guilt pressed on his chest. *Good job there, Atherton. Jesus, could I have screwed up any more badly?*

He watched another bright light fall to its doom on Earth. In the club, she acted like a brat for the killer. It explained her idiotic rebellions like the missing fact in a trial. All those times she'd start to submit, then straighten her shoulders and spit out something outrageous—all pretense. His chest tightened as he remembered how many times he'd punished her. God, how could she ever forgive him?

He'd acted appropriately for what she'd allowed him to know—and realizing that didn't help at all. How the hell would he make this up to her? During his marriage, his wife had demanded presents, jewelry, flowers after a fight. He dry scrubbed his face, his stubble rasping over his palms. Jewelry wouldn't fix this. Nothing would.

In the distance, an emergency siren wailed. Marcus tipped his head back with a sigh. *Hard world*. He did his best to try to make it a better place. Now to discover he'd hurt someone he'd come to...come to what? Care for? *Maybe.*

Probably. She'd appealed to him from the beginning, even with her outrageous behavior. Of course, not all that brattiness was acting. Marcus smiled and took a sip of brandy. No, she had a mouth on her.

She'd hidden much of herself, but everything he did know attracted him. Her laughter. "*I felt sorry for myself since my wimpy dom can't catch a snail crossing the sidewalk.*" He wanted that laughter in his life.

"*They shot my Danny and Rock. I was so mad, and I wanted to hurt them.*" So matter-of-fact when she'd told him, as if her loyalty and courage weren't remarkable.

He tilted his head back, remembering her wistful voice. "*You know, he'd buy me romance novels. We were broke, but somehow he'd still find me books.*" Such a little thing to mean so much to her. He wanted to be the one to comfort her. To take care of her. He smiled. To buy her romance novels.

But she'd undoubtedly run from him now. What if she didn't return to the Shadowlands? She might not want to give him a second chance. His mouth tightened, and determination settled inside him.

Such a shame that a sub doesn't always get what she wants.

On Monday, Gabi rode the elevator in the Clearwater hotel two flights past the FBI agents' floor, then took the stairs back down. Her dread of the coming interview increased with each step closer to the room.

She opened the stairwell door, stepped into the hallway, and trudged across the thick carpeting. She and sleep hadn't been on speaking terms, and her exhausted body felt as if it was wading through water.

At the door, she hesitated. What could she say? She still didn't understand what had happened to her last Saturday, so how could she explain it to the agents?

Maybe Master Z had called? But all contact was supposed to go through Rhodes. And she already knew his reaction. Her mouth twisted. When she'd finally reached him late Sunday, he'd completely lost it. "*What the hell is wrong with you? You're undercover* —un-der-co-ver—*or doesn't that mean anything to you? So he fucked you and you decided to spill everything. What is that—pillow talk?*" He'd finished his rant with what she'd expected. "*I'm going to have your ass for this.*"

Even before she'd called him, she'd known her career in the FBI was over. Finished. *Kaput*. No one would understand. They'd simply see she'd exposed an ongoing investigation to a whole lot of people. Yeah, serving as a decoy wasn't her real job; yes, she'd volunteered to do it; but after destroying a covert operation, it wouldn't matter.

So. *I might as well get this over with and then start seriously job hunting*. She tugged her T-shirt down—why dress up to get fired? —straightened her shoulders, and knocked on the door.

The door opened, and the big agent, Vance Buchanan, let her in. He wore faded jeans, a blue T-shirt, and beard stubble. He looked her over slowly as if assessing her condition. "Bad week, eh, Gabrielle?"

At the rough sympathy in his voice, tears burned her eyes. She turned her head away and sucked it up. "I've had better."

"I bet. Z gave us a call yesterday." He pointed toward the L-shaped couch and chairs where Galen waited. "Go sit."

As she took a chair across from Galen, Vance took a soda from the small refrigerator, opened it, and set the can on the coffee table in front of her.

"Thank you." Okay, confession time. Rhodes had already told them—God, she just *bet* he'd told them—but she needed to also. "Some of the Shadowlands Masters learned I'm working undercover. It's my fault." She started to pick up her drink and realized she couldn't swallow past the lump in her throat. Instead she folded her hands in her lap and forced herself to meet Galen's eyes. "I told them. By accident. But it's still my fault. I—"

"Stop," Galen said, holding up a hand. "I'm not sure I understand your logic. You have a dom, one experienced enough that Zachary Grayson trusts him with the Shadowlands trainees. He strings you up, drives you straight into subspace, and asks you questions. Why the hell do you think that's your fault?"

"But—"

"Shut up and drink your soda." Galen's baritone was actually kind.

"You don't blame me?"

"You've played a brat too long, Renard. What did I tell you to do?"

Oh hell, that answered one question. The guy was definitely a dom. She picked up the can and took a tiny sip.

Standing behind the couch, Vance leaned his forearms on the back cushions. "Gabrielle, the sole reason we accepted you as a decoy is because you're submissive. You had no defenses against a determined master like Marcus Atherton." He fixed her with a level gaze. "Am I clear? We don't blame you in the least."

She let out the breath that she'd held since...oh, since yesterday when Rhodes went ballistic.

Galen's brows drew together. "You figured we'd fire you?"

"Seemed logical."

Vance's blue eyes turned hard. "Rhodes is an asshole. He had the contacts to get him assigned to this case and plays the game well enough we can't justify yanking him off, but do us the courtesy of not thinking we're complete idiots."

A gasp of laughter escaped her, and both men grinned.

"Much better." Galen leaned forward, elbows on his knees. "We didn't ask you here today to ream you out. Quite the opposite. Gabrielle, are you willing to return to the Shadowlands?"

That was so far from what she'd expected that her head spun. "I will. You know I will, but Master Marcus—he knows. He knows I've lied to him and been faking it all."

Vance tilted his head. "Personally I'd say you only fake about fifty percent. What do you think, Galen?"

"I think sixty-forty, with the weight on the sassy side."

Her mouth dropped open, and then she glared.

Vance chuckled. "You win. There's more brat there than fifty percent."

"And that's not funny. Did you hear what I said?" Gabi crossed her arms over her chest, less to appear confident than to conceal her trembling hands. "Marcus won't tolerate me coming back, and even if he did, I don't want to...to do anything with him. Ever." She'd trusted him, and he'd taken advantage of her. She shook her head and tried to keep her mind on the subject. "Besides, the other Masters know also."

"It's all right," Vance said. "Z explained it all. The Masters aren't stupid, and they understand why we kept your identity secret. It won't be easy for them now. They'll have to fight back the need to protect you, not punish you."

Galen interjected, "But they swore to do their best." The corner of his mouth tipped up. "Not the most reassuring thing in the world for you to hear, I'm afraid."

Go back. Be terrified of a kidnapper. Be punished.

Be with Marcus. Her hands curled into tight balls of dissent. He'd seen her at her most vulnerable and taken advantage of it.

"I'll go to a different dom?" Could she bear having someone else in charge of her? She bowed her head, watching her knuckles tighten. *I don't have a choice.* She'd woken before dawn covered in sweat from another nightmare about Kim being whipped. Her screams had dug into Gabi's mind until she could hear them echoing off the walls of her apartment.

A tap sounded on the door, and she raised her head.

Galen glanced at his watch. "Damn lawyers are way too punctual."

"This is your decision, Gabi," Vance said over his shoulder as he crossed the room. "We're going to let you two work out how you want to handle it." He opened the door.

Master Marcus stepped in. He glanced around. Then his gaze zeroed in on her like a targeting control in a video game.

Every blood cell in her body leaped in joy until she remembered what she'd done. What he'd done. The joy fractured and died, leaving her with the bitter taste of betrayal on her tongue.

"Marcus," Galen said, rising. He held his hand out. "I'm glad you could make it."

"Galen." With his silent grace, Marcus walked over to shake hands, then nodded at Vance before turning his gaze back on Gabi.

She couldn't meet his eyes. The lethal blue color hadn't changed from when it had filled her world like a desert sky. And his voice—soft and deep, so different from the sound he'd made when she'd told him she was FBI. Like he'd been stabbed. She concentrated on picking up her soda gracefully, although from the way her stomach churned, she sure didn't need a drink.

Vance huffed a laugh. "Take her for a walk, Marcus, before she turns any greener."

Galen said, "She's willing to return—got more guts than a lot of so-called agents—so when you've worked out how you'll handle this, come back here so we can finish planning."

Go with him? As she realized the agents had cast her to the sharks, she stiffened in disbelief.

Marcus pinned her with his gaze. *One shark.* With piercing blue eyes. He held his hand out. "Come, Gabrielle."

"No. I won't go anywhere with you." Back stiff, she rose, heading for the door. She gave the other two men a wounded look.

"Little spitfire." Vance caught her wrist and pulled her to a stop. His eyes were a darker blue than Marcus's but surprisingly kind. "We talked with Z, with the other Masters, and with Marcus. All anyone wants is to let you serve as a decoy in the safest, gentlest way we can arrange...and we all agree Marcus is the best choice. Talk to him, Gabi, and if you decide you can't work with him, we'll figure out something else."

Talk with Marcus. Could she stand it? Did she have a choice? Vance held her gaze until she nodded her surrender.

"Good girl." He set her wrist into Marcus's hand. Strong fingers closed, trapping her more completely than any restraint.

The agents had planned for Z to attend this meeting, but Marcus had played the guilt card on them. He might have employed a few courtroom techniques, but he'd told the truth. Their secrecy bullshit had not only given him a rough few weeks, but also led to the fiasco last Saturday. They sure as hell owed him a chance to make it right with Gabrielle. They'd reluctantly agreed, with the stipulation that Gabi had the final choice.

Marcus had pondered long and hard about today—what to say and where to go so she'd feel comfortable. Obviously nowhere alone with him. So now he guided her out of the lobby toward the beach. On the grounds around the hotel, the palm trees rustled and swayed in the stiffening breeze. Gulls cried as they rode the air currents, diving at the white-capped waves. People were scattered here and there, their towels, blankets, and umbrellas bright splashes of color against the white sand. A child with flaming red hair used a stick to write his name in the sand.

As Marcus guided Gabi onto the sidewalk paralleling the beach, his spirits rose. Damn, he liked seeing her, even if she was under duress. The sea wind ruffled her shaggy hair and brought him her sandalwood scent. With an effort, he put away the memory of how the fragrance deepened, darkened in the tender crease between her hip and thigh.

Instead he studied her. Shoulders still rigid, walk stiff, the small muscles around her eyes and mouth tense. "Gabrielle."

She looked up at him, her brown eyes wary. "I'll listen to what you have to say, but just so you know, I don't want to...to *work*... with you." Her mouth twisted bitterly at the word. "You're wasting your time."

The stab hurt. "I understand." And she was perfectly justified in her feelings; however, if she stayed enmeshed in the past, she'd not listen to him at all. How could he get her to relax? *Got it*. He stopped, right in the middle of the sidewalk. After removing his shoes, he stuffed his socks in the toes and rolled up his jeans.

She stared at him as if she'd never seen bare legs before, and a spurt of humor broke through his guilt. Did she really see him as that stuck in the mud? He tied the laces together, slung his shoes over his shoulder, and nodded toward the wide expanse of beach. "Coming?"

After eyeing him suspiciously, she said, "Fine," and followed suit, removing her shoes and socks. Although she'd worn a black T-shirt and jeans, her sneakers were blue and her socks a flaming red that matched her toenails. Damn, she made him smile every time he saw her.

She walked beside him toward the water. The warm sand was deep and soft, the footing a little unsteady. He watched with satisfaction as she gave up hating him and concentrated on avoiding clusters of seaweed, broken shells, and enthusiastic dogs.

When they reached the wet sand, flattened into firmness by the waves, he took her hand.

Startled, she frowned up at him, gave a token tug to see if he'd cooperate, and then shrugged, obviously deciding not to fight about it. She turned her head, staring at the water. "So talk."

He snorted a laugh. "Tough little sub, aren't you?"

Her mouth tightened, but she didn't look up.

He stopped, took her shoes, and dropped both pairs onto the sand. Cupping her cheek with one hand, he used his thumb to tilt her head up. Her stormy eyes met his. "Gabrielle, I'm sorry."

"Uh-huh," she said cynically. "What are you sorry for, anyway? I'm the one who lied."

She didn't want to admit they had anything between them that he could have damaged. He couldn't quite read her; too many emotions warred across the face. Defensiveness. Hurt. Anger. Something else. "Z lied too, Gabi. Did either of you have a choice?"

"No, but—"

He sighed. "I don't like this matter at all, but *you* didn't do anything wrong."

Her brown eyes lightened slightly, and then a crease furrowed her brow. "What are you apologizing for?"

He lifted his other hand, holding her face between his palms. Her cheeks were soft and warm. The sunlight glinted off her long red-blonde eyelashes. "I might not have known about the role you played, but still, the thought of how rough I was on you sits poorly with me."

"Not your fault, Sir."

The inadvertent slip warmed his heart. "But what I truly regret—"

Gabi waited for him to gather his words, and actually felt a bit of amusement. Was the fancy lawyer at a loss for the right thing to say? Her humor faded quickly, for his firm hands kept her from retreating and assuming a more comfortable, distant manner. He'd placed them face-to-face and shared his emotions openly, just as he demanded from her.

His thumb rubbed over her chin. "I regret the loss of your trust, Gabrielle. I deliberately kept you after closing on Saturday. I could tell you had a reason for all the defiance, and I wanted to discover what it was so we could deal with it." His lips twisted into a wry smile. "Questioning you when you couldn't think was to help, not undermine you. Instead it turned into a betrayal of your trust. I'm sorry, Gabi."

He hurt too. The open pain in his eyes crumpled her hard-erected defenses as if she'd constructed them of paper. Somehow he'd gone straight to the heart of her anger. He'd known that she *did* feel betrayed. Did feel as if he'd taken advantage of her, and she wouldn't have if she hadn't trusted him so much. Her breath hitched, and her eyes flooded with tears. *Oh hell.* She tried to jerk away, choking out, "Let me go."

"No, darlin', that I won't." He wrapped his arms around her and pulled her against his solid chest. His hand pressed her head into the hollow of his shoulder and the comfort...the sheer wonder at being held finished her off. And she cried, sobbing out her pain, even her smoldering anger at the punishments she herself had forced him to mete out. *He hurt me and hit me, and he means so much to me...*

He enclosed her in his hard arms, rumbling unintelligible, comforting sounds, and rocked her slowly in his cradle of safety. As the storm of her emotions died down, she managed somehow to find a semblance of control and pull herself together.

His arms loosened, and he let her go...and she wanted to crawl back into his embrace.

"Little sub," he murmured and used his thumbs to wipe the tears from her face.

"I got your shirt wet."

He didn't look like himself, thick hair windblown, jeans, his cotton shirt rumpled and wet, but his blue eyes hadn't changed, and neither had the way he studied her. "It'll dry. Hopefully you feel better."

She felt...hollow, emptied of anger and pain. Her fear hadn't left, but—

"What?" He frowned, tilted her chin up. "Something is still wrong."

"It's not you." She shrugged, trying to act nonchalant. "I'm just scared. Nothing new."

The word he said under his breath could never have come from Mr. Conservative, and she stared at him in shock.

He laughed, his deep, infectious laugh that was almost as startling as hearing him curse. He pulled her hand away from her scar and kissed her fingertips. After picking up the shoes, he put his arm over her shoulder and started walking again.

As the tide came in, the waves flowed farther up the sand, engulfing and tickling their feet in frothy white water. She smiled. Then the tightness returned to her chest. What would it be like to never be part of any of this again?

He squeezed her shoulder, breaking into her thoughts. "Do you think less of yourself because you're afraid?"

"A little. Other people manage to do this kind of thing all the time."

"And some hide in their houses scared to come out," he said. "You learned about violence at an early age and in a particularly ugly way, Gabrielle. But more than that..."

She glanced up at him, and his eyes met hers.

"You have a caring personality. You understand people and want to help. That's different from a soldier's mind-set. You're more vulnerable to the damage that evil can create." His brows drew together. "You must have studied this in college, and you had counseling. You should know this, sugar."

She gave him a wry smile. "I do. I did. But deliberately setting myself up for—" She halted. She hadn't planned to mention—

"I heard you volunteered because of your friend." Despite the concerned expression on his face, his gaze held only warm approval. "You're a loyal friend, Gabi."

Her laugh came easily, as if her tears had hollowed out room for happier emotions. "Nah, I just wanted an excuse to hang out in a BDSM club."

He chuckled, then cursed as an incoming wave soaked the bottoms of his rolled-up jeans.

She giggled.

One second before the next wave hit, he swung her around to reverse their positions. She squeaked as cold water splashed up her calves, soaked the material over her thighs, and ran down her legs, turning her skin to goose bumps. "You...you scumbag dipwad."

His eyes narrowed. "Did you call your dom a name?"

She giggled, then protested, "You're not my dom."

"Am I not?" Deliberately, he tossed their shoes onto the dry sand and advanced on her.

"No, wait." Hands up, she waded farther into the water until it hit her knees and each wave tested her balance.

He stopped, and his smile faded. "Seriously, Gabi, do you want me to arrange a different dom for you?"

The thought of losing him actually hurt, like a cruel blow somewhere deep inside. Obviously she'd ventured farther with him than was safe. A wave surged into her, and she staggered on the shifting sand—the footing was definitely unstable. She and Marcus had no solid foundation either, but...for right now, she'd cherish the time with him. Hell, she could end up enslaved or dead before this week ended—might as well take what she wanted from life. "I want you," she said, then winced. "Uh. I still have to behave like a brat."

He chuckled and heaved a mock sigh of complaint. "You planning to make this here weekend a nightmare for me?"

"You bet." And what a relief he now realized it was an act—well, some of it was an act.

"In that case, I'm fixin' to feel bad every time I punish you." His face sobered. "I truly will, Gabi. I understand why Galen and Vance demanded secrecy. I don't think I could have..." He shook his head.

He was the kind of dom who would hurt for doing what must be done. "I know. It's okay."

"Well, that's good then." He curved his hands around her waist in a hard grip. "However, li'l brat, I reckon I'm not going to regret *this* at all."

She frowned at him. *This?*

He actually grinned. Then he lifted her and tossed her through the air into the water.

CHAPTER SIXTEEN

When Gabi walked into the Shadowlands that Friday, apprehension crept up her spine. How would the Masters treat her now?

She spotted Agent Rhodes sitting at the end of the bar and snickered at his glare. Had Vance or Galen taken him down a peg? Or maybe the fact that they hadn't reprimanded her torqued his jaw. She veered to avoid him and headed for the other end of the bar, where Master Raoul talked with the big bartender.

"Ah, if it isn't our wayward trainee." Raoul smiled at her, his dark eyes warm.

She flushed, remembering how he'd held her...and how rudely she'd behaved afterward. "Good evening, Master Raoul...oh, Master of the Universe," she amended quickly. Damn these doms for making it so easy to forget her role.

"Master of the Universe? That doesn't sound too bad." Cullen leaned an arm on his bar and grinned. "So how do I get greeted, little sub?"

"Well..." He was baiting her. Deliberately. She tried to forget that he'd put a ball gag on her for being mouthy and raised her voice so the people seated around the bar could hear her. "You know how really big guys are always nicknamed Tiny?" She didn't wait for any response, afraid she'd chicken out. "Guess that would make you Master Munchkin, huh?"

Raoul choked on his beer, sputtering so hard Gabi helpfully slapped him on the shoulders. Several times, although his back felt like a concrete wall.

Success—now she had two doms glaring at her, and Andrea stood behind Cullen, hands over her mouth, trying to smother her laughter and failing miserably.

The other reactions around the bar varied. Some of the doms grinned. A few looked displeased, their expressions similar enough to her father's that she retreated a step as her backbone of oak turned to willow.

"Is this trainee acting out again?" At the sound of Marcus's soft drawl, excitement replaced her dread. She started to spin, only to have him yank her back against his body. His hard chest pressing against hers and his unbending strength somehow emptied her mind like someone had opened a drain.

"Impertinent submissive," Raoul snapped, and his dark brown eyes turned mean. "Nothing new for this one. You're doing a lousy job of bringing her to heel, Marcus."

"Bring me to heel? Like I'm a dog?" Without thinking, Gabi instinctively yanked away and snapped out, "Bite me."

"I'd say she does need to be brought to heel." Marcus's blue eyes chilled. "Cullen, do you still have the toys Margery left?"

Cullen laughed, loud and strong. Her stomach sank. Dammit, she'd only arrived a few minutes ago. A little warm-up would have been nice.

He rummaged in the shelves under the bar, and she felt a glimmer of hope. Considering how much junk he had stored, maybe he wouldn't—

"Bingo." He shoved a brown paper sack across the bar to Marcus.

"Is there a problem here?" Master Z strolled up to the bar.

Oh God, they're conglomerating. Nooo.

"Afraid so, Z," Raoul said, pulling the sack closer. He smiled at her. "Lose the clothes, subbie."

"No way. I've only had this on a half an hour," she protested without moving. "I like this dress."

Marcus lifted her chin. "You've been disrespectful to the doms and disobedient. Since a spanking didn't work, let's see if humiliation will incite you to more attractive behavior."

The relentless look in his eyes and the controlled power in his voice turned her body into a forge of heat, melting her bones. It took a minute for the meaning of his words to catch up. *Wait, wait, wait. Humiliation?*

He pulled her closer and unzipped her skintight, black latex dress. Her skin seemed to yearn toward him, and as if he knew, he slid his fingers under the material and fondled her breasts. He held her gaze as he touched her, rubbing his thumbs in circles over her nipples until the peaks bunched painfully and a tremor of need shook her body.

"There we go," he said. "All warmed up and ready for action."

What kind of action? The nipple clamps came to mind, and she tried to take a step back.

He pulled the dress over her head. "I've always preferred my subs naked anyway."

His strong hands held her waist firmly, warm against her skin, and she stared up, bathed in the clear blue of his eyes. Every time she looked at him, the world seemed to slip sideways.

Then she shook her head. *Get over it.* She saw Raoul pick up her dress and hand it to Cullen. *Naked, dammit.* Even worse, she had a hunch they'd barely started.

Marcus took a dog collar off the bar and buckled it around her neck. The controlled heat in his eyes pinned her far more securely than any restraint. Something shook deep inside, like an earthquake so far below the surface that nothing moves above.

"I like seeing you in a collar," he said softly. His fingers checked the fit, tracing along the edge of the leather. Arousal bloomed in her body as if he'd touched her pussy instead, and he smiled into her eyes and ran his fingers the other direction.

He slid fur mittens over her hands, fastening small buckles, which would prevent her from removing them unless she used her teeth. Furry mittens. A collar. Her stomach tightened as she began to suspect what they planned. "*Bite me*." She'd made a really poor choice of words.

Marcus took a hair comb from the bag, displayed the brown, furry ovals hanging from each side, and slid it into her hair. He adjusted it so the furry...*ears*...dangled against her cheeks.

She stared at him in horror—they actually planned to dress her up like a dog. A floppy-eared dog. Fury rolled through her. Spanking was one thing, this was... "You sorry-ass bastard, you are *not* going to do this!"

She heard laughter around her. Then Master Marcus yanked her off her feet and flattened her on the bar. Her bare stomach lay on the cool, polished wood, and her legs dangled over the side. He leaned against the backs of her thighs, immovable and heavy, and patted her bottom. "You might could be less sassy, sugar."

Cullen tossed Marcus something, and she heard paper tear. "That's a fine size," Marcus said approvingly.

Oh no. Oh God. The last time he'd set her in this position—

"Raoul, if you would?" Marcus said.

"My pleasure." Raoul's hard hands pulled the cheeks of her bottom apart. Cold liquid dripped into the crack.

"Oh no, you don't," she yelled, struggling to pull away.

The weight on her legs increased. Something touched her anus. Marcus made a little circle around the rim with the slick lube, and nerves jolted awake and fired straight to her pussy. "Easy, sugar. Push back so it doesn't hurt."

"You bastard, I—"

A slap across her bottom silenced her. "I do believe you're trying my patience, sugar." Without mercy, Marcus slowly pushed the anal plug in. Bigger than before, burning as it stretched her, and she moaned and squirmed.

She couldn't move. Couldn't escape. And then, with the feel of Marcus's body pinning her to the bar, his fingers warm between her ass checks, and his determined invasion of even her most private place, she surrendered completely. It was as if his use of that area reinforced his rights over her as effectively as putting a collar on her. As her will to fight disappeared, she looked over her shoulder at him. He was watching her intently. When her yielding gaze met his, his eyes fired with possessiveness.

For long moments, he held her transfixed until he finally looked away, breaking the spell.

She hauled in a shuddering breath, recalled to her surroundings. She realized she was wet between her legs from more than the lubricant, and her body craved, screamed for him to touch her there. To take her. In front of everyone? Oh God, was she insane? *I'm on a bar. Exposed.* How could this possibly turn her on? Unable to bear the humiliation, she started to struggle again.

Raoul's hands tightened.

Then it was in; the pain stopped. She felt a slight tug at the plug that made her jerk. Looking over her shoulder, she saw Raoul holding a long fuzzy...tail.

The damn thing had a tail attached. *I'm going to kill them. Kill them all.*

"What do you think, Master Z?" Marcus asked politely, wiggling the plug, undoubtedly to watch her wiggle.

She did.

"She does make a pretty puppy, Master Marcus," Z said, amusement clear in his smooth, deep voice. *Damn you, Z.*

"Yes, she does." Marcus patted her bottom and ordered, "Open for me, Gabrielle."

She didn't want to, not here, but oh she wanted his hands on her. She spread her thighs and gasped as he set his hand against her pussy. "A nice wet start," he murmured. "Let's make this more fun for you." He slid his fingers between her folds and over her clit, deliberately arousing her until her sex ached with need, until her mind emptied of anything except his touch.

He patted her bottom. "Now kneel for me."

"On the bar?"

"On the bar." He lifted and steadied her as she knelt on the polished wood. Her butt rested on her heels, and the plug shifted every time she did, keeping her nerves far too awake. Her pussy throbbed. As she stared at the grinning faces around the bar, the fake ears flapped against her cheeks.

"Lie down, puppy." Marcus patted the wood.

She considered refusing, but God knew what he'd come up with next. And she had done enough bucking orders for the moment. She bent over, resting her forearms in front of her knees. She stared down at the wood of the bar. Cullen liked to polish it, she remembered, seeing her reflection in the glossy finish. And now they'd put her on top of it, naked. Humiliation seemed somehow worse than getting walloped. And it was lonely. Really lonely.

Marcus pulled her sideways to the edge of the bar until her shoulder rested against his. The warmth of his body hardly registered, dropping into the big well of unhappiness inside her. "Look at me, Gabrielle."

She didn't move.

With an exasperated sound, he turned toward her, setting his hands on each side of her face.

She looked up at his strong jaw, his unsmiling mouth, intent eyes.

"Li'l sub." He stroked her hair, tugged on one floppy ear. His voice dropped low. "Sweetheart, Galen and Vance wanted at least one punishment tonight that involves the other doms and keeps you front and center. This is what I came up with. I'd hoped a few insults from Raoul would get you riled up, but you only needed one."

He'd set it up? "You want to humiliate me?"

"I chose the scene for several reasons, Gabi. For one, you'll have the attention of pretty much the whole bar. For two..." His lips tightened, and his eyes darkened as if clouds had covered a summer sky. "None of us can bear to beat on you, darlin'. Not hard enough to make it realistic."

The knot in her stomach loosened slightly. "Oh."

"The third reason..." He ran his knuckles gently over her cheek, and she felt the scrape of his scars and calluses. "You wanted to find out if you could handle more than one man touching you. Do you remember?"

"I..." At his house. She had wondered what might trigger a flashback. "I did, didn't I?"

"In this way, I can watch and control what happens and also make it clear there's nothing going on between us."

Nothing between us. The words made her heart squeeze. She pushed the ragged sense of loss aside. Galen and Vance had said Marcus might have an occasional scene with her, but not every scene. He was just following orders. And trying to fullfill her wishes. "I see. Okay." She hauled in a breath. "I can handle the embarrassment."

"I'm beginning to think you can handle just about anything," he murmured, and the respect in his voice almost undid her right then and there. "Your safe word is...?"

"Red."

"You can use yellow if you're getting a little overwhelmed and need a break but still want to continue." A muscle in his jaw flexed. "You *will* use your safe words, Gabrielle, if it gets to be too much. No heroics."

"Yes, Sir." He cared. The warmth running through her wasn't arousal this time.

"Good." He brushed a kiss over her lips. "Kneel up."

She straightened back into a normal kneeling position. He gave her a nod and a loud order. "Puppy. Stay."

He left her sitting on top of the bar, a floppy-eared dog, and heat rose in her face as she realized she'd become the center of attention for the entire bar. But instead of derision, she heard approving murmurs, compliments on her breasts, her ass, how sexy she looked. Although the doms sounded amused, it was a friendly amusement, and the sting of humiliation disappeared.

As Marcus talked to Master Z, Master Cullen wandered closer, carrying the makings for a drink. The huge bartender set everything on the counter a few feet from her, gave her a wink, and started mixing the ingredients.

If she was a puppy, then he was a guard dog. Marcus left nothing to chance.

"Gentlemen." Marcus raised his voice for the bar area, not loud enough to disturb the scenes around the perimeter of the room. "This li'l Irish setter puppy is in obedience school. She can growl, whine, whimper, or yelp. Nothing else." His eyes met hers, checking that she understood.

She nodded.

"Her name is Gabi or Puppy, nothing else. Anyone using derogatory language to my puppy will be escorted from the bar."

He wasn't taking any chances with them saying her trigger words. The fact that he'd remembered, that he cared felt...good.

One of the doms close to her said sarcastically, "And will the fancy suit do the escorting if they don't want to go?"

An older dom snorted. "Atherton uses the word *escort* loosely. The last time someone messed with a trainee, he threw the guy across the bar. Strolled over, waited for the idiot to stand up, punched his lights out, and dragged him by his jacket collar out of the place. *Escorted* him, my ass. Didn't even wrinkle that *fancy* suit." He took a sip of his beer and added, "Atherton is invariably polite, but nobody in their right mind fucks with his trainees."

Marcus waited until the noise diminished. "She's going to make a circle of the bar, showing off the commands she has learned. Since she's a little slow, her only commands are: come, sit, lie, stand, and stay. Please pet her if she's a good puppy; swat her hind end if she disobeys."

Oh. My God. Surely he meant for her to *walk* around the bar... not crawl on it. Didn't he?

He chuckled. "I do mean to say that in this case, *come* means *crawl over here*, not *have an orgasm for me*." As laughter ran about the bar, he edged between two seated men, gave her a level look, and snapped his fingers. "Puppy, come."

He meant for her to crawl. She stared at him and shook her head. *No*. Right this minute, her orders to act defiant merged completely with her inclination. *No way*. And since she sat on her bottom, no one would be...

Someone swatted her upper thigh hard enough to sting. "Ow!" She jerked around.

Master Dan had pushed between a couple of the men. "Growl, whine, whimper, or yelp," he reminded her and slapped her thigh again, lighter this time.

Goddammit. She lifted her upper lip and snarled at him. *I hate you, and if you hit me one more time, I'll bite you.*

Amusement lit in his brown eyes, and he grinned. She stared in shock. Stone Face was human?

"Go, sweetie," he said softly and jerked his head.

Crawl. She gave a long, loud sigh and started down the bar. The anal plug sent little nerves pinging inside her, and the fluffy tail brushed against the back of her thighs with each movement.

Why did Master Z have such a big bar? Doms reached out and patted her butt. One raised his voice, a sound like a gravel truck on a bad day. "Puppy, lie down."

She glanced over. Master Nolan. She hesitated. Marcus had said come. Only he'd disappeared. Her hesitation earned her a light swat on the rear and a firmer, "Lie down."

She crouched, arms resting on the wood.

"That's a good girl," he said. He ran his hand down her bare back, her arm. "Don't you agree, gentlemen?"

Other hands reached out, and she jerked as they touched her.

"Easy, Gabi," his rough voice murmured, his hand wrapping around her arm, less to restrain her than to support her. Shaking inside, she stared at him, saw the way he studied her with dark, dark eyes, and she knew Marcus had explained the purpose for the puppy play. As a gray-haired dom patted her bottom and another stroked her ribs, she found her breathing had steadied. She wasn't alone here.

Nolan gave her an approving smile and stepped away.

Down the bar, Master Raoul leaned forward. "Come, Puppy."

She almost smiled. So Marcus had hedged his bet, planting the Masters both to help her and to demonstrate to the doms what he'd allow. Her heart lightened, and despite the way the ears flopped against her face and the weird tail brushed her thighs, she did a bouncy crawl down the bar to Raoul.

His teeth flashed white in the dark skin. "Pretty puppy. Sit."

She planted her butt on her heels and jumped when it pushed the plug deeper. This was just too weird. Her heart still hammered from fear, her face burned from embarrassment, and yet she was wet between the legs. *Aroused? God help me*. She settled more carefully into position.

"*Bueno*," Raoul said and ran his hand down her arm, glancing at the men next to him. "Pet the puppy and show her she's a good girl," he said.

Hands seemed to come from everywhere, stroking her bottom, her thighs, her back.

Then Raoul, with a firm grip on her arm, cupped her breast.

She jerked and whined.

"Shhh, Puppy," he said, and his eyes held the same watchful intelligence as Nolan's as he stroked her breasts, the calluses on his fingers scraping lightly over her nipples. The other men kept touching her. Too many hands.

She whimpered, her fingers clenching together, fear rising inside her like the tide.

"Gabi, look up," Raoul said in a low voice.

When she turned to him, he tilted his head to the right.

Several feet farther down, Master Marcus stood at the bar. His eyes held blue fire, his gaze almost palpable, silently reassuring her that nothing horrible would happen.

He hadn't left her. He'd keep her safe. She relaxed.

He smiled, and then his gaze ran over her, lingering on her breasts, her slightly open thighs, before returning to her face. The heat in his eyes seared her.

God, she wanted him.

He glanced at Raoul and nodded. As Raoul started stroking her breasts again, Marcus watched, his attention increasing her awareness of how Raoul's broad fingers pinched her nipples, of someone tugging her tail, another massaging her bottom. Excitement rose inside her. Under his gaze, everything seemed to change as if each man's hands were his...as if it was him touching her.

Raoul chuckled, pulling her attention to him. "That's much better. Stand, Puppy."

Her breasts swung, swollen and heavy, as she took the crawl stance. At the far end of the bar, Master Sam snapped his fingers. "Come here, Puppy."

She set off down the bar. Halfway there, she felt a hard pinch on her thigh and yelped in surprise and pain.

Rhodes grinned at her nastily—and then Cullen grabbed the agent's hand and slammed it onto the bar. "Since you can't follow instructions, I suggest you step away from the bar," Cullen growled. "Now."

Rhodes scrambled away so fast he tripped on the bar stool and almost fell.

"Sorry, Pup." Cullen leaned an arm on the bar and smiled at Gabi.

Giving him a grateful look, she licked his knuckles and wiggled her butt hard enough to make her tail swing.

His laughter should have shaken the bar. He pointed to the end of the bar. "Keep going, Pup. You don't want to piss off Master Sam."

Giggling, she headed down the bar, actually enjoying the little pats from the various doms, the murmured, "Pretty puppy." "She's adorable." "Is Marcus letting her scene yet?"

Maybe this punishment wasn't so bad after all.

When she reached Master Sam, he pointed to the bar. "Sit, Pup, and stay."

She eyed him and had a thought. She needed to act up again, but Marcus said the Masters felt bad about punishing her. Master Sam was a sadist, so he'd do okay with it, right? Instead of sitting, she growled and bit his wrist. Very, very gently, but a definite bite. He gave a startled shout and yanked his hand away. "You little—" He caught himself and snapped, "Bad puppy."

One look at his menacing expression and she decided only a complete idiot would bite a sadist. She scrambled past him as fast as her hands and knees could manage.

He grabbed her ankle, pulling her mercilessly back down the bar. She whined.

"Let's try this again." His growl came out a lot lower than hers as he yanked her to the edge of the bar. He put his right arm under her pelvis, holding her butt up, and gripped her thigh. She had a second to realize how he'd secured her, and then his hand hit her bottom. Hard.

She managed to change her scream into a yelp. Three brutal swats and her bottom burned with pain. One more and her eyes filled with tears.

He released her and snapped, "Now sit, dammit."

She started to, until her tender ass cheeks touched her heels, and she almost didn't. Very carefully she lowered her butt. Hopefully the bad guy had seen her wonderful defiance and punishment so it wouldn't be wasted. That had really, really hurt.

He nodded, his eyes still icy. “No petting for you. You don’t deserve any.”

The doms around him made sounds of disappointment. Sam stared at her for a minute, then leaned forward and fisted her hair. She cringed when he bent forward, but he whispered in her ear, his voice a rasp, “It so happens that I only like hurting people who want the pain. I didn’t enjoy that, girl.”

When he let go, she saw the tense muscles in his cheeks. He’d meant it. *Oh hell.* Guilt stabbed deep inside her. Weren’t doms supposed to be tougher than this? She gave him an apologetic whine and pawed his hand with her furry mitten.

One corner of his mouth turned up, and his eyes lightened a little. “Off you go, pup, and behave.”

Holt called her down the bar next, and he simply gave her a command and kept her long enough for everyone to pet her. Then she went to an older dom with gray peppering his hair. Between them, she watched for Marcus. He moved from place to place, staying in front of her, staying within sight. And his smoldering gaze transformed each dom’s touch to something erotic. She grew increasingly wet. Aroused.

Dammit.

As she neared the end and veered around some glasses, she heard: “Li’l puppy.” A baritone with a southern accent like warm sunshine. *Marcus.*

Standing at the end of the bar, he snapped his fingers. “Come here, Puppy,” he said.

Relief washed over her, followed by a wave of excitement. She crawled to him and whined, pawing at his arm with one mittened hand.

Cupping her face, he regarded her for a long moment. The pad of his thumb traced her lower lip. “Almost over, sugar,” he murmured for her ears only, “then you’ll get a break. Are you up to playing a brat in a threesome?”

She cringed. Strangers taking her. Two strangers. Her heart sank.

He must have seen, for the sun lines beside his eyes deepened. "With me, darlin'. And Raoul. You did request it."

Oh my God. Marcus *and* Raoul? She inhaled sharply, need and uncertainly mingling inside her. Taking refuge in her act, she barked a couple of times. Then bit his hand.

His uncontrolled bellow of laughter sent chills all the way down her spine and had her lips curving up. *Dammit. No smiling. I'm a brat*. When he reached for her, she grabbed the sleeve of his suit in her teeth and shook her head, growling.

"What in the—"

Planting her mittened hands, she tugged. Serve him right if she put holes in his suit.

"Bad puppy." He swatted her sore bottom, pulling his sleeve away when she yelped. Her butt started burning all over again. She growled at him.

He chuckled, picked her up, and slung her over his shoulder, knocking the air right out of her. He anchored her with one hand...and the other fondled her sore bottom.

When she whined, he laughed. "I like seeing you all pink-assed, sugar."

He set her down on a long wooden coffee table beside his already open toy bag. "Stay, Puppy."

Oh, man. She gave him an uncertain look, then waited on hands and knees. *Me. With two men*. Her heart rate increased. When boots appeared in her line of vision, she lifted her head to see Raoul.

CHAPTER SEVENTEEN

"Awfully sad-looking little puppy you have here, Marcus." A big hand stroked her hair. "Looks pretty used."

"She'll look even worse in another minute," Marcus said, his voice louder than normal again. "The li'l pup bit me." His own way of helping, she realized, making sure everyone knew she was being punished.

Raoul choked on a laugh.

"I believe puppies like to lick everything in sight," Marcus said, amusement clear in his voice. "Master Raoul, would you give her something to lick, please?"

"My pleasure," Raoul said.

Lick? Oh God. A little stunned, she watched him open his leathers. His cock was hard, long, the same darkness as his skin, with a mushroom tip tending toward purple and a slight bend to the left. He fisted it. When she stared at him, he grinned, his teeth white in the swarthy face. "Come, Puppy, let's see if you're as good as I've heard. No biting," he warned.

She tensed and prepared to obey. She closed her eyes and opened her mouth.

Nothing. She looked up. He waited with a patient expression. He wouldn't push her into something she wasn't ready for.

But Galen said the kidnapped women had participated in public sex. She needed to do this.

And...she'd asked Marcus for it. Uncertain or not, excitement bubbled inside her. A threesome. *God.*

At least Marcus had given her someone she liked. She remembered how patient Raoul had been in her apartment, cuddling her until she'd stopped shaking. Okay. *Here goes nothing.* She carefully licked up his cock, tonguing the fat veins.

"Very good, querida," he said softly. He pulled a condom from his pocket and sheathed himself. "Master Sam mentioned you like orange."

She snorted a laugh as he put his cock between her lips and she tasted the citrus. These guys. He eased farther into her mouth. She started to rise up, wanting to use her hands, and heard from behind her, "Nice puppies don't jump on people. Stay on all fours, sugar."

Oh, hell. Raoul set a hand behind her head and started thrusting. "Tighten your lips, Gabrielle," he murmured, "and use your tongue."

She did her best, trying not to get intimidated, but... *What if he shoves it down my throat?* Then she noticed he still had his hand around the base of his cock. It would keep him from pushing too far, she realized. Relief filled her. *I can do this.* Using her tongue and lips, she did her best to pay him back, even as excitement rose in her.

And all the time she felt the heat of Marcus's gaze. His hands massaged her bottom, making her insides melt.

Raoul's hand fisted in her hair.

"Ah, that's very nice, Puppy," he growled in a low voice.

After a bit, Marcus set something on her low back. She tried to turn, but Raoul's grip in her hair kept her in place. The rhythm of his cock thrusting—the knowledge Marcus planned to take her from the rear—started a burning low in her belly.

Marcus ran his fingers between her legs, sliding easily in her very wet folds, and he made a satisfied, "Mmmph." A condom wrapper rustled, then he ruthlessly separated her thighs, opening her.

She tensed and moaned around the cock in her mouth.

Marcus's cockhead bumped against her entrance, making her jolt. Her fingers curled inside the mittens. *Please.*

He steadily pushed inside her. *Oh God.* His thick shaft stretched her swollen tissues, glided past the anal plug, tugged at the folds around her engorged clit.

She'd been so excited for so long... Her mouth full, her pussy full, held in place at each end, and it was too, too much. Everything inside her coiled tight, tighter, and then snapped in a wholly unexpected, long, rolling orgasm.

"Bueno," Raoul murmured.

"There's a good li'l pup." Marcus pushed farther into her. As he tilted her ass higher in the air, she realized it let him go deeper. *Too deep.*

She whined, his size uncomfortable and so, so erotic.

"Your puppy sounds a little upset," Raoul remarked. He caressed her hair and plunged in far enough to touch the back of her throat as if to remind her she had a cock at each end.

"Let's set her to yipping instead," Marcus said. He felt huge inside her, filling her completely. And then he tugged on her tail, wiggling the anal plug and shocking awake the nerves in her backside. She couldn't keep from moaning.

Raoul laughed, thrusting rhythmically into her mouth, and she accepted helplessly, wanting Marcus to do the same. "I didn't hear a yip."

"She will." Marcus's hands closed on her hips in an unyielding grip. He withdrew slightly, then thrust into her again, steadily increasing his pace. It felt good—so good to have him inside her.

She concentrated on Raoul for a bit, sucking and licking, tightening her lips around his cock. He murmured something in Spanish and increased his speed until he was pistoning into her mouth. With a low groan, he came, the jerks of his cock a kind of reward, his hand clenched in her hair somehow sexy as hell.

Marcus had given her, and he'd taken her.

When Raoul stepped back, Marcus started to thrust hard and fast. She pushed back against him, keeping his rhythm, pleased that she'd already come and could concentrate fully on him.

Marcus lifted the thing he'd set on her back, and a second later, it buzzed. A vibrator. *Oh man.*

Rrr-rrr-rrrrrrr, rrr-rrr-rrrrrrr sounded in surges of steadily increasing vibrations. Marcus reached around her and set the vibrator against her clit.

"Aaah!" Her yelp made him chuckle, the bastard.

"Now that's a yip," he said to Raoul.

Gabi dropped her head as need started to burn inside her again. As her concentration fragmented, she realized it was another way Marcus took control from her. She couldn't think, could only move as he dictated, take what he gave her.

Between Marcus's cock and the anal plug, she felt too full. Too stretched. The vibe pulsed against her clit, and the increasing waves demanded a response. Her clit engorged, the skin tightening over the swelling tissues. Almost there...

But before her clit hardened enough to send her over, he moved the vibe, rocking it up to press on the hood of her clit, then rolling it to one side and the other. In between, he'd hammer into her, his cock a tool he used to command her submission.

She wanted to curse him. Each time she neared the peak, he put the vibrator somewhere else. Sam wasn't the sadist, dammit; Marcus was. As he kept it up, her labia swelled, her flesh burned. Everything he did tensed her insides until she felt like an overstretched rubber band.

Each thrust buried him to the hilt, and the vibrator on her clit sent electricity shooting through her veins, sizzling and burning away every thought in her head except the way he felt inside her —and the uncontrollable beginning of her climax. She moaned, her legs shaking.

"That's my puppy," he drawled. She felt the vibrator move... and come to rest directly on top of her swollen, sensitive clit. "Come for me now, sugar."

"Ooooooh." The rubber band of her climax broke with a hard snap, and then she was coming, wave after wave of exquisitely brutal pleasure. Her spasming vagina rebounded around his cock, bounced off the anal plug, and sent her into more spasms until her whole body shook. Her arms collapsed, and her weight landed on her forearms.

The vibrator dropped to the table. Before she could slide completely down in a boneless heap, Marcus closed his hands on her hips, pulling her ass upward, yanking her back onto his cock. And then he pounded into her, short hard strokes, finishing with one so deep that she felt impaled. As his cock jerked with his climax against her cervix, her body spasmed again.

Marcus bowed his head, sucking in air, still buried inside her as the inner walls of her cunt rippled around his cock in the most intimate caress known to man. She came more beautifully and more wholeheartedly than any woman he'd known. He'd never felt like this before, as if when she took him inside her, she accepted all of who he was.

He'd worried that she'd never trust him again. Instead, as she fought her fears on the bar top, she'd used him as her anchor, trusting him to keep her safe. The feeling she'd roused in him with her faith in his protection had been better than any climax.

With a sigh of satisfaction, he bent to kiss up the delicate ridge of her spine, across her vulnerable nape, to the sweet curve of her shoulder. During the puppy play, knowing his presence turned her fear to excitement had left him harder than an iron bar. But watching other men touch her had created an undeniable need to take her, to mark her as his own. Territorial? Damn right.

He still gripped her hips, soft hips with a beautifully rounded ass. It jiggled as she walked, enticing a man with the urge to grab and plunge balls-deep. He uncurled his fingers. She'd have some bruises there on her fair skin, more marks to add to the pretty red handprints on her ass. He ran his hand over the redness, enjoyed the resulting wiggle and squeak...and the way her pussy clenched around him.

Unfortunately he couldn't stay here forever, tempting as it was. With a feeling of loss, he pulled out, removing the anal plug at the same time, smiling at the way her back arched in response to the sudden sensations. She started to slump, and he put an arm under her waist.

"I'll hold her for you, my friend," Raoul said.

"Thank you." When Marcus stepped back, Raoul swung her up into his arms, waiting patiently.

Marcus disposed of the plug and condom and fastened his slacks, then grabbed a subbie blanket from the stack near the wall. After wrapping the blanket around her, he took her from Raoul.

Her mouth was swollen and pink, her eyes glazed. Droopy dog ears flopped on her flushed cheeks. "You are so cute," Marcus said under his breath.

Raoul grinned at him in agreement, slapped him on the shoulder, and left.

Marcus settled into a chair with the little sub against his chest. She glanced up, focused on his face for a second, then, obviously content, lay her head back down.

"Master Marcus." Andrea stood in front of him. "Cullen said your puppy needed water, and you might too after all your hard work."

Marcus lifted his eyebrows. "Who said?"

She flushed. "*Dios*, you're fussy. Master Cullen said."

"Better. Open the bottles for me, please, and set one on the coffee table."

She did and handed him the other bottle.

"Thank you, sugar, and please thank your dom for me."

"Will do." She grinned at him and walked quickly away before he could reprimand her again. He shook his head. Andrea was a beautiful woman, but he'd never envied Cullen her sassy mouth. And now look what he had: a little sub who outdid Andrea in brattiness without even trying. He knew damn well Gabi didn't make up all the defiance—a hell of a lot of it was just her nature.

He kissed the top of her nose and chuckled when she frowned up at him. "Making me crawl on the bar was a very mean punishment, Sir."

He tried not to smile but couldn't help it. She had the satiated look of a woman who has come and come hard, and she still found the energy to glare at him.

"It was, wasn't it?" He nuzzled her cheek, enjoying the playful fragrances of rose and sandalwood mingling with the scent of her arousal. "How much did it bother you to have so many men touching you?"

She looked away, stiffening slightly.

"Uh-uh. Look at me, Gabi."

Big vulnerable brown eyes met his.

"Tell me."

"It scared me at first, but you—When you watched me, I felt safe. And I saw that you wanted me to enjoy it, and somehow then I did. Thank you." The gratitude and warmth in her gaze made him feel as if he'd grown another foot in height.

"And with Raoul? Did you like the threesome?" He kept his tone easy, knowing if she really wanted multiple men, he'd try to manage it for her. Somehow. His jaw tightened. He'd wanted to break Raoul's neck for touching her. *My sub.*

A line formed between her brows. "I like Raoul and having you both excited me, but mostly because of you. Knowing you were watching, and when you took me, all I could think about was you inside me." She bit her lip. "I'm glad I tried it, but I'd just as soon not do it again."

Again. She had only one more day at the club. Did she even remember? He pushed the thought away. "And playing puppy?"

She giggled. "I rather like biting and growling. Especially biting."

Brat. "Once you got started, you seemed to enjoy yourself. We did too, watching you heat up from being petted, seeing your breasts swing and your tail swish. I do believe the entire bar cheered when you screamed a minute ago."

Red rolled up into her already pink cheeks.

"You come beautifully, sugar, and it's a pleasure to watch. I'm sure the doms enjoyed knowing they helped you get there."

She opened her mouth and obviously couldn't figure out what to say, settling for a "Now what?"

"Now you can put your clothes back on. I'm being generous, darlin', so you'd best thank me. I'll take myself a kiss."

Her lips curved. "Thank you, Sir."

He got his reward in a long, lingering kiss, one that made him remember how much fun simply kissing a woman could be. Especially this woman.

Most amusing. The spotter for the Harvest Association observed the ending of the puppy play and shook his head. The sub made an excellent dog. He diverted himself for a few minutes wondering how she'd react to pony play. To wearing a bridle and harness and a long tail attached to an oversize anal plug that would make her scream as it went in.

Perhaps pulling a cart.

He did enjoy whipping ponies to a faster speed, watching how their muscles contracted with strain and sweat poured off their naked bodies.

Glancing over at Gabrielle, the newest addition to the Association list, he smiled.

A couple of hours later, Gabi admitted she was having fun. Every dom in the place treated her like their pet now. She received a lot of "here, little puppy" calls from the doms who wanted drinks. She sassed them mildly and saved her good insults for the Masters.

Her feet hurt though, almost worse than her bottom. The trainees were all working harder. Z said Sally had gone to visit her family. That had been a rather sudden vacation, Gabi thought, but it eased her mind. Sally fit the profile of the kidnapped victims perfectly.

A thought struck her, and her eyes narrowed. Had someone whose name started with *Z* made sure one potential target got out of range? Oh, he damn well had; she knew it. Grinning, Gabi picked up the tray of drinks from the bar.

As Gabi checked to see if anyone needed a drink, her heart missed a beat. Marcus stood by the St. Andrew's cross, talking to that blonde, the one who always came on to him. His girlfriend, Celine, Sally had said, although it seemed strange that Marcus would have a lover and still screw around with other women. Then again, Gabi didn't have much experience with people in the BDSM lifestyle. Maybe everything Marcus had done with her was just considered part of the master of the trainees job. Nothing special. Nothing to threaten a girlfriend.

The woman was beautiful, damn her, like a glowing version of Marcus, with golden blonde hair, light blue eyes, and a dark tan. Tall and slender. Jealousy seared Gabi's veins as if they flowed with acid instead of blood.

The woman knelt, as gracefully as a ballet dancer. Perfect manicure and pedicure, perfectly styled hair, perfect makeup. She wore what looked like a custom-fitted leather corset. So she was rich too. She and Marcus looked... right... together.

Marcus said something to the woman. She bowed her head and kissed his shoe, her golden hair spilling prettily over her back. The way she gazed at him in adoration made Gabi's teeth clench hard.

Leave him alone, you piece of perfect. He's mine. Gabi blinked and took a step away from the scene area. Then another.

He's not mine. What am I thinking? And yet...she'd definitely headed herself right down that path. *Not smart, Gabi.* Nothing would last past this weekend. He'd agreed to work with her as his trainee. Nothing more.

Gabi bit her lip. The pull toward him felt like a riptide, impossible to escape. *I want more.*

The blonde picked up a flogger from the floor and held it up to him, waggling her butt in invitation. Gabi couldn't stand it anymore. After last Saturday—with Marcus—she now knew exactly how intimate a flogging could be. *I can't watch this.*

Turning her back on them, she took her tray to the bar, depression settling around her shoulders like a black cloak.

And when Cullen spoke, she sassed him so bad he tossed her on the bar top and walloped her a few times with his bare hand.

It didn't make her feel better, but at least she wasn't watching something that made her chest hurt.

Exasperated, Marcus frowned at the woman kneeling at his feet. Even though he hadn't dated her in a couple of months, she still clung to him like kudzu. He'd scened with her occasionally when she'd begged—mild flogging, no sex, no real emotion. Not that she complained. She actually preferred lightweight scenes, didn't like her boundaries pushed, didn't want a significant connection.

I do. Even before he'd met Gabi, he'd known he needed more. And now, having made love with her and connecting with her on so many levels, he'd never settle for less.

He studied Celine for a second. She hadn't taken his hints. Then again, she wasn't a perceptive woman. When they'd first met, she'd delighted him with her apparent sweetness, her graceful submissiveness. Now her behavior felt cloying, for her submission was all on the surface, not soul-deep.

She wanted him to do a scene with her.

Marcus sighed. Galen and Vance had made it clear Gabi should appear uncommitted. She must play with various doms—and they'd encouraged him to do the same. Dammit.

After setting up the puppy play punishment, he'd steeled himself to watch her fuck another man—or two men if she'd wanted the threesome. But when she'd almost panicked and never taken her eyes off him, he'd known she wouldn't willingly have sex with someone else.

He felt the same. And yet he really should reinforce he wasn't involved with Gabi and wouldn't notice if she disappeared.

He couldn't do it.

"Please do a scene with me, Master," Celine repeated, making him grimace.

She knew full well that calling him *Master* rather than *Master Marcus* implied that he owned her, and if she thought that was an enticement, she didn't understand him at all. *Master* meant commitment. To a submissive. To a woman. And love...love would be in there too. "I'm not your master. Use my name."

"May I give you pleasure?"

"No." He hadn't wanted to hurt her by being blunt, but apparently he'd made a mistake. "Celine, you're a lovely woman, but I don't feel about you the way I should for a girlfriend or a submissive."

The muscles of her face tautened until her cheekbones turned white. "I'm perfect for you, Marcus. Let me show you."

"No. I won't scene with you again." He paused. "Would you like me to introduce you to some doms?"

"No!" She stayed on her knees as if she expected him to change his mind. She was stubborn, he'd give her that.

"I hope you find a good master. Take care of yourself, sugar." He walked away before she could respond. After he did a quick check of his trainees, he'd damn well get himself a drink.

Later this evening, he needed to get Gabi into a scene where she could display all her bratty talents. He chuckled...and his smile faded. He couldn't top her again; they'd spent enough time together tonight.

As he pondered on the doms he'd trust with her, his jaw tightened. He was an idiot, getting so territorial when they hadn't talked about being together after this weekend. Nonetheless, that's the way he felt.

But she did need to play with someone else tonight. Maybe a lightweight flogging with nothing erotic at all.

And for his own piece of mind, he'd find her an ugly dom.

Close to two in the morning, Maganti waited patiently for his last target to show up. Soon now, since Jang had called from the off-ramp to say she'd driven past. With the Shadowlands so far into the country, Jang had to watch from a more public location.

Number four chickie. The last one. Pretty too. He smiled. Maybe he'd delay calling for the boat so he and Jang could enjoy themselves longer.

With a sense of anticipation, he spotted her car pulling into the lot. Right on time.

Flashing lights appeared behind her, and Maganti's jaw

dropped when a cop car turned in and headed straight for the apartment building where he stood. What the fuck?

Son of a fucking bitch, had he been made? Sweat trickled down his face as he ghosted back through the breezeway to the rear of the building, and from there watched two cops jump out of the patrol car and race up the stairs. They pounded on a door.

A man shouted, "Go away." Through the breezeway, Maganti saw lights blink on in the other buildings. Doors opened. The asshole had woken up everybody in the entire fucking apartment complex.

Maganti watched, teeth grinding together, as his target walked into the breezeway and up the steps to her apartment.

Gabi'd felt so jumpy on the drive back that she almost crashed when a cop car appeared behind her. It followed her into the parking lot, then raced past and over to her building.

It's not here for me. Yet as she got out of the car, her skin prickled as if every little nerve ending sensed someone watching her. She knew Rhodes hung around somewhere, but somehow this felt more...ominous. Yet no one appeared. Maybe the weather'd made her jumpy. A storm system had moved in off the Gulf, and black clouds blotted out the stars. A blustery wind swayed the trees and tugged at her clothing.

She walked across the lot as the cops pounded on a door a ways down from her own apartment. Before she'd reached the building, another police car pulled up, then an ambulance. Damn.

After climbing the steps to her floor, she spotted her neighbor peeking out and asked, "What's going on?"

The tiny white-haired woman lit up at the chance to share gossip. "Oooh, that man in 282 came home beastly drunk and beat up his girlfriend. We heard her screaming all the way down here. Clara from 280 called me, and I told her to call the police."

Nothing to do with me. The relief made her grin. "Pretty disgusting—a man beating on a woman." The switch marks on her bottom burned.

"I never liked the look of him anyway. I told Clara that he looked like a brute." Drawing her cotton robe closer against a spatter of raindrops, Mrs. Peters edged out onto the walkway to watch the brute get hauled away.

Gabi glanced over the railing. Drunk and belligerent. She hesitated, wondering if she should check on the girlfriend, then saw a policewoman enter the apartment. So she patted Mrs. Peters on the fragile shoulder. "Have a nice rest of the night."

"You too, dear."

After a quick shower, Gabi sprawled on her bed, still too awake to call it a night. As rain hit the windows in waves, she snipped off the leg of a snagged pair of panty hose and rolled it into a mouselike cat toy. She left a realistic tail on the end and tossed it onto the carpet. Two furry bodies sprang in pursuit.

Horatio won. The brown ball in his mouth drooped in a convincingly mousy manner as he growled at Hamlet and lashed his tail.

Hamlet hesitated. He licked a rough patch of fur to show he didn't really want the mouse ball, then jumped on the bed to cozy up to Gabi.

Lying on her side, she rubbed her nose in his soft fur. When she'd walked on the beach with Marcus, she'd asked that he find good homes for her babies...if anything happened. His expression had been frightening, and then he'd yanked her into his arms and held her. But he'd promised.

"You'll be safe, my boys, no matter what," she murmured. "Just one more night."

Then what?

She scritched Hamlet under the jaw, winning a purr. Then she'd go home to Miami and forget all about the Shadowlands? Marcus?

Could she? Return home, yes. Forget? Probably not.

Until the Shadowlands and Marcus, she hadn't realized how deep her need went for more than—what did Marcus call it?—vanilla sex. After all, in the BDSM clubs in college, she'd never really submitted.

But Marcus had shown her the fulfillment of handing over the reins and surrendering all of herself. She couldn't give that up now, even if she had to look for it with someone else. So she'd continue to explore the scene, even when she left. Master Z could probably recommend a safe club.

Marcus wouldn't be her dom though. Needing something to fill the black emptiness inside, she pulled the cat on top of her stomach. He blinked at her and settled back down to snooze, ears cocked forward to listen.

"You know, Hamlet, I don't understand him." When Marcus had taken her home with him, she'd had so much fun. Cooking, bantering, swimming. Just talking. The way he stepped in and out of dom mode had kept her half-aroused the entire time. On the beach, he'd been so sweet and playful...and she'd thought she meant something to him.

But she could tell from the way Celine acted that they had a relationship.

"You're a guy," she told Hamlet. "So tell me, how could he make love to me if he and Celine are an item?"

His eyes opened a slit as if to remind her that men were bastards.

Last night Marcus had handed her over to another dom to scene with. Not the behavior of someone who gave a damn, right? And she'd seen how well Celine suited him. So damned perfect. "They look good together, Hamlet." Gabi sighed. "I guess I really don't know him all that well."

Only she did. With her disobedient, insolent behavior, she'd made him furious, and he still controlled his temper. *And me.* The thoughtful, generous way he made love told her a lot. So did how he argued—fairly, acknowledging when she brought up a good point—and how he listened.

She gave him the same things back. *And I make him laugh. Can oh-so-sweet Celine do that?*

Dammit. Tomorrow would be her last night. She'd watch, maybe ask him...somehow...if he thought...wanted... She groaned. *Right. That'll go over well; ask him a question you can't even manage to articulate.*

CHAPTER EIGHTEEN

Sitting quietly—and nakedly—in a roped-off scene area, Gabi waited for Marcus to return. The plastic drape covering the waist-high bondage table crackled under her butt. Around her, the Shadowlands warbled and soared with its own unique music: the Goth music of Cruxshadows pounding, impact toys cracking on bare flesh, a caged submissive crying in a high voice, a sub in a flogging scene moaning.

The fragrance of leather mingled with sex and sweat and perfume. She held her arm to her face and inhaled the lingering scent from where Marcus had gripped her wrist.

This was her last night here, Gabi thought. It was almost over, and no one had made an effort to lure her out of the building. Would the perp try for her later, after she left? Or maybe he hadn't taken the bait. Had he targeted someone else?

What if nothing happened now? She felt like dancing in relief...and crying. What about the women he'd kidnapped? What about Kim? Her hands fisted; then she forced her fingers to open. *You can only do what you can do.*

Tonight, she'd act like a brat; this was her part to do. And she'd enjoy it as much as possible. Because, as Kim and the other women had found, sometimes things go bad. If the kidnapper did manage to get Gabi, at least she'd have lived.

And loved? She shook her head. *Live for today. Tomorrow can wait.*

A scream of release turned her attention to the flogging scene where the submissive writhed against the St. Andrew's cross. The dom dropped his flogger and pumped his fingers into her pussy, and she shrieked higher, obviously coming again.

At least someone was having a good night. *I'm not sure I am.* While serving drinks, she'd acted obnoxious enough to collect some nasty reprimands from the Masters. Now Marcus planned to play with her—with hot wax.

And he calls it playing? Like, whatever happened to chess? Or cards? Or tag?

As he strode into the roped-off area, carrying a tray of ominous-looking things, excitement speared low in her belly, along with a hell of a lot of anxiety.

He set the tray on a table and moved it closer. "There we go. All ready."

Her hands turned clammy. "I don't think I want to do this."

Marcus smiled at her and pulled her legs open, securing her knees to the straps on each side of the hip-wide table. He kissed her lightly, then put his hand over her face and pushed her down, making her giggle, at least until he put a strap across her hips. Oh man.

"Do you prefer your arms above your head or at your sides?" he asked, ever so polite, the bastard, as if she didn't see the amusement in his eyes at her squirming.

She wiggled—tried to, at least—and the knowledge that she couldn't escape sent a wave of heat rolling over her even as her breathing increased and fear trickled into her belly. No, hot wax wasn't a good idea. "I prefer not to do this. I changed my mind."

He rubbed his jaw and looked at her quizzically. "Did I ask your permission? No, I didn't. Little *trainee*"—he emphasized the word—"if you didn't mark something as a hard limit, then you get to try it."

Oh God. "But—"

He leaned his weight on his forearm beside her head, his eyes intent on hers. "If after we've started, you find this too much for you, for whatever reason, use your safe word. Do you trust me, Gabrielle?"

"Too damn much if you ask me," she grumbled. "Look at the stuff you've gotten me into."

"Look what you've learned about yourself, sugar." He kissed her, taking charge of it and letting her feel that he had. By the time he lifted his head, desire bubbled in her veins and turned to a hot sizzle when his hand cupped her breast. How did he do this to her, take away all her willpower to fight?

How could he turn her on with one single smile?

Still leaning on his arm, he caressed her breasts. His licked finger stroked wetness in circles over the areola. As if he had nothing better to do, he studied how her nipples bunched into peaks. A mild pinch on each tip shot a roaring blast straight to her clit as if she had a freeway running from her breasts to her pussy.

His eyes stayed focused on her face as he slid his hand down to the junction between her legs. "For someone who doesn't want to do this, you're a tad wet, sugar," he murmured. His fingers played in the betraying wetness, tugging at her folds, sliding over her clit, teasing her entrance.

Her clit tightened, and she actually felt blood swelling her labia until she throbbed. "It's not the wax; it's you." Her voice came out breathless.

His eyes crinkled. "Now that is purely nice to hear, sugar."

He straightened and pulled a strap across the table, positioning it below her breasts to restrain her arms at her sides. Another strap went a few inches above her nipples, and the two squeezed her breasts between them, pulling the skin taut. "Very pretty," he said and tugged the hard peaks lightly, showing her how sensitive they'd become.

She bit back a moan and tried to remember she needed to act disobedient. He made it so difficult. One stern look from him and she waved the white flag every time.

Or at least until she regained her wits.

After drizzling massage oil onto her stomach, he massaged it in, from above her breasts to her inner thighs. When he dripped more over her clit, the electrifying impact of the tiny drops made her shudder. Then she gulped. There? Why was he putting anything anywhere near her pussy? "Why oil?"

"You have beautifully delicate skin, Gabi," he said gently. "The oil keeps the wax from sticking as much. Maybe someday we'll try it without."

They had no someday. The thought sent a stab of regret through her. But what if there were? Would he want to see her after this?

He shoved the small table closer and lit a white candle. Her arms tried to lift against the restraints. *Get it away*. Oh God, he really planned to do this.

After rolling up the sleeves of his white tailored shirt, exposing those muscular forearms that really didn't belong on a lawyer, he picked up the candle. He dripped some wax on his inner elbow, grunted, and raised the candle higher. More wax splatted onto his arm. "That'll do."

She couldn't take her eyes from the dancing flame. No, this was so wrong. Candles should be used for meditation...for romance. Or on a birthday cake at least.

So where was the cake? The present? The *song?*

As he stepped closer to her—as the damned flame got way too close—she started singing. "Happy birthday to me. Happy birthday to me..."

Marcus paused, looking at her in disbelief.

See. I knew he didn't have a sense of humor. "Happy birthday, dear

Gabi"—she lifted her head and blew out the candle—"happy birthday to me."

He stared at her, and she tensed, and then he burst out laughing, so loud and strong that she giggled. God, he was so incredibly sexy when he laughed.

The stony-faced Master Nolan walked into the roped-off area and stared at her with unforgiving, dark eyes. "Marcus, you're a pitiful excuse for a dom, let alone a trainer," he said in his rough voice. And loudly too. "Beat her. Don't laugh at her."

She scowled at him. "We don't need you here."

With a snort of disgust, Nolan held up a tiny, tiny flogger with a palm-sized handle and thin suede strips. "Z got these today and sent one as a gift for your trainee."

It was totally cute. Marcus could lash her all day without doing any damage. She grinned. "A widdle flogger. Oooo, I'm scared now."

"I do believe you're right. The trainee is getting ornery," Marcus said in his soft voice. He took the flogger and smiled at her. "It's little, sugar, because it's meant for little places." With a flick of his wrist, he brought the strands down right on her pussy.

"Ack!" Her back arched as she fought the straps, tried to bring her legs together as he gave her two more whaps. "Jesus Christ! What are—"

He lifted an eyebrow and the flogger at the same time.

She shut right up. Her clit had been swollen from his fingers. Now it throbbed and burned. Wetness trickled through her folds, and she sucked in a breath. God, if he lashed her again, she might come.

Nolan glanced at her pussy and snorted a laugh. "It's not a good punishment for her, Marcus. She likes pussy whipping too much."

Smiling, Marcus pressed his palm between her legs, his intent blue eyes on her face as his fingers slipped and slid in her folds.

"Well now, darlin', we might could have some fun with this later tonight."

The threat—promise—made her her pussy clench, and he laughed.

Nolan shook his head, slapped him on the shoulder, and returned to the redheaded sub waiting outside the roped-off area.

Marcus circled his fingers around her entrance, sliding so easily she knew her pussy must be drenched. "I do think you need something in that li'l cunt." He turned away from her, leaving her throbbing, and rummaged in his leather toy bag.

Her eyes widened when he held up the vibrator from the previous night. "I forgot to tell you that this is yours now, sugar. Before you take it home, we might as well get one more use of it."

"You wouldn't."

He glanced at her in amusement. "Of course I would. Haven't you learned anything yet?" He pushed the nubby penis shape against her entrance, and despite how wet she was, she was also still swollen from yesterday. She groaned as sensitive tissues stretched. He seated it deep inside her, and her vagina pulsed around the intrusion with each beat of her heart.

At least he hadn't turned it on.

Marcus stepped closer to the tray, picked up the candle, and frowned at it. After a second's thought, he pulled a blindfold from his toy bag and firmly tied the soft silk over her eyes. "I don't want to gag you, sugar, but one blown-out candle is your limit. I figure if you can't see the flame, you can't huff and puff at it."

She couldn't see anything...couldn't tell what he was doing. A tremor shook her.

"Yes, blindness makes everything more intense."

Ears straining, she caught the crack of a paddle. Not close. Moaning. A man somewhere on her right cried in gut-wrenching sobs. A woman gave hard-voiced orders. Cullen's hearty laugh.

The lighter clicked. Oh, God. She sniffed, trying to tell if he'd moved the candle closer.

"I use candles without fragrance, Gabi," he said and chuckled. "For safety. You won't smell anything approaching."

Something hit her stomach. She jerked at the momentary burn, then relaxed as it faded to warmth.

After a second, Marcus pried the wax from her skin and ran his finger over the spot. "Just right," he murmured.

Then she had no chance to process anything as hot drips of wax created a line across her stomach, slow drip after slow drip, each burning sensation blossoming over her nerves before fading. He drew one line down to her lower stomach and back up. Circled her belly button. The heat became more intense, then cooler. She couldn't predict where the next drop would start, and her skin grew more sensitive, waiting for the slight pain, then the warmth.

He covered her stomach, gradually moving upward to between her breasts. She held her breath as the splats of wax headed left, circling the curve of her breast, around and around, closer and closer to her nipple. Sometimes very hot, sometimes just warm, so she couldn't predict what any one would feel like, but she cringed, anticipating—

A splat of wax hit right on the very peak. Her back arched uncontrollably. Hot, hot, it pulled like wet sucking lips around her nipple. As the sensation spread through her breast, she almost came right then.

She panted, aroused beyond bearing, and heard him murmur, "You're doin' fine, sugar. Just fine." He stroked her hair back from her face and kissed her forehead.

Wax dropped onto her stomach again, the heat soaking into her skin and heading in an unrelenting line straight upward to her right breast. By the time wax impacted her other nipple with the bite of pain, she seemed to be submerged in cotton balls, feeling nothing except the sensations crawling across her body and the sheer need coiling inside her.

She felt his hand between her legs, and the vibrator clicked on, clicked more times as he cycled through the choices to one where the intensity of the vibrations surged up and down like ocean waves. All the nerves inside her awoke as if she had a second clit deep in her vagina. Her hips tried to lift, held in place by the strap, and her pussy clenched over and over around the intrusion.

Suddenly more wax drizzled back and forth across her stomach, hotter this time, but it didn't seem to matter. Lower, criss-crossing to her hips in measured splat after hot splat, venturing down her thighs and up. As the lines drifted farther toward the inside of her legs, she realized his goal and could only moan, unable to verbalize anything.

Her clit throbbed and swelled in anticipation. Ruthlessly he dripped the wax in an arc from her left inner thigh to high over her mound, down the right thigh, and back again, each set of hot drops closing drip by drip on her very center. As the vibrations inside her intensified, he changed direction. A drop of wax hit the top of her mound, a pause, another a little closer to her pussy, a pause, and another. Her lower half tightened more between each searingly hot impact.

Closer...and the wait for the next seemed eternal.

It hit—*oh God*—the hard, hot splat hit directly on her impossibly sensitive clit.

"Aaaaah!" Everything inside her exploded outward in waves of excruciating pleasure, over and over. Every time they slowed, the vibrator inside her changed its rhythm and another inescapable climax shuddered through her. Her hips bucked against the immovable strap; her whole body tried to arch upward.

When everything finally stopped, she struggled for air. *God, that had been—*

Liquid poured directly onto her pussy—*hot, hot, hot*—and she screamed as another orgasm hit, brutally hard, shaking her like a rag doll.

As the spasms faded, as the roaring in her ears receded, she realized the liquid hadn't been hot at all—he'd poured ice water onto her pussy.

"You...you sadist," she gasped. He gently removed the vibrator, and she shivered at the cold, lonely feeling of being lost inside the clouds.

With one hand he pulled off her blindfold. His other stroked soothingly over the tender area between her hips and thighs, his grip pulling her back to earth. "Easy, sugar, I'm here."

She met his gaze, and everything inside her melted like the wax he'd poured on her. *I love you.*

Despite the oil, removing the wax from Gabi's skin overloaded her senses and sent her back into subspace. Now buried in the blanket he'd wrapped her in, she blinked at him, her smart little mouth silent, as he cleaned up. Once finished, he put her corset and skirt in her arms and picked her up.

He nuzzled her temple and inhaled her fragrance. Adrenaline still sizzled through his veins, the high of topping a little spitfire, reading her responses and reacting in turn, and taking her to the ultimate of pleasure. Sometimes topping a sub reminded him of working a jury until they reacted as he wanted, glaring at the accused and sympathizing with the victims.

A good scene with a responsive sub was even better. And with Gabi? As his arms tightened around her, she sighed and rubbed her cheek against his chest. Had there ever been such a sweet, snuggly brat? His heart squeezed.

Before the night ended, they needed to have a long talk.

As he searched for a good place to relax, he spotted Dan and Kari, Cullen and Andrea across the almost empty room at the chain station, watching Nolan play with his sub. Hell, in the Master's meeting before opening, Nolan had mentioned that near the end of the night, he planned to nudge Beth forward and had invited the others to watch. Marcus had almost forgotten.

With Gabi still in his arms, he took a chair across from Dan.

Dan grinned. "Heard a lot of screaming from your direction." He frowned at Gabi and nodded at Marcus's feet.

It took Marcus a second before he realized she shouldn't sit in his lap. Cuddling didn't make for bratlike opportunities. With a silent sigh, he shook her, wanting to kiss her instead.

"Mmmm?" She blinked at him.

My puppy. He set her on her feet and nodded at the floor. "Down where you belong, darlin'."

She gave him such a meltingly sweet look, he almost pulled her back on his lap. Then she remembered her role. "*Belong*? On the floor?"

He pointed to his feet in answer.

"Rat bastard," she huffed. She knelt, and just when he thought she'd lost her touch, she glanced up at him and said loudly, "I can't believe that out of one hundred thousand sperm, *you* were the fastest."

Dan choked on his drink, and Cullen's loud laugh filled the air. Kari buried her head against Dan's chest, her shoulders shaking. Andrea was laughing like a loon.

Trying to seem angry, Marcus yanked her back so he could lean over and talk in her ear. Hopefully he'd appear to be giving her hell. Instead he told her the truth. "I'm liable to split a gut if you keep acting up, sugar."

She bowed her head, choking on giggles. Little brat was too cute for her own good, and where did she come up with those insults? "How do you feel? Are you able to kneel?" He half hoped she'd say she needed him to hold her.

She was of stronger stuff. "I'm okay." Her voice didn't sound convinced.

He straightened and said loudly, "I'd best keep you close so you don't rile me up anymore." After settling himself forward on the chair, he pulled her back until his legs enclosed her, and he gripped her nape in a mock hard grip. "Let me know if you get uncomfortable, darlin'," he murmured for her ears only.

As she relaxed against him, he traced a finger over the black chain-link tattoo around her neck. She had matching ones on her ankles. One unpredictable, fascinating woman.

What did she plan to do after today? Would she return to Miami right away?

That wouldn't work. They needed time to explore what they had together. She was attracted to him. A little sub couldn't disguise that or her response to him in bed.

And now that he could distinguish what portion of her brattiness was acting versus pure ornery Gabi, he found her behavior more amusing than annoying. In the future—if they had one—when she sassed him, his taking her to task would reward them both. *Funishment*—not truly discipline.

"This is your last night here," he said, testing to see if she'd give a hint as to her plans.

"Yeah." She didn't sound happy.

Leaning forward, he massaged her shoulders. Her tense little body should still be relaxed, considering how far she'd gone under in the scene. He kissed the top of her head and said softly, "Something is bothering you."

She brushed her cheek against his with that unconscious affection he'd grown to love. "What if he isn't caught? What about my friend? The other women?"

Her loyalty squeezed his heart, and he offered the only reassurance he could. "Our...friends...won't give up."

Her shoulders relaxed slightly. "No, they won't." Her lips curved. "They're almost as stubborn as you are."

He nipped her earlobe in retaliation and smiled at her husky giggle. As she rested her cheek against his leg, he realized in surprise that he felt...content. Relaxed and happy in a way he hadn't for, perhaps, years.

Kneeling between Marcus's legs, Gabi felt enclosed in safety as he played with her hair and traced his fingers across the back of her neck.

The other two couples were watching the scene where the harsh dom, Master Nolan, caned... What had Andrea said his sub was named? *Beth*. Chains held the redheaded sub's arms over her head, and a spreader bar kept her legs wide apart as Master Nolan beat on her. A flogger lay discarded on the floor, and now he tossed away the cane and picked up a leather tawse. Beth had tears in her eyes, but her nipples had peaked hard and her face was flushed. She waggled her hips and arched into the blows with more excitement than pain.

Gabi shivered, remembering the flogging from Marcus, how the burning had somehow changed to pleasure until she couldn't tell the difference. The redhead's moans sure didn't sound unhappy. Her dom worked her higher and higher, then switched to the little pussy flogger Marcus had used. Had Z given them to all the Masters?

Nolan slapped the flogger across Beth's breasts, then landed one right between her legs. The sub's back arched as she screamed and shuddered in a long, awe-inspiring climax.

Master Nolan's face changed entirely as he smiled, and Gabi saw why his sub found him appealing. The rumble of his voice reached the people watching as he fisted a hand in Beth's hair, leaning his body against hers. Her tremors eased. And then Nolan stepped back and swatted the flogger three more times right on her pussy, hard and fast. With an incredible look of shock, Beth climaxed again so violently that the chains rang.

The watching doms grinned, murmuring approval of his skill.

The rest of the Masters had arrived while Gabi had stared at the scene. Sam, a whip dangling from his belt, stood with arms folded across his chest. Mistress Anne sat in a leather chair, and a sub in a chain chest harness knelt at her feet. Raoul leaned against the back of the couch where Dan and Kari sat.

Dan pulled Kari onto his lap, freeing up more space. His big hand splayed over her pregnant stomach, and he smiled at her like a man who had all his dreams right there in his arms.

Gabi sighed. Would anyone ever look at her like that?

Mistress Olivia sat down beside Dan and Kari.

Master Z had stood off to one side and now chose one of the two empty chairs. He had his short, curvy sub with him tonight, although Gabi didn't remember seeing her recently. Z pointed to the floor. Jessica sank to a kneeling position, her face expressionless.

As Nolan wrapped his arms around his restrained sub, Gabi glanced at Marcus and the other Masters. "Why's everyone so happy?" she whispered to Marcus.

He leaned down, crossing his arms under her breasts, and murmured in her ear: "Beth was married to a sadist who scarred her up simply to hear her scream. She ran away."

When Gabi squinted her eyes, she saw Beth's white scar lines and puckered circles, marks like she'd seen on some of the victims she'd worked with. "The bastard. I hope he's rotting behind bars."

"Underground actually, I believe. At any rate, when Beth came to the Shadowlands, she was too terrified to give up control. Z made her take Nolan as her dom."

Gabi suppressed a laugh. The meanest-looking dom in the place? If she'd been Beth, she'd have run like hell.

"He's worked with her for months to get her over her fear of restraints. She trusts him now. Totally. So much that when he brings out floggers and canes, she doesn't have a panic attack. He considers tonight her graduation in a way, and he wanted to show her that she could do it all."

Gabi watched as Nolan released his sub from the restraints, one big arm around her to hold her up. Beth's eyes were fixed on the dom as if he held the sum total of her world. "I think she passed the test."

CHAPTER NINETEEN

Jessica sighed as Nolan swept Beth up, carrying her over to join the group.

Z turned, motioned for one of the trainees, and nodded to the scene area. The members knew to wipe up after playing, but sometimes a sub needed the attention more, so Z kept a cleaning person available. The trainee nodded and trotted off.

Although a bit glassy-eyed, Beth appeared incredibly happy, snuggled into Nolan's lap with her head against his shoulder. He murmured to her, his face as gentle as Jessica had ever seen. God, they looked good together, and she felt pleased for them...if a little envious.

Nolan's voice lifted slightly. "Beth, do you love me?"

She tilted her head back to smile up at him. "You know I do."

"Do you like living with me?" He framed her face, his hands almost as scarred as his sub's body.

"Of course."

"You trust me."

"With everything in me," she whispered.

"Am I your dom, little rabbit?"

"Yes." Her red-brown brows drew together. "What's wrong?"

"Not a thing." He gave her a faint smile, and his gravelly voice deepened. "I thought I'd tell you we're getting married next month. We need to get a plane ticket for your mama."

Jessica could almost see Beth's mind try to process Nolan's declaration. The redhead sat straight up. "What?"

"You heard me, honey."

"That's...that's not any kind of a proposal. You can't..."

Nolan's mouth tightened, and he gave her a look any sub in the world would recognize, the one that said someone was getting far too close to pissing off a nasty dom.

Beth stopped. She frowned at her hands.

"Beth, do you love me?"

"Yes," she snapped, lifting her head.

"Do you like living with me?"

Beth gave an exasperated snort. "Okay, you jerk. You don't need to go through it all again, although you really should have finished with a 'will you marry me' question."

He smiled slowly. "I didn't want to take the chance you'd say no."

"You're such a dom," she grumbled and then gave him a breathtaking smile. "Of course I'll marry you."

As everyone broke into applause, Cullen handed Nolan a ring, and he slid it onto Beth's finger. She let out a squeak of delight, her eyes wide. Hands bracketing her dom's face, she gave him a very long, very sweet kiss.

And then she shoved herself off his lap to hurry to Kari and show her ring off.

Jessica grinned as Nolan winced and adjusted a conspicuous erection.

Dan snorted and told Nolan in a low voice, "You'd better take her home soon before you damage something."

"Hell with that. We're heading upstairs the minute she stops showing off her ring." Nolan grinned as Beth trotted from Kari to Andrea. "Then again, if she takes much longer, I may just bend her over this chair."

As the men laughed, Beth dropped down beside Jessica. "Look, Jessica."

Jessica smiled at her instead, seeing the glow in her eyes, the utter happiness with no reservations whatsoever. "I'm so glad for you."

Beth hugged her. "Without you holding my hand and encouraging me, I might have run. Thank you."

Blinking away tears, Jessica hugged her back. "Okay, show me."

The ring was lovely, a diamond in the center of smaller multicolored gems, giving the impression of a flower in bloom, perfect for the landscape designer. "I'm envious," Jessica said, trying to make her words light even though she meant them with all her heart. "And I know you two will be wonderfully happy together."

"Thank you." Beth kissed her cheek before grinning at Z. "Thank you, Sir."

Z stroked her hair. "Be happy, Elizabeth."

Feeling a little excluded and a lot envious, Gabi watched Beth return to Nolan.

His black gaze had never left his submissive for more than a few seconds.

Beth flapped her subbie blanket at him. "Want to go upstairs, my lord and master...or just bend me over the arm of your chair?"

Everyone burst out laughing.

Nolan's face darkened, and he rose.

Beth warily took a step back.

Gabi giggled when Nolan stripped the blanket from Beth and tossed her over his shoulder. He slapped her butt, glanced around at everyone, and grinned. "We're going upstairs for a bit, Z," he said.

Master Z inclined his head. "Feel free to spend the night, Nolan. Use as many rooms as you deem necessary to get her properly engaged."

Nolan chuckled, caressing Beth's slim thigh. "Good suggestion, Z. It shouldn't take more than a handful of rooms to obtain a quiet little fiancée."

A muffled "What!" came from the redhead, even as the rest of the doms grinned.

Cullen had picked up the various toys in the scene area. Now he hung the leather bag over Nolan's shoulder. "You'll need this, buddy."

Gabi shook her head, a bit appalled. Each of the private rooms on the second floor had a different piece of equipment—from spanking benches to St. Andrew's crosses to bondage tables. By morning, poor Beth probably wouldn't be able to walk.

"Well, that exhausted me." Dan nuzzled his pregnant sub. "Brought back all sorts of horrible memories of getting engaged."

"Oh, it did not," she said. Gabi gasped as the round little sub poked her hard-faced dom in the ribs. Was she insane?

"Do you get the impression we have an overabundance of smart-ass subs?" Master Dan growled to Cullen. He grabbed Kari's wrists and hooked her cuffs together over her protruding belly.

Cullen's sub, Andrea, grinned. "Not me. As a past trainee, I'm the very epitome of a submissive, an example to the other subs in my attire and demeanor and obedience."

That sounded like a quote, but if that had been in the trainee instructions, Gabi had sure missed it.

Cullen stared at his sub in disbelief. "For that absolute whopper of a lie, you may fetch me a beer—and just water for you."

When she scowled at him, he yanked her dress over her head, leaving her in only a thong. His fingers curled under the thin band on one hip. "Look at me in that tone of voice again, and you'll lose this too, love."

As she flounced away, Cullen grinned. "You know, I never get tired of watching that ass, especially when she's stomping."

Marcus laughed. He rubbed his cheek against Gabi's, his beard shadow tantalizingly abrasive, and murmured, "Get dressed, sugar; then fetch us both a drink. Since you've been a good girl—for oh, at least the last five minutes...you may have whatever you wish."

God, she could listen to his voice forever. She turned her face up and whispered, "Thank you, Sir."

He gave her a kiss as slow and sweet as his Southern drawl.

After squirming into her vinyl skirt and hooking up her corset, Gabi waited at the bar to give her order. An older couple had taken over the closest scene area. In a pink bustier and matching collar, the woman was carefully helped onto a spanking sawhorse by her white-haired dom. They must be around seventy and looked so sweet together. Imagine living with—and loving—someone for half a century.

With fingers knotted by arthritis, the dom stroked his sub's cheek, and they exchanged a kiss and laughter.

Gabi's heart squeezed. *I want that. I want Marcus to be my dom. My man.*

She ordered Marcus's vodka and a soda for herself from the dom serving as bartender, then made circles in a streak of spilled beer. Marcus acted affectionate. But did he treat all his trainees like her? Wouldn't he have said something if he figured on seeing her after tonight?

Her insides fluttered as if she'd eaten an anxiety sandwich for lunch rather than tuna. Maybe he thought she wasn't interested, that she planned to go home and never think of him again. He's a dom, Gabi; he'd know, one part of her said. The other more optimistic side insisted she should make an effort before giving up.

"Hi there."

Gabi glanced over and saw the blonde submissive who adored Marcus. Miss Golden and Perfect. "Hi."

"My Marcus said you're one of his new trainees." The woman's voice was soft and sugar-sweet. "My name is Celine."

My Marcus. The pain of her claim slid into Gabi's heart so quickly she had no defense against it. She inhaled carefully and attempted a return smile. "It's nice to meet you." *And that is so not true. I could have happily lived my whole life without meeting you.* "I'm Gabrielle. How long have you two been together?"

"Since spring. He's everything I ever wanted." Celine smiled and patted Gabi's hand. "I've watched you, bless your heart. Don't you realize the doms don't like bratty submissives?"

"Oh. Really?" *Some village somewhere is missing an idiot.* "Why, I hadn't noticed."

Celine pursed her lips into a moue of disapproval. "That's why that trainee Sally still hasn't found a dom who can stand her. I'm surprised Marcus puts up with her. He hates disrespectful behavior."

Gabi managed not to wince and kept her voice level. "Well, damn. Who knew?"

"Now don't be hurt," Celine said. "I'm trying to help."

On the other side of Celine, Master Dan's pregnant submissive frowned; maybe she didn't approve of sarcastic subs either.

"You see, that's why Marcus loves me so much," Celine said. "I never give him any trouble or back talk. Whatever he wants is what I want."

I should punch her. Tear some of her perfect hair out. No submissive in the place would blame me.

The bartender showed up—finally—and set Gabi's order down. "One Grey Goose, one Coke."

"Thank you," Gabi said.

"Oh, is that for my master?" Celine picked up Marcus's drink. "I'll save you the trip, and you can get back to waiting on people." She moved away, gracefully and amazingly fast. Gabi would have had to chase after her like a hound on the hunt.

Gabi watched as Celine, the perfect submissive, handed Marcus his drink and knelt at his feet.

That's my place.

Marcus said something, and Celine laid her face against his knee.

When Gabi let out the breath she'd held, it felt as if her ribs had collapsed into jagged bones. That completely answered any questions she'd had about...anything. He had someone already, and even if he didn't, Gabi sure wasn't the type of sub or woman he wanted. He'd made it clear right from the beginning he wouldn't tolerate brats. Why had she thought he'd changed his mind?

She glanced at her drink. Bubbles rose in the dark liquid to burst and disappear. *Time is up, Cinderella sub*. The fairy tale had ended, and she needed to go home. What a shame she'd screwed up the story and her future held no Prince Charming. Heart aching, she headed for the exit.

Before she reached the door, she heard, "Gabrielle." Not Marcus, with the extra lilt he gave to the end of her name, but Z's deep voice. She turned.

His brows pulled together. "Were you leaving without saying good-bye?"

She swallowed past the lump in her throat. "It seemed easier."

"Easier isn't always best," he said softly.

"No. But it is this time." Her gaze slid back to Marcus. His blonde submissive had wrapped her arms around his legs. One clinging vine, made-to-order. "Please tell everyone I appreciated their help."

And saying that reminded her of what was really important. Why was she giving in to these stupid, petty emotions when Kim might be fighting for her life? "I wish we'd caught the guy."

His gray eyes turned the color of gunmetal. "We won't stop trying to find them, Gabrielle."

"I know." She managed a half smile. "Well. Thanks."

He silently opened his arms.

She went into his embrace without a second thought, and he held her firmly as she fought tears. Once she had herself under control, she pulled back, and he let her go. Lifting her chin with a finger, he stroked away a tear. "Be safe, little one."

She fled.

Well, that answered that, Jessica thought, as Z strode across the room after the damn trainee.

And then Gabrielle walked into his arms like...like she'd already spent a lot of time there.

Every hope inside Jessica shriveled up and died. Only she hugged him like that.

He hadn't wanted me here tonight. She might not be a psychologist and mind reader, but she could tell when he was displeased. Z had let her come only because of Nolan's plans, but she sure as hell didn't feel wanted.

Now she knew why—she'd been replaced. The certainty slid into her so insidiously she didn't notice until pain swamped her senses. Until she couldn't breathe. Around her the Masters talked, comparing notes on their most disastrous scenes. No one paid attention when she slid back and rose. She needed to get out of here before Z returned—if he did.

Jessica detoured to one side of the room and headed for the exit.

Near the front, she glanced around. Z was on the other side of the bar, his back to her. Even though nothing ever erased his military-straight posture, she saw weariness in his stride. She hesitated. Could she be wrong?

Doubtful.

As she passed the office door, she slowed. Z stored the membership records on the computer, and since she did the accounting, she could pull up any information she wanted. Like a trainee's address.

Maybe she'd go and chat awhile with the sub. Z might not be

willing to talk, but she'd bet Gabrielle would have no such compunctions. Jessica's fingers were numb as she punched in the code and entered the office. She'd find out how long Z had been seeing her, and maybe then she'd know what to do.

In her apartment parking lot, Gabi slid out of her car, inhaling the clean, crisp air. The storm had passed, and now palm fronds and debris skittered across the concrete in the light breeze. She shivered as the cool air hit her bare shoulders and legs. Not exactly dressed for the weather, was she? She gave a bitter laugh.

She hadn't stopped to change or even put on her shoes, just emptied everything from her locker and left. Lingering meant Marcus might notice her absence. Then again, he'd seemed pretty occupied when his *real* sub had brought his drink. She gave a cynical laugh; he probably wouldn't think of her until closing time.

She stopped and closed her eyes. No, that wasn't fair. She'd known few men as responsible as Marcus. He'd eventually have searched for her...and then rounded up a kindly dom for her to play with like he had last night. So she'd saved him all sorts of work by leaving early.

As she bent over to reach for her purse and clothing on the passenger seat, she heard, "Nice ass."

Dickhead. Could the evening get any better? She turned, trapped between the open car door and his body, regretting her lack of clothing. Clenching her hand around her car keys, she said, "You're blowing your cover."

"Case is over. Thompson caught the kidnapper."

Hope spiraled up inside Gabi, wiping out every other emotion. *Kim. They can save Kim.* "Where? When? Did he go after one of the decoys? How did you find out?" *Why didn't someone call me?*

Rhodes's expression turned sour. "Thompson made the bust at the St. Pete club. He was waiting outside for the decoy and heard noises from the alley and went to check it out. The unsub had attacked a woman who'd come out the back door." Rhodes shook his head. "Why she was stupid enough to leave the club through the alley..."

"But he's caught? Did anyone get hurt?"

"The woman got knocked out when Thompson charged into them, but the paramedics are there."

"Wow. I guess my part is over then." She felt off-balance, as if she was still running even after the race ended.

"Dammit. I wanted the collar." His gaze turned to her. "You should have tried harder."

"I did my best." Gabi sighed, understanding his sour grapes. After all the work, that was it. Time to go back and try to pick up her life again. A sadder life now she'd seen its emptiness. No deep laughter, no hot sex, no warm snuggles. She rubbed her arms as if that would stave off the cold.

The movement drew Rhodes's attention to her lack of clothing, her bare shoulders and legs, the cleavage made by the corset. His expression changed. "You might have done better if you hadn't gotten such a kick out of everything." His gaze slid over her body like a spray of filth. "But since we're both here together, why don't we keep enjoying ourselves." He jerked his chin toward her apartment. "I can show you as good a time as that asshole trainer did."

"In your dreams." Substitute him for Marcus? *Oh God, I want my Marcus*. Her throat tightened until she was afraid she'd burst into tears, so she snapped at him instead. "You are such a sleazeball, Rhodes—walking, talking proof of why siblings shouldn't marry."

It took him a second, and then anger distorted his face into something ugly.

That was stupid, Gabi. Exhausted, she leaned against the car.

Just leave, dammit. "Go home, Rhodes. I don't want to have to report you." She fully planned to note his behavior in her account anyway, although it probably wouldn't do any good.

His color darkened. "You report away. You know, Renard, if I document how much you enjoyed your assignment, you won't have a job to go back to."

Sickness spread through her; she'd known this might happen. But to have her entire life and hopes destroyed in one evening... "You're a real bastard, aren't you?" she said slowly.

"Oh, I'm sure we can work something out." Leaning on the side of the car, he put his hand on her. On her breast. Squeezing.

"No!" With a growl she couldn't control, she slapped his hand away and slugged him square in the nose. The crunch of shattering cartilage made her stomach clench, and his high-pitched yell reverberated back from her nightmares.

He grabbed his face, and blood gushed through his fingers.

She raised her fists, despite the bile burning her throat. "Go, Rhodes. Leave now."

Eyes crazy, he backed away. Before he'd gone ten feet, she slammed the car door and fled across the parking lot, easing up only when an engine revved.

Car tires screeched on the pavement as he drove out of the lot.

As her heart hammered in her chest with lingering adrenaline, she tried to laugh. He'd left.

I broke his nose.

Trying not to remember the ghastly noise it had made, she snorted. Dickhead shouldn't have provoked a woman with a broken heart.

Her mood flattened into dismal again.

As she walked to her building, a small car pulled up at the fire lane, blocking her path. The car shut off, and a short blonde jumped out.

Z's sub, Jessica. The blonde's face was drawn, her hands clenched as she glared at Gabi.

Jesus, what is this? Pick on Gabi night?

Maganti shook his head. *Jesus, what is this? Screw up Cesar's night?*

What was it going to take to grab this cunt? Last night, fucking cops all over the place; now, some chick wanting to do a smackdown.

He needed to get this bitch tonight. Now. *Get lost, blondie, so I can do my job.*

As he watched from the shadows, the little blonde said in a hard voice to his target, "I want to talk with you. How long has he been seeing you?"

"What? Who?"

"Z."

The redhead rolled her eyes. "If you and Z are having problems, it has nothing to do with me. Go talk to him."

Wait, wait, wait. Maganti stiffened, losing track of the conversation. The curvy blonde had been on his list. He'd done a background check and crossed her off because she had a lover. But if she'd fought with her fuck buddy, she could go right back on the menu. If a chick's dude screwed around on her, no one wondered why she up and disappeared.

He looked at her and saw dollar signs.

His target scowled and started to walk away, but the bulldog blonde grabbed her arm. "I need answers. Please."

The redhead gave a long-suffering sigh. "God, you're stubborn. Fine. Let's go upstairs and talk. It's really not what you think."

"Sure it's not."

The redhead leaned forward and whispered something in the blonde's ear, making her jerk back and stare. "No way."

"Way. We'll discuss it in my apartment."

An okay night changed into a fucking great night when they both headed toward the stairs at the center of the building.

As they entered the thruway, Maganti pulled his backup Taser and waited until they'd turned to climb the steps. He moved out far enough to get a clear line of fire and shot one and the other. *Pow, pow*. It only took a minute to pull the prongs out of their bodies and heave the women into the box—a little tangled, but what the hell—and secure the box to the handcart. He backed his van up, pushed the handcart up the ramp, and was on his way.

Now this was a fucking fine haul.

Gabi woke, head pounding, stomach wrenching with nausea. Her mouth felt as if she'd licked up beach sand, and her foggy brain seemed to think she'd spent the night drinking. Only...she hadn't, right?

She tried to sit up, realized she lay on a metal floor—not her bed. Something rattled when she moved her arms. Restrained? Was she still at the club? She raised her head carefully so it wouldn't fall off. She wore handcuffs. A two-feet chain strung through the cuffs was padlocked to a bolt in the gray metal wall.

The world spun dizzily as she wiggled to a sitting position. She swallowed hard. *Am I at the Shadowlands*? No sounds. Not Marcus's place. She'd left him at the club. So why the bondage?

She'd driven back to her apartment. Right. And she'd punched Dickhead? She flexed her fingers, gritting her teeth at the soreness in her right knuckles. That part wasn't a dream. Then...Jessica'd arrived, and they'd started to climb the steps. A man in the shadows. *Pain*. Gabi tensed, remembering the horrible pain, how every muscle had shrieked in agony. Then...

Here. She turned her head. Jessica lay beside her. Unconscious. Handcuffed.

They weren't at the club. Not playing, not a scene. *No no no*. A scream tried to escape, couldn't get past the constriction in her throat. The nausea, the headache, the grogginess...drugged.

The horrible realization came from deep inside and slammed into her brain. *Kidnapped.* Thompson hadn't caught the perp.

I've been kidnapped. With Jessica. Terror rose in her, as inescapable as waves breaking on the rocks, swamping her thoughts until the room itself turned red. Cold.

I've got to get out of here. She jerked on the bolt, and it held her implacably. *No. Oh God, please.* She rattled and yanked the chain. *Let go, dammit, let go*! Pulled over and over, until the metal handcuffs ripped her skin.

Pain. The increasing pain pushed her beyond her panic. Panting, she slumped against the cold wall. What was she doing?

I panicked. She shook her head, forced her breathing to slow. *Don't do that again, Gabi.* As she stared at the blood trickling down her wrists, terror waited on the edges of her mind, pushing against her control.

Using all her willpower, she turned her attention away from the restraints.

Where are we? Gray walls, gray floor. Metal. Not a room. A cargo van. It stank of sweat and fear and sickness. And sex. She pushed farther back against the wall, pulling her legs in, curling into a ball.

The only light came from a small mesh window in a door between the cargo part and the cab section. The cargo area held a cooler, a porta-potty, and a big corrugated box for a washing machine with a handcart leaning on it. Nothing within reach.

Her chest started to tighten, but Jessica groaned.

A minute later, the blonde raised her head, squinting against the light. "What happened?"

"We've been kidnapped."

"Excuse me?"

Do better, Gabi. "Sorry. At my apartment, I think somebody Tasered us and drugged us. We're chained up." Gabi listened. No traffic noises, no people shouting or laughing or talking.

The chains jangled as Gabi rubbed her aching head. "No one

knows where we are—or even that he's got us." The FBI thought they'd caught the perp. How long before anyone called Gabi? *Oh dear God.* Fear spiraled outward. *No rescue. No hope.* Her hands closed into fists as she fought for control.

"Easy, girlfriend, easy." Jessica slid closer.

Not alone. She had someone depending on her. *I can't lose it.* "Sorry," Gabi whispered. Heart hammering, she mentally edged back from the chasm. After a second, she turned and leaned against the wall of the van, facing the other woman. "We're kind of in trouble."

Hands clenched into fists, the blonde stared around the van, her face white. Then her chin lifted. "I reserve the right to yell about you and Z later. For now, tell me what's going on."

Despite the ice creeping up her spine, Gabi almost managed a smile. Trust Z not to have a wimpy girlfriend. "It's like this..."

As Gabrielle talked, Jessica tried various ways to get out of the handcuffs. No deal. By the time Gabrielle finished the story, Jessica wanted to kill Z, dead as a doornail. That's why he'd come down on her so hard for her brattiness. Why he'd kept gagging her. And why... "He tried to keep me out of the club completely," she said slowly.

"I bet." Gabrielle shook her head. "Anyway, the only thing he feels for me is sympathy. I'm sorry that he couldn't tell you." She grimaced. "Marcus was furious when he found out."

"But if you're with the FBI and a decoy, then someone will rescue us." Hope bubbled up. She could almost hear the good guys sneaking up on the van right now.

"No. God, this is so screwed up. My backup, Dickhead, treated me like a slut and kept getting nastier. Last night, someone told him they'd caught the kidnapper, so he figured the assignment was over and came on to me." Gabrielle shuddered.

"Oh."

"Yeah. Name-calling was done. Groping happened."

"And?"

"And I broke his nose. He left."

Outrage burned through Jessica. "Your protector abandoned you?"

Gabrielle shrugged. "Well, supposedly they'd caught the bad guy. Not."

"So no one knows we've even been kidnapped." *Oh God.* Jessica's fingernails dug holes in her palms. "I don't suppose you have any wonderful FBI skills?"

Gabrielle gave a bitter laugh. "I'm a social worker, not an agent. I volunteered because I'd played in BDSM clubs—years ago."

"You're not an agent?"

"I'm sorry. I can't believe he got you too," Gabrielle whispered. "He'll s-sell us." Her face was white enough to match her scar, shivers shook her constantly, and she looked right on the edge.

"You okay?"

"I've had so many nightmares of this. And now it has happened." Gabrielle stared at her hands, breathing way too fast.

Jessica remembered how a few members had laughed at the bratty trainee's punishments. Except she wasn't a brat at all. For a month, this poor woman had played decoy, hoping to be kidnapped. Jessica shook her head, sympathy overwhelming her fear. *Time for me to shoulder a little of the burden.*

She considered options, then slid as far as the chain would let her. She bumped her arm companionably against the woman's shoulder. "Hey, if two brats can't figure out how to get out of this, who can?"

Gabrielle stiffened and stared at her in disbelief.

Jessica gave her a level look and tilted her head in the way Z did when he challenged her to try something new.

Gabrielle's shoulders straightened. "Oh. Okay." Her eyes cleared. "Get out of here? Sure. We'll just do that little thing."

"You bet."

"Thanks."

"My pleasure." Jessica waited a beat. "Guess I won't get to knock you on your ass when this is over, huh?"

This time Gabrielle actually chuckled. "No wonder Z adores you."

Jessica stared.

"Oh, please. I'm not blind. I've seen the way he looks at you, how he treats you." Gabrielle gave her a derisive sniff. "Personally I thought you were a real bitch, but if you believed I'd poached on your man—and that he'd actually look twice at me—I might have come across all pissy too. But get over it. The man loves you."

A knot in the pit of Jessica's stomach disappeared, and her eyes pooled. "Thanks."

"No problem."

"You know, I feel better. I'm still terrified, but...better. I'm so happy I could even...scream." She waggled her eyebrows.

"Sounds like a plan."

Jessica let out an earsplitting scream, and Gabrielle followed suit.

As the back door of the van rolled up, Jessica's eyes watered at the sudden blast of daylight.

"The bitches are awake, Cesar."

"Good." Another man's voice. "It's almost time to leave."

CHAPTER TWENTY

Unable to sleep, Marcus had risen at dawn and tried to prepare questions for a witness in his next court case. Useless. He couldn't concentrate. He picked up the phone in his home office and punched in Gabi's number. Still no answer.

Damn the little sub, walking out of the club without even a good-bye or *have a nice life* or anything. Damn Celine too. After handing him his drink and saying Gabi was using the restroom, she'd started in with her "you're my master" bullshit. She probably wouldn't pull that again, since he'd called over some doms and told them she was looking for a master.

Finally freed up, he'd gone to find his missing sub, only to discover she'd left.

He rubbed his face wearily. He'd almost called Z to demand Gabi's address, but showing up at her home might screw up the FBI investigation. She'd best get her pretty ass out of bed and answer her phone.

Why had she left like that?

Maybe, with her assignment concluded, she figured they were done with each other. She'd be wrong.

Hands laced behind his head, he leaned back in his office

chair. Smiling, he remembered how she'd blown out the candle for wax play. *Little brat*. He needed to convince her to remain another week—and stay here with him. If he could win a jury over, you'd think he could argue a case for himself. Or he might could wrangle some vacation time from the DA and visit Miami.

No, sugar, we're not done.

When his phone rang, he picked it up, anticipation rising. No one would call him this early, except maybe a repentant trainee. "Hello."

"Marcus, is Gabrielle with you?" Z's voice.

Disappointment gave way to concern. "No, she isn't. Why?"

"She's not answering her phone, neither is her backup from last night. The agent coming on duty says she's not in her apartment, but her car's in the parking lot."

Marcus was on his feet with no memory of standing. He forced a breath. *Get the facts, Atherton, before going off half-cocked.* "Maybe she and the agent went for a walk?"

"Apparently the next man would get notified of their location."

A cold hand squeezed Marcus's spine at the implication. "Are you at her place?"

"On my way. Galen and Vance are there."

"Give me the address."

Twenty minutes later, Marcus pulled in to the parking lot of Gabi's apartment complex. Three-story building, dull brown, no landscaping. It hurt him to think of her living here. He squinted at the numbers on the doors and spotted hers.

A light rain spattered against him as he ran across the lot. He veered around a small Taurus parked in the fire lane and took the steps two at a time.

Gabi's apartment stood open, a man in a dark suit blocking the door. "Let him in," Z called from inside.

Marcus pushed past the man.

Vance and another man were in the living space. Z stood in the tiny kitchen area, his face drawn with exhaustion. "Marcus."

"News?" Marcus asked.

"Nothing good." Z kneaded his neck. "That's Jessica's car in front. Unlocked. Her purse is in it. Her phone too. She's not answering at home."

Marcus stared at him. "Both of them are missing?"

Galen stepped out of the bedroom. He carefully used his foot to push a cat back and closed the door behind him. He nodded to Marcus and spoke to everyone. "I called in. The tracking devices are operating, but they're worthless. Both Gabrielle's shoes and purse are still in her car."

"No chance you've made a mistake?" Marcus asked.

Galen gave a bitter glance at a set of keys on the kitchen table. "Vance found Gabi's apartment keys on the sidewalk by the steps."

The fury rising in Marcus's veins was matched by sheer fear. *Where are you, Gabi?*

"You gonna scream again, bitch? We're in the middle of a swamp—won't do you much good." In a tank top and jeans, a repulsive man with pitted skin and stringy black hair stepped up into the van, rocking it with his weight. Gabi saw the gang tattoos covering his arms and almost panicked again.

His mouth twisted in an ugly grin as he stared at Gabi, his gaze lingering on her breasts. "Cesar knows I like it when bitches scream."

Her heart hammering, Gabi stared past him and out the van door. Oaks with hanging moss, thick underbrush, a dirt road. Silent except for the dripping of water from the trees and a few bird calls. She glanced at Jessica and saw her unhappy comprehension. No one would come to investigate their screams.

The man called Cesar stepped into the van and pulled the door down behind him. Dyed blonde hair, mud brown eyes, just under six feet, and thickly muscled. He wore a coverall with an appliance store brand. "I don't like cleaning up my van when you chickies piss in your clothes, so use the porta-potty now. You won't get another chance till you're on the boat."

"What's going on? Where are we?" Jessica asked, her voice shaking slightly.

Cesar snorted. "Always the same questions. You're getting sold to buyers who will appreciate your special...qualities."

"Now?" Fear combined with the nausea from the drugs, and Gabi's stomach roiled. *How much time do we have?*

"Soon enough. A boat'll pick you up in downtown Clearwater in a couple of hours. We'll be on our way in a bit."

"Then what?"

He shrugged. "Don't know. Don't care." He glanced at the other man. "Jang, one at a time. I'll cover." He patted the Taser holstered on his belt.

When Jang pulled a key from his jeans pocket, Gabi saw the outline of a cell phone. Her nostrils flared as if she could scent hope. *A phone.*

"You first, bitch." When his eyes raked over her, Gabi's skin crawled. "We gonna have us some fun on the drive. I am, at least. You're gonna scream." He grabbed her wrists and shoved his other hand in her corset.

Without thinking, she kicked him in the balls as hard as she could.

He made a horrible high-pitched sound as he staggered sideways. His legs gave out, dropping him to his knees as he clutched his groin, gagging and sucking air.

Gabi pulled her legs back, the momentary sense of victory eclipsed by fear. Then she raised her chin. She'd pay for kicking him...but it had been worth it.

When Jang moaned, the other guy gave a nasty laugh. "You

forget we divided the cuffs so each bitch got one set? Legs are free, you fucking idiot. Now move it."

Jang pushed to his feet, his gait unsteady, his face pale. He detoured around her legs. Before she could move, he grabbed her hair and slammed her head against the side of the van.

Pain ripped through her head in a searing explosion. Her stomach turned over, and she gagged.

"Shit." Jang released her and stepped away hastily.

"Fuckhead." Cesar made a sound of disgust. "It still stinks from the last one puking her guts out. Just let her piss and lock her back up."

Growling, Jang unlocked one cuff, yanked the chain free, and hefted her to her feet. He shoved her toward the portable toilet.

She let herself stagger, which wasn't hard considering she felt dizzier than hell. Turning to sit on the commode, she deliberately fell forward, knocking into him. As he staggered back, he grabbed her upper arms. With Jang's body blocking the other man's view, Gabi thumped her head on his chest to divert his attention, and slid her hand into his pocket.

Her fingers closed around the phone.

She dropped onto the toilet, hiding the phone in her hand and hunching over her stomach as if she needed to throw up. And if her head got any worse, she might. After a quick breath, she lifted her head and glared at Jessica. "What are you staring at, you loser? This is all your fault."

Both men turned to look at Jessica.

The blonde's mouth dropped open.

Hell. Catching Jessica's gaze, Gabi mouthed, *Yell.*

Jessica blinked. But she caught on fast. "My fault? You're the skanky bitch who tried to steal my man." She yanked at her restraints.

While the men's attention was on Jessica, Gabi shoved the phone into her corset, hiding it between her breasts. Then, taking her time, trying to get her stomach to settle, she did her business, humiliated at the sound.

Still walking bowlegged, Jang hauled Gabi off the toilet, locked her back up, and gave Jessica a turn.

Leaning back, Gabi watched under her lashes, praying no one called Jang's phone. She figured, no matter how dumb he was, he might notice if ringing noises came from her breasts. To her relief, they simply chained Jessica up, walked to the front, and shut the door to the cab section behind them.

The engine started with a rumble, and the van pulled out.

Gabi frowned. The door between the cargo section and the cab held a tiny window. They could see into the back, but probably not easily since the only light came from that window. Why have a door at all?

Her stomach twisted. Probably so no one on the street could look through the windshield and see the handcuffed women. Her breath hitched. *No. Can't panic now.*

"What's with all the acting?" Jessica whispered. She must not have seen Gabi pick his pocket.

If you're watching from the other side, Danny—thank you for the lessons.

"I got his cell." Head splitting with pain, Gabi fumbled around the restrictions of the short length of chain and handcuffs, finally managing to fish the phone out of her corset. She punched in 911. *Busy.*

Tried again. *Busy.*

Dammit all. She put in Rhodes's number. No answer. "I don't remember Galen's number. Give me Z's number."

Jessica reeled off a number. No one answered, and Gabi used voice mail, trying to be clear. Kidnapped. Clearwater. Docks. Cargo van.

"Describe the guys—tell them about the tattoos," Jessica whispered. Gabi did and finished, telling him not to call the cell's number. She put it on silent too...just in case.

"Shit, shit, shit." Jessica gave Gabi the number to his office.

Another voice mail, dammit. Gabi left the same message, then deleted the phone log. "Let me try 911 again." She punched in 9, then 1—

"I can't find my fucking phone!" Jang yelled in the cab.

Gabi felt the blood drain from her face. *Oh God.*

The van pulled over and stopped. Heart pounding, Gabi unsilenced the cell and slid it across the floor. It stopped beside the porta-potty. She slumped, trying to control her breathing.

The door to the cab burst open and hit the wall with a crack that made her insides cringe. Light from the windshield highlighted Jang's body as he stepped into the back. "Where is it, you fucking bitches?"

Gabi mirrored Jessica's baffled expression.

"Fine, I'll find it myself." He still walked as if his balls hurt. Avoiding her feet, he yanked Gabi sideways until the restraints pulled her arms straight. The handcuffs dug into her raw wrists. He tugged at her corset unsuccessfully, cursed, and started to unhook it.

Gabi struggled futilely, sick with revulsion. With fear. When her corset opened halfway, Jang grabbed her breast.

When he touched her, her thoughts fragmented with terror. She couldn't move, couldn't breathe.

"What's taking so long?" Cesar stepped into the back and glared at Jang. "You asshole, I don't have time for this crap." Pulling out his own cell, he punched in a number...and the phone by the commode buzzed softly. "You clumsy fuck, it's over there."

"Fine." Jang squeezed Gabi's breast viciously. "Consider this a sample for later," he whispered and shoved her against the metal wall.

She grunted as she hit, and tears filled her eyes. *Please, someone, get us out of this.*

After retrieving his phone, Jang hit a few buttons, obviously checking the outgoing calls.

Not moving, Gabi watched, thanking God she'd erased the numbers she'd dialed. Her head pounded; her shoulder and wrists and breast throbbed with pain. If he came back for her, she might cry. Her jaw clenched. No. No, she wouldn't.

With a shrug, he told Cesar, "We're good."

"Yeah, good thing for you, fuckup." Cesar motioned him into the cab and followed.

"You okay?" Jessica whispered.

Gabi nodded, grateful she wasn't totally alone. Not that it would matter.

Leaning her head on the wall, she stared at her wrists, at the mangled flesh and purpling bruising under the metal handcuffs. Blood smeared the metal floor. Maybe that's why Marcus only used leather cuffs. She remembered how he'd stand close enough that her every breath brought her his masculine scent, how he'd hold her arm with a firm, warm grip while he ran a finger under the cuff to make sure it wasn't too tight. She'd look up to see him watching her intently. His lips would curve—just barely those first few days, then more. The last two nights, he'd had a different smile: one that said he knew her, all of her—the possessive smile of a man who'd had a woman and intended to have her again.

Each time, even though she wouldn't move at all, she'd yearn toward him. Toward his possession. No longer *make me, Sir*, but *take me, Sir*.

And now she'd never see him again.

A slave. Would they break her? Maybe? Or maybe she'd die first, her body as mangled as her wrists, her voice gone from screaming. A shudder seized her. She wasn't especially afraid to die. Everybody did, sooner or later. But the thought of what came before death, that someone would deliberately inflict horrible, crushing pain on her... As her hands trembled, the blood oozing from her wrists splattered on the floor.

Okay, I'm terrified. They could so easily turn her into a panicking, mindless animal. *I don't want that again*. So she'd damn well do absolutely everything she could to escape, no matter how small the chance. No point in waiting and hoping for something better to come.

And if she managed to attract attention, then maybe—even if she died—maybe Kim or Jessica might get rescued.

Her spine straightened. Pretty weak plan, but it helped take her another step away from losing control. *I'm more than an animal.*

As the truck rumbled down the road, she mentally pulled up her big-girl panties—and she really, really wished she'd worn panties rather than a thong—and turned to Jessica. "You know, I had all these great insults to use at the Shadowlands, but I forgot to yell them at Jang. Wanna hear them?"

Jessica stared at her, then sucked in a shaky breath and grinned. "Sure. I'll trade you some of my favorites."

"Cool. My favorite is: Your birth certificate is an apology from the condom factory."

"Nah. Jang's too stupid to get the meaning." Jessica thought. "How about: Why don't you check eBay and see if they have a life for sale?"

Gabi grinned. "Not bad. Hmm—oh, I know... Is that your face or did your neck just throw up."

The sputter of laughter Jessica gave made Gabi's heart lighten. It was good not to be alone.

In increasing frustration, Zachary watched as the FBI agents tried to find something, anything to point them in the right direction. Dammit, where would the pickup happen? His fear for Jessica knotted his guts until he stood and paced the kitchen. Again.

From the bedroom came the sound of plaintive meows. He'd been in there earlier, holding and petting the two felines while Vance searched the apartment. The cats wanted

Gabrielle. Maybe as much as he wanted Jessica. He ran his hand through his hair, craving her so badly his arms ached. Needing to shake her silly for scaring him, to hold her and let her know what she meant to him. All he could think about was how unhappy she'd been last night. Because of him.

He stared at his hands, useless with no target in sight. This not knowing...not being able to act...

On the decrepit sofa, Galen had his bad leg extended. As he talked on his cell phone, his face slowly reddened with anger, and his low voice sharpened to such a cutting edge that the other person probably had blood pooling at his feet. With a low curse, the agent snapped the phone closed and called over one of the local agents. "Campbell, meet Rhodes at your office. Grill him for anything he saw last night."

"What happened to him?" Campbell asked. "Why isn't he here? Is he okay? Where's Ms. Renard?"

Galen's eyes had darkened to total black. "The fucking asshole says Gabrielle lost her temper and punched him. Broke his nose. He spent the night in an ER, waiting to get it set."

Campbell stared. "He left her and didn't call in?"

"What kind of training do your agents have?" Marcus snapped.

Galen took the verbal hit without wincing. "He thought the investigation was over. Last night an agent assigned to another decoy caught a man attacking a woman behind the St. Pete club. The woman was knocked unconscious during the fight, and Thompson believed he'd got the unsub. He called Rhodes to gloat."

"It wasn't the kidnapper?" Zachary asked, already knowing the answer.

"Just a couple from the club wanting to play out a rape scenario. Once the woman woke up and explained, we released the man. But Thompson didn't bother to call Rhodes back."

"So Rhodes is free and clear?" Marcus's hands had fisted. Zachary gave him a warning look.

"No, Marcus," Vance said. "No matter what, he should have arranged coverage for her. We'll deal with him later."

Marcus stilled and visibly forced himself to relax. "I overreacted, gentlemen. Please forgive me."

Galen gave him a thin smile. "Consider him dead meat, Marcus. You have my word."

Zachary turned and paced back across the room, his need to do something ratcheting up another notch. Do anything—take the car and yell their names at every corner. *Dammit, Jessica.*

With the noise of the various conversations, Zachary at first didn't hear the music coming from the bedroom. Mangione's "Feels So Good." His cell's ringtone. "No!"

He tore across the apartment, shoved the door open, tripping over the cats and somehow managing to kick the door shut behind him before they escaped. He grabbed his jacket from the bed and yanked the cell out of the pocket.

The ringing stopped. *No, dammit.*

He flipped the phone open. One message. He almost listened, then forced himself to return to the others before punching Play.

"Z." Gabrielle's voice. Hoarse. Strained.

"Silence!" he snapped at the others. He set it on speaker and turned the volume up.

"He got us—me and Jessica. Taser and drugs. We're in a big van—cargo-sized. A boat is picking us up at the Clearwater Docks, downtown, in about two hours." Zachary heard a whisper. Jessica's voice saying something about tattoos. His heart thumped hard enough to hurt. She was *alive.*

Gabi's message continued, "Two men. They call each other Cesar and Jang. Jang has gang tattoos covering his arms. Don't call this number back. It's their phone."

Silence.

Galen was already on the phone, barking orders. Vance had his cell out but paused to look at Marcus and Z. "Most women would be in hysterics. Those two are keeping it together. Thinking. Give me a brat any day." He handed Zachary a slip of paper with a number scrawled on it. "Forward the message to this number for a sound analysis. I doubt we'll get anything useful, but we'll try."

Zachary nodded.

Marcus tapped his fingers on the table for a second. Then he glanced at Zachary and lowered his voice. "I'm not waiting for them to say I can't help. I'm leaving now."

Zachary checked the agents, occupied with their planning. "I'll drive."

CHAPTER TWENTY-ONE

Chuffing mufflers, whining motors, the screech of brakes. A car horn. Gabi knew they'd reached the city. The van slowed, sped up, slowed, jarring the cuffs on her wrists, making them burn. More blood trickled down her arm.

Jang stepped into the cargo section, leaving the door open. Holding a rag and a roll of duct tape, he walked over to her.

Her heart hammered against her ribs. They were in the city, people around. Probably going too fast for anyone to hear them. Still... *Don't miss a chance. We'll die anyway*. She screamed as loud as she could, and Jessica joined her a second later.

He backhanded Gabi. Her head snapped back, her cheek flaring with pain.

Then he kicked Jessica in the stomach. Her groan made him laugh before he turned back to Gabi.

"Watch the merchandise, asshole," Cesar yelled.

Her face on fire with pain, Gabi struggled, jamming her shoulder against him, trying to knock him away. Jang seized her jaw and forced her mouth open. He stuffed a filthy rag in. Despite her attempts to head butt him, he got several strips of duct tape across her face, muffling her completely. When he stood up, she managed to twist far and fast enough to kick his knee. He shouted and staggered back.

With a filthy curse, he evaded her feet and slapped her hard to the floor. Her head struck, a hammer blow reverberating in her brain.

His boot caught her in the ribs. A firebomb of pain burst through her. She retched and choked, unable to inhale.

"If you puke with a gag on, you'll die, bitch." He watched for a second, grinning, then cuffed her hands behind her back.

Too dizzy to sit up, Gabi lay on her side, lungs heaving for air. *Don't throw up*. She could only breathe though her nose. *I'm suffocating...* Stars filled her vision. *Slow breath. Slow breath*. More stars wheeled in the black sky. *Helpless.*

Jang had moved to Jessica, but Gabi couldn't help. She heard a thud and a high cry of pain, then footsteps. Gabi lay still, heart rate easing as she drew air in. Carefully. *Don't panic.*

A few minutes later, the van pulled to a halt, and the engine stopped.

"The boat here?" Jang asked.

"They haven't called yet. The storm probably slowed them down. At least the rain will cut down the number of people on the docks."

We're at the docks. Once on a boat, there'd be no escape. *God.* Gabi's fear rose until she strangled with it, but she pushed it away. If she panicked, she'd die. *Think, stupid*. Could she get to her feet?

"Box the redhead first," Cesar said.

"No fucking ankle cuffs, remember?"

"Hell." Cesar narrowed his eyes and stared a second. "Use duct tape and the chain. Hogtie them."

"Got it." Jang turned to Gabi. Too nauseated to fight back, she lay still as he did a couple of turns of duct tape around her ankles. He used the chain to secure her feet close to the handcuffs. "Done."

She tried to wiggle, tried to move, and had to force panic

down again. Jessica met her gaze, and she gave Gabi a sharp nod. Not giving up yet. Neither would Gabi.

"One little trip left, chickies, and then you can scream yourselves blue," Cesar said from the driver's seat.

You bastard.

"We gonna have some time before the boat shows?" Jang asked.

"You think your dick's going to work by then?" Cesar gave a nasty laugh.

Jang touched his crotch gingerly and growled something foul.

Please let his cock stay limp. She stared at his crotch. As long as she was wishing, let it rot and fall off too. *Please.*

Cesar stepped into the cargo area, sliding a pistol into one coverall pocket. He pulled the washing machine labels off the sides of the box, leaving only THIS SIDE UP markings. "Let's get her loaded."

He grabbed Gabi under the shoulders, Jang grabbed under her thighs, and they hefted her up. They lowered her most of the way into the box, then dropped her the last couple of feet, knocking the air out of her. Lights danced in her vision until she managed a breath.

"Tape it shut?" Jang asked, leering down at her, lips pulled back to show yellowing teeth.

I'm so glad I kicked your balls into your throat.

"Slap on a couple of strips to keep the top closed. I don't want to fuck around with peeling tape off between loads."

The flaps shut, leaving her in darkness. Her heart hammered, and blood pounded in her veins so loudly she barely heard Jang apply the tape to the top.

"Fucking shitheads, if they got delayed, they should have called." Cesar's voice came faintly through the box.

Take your time, boat. Gabi arched backward until her spine felt as if it would snap, and managed to touch the duct tape wrapped around her ankles. She inched a finger along the tape, swearing silently. The chain holding her wrists to her ankles had rolled much of the tape over, rendering it untearable. Dammit. *I only need an inch or two—and a little time.*

A cell phone rang. "Yeah." Cesar's voice. "Got it. Be right there."

"They're here?"

"Tying up now," Cesar said, satisfaction thick in his voice.

Boots thumped into the cargo area, and Gabi heard the rattle as the back of the van slid up.

"Get the ramp. I'll take her and tell them I got an extra," Cesar said. "Have Blondie ready to go for when I get back."

Dammit. Gabi wanted to groan—she'd just found an uncurled area of the duct tape. She ripped at it.

The box tilted, dislodging her grip. They'd put it onto the hand trolley, Gabi realized. She frantically tried again as things scraped on the box—straps securing it. The floor of the box came up, sliding her sideways, as the trolly thumped down the ramp. She heard a metallic rattle as someone pulled the van door down.

Soft tapping noises confused her. Rain? She twisted to reach the tape again. The cart rolled erratically, ruining her grip.

Eventually the grating of wheels on the street changed, and she heard the lapping of water. They'd reached the dock.

God, she was out of time. The cart bumped over something, tilting slightly, and she blinked. *Maybe...*

Motion stopped. Low voices.

Gabi squirmed until her feet faced forward, then rolled over her cuffed hands to hit the side of the box with her knees and head. The cart rocked slightly. She rolled back to thump harder into the other side.

The box dented. Cesar cursed.

The Clearwater Downtown Docks were way too big. Cursing under his breath, Marcus wiped rain out of his eyes. Thunder rumbled, drowning out the hum of traffic on the Memorial Causeway Bridge that loomed high over the waterside. He could feel time disappearing, and his gut knotted more with each unrecoverable minute.

How the hell was he supposed to differentiate a boat doing the pickup from an innocent one? Despite the weather, the place was busy—mostly Sunday sailors and those that knew a good rainstorm helped fishing.

A yacht chugged away in a billow of blue-gray smoke. He stiffened. What if Gabi was on board? If they were too late?

He saw Vance and other agents on the adjacent docks. He and Z had already been prowling the wharf when the FBI had arrived. Accepting the inevitable, Vance had given them assignments. Z to the south parking lot, another agent to the north to search for the cargo van among the daunting number of vehicles. After seeing the size of the waterfront, Galen had gotten back in his car to call in the Clearwater police.

Glancing at craft after craft, Marcus kept walking. At the end slip, two men in dark green slickers and jeans finished tying up their fishing boat. One stepped onto the dock and leaned against a concrete post, arms folded.

Marcus studied the vessel for a minute. Lower hatch open. Nothing showed inside. No noises. And he knew anything and anyone might be stashed in there. With a growing sense of despair, he headed back.

A man in a coverall, pushing a box on a hand trolley, veered around him.

Marcus nodded to him and stopped after a few steps. *That's a very big box*. He turned.

The man from the fishing boat stepped forward to greet the delivery man. As they shook hands, the box on the trolley rocked slightly, and one side dented outward.

The man cursed and slapped his hand on the box.

Fury raged through Marcus, searing the blood in his veins. He hesitated—if he yelled, the boat would get away. But he couldn't risk them loading whoever was in the box...

"Here!" he roared, the sound echoing across the water. "Vance, here!"

As the men turned, he slammed into both, knocking them away from the box. They staggered back. The hand trolley tipped over, landing right on the edge of the dock. A cart wheel caught, hung for a second, and the weight of the box dragged it toward the water below.

God. Marcus made a frantic grab for the wheel, seized it, and yanked the trolley and the strapped-on box back. The cart clanged onto the concrete dock. From the corner of his eyes, he saw a pipe swinging straight for his head. He jerked back. The metal grazed his skull. Pain exploded in his head, and his vision sheeted to red. He lurched sideways.

From instinct alone, he managed to block the next blow, spotted another incoming, and kicked the man in a coverall to his knees.

"Here! Vance here!" Zachary spun toward Marcus's shouts. Hope outraced the rush of adrenaline.

A man near the end of the parking lot stepped out of a van to stare at the docks. Tank top—tattooed arms. Zachary broke into a run.

The man spotted him. He swung back into the cab and slammed the door shut.

Zachary tore across the lot. "Galen! Over here!" Too far, dammit, too far. The van started with a roar and backed out of the parking space. Tires squealed as the truck accelerated toward the exit lane at the end.

Zachary cursed. He'd never catch it. Sirens wailed in the distance—too far away.

Nearing the end, the van swerved sharply, skidded, and rammed into a parked car. And stalled.

What the hell? Zachary raced toward the van. He heard the *rrrr* of an attempt to start the engine. Through the side window, he saw the driver. Blood trickled from his nose.

A foot materialized out of nowhere and booted the man in the face. Two people. One in the passenger seat.

Zachary slid into the side of the van with a hard thud. He pulled open the driver's door.

The driver struck at him backhanded.

Grabbing the arm, Zachary yanked him out onto the pavement. The man staggered, caught himself. Spinning around, he punched.

Zachary blocked the incompetent blow, seized his arm, twisted up and back. A crunch of bone and gristle—dislocated.

Screaming in pain, the guy swung blindly. Taking a quick side step, Zachary buried his fist in a soft belly. With an explosive grunt, the driver folded in half. Zachary rammed his knee into the guy's face.

Another crunch. Another scream. And not nearly enough.

His knee had straightened the bastard up sufficiently for another punch. Zachary was happy to oblige. He channeled his rage in a fist to the ribs. The satisfying crackle of bones breaking, caving in—and the way the man's eyes rolled back in his head—dissipated Zachary's fury.

The bastard fell. Out cold.

The harsh snapping of gunfire coming from the docks tightened his gut. Marcus hadn't been armed. But Zachary's job was here.

He stepped toward the driver's side. Cautiously. He'd recognized those feet, and his kitten would be pretty upset.

Blonde hair in a tangle, Jessica lay half-sprawled across the passenger seat. Hands behind her back. Duct tape over her mouth. Green eyes blazing. Legs up, ready to kick a man into hell and beyond.

Damn, he loved her.

She saw him, and her eyes widened. The look she gave him—fury and relief and love...oh yes, there was love there—made his world right again.

He inclined his head and smiled. "Rough day, huh?"

She choked on a hysterical-sounding laugh, obviously recognizing the question from the night they'd first met.

Swinging into the cab, he helped her sit up. His fury ignited again at the bruises on her cheek, the ripped skin on her wrists. But she was alive. Safe. He buried his face in her hair for a self-indulgent moment.

Gabi'd heard Marcus shouting before her box had gone crazy, toppling and spinning and swinging. Her head still whirled. Her shoulder sockets felt wrenched from landing on her cuffed hands. The box lay on its side, and cracks of light showed through the torn flaps.

Was Marcus really here?

Must get out. She inched her fingers down the duct tape again. There, an intact edge. Fighting the handcuffs, she managed to get the tape between her fingertips and ripped. It tore—*oh God, yes*! The chain, looped around the cuffs and tape, came loose.

Frantic with the need to get free, she scissored her legs to peel the rest of the torn tape from her ankles. Her wrists were still cuffed behind her, but *move, move, move*. She squirmed to the end of the box and kicked the flaps. The top burst open, and Gabi rolled out.

Too much light. Her skull blared with pain. Rain splattered against her. On the wharf, men were yelling and running toward the docks. She turned her head. Cesar sprawled on the dock near her. Farther away, men fighting. Grunts and curses. The figures blurred, cleared.

Marcus. A man in a slicker swung a thick metal pipe at him, and Gabi screamed behind the gag.

No, please, no. She struggled to rise. The blow missed Marcus somehow, and he hit the man, knocking him back.

In front of Gabi, Cesar pushed to his feet and drew the pistol from his coverall.

No! Gabi pulled her legs under her and dove at Cesar. Her shoulder slammed into the back of his knees. His legs buckled, and he yelled as he toppled backward.

A ton of weight landed on her back, almost yanking her arms from the sockets. Her knees scraped the concrete. Mouth still taped, she struggled for air.

"Bitch." Cesar rolled off, lunged for the pistol just out of his reach. Sucking in air, she twisted and kicked his leg, sending him to his knees. A moment of satisfaction.

Face contorted with rage, he lurched toward her. *Oh God*. She rolled frantically away, over her bound arms.

"Gabi!" Marcus yanked her to her feet and whirled her aside. A pipe flew past her head. A man turned and ran toward a boat slowly pulling out of the slip.

Dizzy, Gabi staggered sideways. She caught her balance and turned back toward the men. Her breath stopped as Cesar pointed the pistol directly at her. "You fucking cunt."

"Fucking cunt." Hands tearing her clothing, yelling horrible names... Gabi's body froze as her brain went blank. Marcus's yell, "Gabi, down!" hit the surface of her mind and bounced away.

A brutal shove knocked her to one side. She hit the ground hard, breaking the paralysis. Marcus blocked her view of Cesar.

The sharp crack of a pistol shattered the air. Marcus made a low, horrible sound and jolted back, turning slightly. Blood, terrifyingly red, stained his light shirt. Growing bigger.

Nooo.

Snapping sounds like a multitude of fireworks deafened her, and Cesar screamed. He fell.

Cursing and yelling. Men—many men—thudded down the dock.

Marcus. She tried to sit up, failed, tried again. *Oh please.*

Cesar lay, eyes open. A uniformed cop stopped beside him, then kicked the pistol farther away. Another man yelled for an ambulance.

Still standing, Marcus had his hand pressed to his shoulder, and blood in a nightmarish flood flowed between his fingers. *He's hurt. God no*. Gabi choked, rolled onto her knees, trying frantically to stand with legs that had no strength.

Someone grabbed her shoulders, holding her. *Hands touching her. No no no*. A tidal wave of terror took her, and she fought blindly, yanking her wrists, unable to scream.

The hands released her. She was free...and Marcus was there, his face filling her vision. She blinked. Not dreaming. Rain ran down her cheeks like tears as his warm fingers curled around her bare shoulder.

"Easy, sugar. It's over. You're safe, sweetheart." His voice, like no one else's, convinced her.

Her heart still raced, but she could only stare at him. *He's alive*. She tried to talk and choked on the gag.

"Bastards," he said under his breath, as he peeled the duct tape off her lips ever so slowly.

"Sir, you're hurt." A man bobbed at his elbow.

"In a minute." Marcus pulled the rag out of her mouth. When she sucked in air, his eyes crinkled at the edges. "There, now you can sass all you want."

As he touched her face with gentle fingers, someone knelt behind her and gripped her arms. She jerked, trying to escape, but Marcus held her shoulders, murmuring, "Easy, Gabi."

Handcuffs. The man was unlocking her handcuffs. She held

still, barely breathing, ignoring the pain as he pulled away the metal that had dug into her flesh. "There you go, sweetie." She knew that voice.

As she brought her arms forward, the wrench of agony in her shoulders mattered not at all. *Free.*

Vance stepped out from behind her. "I want a blanket for this woman, and get this man to the hospital," he shouted. "You asshole," he said to Marcus. "Sit down before you fall down."

He looked so white.

Gabi sat next to Marcus's bed with her arm pushed through the side rails so she could hold his hand. He had intravenous lines in his arm, and wires ran to a monitor showing his heart rate. She tried not to stare at the display, terrified the lines would suddenly go straight like they did in the movies.

But he'd made it through surgery, right? If he was in danger, the doctor'd have sent him to the ICU, not a surgical unit. *Right?*

"God, I hate hospitals," she whispered to him. "Wake up, dammit. They said you woke up in recovery. Do it again."

It had been a long, long day. When Marcus had been wheeled out of the emergency room, she'd pulled out her IV and followed. Sitting in the surgery waiting room, she'd stared at the television set and had seen horror instead. The gun. "*Gabi, down*!" Marcus stepping in front of her. Staggering back. The blood.

My fault.

When his grandparents had arrived, the nurses had freely offered up information about the progress of the surgery, so Gabi had moved closer to eavesdrop. She'd regretted it when the older couple started discussing the girlfriend they'd met in June, Celine, and arguing whether to call her. Thank God, the grandfather had said no.

The waiting had been interminable. Unable to sit still, she'd cuddled a teenage girl whose mother was in surgery after a car accident, then comforted an old woman whose husband wasn't likely to survive.

After Marcus left the recovery room, his grandparents had sat with him for a while, then gone to make calls and get something to eat...and Gabi had slipped in.

Would he ever wake up?

Voices in the hallway caught her attention. Galen's clipped New England accent and Vance's rumbling baritone. *Damn them.* They were undoubtedly looking for her and would drag her back to the emergency room to finish getting treated. But she couldn't leave Marcus. Not yet. Not until she saw him awake.

So maybe she wasn't firing on all cylinders right now, but she didn't care. He had to wake up. She had to say she was sorry.

She limped into the tiny bathroom to hide. Too dizzy to stand long, she sat on the toilet and waited.

Once they left, she resumed her vigil. She stayed upright, afraid of falling asleep. Her head felt like someone was pounding on it with a mallet. Her jaw didn't want to open. She fingered it and winced. With every movement, her shoulders screamed as if they were hinges that had rusted shut after a decade in the rain. And her ribs... Well, although the X-rays said cracked, not broken, she sure couldn't tell the difference. Damn Jang anyway.

None of her injuries compared to a bullet in the shoulder. "I'm sorry, Marcus. So, so sorry."

If she hadn't frozen, if she'd jumped away, he wouldn't have stepped in front of her and gotten shot. She put her head into her hands and moaned. *Be all right, please. Just be all right.* Once she saw him awake, she'd leave and do whatever Galen and Vance needed. She wouldn't stay—he wouldn't want to see her.

She was just another trainee. One he'd felt he had to protect. *He could have died.*

More minutes ticked by.

Marcus groaned.

Gabi jerked upright and moaned as pain battered her nerves. She leaned forward, her hand clamping around his.

His eyelids fluttered. He looked at her, his gaze unfocused. But awake. Alive.

Thank you, God. Oh thank you.

She managed to stand. Bracing herself on the side rail, she touched his face. Warm. She ran her finger over the scratchy beard stubble, slightly darker than his hair, and traced a darkening bruise on his forehead. Beat-up...but alive.

His eyes cleared, and he frowned at the room, the IV stand, and the monitors.

"You're in the hospital," she told him, her guilt so heavy she had trouble speaking. "You got shot—because of me. But you're going to be fine."

When she released his fingers, his hand turned over to capture hers. He tried to speak, then cleared his throat. His voice rasped, the smoothness gone. "Are you all right?"

She choked. "Oh yeah. You're the one who got shot." Her throat constricted until her voice sounded as rough as his. "It should have been me. I'm sorry, so sorry."

He tried to say something, but she couldn't take more. She brushed a kiss to his cheek. "Good-bye, Marcus," she whispered.

She limped out of the room as fast as she could. With relief, she spotted his grandparents coming down the hall. He wouldn't be alone. Averting her gaze, she made for the elevators. A wave of dizziness crashed over her, and blackness edged the corners of her vision. *No. Passing out not allowed, Gabi.*

Everything was finished now. The case. Her stay in Tampa. Her time with Marcus.

She wanted to go home.

CHAPTER TWENTY-TWO

The sound of songbirds in the garden drifted in through the open window of Zachary's bedroom, and he smiled at the peaceful melodies.

Snuggled in the bedding, Jessica breathed slowly, still deep in sleep. One half-curled hand nestled under a round cheek. Her long golden hair spilled over the pillow, the light strands glowing against the dark fabric.

Just as she glowed like a beacon in his dark life. He pulled his chair closer and wrapped his hand around her delicate fingers. Did she have any clue how much she meant to him? He worked with children, sad, broken, abused children who'd seen more horror in their short lives than most adults. Sometimes to heal, they needed to know someone—anyone—understood their sorrow and rage and confusion. He'd listen. He'd take in their pain and relieve them of some of the burden.

But pain accumulated, and even the love of friends and family hadn't been able to lift his increasing sadness. Then Jessica erupted like a small hurricane into his life. Her keen intelligence and logical mind was balanced by her spirit, her courage—and her love. She reminded him that the world held as much good as it did evil.

God, he'd almost lost her today. His shoulders tightened. Leaning forward, he pushed her hair away from her face. Silky hair—soft, soft cheek.

When she blinked, he cursed himself for his lack of discipline. She needed the sleep.

Her hands fisted, and she stiffened. He felt her fear, saw it overwhelm her.

"Jessica," he said in a level, clear voice.

Her eyes focused on his face, and he saw—felt—relief flood through her. "You're safe, kitten," he said, affirming it verbally.

She pulled in a breath, looked at the room, the bed, the window. When her eyes met his again, her smile blossomed. "You saved me."

"I think you might have managed to save yourself."

She considered it, his logical sub, and shook her head. "No. If you hadn't come, he'd have won eventually. I was cuffed. Even if I'd gotten out of the van, I couldn't run. Not after hurting my ankle." She pouted. "I'd like to think I sprained it when I kicked his face, but I think the steering wheel did it."

"Bloodthirsty little sub," Zachary murmured.

"Oh sure. I saw Jang after you got through. I didn't do nearly as much damage."

Zachary's hands closed as if he had the man's neck in his grasp. He should have bloodied him a little more.

She smiled at him, her green eyes glinting with laughter. "I'm afraid you're going to have to be a hero. Saving the subs like a proper dom."

Saving. He frowned. "You shouldn't have needed saving or been anywhere near those men. Jessica, why did you leave last night without speaking to me?"

He caught a flash of *oh shit* before she stalled. "Well." Obviously needing to be on a more equal level, she pushed up in the bed and winced.

Dammit. He couldn't stand seeing her in pain. Grasping her under the arms, he gently pulled her up in the bed and tucked pillows behind her back. Her face had paled. Nonetheless, he couldn't put off this talk any longer. They'd had enough silence between them. His jaw clenched. If she wanted to leave, he needed to know. "Now tell me. Why?"

She looked down and fingered the abrasions from the damned metal handcuffs the kidnapper had used. "Things had... You haven't been the same. For a while. You've acted so...distant. And mad at me. Every time I sassed you or anyone at the club, you'd gag me as if you didn't want to hear me. I knew you were unhappy. I thought it was because of me."

"But—"

"No, Zachary, let me finish."

Zachary. He rarely heard her use his real name. Usually only in bed or when she was moved, as if it had special meaning to her. He took her hand. Everything in him wanted to object that she'd not understood, to coax her to let him fix it and make it right, to help her understand their relationship wasn't broken completely. Instead he tilted his head and kept silent.

"I saw you with Gabi. I could tell you had a secret, the two of you. And you treated her...differently...than the other subs. Almost like you treat me."

He frowned. "I don't understand."

"The amount of caring you show me...her...is exponentially higher," said his little mathematician. "More protective."

"But—"

She stared at her hands again. "And then I met your sons." She bit her lip. "Eric doesn't approve of me. He obviously thinks you should find someone more—more like you. I'm just an accountant, from a middle-class family. I'm not rich or sophisticated or beautiful, and I've seen pictures of your ex. She is. If Eric can't get you back with his mother, he wants you to have someone classier...and older."

He nodded. Eric saw first with his eyes, not his heart.

"So. I felt like you'd pulled away, not wanting me around—you even told me not to come to the club—and I was jealous. And insecure. I thought maybe you had second thoughts about being with me."

Past tense. She'd used the past tense. "You know differently now, don't you?"

"Some. I understand about Gabi being a decoy, and you wanted to keep me from getting targeted. But that still doesn't... Nolan and Beth are engaged. Dan and Kari are married and having a baby. And they all met after we did."

He rubbed his face. The best-meant ideas didn't always work out in the way a person expected. "Jessica, as my boy so kindly pointed out, I'm older than you are. I have grown children. You're just starting your life, kitten, and I don't want to push you into something you might regret. Especially since a person first entering the lifestyle can confuse the desire to be dominated with desire for the dom."

She stared at him for a moment, and then her eyes narrowed. "We can't have a relationship because you think I'm too young? God, Z, I'm thirty. How old do I have to be to know my own mind?"

The sparks lighting her eyes delighted him—she was rapidly returning to normal—but he had enough experience with women to realize that if he smiled, she'd throw something at him. "I might have been overly cautious," he admitted.

"I'd say so. I'm still here, aren't I? I know where the door is, and I know how to say 'no thanks.' You're being stupid. Get over it."

He sat back in his chair, a bit stunned. Her cheeks had flushed with—ah, that was definitely anger. And there wasn't a single doubt in her mind. *Well, then.*

Uh, oh. He'd gotten a look on his face that boded no good for her, yet everything in her rejoiced because the expression wasn't that of a man who was bored with his girlfriend, but the possessive look of a dom.

She winced. Had she really called him stupid?

"Let me see if I have this straight," he said in a chillingly smooth voice. "You want a commitment. And do you want children to go with that?"

She sputtered. "You make it sound like, 'Here's your order. Do you want fries with that?'"

He raised an eyebrow.

"Yes, I want fries—I mean children. With you." Telling him about her hopes made her feel as if she stood naked on a cliff in a cold wind. Why could they discuss everything else, but this...this seemed harder? "I want at least one baby, maybe two. And considering how rude one of your kids is, I'll probably do a better job of motherhood than your ex."

His lips twitched as if he'd started to smile. But this baring the soul was too one-sided, and she faltered. "W-would you want more children?"

He steepled his fingers and gave her a level look over the top. "Jessica, I work with children. I like children. And I'd enjoy actually being present this time. I've always regretted being out of the country so much when Eric and Richard were growing up."

Oh. She breathed out as her ballooning anxiety started to deflate. "Really?"

"Really. And maybe I should add that Eric asked me to convey his apologies for his rudeness." Z smiled. "He'll come around, kitten. Now go on, give me the rest."

The rest. She mustered her thoughts, lined up his objections. Her wants had been tabulated; she needed to sum it all up. Like their ages. *The idiot*. "Okay, you're older. Not much, really. And considering you love staying in shape and I refuse to run, we'll probably get all old and crippled at the same time. If not, then

I'll learn to use a cane, and I'll get to beat on your ass for a change."

He laughed, actually laughed, and she grinned. Maybe her hopes wouldn't materialize, but she felt the healing between them, the sense of rightness return.

"You are an awful submissive," he said softly. "Quite the brat. Are you going to also address that small problem of yours now?"

She hunched her shoulders. He was tired of her mouthiness, wasn't he? Her hopes shriveled. Then she remembered what Gabi had said: "*No wonder Z adores you.*" The jerk was playing his psychology tricks on her. She pushed her hair back over her shoulder and wrinkled her nose at him. "Nope. You like me as I am."

He shook his head, smiling faintly. "No, Jessica—I love you as you are." He rose and stripped the covers right off her, and she realized he'd removed her clothes when he'd helped her to bed. She squeaked and instinctively grabbed for the sheet.

Grasping her forearms, avoiding the sore spots from the cuffs, he looked into her eyes. "I won't restrain you...today...since you've had enough of that. Instead, you will turn over and kneel. Hold on to the head of the bed. Open your legs to me. For every time you move from that position, I'll add another swat from Mistress Anne's favorite paddle."

She winced. The domme had a paddle with MINE carved out, so a smack not only pinkened a butt cheek but left raised white areas spelling out the word. He watched, his jaw stern, as she rolled over onto her knees and grabbed the headboard.

"Wider, Jessica."

Oh, God. But she felt moisture gather between her legs and how her heart rate hammered. She looked over her shoulder and saw his gray eyes darken with pleasure as he looked at her. Her excitement skyrocketed. His ruthless hands opened her even more widely, and then he touched her, running his fingers through her folds, teasing her clit until she squirmed. Dammit, a year ago he'd scared her with how well he could play her body. Now he was terrifying.

She heard him unbuckle his belt and open his slacks. He came up behind her, his knees between hers. The coarse hair on his thighs teased her buttocks. Oh God, she needed him so badly, she whimpered.

He pulled her back against his chest, turning her slightly. Threading his fingers in her hair, he tethered her as he took her mouth, his lips firm, his kiss blatantly hard and possessive until she felt as if she was drowning in sensation. Held by his fist in her hair, his mouth, she couldn't move as his free hand played with her breasts. He teased her until they swelled, and each pinch of her nipples sent a sizzling current of electricity to her pussy.

Until her need stretched out past endurance. She burned. When her bottom pushed back against his thick erection, he freed her lips long enough to let her whine. "Pleeease."

His almost painful grip on her hair kept her head tilted up and back as he studied her for a long moment. Her sex throbbed in time with her pulse; her urgency grew. Then he rubbed his cheek against hers. "I believe I'd like to hear more begging first." And he released her hair, sliding his hand to her pussy instead. He caged her there, one hand rolling her nipples as his other traced figure eights around her clit and entrance. *Too light, dammit.*

He changed to firm, slow strokes. *Too slow, dammit*. Sadistically, he drove her upward at a snail's pace until she reached the edge, her legs trembling, her head back against his shoulder, her hands white-knuckled from trying not to shift position.

"God, please."

His finger paused and then resumed circling her clit. She pushed her hips forward. If he'd just go over the top of it...

He released her breast and set his hard arm across her pelvis, pinning her tightly against him, permitting her bottom no movement at all. His finger circled again.

Her whole body shook. "I can't take it anymore. Please." She used her ultimate weapon. "Master, please, I love you..."

His low, satisfied laugh almost sent her over. "Clever little sub," he murmured in her ear and nipped her earlobe. When he took his hand from her pussy, she groaned in frustration.

"Shhh." He swirled his cock in her wetness and brushed the velvety head against her clit.

Oh yes. She held her breath. *Please please please.*

And then he drove into her with a long, heavy thrust, filling her to the point of pain.

"Aaaah." So thick and hard and... She strangled on the next cry, panting at the incredible feeling of him, at the way her body melted under his firm hands.

Merciless thrusts bent her forward. Only her grip on the headboard and his iron-hard arm across her pelvis kept her upright. He pushed her knees farther apart and set a finger on either side of her clit so each powerful thrust tightened the skin over it and sent forks of desperate pleasure careening through her body. Her toes curled, and her fingernails squeezed the headboard, the need to come building higher.

Something was different, but she couldn't think, her attention narrowed until she felt only his fingers stroking over her clit and the thick, hot slide of his cock. He held her right at the edge as she shook uncontrollably.

"Tradition says a man should be on his knees when he proposes," he murmured in her ear and pushed farther inside her until she moaned.

Wait. "What?"

"I'm a traditional man, after all." He kissed the little spot right under her ear, sending goose bumps over her skin. "I love you, kitten. Will you marry me?"

He drove into her harder, until she felt the jolt of each thrust deep in her belly. And then he slowed, leaving her teetering on the precipice of an orgasm. "Answer me now, Jessica."

Her vision blurred as she only clung to this world by her fingertips. *Oh God.* "Yes. Yes, yes."

"Excellent." His rhythm changed. His thick cock stretched her with each deep plunge. Each time he pulled back, his finger would slide up and over her clit. Her engorged nub tightened more and more, and her pussy clenched around him. Her orgasm rolled toward her, as inevitable as the turning of the tide.

She poised on the crest for one agonizing second, and then her insides exploded into pleasure so intense the room blurred and only his hard hands seemed to hold her in this universe. She convulsed around him, wave after wave consuming her until even her fingers tingled with the sensations.

As she gasped for air, he murmured into her ear, "However, when we're old, I will still keep the cane."

Her choked laugh turned to a yelp when he pinched her clit... and she came again.

A second later, he drove into her far enough to bump against her womb. His hands tightened on her hips. As he pulsed inside her and his heat filled her, she realized what had changed.

She'd heard no crinkling sound of a condom wrapper. His cock felt different—velvety and hot and *real.*

His big hand splayed over her abdomen, and in a dangerously low voice, he murmured, "We'll get started on those children right away."

"Good morning, Mr. Atherton."

Marcus forced his eyes open. A figure blurred, then came into focus. A gray-haired nurse, wearing green scrubs with pink dancing bears. She pulled his covers down to his waist. White gauze dressings covered his shoulder, and it hurt.

Some of the fog cleared from his brain. He'd been shot. Had surgery. His mouth felt like it had the day after he'd discovered tequila. "Uh." He swallowed and tried again. "Good morning. What time is it?"

She nodded at a clock on the wall. "Still early. My name is Mary, and I'm your nurse today. Your doctor should be in soon to do the first dressing change. Can you give me a number for how much pain you're in—on a scale of one to ten, where one is almost nothing?"

His shoulder hurt like hell. "About a three."

She gave a gravelly laugh. "You men. Try again and be honest this time."

With a wry smile, he admitted, "Seven." She'd make a good domme.

"'Bout what I figured." She held up a little device attached to the IV. "I showed you this yesterday, but I doubt if you remember." She pushed the button. "I just gave you a dose, and you should feel better in a minute or two. Next time, when your pain hits around four or so, push the button. It won't let you punch it too many times, so you can't overdose. Got it?"

He nodded and realized his head hurt too. Damn pipe-wielding bastard.

"Breakfast will arrive shortly. And your grandparents said they'd visit this morning, if you don't remember."

He frowned. Had Gabi been with him? "Was anyone else here yesterday?"

"Oh yes." She smiled. "A very beat-up and exhausted young woman kept you company from the minute your grandparents left the room until they returned."

The pleasure that she'd cared enough to watch over him was swamped by his concern. "She should have been in a hospital bed herself."

"She wasn't about to budge. She even dodged the Feds looking for her."

"Stubborn little brat," he muttered.

The nurse smiled and turned her attention to getting his

temperature and checking his lungs. By the time she left, the pain medication had kicked in, and he sighed in relief. Nasty things, bullets. They'd been lucky though; he and Gabi could easily have died. Instead she was battered but alive. And this hole in his shoulder would heal up fast enough.

For a few minutes, he worked on separating his anesthetic-induced dreams from reality. Too much of yesterday seemed like a nightmare—his fear that they'd arrive too late, that Gabi'd be hurt. The box sliding off the dock. Hell, it had all been too close. Another couple of minutes and the boat would have left with her on it. The thought darkened the room for a moment.

He touched the side of his head, fingering the tender lump. He owed his little trainee his life. Instead of giving up, she'd not only gotten free but flung herself to his rescue. He chuckled, remembering how the bastard had toppled when she tackled him. So brave. No cringing on the ground for his spitfire.

Or going into hysterics afterward. He still couldn't believe she'd sneaked in here to check on him. She had incredible loyalty and courage—qualities he'd not considered essential in a lover—but perhaps his vision had been narrow.

He glanced at the door. Dammit, he wanted to see for himself that she was all right.

He frowned at the memory of her in his room. Blood on a swollen lip, her cheek scraped and raw. Whispering to him, asking him to wake up. "*Sorry...*" Had she said she was sorry? For what?

"*It should have been me.*" His mouth tightened as her low husky voice sang through his memories. What the hell did that mean? His eyes narrowed. She'd kissed him...and said good-bye. Not *See you later*. Not *I'll visit tomorrow. "Good-bye."*

An ominous feeling took up residence in his gut. Spotting a phone, he reached over, stifled a groan when he jarred his shoulder, then dialed. Her number rang and rang before a recording stated it was no longer in service.

He scowled, trying to think despite the fogginess from the

pain meds. Her phone... Ah, she'd probably received it for the decoy job. He stiffened. What about her apartment? Was she even in Tampa?

"Hey there, boy." His grandfather stepped into the room and stopped for a thorough scrutiny. A smile creased his leathery face. "You look better today."

"Thank you, sir." Marcus smiled and held his hand out to shake.

His grandmother followed, bending to give him a gentle hug and kiss. Her eyes teared up. "We were so worried," she said, smiling at him. "Your mama called."

"I hope you told them not to come. Marissa needs them more." On complete bed rest in the last month of her pregnancy and with two children under five, his sister needed all the help she could get.

"They agreed only if we both call them daily."

"That'll work."

"Since when do attorneys involve themselves in shoot-outs, boy?" Ex-Judge Atherton pulled up a chair, obviously preparing to show he hadn't lost a jot of his cross-examination skills since retirement.

"Complicated story." How to explain his relationship with Gabrielle? "A woman I...know...was kidnapped, and a friend and I assisted in locating her." Not a bad summary, he decided, then screwed it up by adding, "A bullet is a small price to pay to get her back."

His grandmother's eyes widened. "Really? Is she the woman we met last June? Celine?"

Marcus smothered a smile. When Celine had joined them for dinner one evening, his grandparents had been...polite. Their reaction to her had added weight to his decision to step back. He didn't want a surface-sweet, manipulative woman; he wanted one who'd yell at him to his face, one who could keep him as fascinated as Gramps was with Nana.

In the lifestyle, his grandmother would be known as a brat. "No, Nana, you haven't met her."

"Are we likely to?" she asked bluntly.

He smiled at the thought of a meeting. Gabi had an effect on others like the spring sun on flowers, and it wasn't because she was a pushover, but because she liked people. Despite her sassy mouth, she cared, and they could feel that. The little brat would probably give his domineering grandfather a rough time, and Gramps would love it. "I very much hope so, yes."

"Was she the woman in here yesterday?" Nana asked.

"No one was in here with him," Gramps said.

"Remember when we returned from the cafeteria? A young lady came out of Marcus's room." She paused. "The same one who sat in the waiting room the entire time we were there."

His grandfather frowned, his bushy brows forming one line as he thought. "The one who kept the little teen from having hysterics?"

Nana nodded.

"Curvy. Fair with light red hair." He snorted. "And a blue streak in it?"

"That's her," Marcus said, smiling.

"She looked like somebody beat the hell out of her." His grandfather's face hardened. "Did you get the bast—bad guy?"

"We did."

"All right then." Blue eyes the same color as Marcus's zeroed in. "You going to get the girl too?"

"I am."

CHAPTER TWENTY-THREE

In her car, Gabi sat in the parking lot of the FBI Tampa field office. This emotional stuff was going to have to end real soon, dammit. She studied her hands. Nice and steady. Her face in the mirror looked calm, despite the yellowing bruises on her cheek and jaw.

Her insides felt like a pile of scooped-up Jell-O. If Dickhead had told stories about her, well...she'd just have to deal with it. At least she didn't work in Tampa.

To her surprise, no one gave her any trouble. On the contrary, the ones who recognized her thanked her and promised they weren't giving up. No sidelong looks at all.

"Ms. Renard."

Gabi stopped in the hallway and turned to see four women in business attire. The one in the lead grinned and held out her hand. "I'm Marjorie—one of the other decoys. I wanted to congratulate you on the job you did. Agent Kouros kept holding you up as a shining example of getting into the role, and you aren't even an agent."

"Uh. Thank you."

"And you didn't give up," another younger woman said. "Even

when your backup abandoned you."

Gabi couldn't help asking. "I never did hear what happened to Agent Rhodes."

Marjorie snorted. "Agent no longer. Something else we have to thank you for." She rolled her eyes. "He said you'd come on to him, blahda-blahda-blah. But, although he managed to side-step written complaints, everyone here knows what kind of an asshole he is. When he tried to lay the blame on you, every woman in the office lined up to set the facts straight. Between the complaints about him, the fact you had to defend yourself, and him leaving you without orders or calling in? He's history."

A tall brunette swept a courtly bow. "And the females in this division thank you."

Well, there is a God. Gabi grinned. "Sounds like I owe you thanks, and you certainly brightened my day."

As the women continued down the hall, Gabi opened the door to the office Galen had commandeered. Same dingy decor. He sat at the small table again, talking with Jessica.

"You're here!" Jessica limped across the room to hug Gabi. "I wanted to visit you in the hospital, but Z wouldn't let me leave the first day, and these guys"—she wrinkled her nose at Galen—"monopolized the next morning, and then you disappeared. Where'd you go? Mr. Never-Talk Galen won't tell me."

"I've been staying with my parents in Orlando." Only one more day there and then home for good.

"Are they vacationing in Disney World?"

"No, they live there. My father is a lawyer for Thompson and Dunn International." An important, dignified job. No scandals allowed. When Galen had called them from her hospital room, she'd heard their revulsion that she was involved in something sordid. It might wipe off on them, right? But Galen had pushed, and her parents had agreed to let her stay in their house.

She pressed her hand over the cold lump in her stomach. The visit had been...difficult. Somehow, maybe from having almost died, she'd realized down to the bone that they'd never love her. And the only way to obtain their respect would be to turn herself into a pale reflection of them.

I like myself. Surely if she said it often enough, the pain would diminish. And hey, she had friends who liked her, a grandmother who loved her, clients who needed her. A person could survive without her parents' love. *So get over it already.*

When Gabi smiled, the worried expression on Jessica's face eased.

"Please join us," Galen said, patting a chair on his right.

Gabi settled herself in the chair. Carefully. Even several days after the kidnapping, her head still hurt, her body hurt.

"One last debriefing with both of you," he said. "Give me any tidbit, interrupt each other, add in what else you might have heard."

By the time they finished, Gabi felt depleted and the aching in her owies had increased an order of magnitude. Then again, she shouldn't complain. She could be screaming under a whip. Raped. Have someone like Jang...

Her stomach twisted, and she started to spiral into a panic attack. *Breathe.* She closed her eyes, trying to get control. Think of something else. Marcus's voice saying, "*Easy, sugar. It's over. You're safe, sweetheart.*" The way his gaze could take her elsewhere. *Breathe.*

Her chest loosened, and she opened her eyes.

Jessica had taken her hand.

Galen was frowning. "Let me get you some water."

"Sorry." The panic attacks and emotional crap would improve, she knew. Been there, done that.

After she'd passed out in the elevator by Marcus's room, they'd admitted her to the hospital—just like ten years ago. Same old merry-go-round. Hospital stay, interviews by cops and FBI, dumped on her parents to finish recovering. Panic attacks. Eventually a return to normality.

As Galen handed her the water, Vance walked in. "Hey, Jessica."

"Hi, Vance."

"Gabrielle." The big agent grinned and came over to gently shake her hand. "You look like hell."

Gabi snorted, feeling better. "Thanks a lot." She took a sip of water, pleased when it went down without difficulty.

"You seeing Marcus today?" Vance asked.

Just like that, the water stuck in her throat. She choked and coughed and tried not to whimper at the stabbing pains in her ribs. She said hoarsely, "No."

Vance frowned. "Does he...?" He shook his head. "First things first. Galen, boot up your computer. I have a couple of problems that came up."

Galen picked up his cane. "Excuse us, ladies."

As the two men moved away, Gabi turned to Jessica. "Did you and Z... Um."

The blonde laughed. "We definitely *ummed.* And Gabi? What you said helped—not only the explanation of the kidnapping stuff, but how Z feels about me. We're getting married. Soon."

"Oh. My. God." Gabi hugged her, ignoring the complaints from her ribs. "That is the best news I've had all week."

"I'm so happy." Jessica bounced in her chair. Then her brows drew together. "Although he's still pretty steamed I left the club that night without him. He said something about putting me in leg shackles."

Gabi snickered. "You poor baby." After waiting for her voice to steady, she asked, "So how is Marcus? Have you seen him?"

"Yeah, we've visited him almost every day—got him groceries and stuff. He seemed a little shocked at first about everybody showing up to help out, but he's mellowed a lot. Anyway, he's doing all right, but he's not supposed to use his arm much. The doctor gave him a sling."

Relief felt like a cool breath of air. "Good. That's good."

"Well, well." Jessica raised her eyebrows. "Did you get hooked on him like all the trainees do?"

Just another one of the trainees, huh? Gabi assumed a rueful smile. "Guess so."

"You met his girlfriend yet?"

"Oh yeah. The lovely Celine made a point of introducing herself." *He deserves so much better.*

"She would. She goes out of her way to make it clear he belongs to her." Jessica shrugged. "Damned if I know how she caught him—I still don't know him that well—but men are really stupid sometimes. Still, she's the kind of oh-so-sweet sub he likes. Everybody knows he doesn't like bratty subs."

"Sally mentioned that." *And he told me himself.*

Jessica's mouth curved. "You're a lot like Sally, you know. I bet if the agents had asked you to be a sweet, passive submissive, you'd have had a lot more trouble playing the part."

"Oh thanks," Gabi snapped, then tried to imagine herself being all sweetness and light. *Ugh.* "You're right. You bitch."

Jessica giggled. "So why don't you ask Marcus to introduce you to a dom who likes brats?"

Oh sure, and how pitiful would that be? *Please, Marcus, if you won't have me, do you know someone who would?* "Thanks, but I'm going back to Miami on Monday."

"Already?"

"I need to work. I really do. Sitting around is..." Too filled with memories and wishes and disappointments. Between her parents' disapproval and loving a man who didn't like her personality, she not only needed a distraction but to surround herself with her friends too—*before I throw a pity party to end all parties.*

"Got it." Jessica smiled. "I wanted to go back yesterday, but Z told me I had to wait until Monday. For someone who said he only dominates in the bedroom, he sure gets bossy sometimes."

"And you love it."

"Well, yeah. Still, it's probably better that he doesn't know that."

Gabi raised her eyebrows. "If you think he can't tell, you are so delusional."

Jessica snickered. "Point to you." She glanced at her watch and grimaced. "I've got to go." Her hand curled around Gabi's. "I wish you could stay. When you come back to visit your folks, why don't you call, and we'll get together?"

"I...don't visit my parents. I'm only there because Galen wanted me close to Tampa and I was too dizzy to stay alone." Gabi managed a smile. "They're pretty conservative, and...they don't approve of me. At all." *God, Gabi. Pathetic much?*

"Oh." Jessica frowned. "Well, maybe come back to the Shadowlands for a visit?"

"Jessica, I don't think that would be a good idea."

The blonde's eyes turned unhappy. "You really did fall for Marcus, didn't you? Oh, Gabrielle..."

"I know. Wouldn't work...and I agree." Gabi made a shooing gesture. "Go. Don't draw this out or we'll both end up bawling. Galen would be horrified."

Jessica nodded, gave a quick hug, and hurried out of the room.

Gabi moved her chair to face the windows and pretended to watch the thunderclouds building up on the horizon. When she had her emotions under control, she turned back around and saw Vance leaning on the desk watching her. Galen had resumed his seat at the table and had the same assessing expression.

"Are you two through with me?" she asked coolly.

"Only a few things left," Galen said. "Your friend, Kimberly. I'm sorry, Gabrielle. It's not good. If we can take this organization down, we might be able to trace her. But our best bet—finding them before the auction—didn't happen." He looked so unhappy she wanted to pat his hand.

"I know." When she finally accepted the facts—that there was nothing anyone could do—she'd spent a day crying. Grieving. "Please...just please don't stop looking."

"You know we won't," Vance said.

"Thank you." She looked away for a second. "So what else?"

"Z and the other Masters have all called, wanting to make sure you're all right. We've reassured them that you are."

Hearing that the doms had worried warmed her. "Thank you. Anything else?"

"Marcus has called every day wanting to know how you are and where you are. Wanting your number." Vance grinned. "He got pretty damned annoyed when I didn't hand it over. But regulations say I need your permission. I assume you're okay with it?"

She so didn't want to see him. She'd said good-bye. If she'd had any lingering hopes, Jessica had crumbled them like dead leaves on a vine. She pushed her emotions into a box and shut the lid. "No, I'm not."

Vance's smile disappeared. "What?"

"My job is finished. I'm going to put this behind me, and I'd rather not have any reminders. Please don't give him—or anyone —my information."

"Marcus didn't sound as if he thought everything was finished," Vance said slowly.

Her eyes prickled with unshed tears. "He's a nice man. I'm sure if you tell him I'm fine, that's all he needs."

Galen leaned back in his chair, his gaze intent. "I got the impression he cared more than that."

"He's very protective of his trainees."

"I...see." Vance sighed. "Well, Gabrielle, the protective bastard isn't going to believe us that you refused, and he'll hound us. Would you mind calling him and explaining?"

The wish to hear Marcus's voice again dissolved in the knowledge of what it would do to her. *No more crying.* "Sorry, you'll just have to cope." She pushed her chair back, needing to be gone.

Galen's mouth tightened. "He deserves more than being blown off, Gabrielle. The man risked his life for you."

Guilt stabbed worse than the pain in her ribs. But Marcus

didn't really want her; they just didn't understand. She said in an even voice, "I know he did, and I'm very grateful."

"Gratitude, hell." Galen tossed a piece of paper and a pen across the table. "You write him a note explaining, or I'll give him every number we have on file for you."

She took a step back, feeling as if he'd slapped her.

His black eyes were cold. Implacable. "Do it now."

You bastard. She shoved her tears down. "You know, any resemblance between you and a human being is purely coincidental."

"I've heard that." He rapped the table with his knuckles and pushed to his feet. "Leave it here and I'll see that he gets it." He turned to Vance. "We're due in Benton's office now."

Vance nodded.

Galen limped to the door, glanced back once. "Be well, Gabrielle."

She looked away.

Vance hugged her. "We enjoyed working with you, Gabrielle. Take care of yourself."

"You too." As he walked toward the door, she cleared her throat. "He was only kidding about writing a note, right?"

Vance gave her a level look. "Galen never bluffs."

On Saturday, Marcus stalked into the Shadowlands. A sub said hi, met his eyes, and backed away. He tried to be amused and failed. Thank Christ Z had assigned the trainees to Mistress Olivia for the rest of September, or he'd probably terrify them too.

The music from the dance floor reverberated through the room, the bass hitting his bones in repetitious blows. He nodded curtly as people greeted him, grateful the doctor had let him abandon the sling and he didn't have to explain to every nosey parker how he'd been hurt.

He glanced around. Z said the FBI agents planned to drop by

tonight to give the Masters an update and their thanks. Marcus intended to ask for an update also. The bastards had refused to tell him Gabi's location; perhaps they'd be more cooperative in person.

"Hey, Marcus." Behind the bar, Cullen waggled a bottle of beer.

Marcus hesitated, then walked over and took the drink. He'd stopped his pain meds yesterday, and his shoulder throbbed like a sadistic dentist had drilled holes in it. "Thank you, Cullen."

"You look a bit pissed off. Anything I can do?"

Marcus's mood lightened slightly. To his surprise, all the Masters had visited him in the hospital. Once he'd gone home, their care continued. Z and Jessica had brought groceries and books on Monday, followed by Dan and Kari, who'd cooked and frozen meals for him to microwave. On Tuesday, Nolan and Beth had stopped by to run errands and had found Sensei and a batch of his teenagers there. Beth had commandeered the boys to do his yard work. Impressed by their enthusiasm, she'd hired two for her gardening service.

Wednesday, Anne, Olivia, and Sam had visited in the morning. Then Andrea had cleaned his house—over his objections—while Cullen had put together a meal. Z and Jessica on Thursday—as well as some associates from the DA's office. On Friday, Raoul had barbecued steaks he'd brought, and the rest had arrived to hold an informal engagement celebration for Z and Jessica, and Nolan and Beth. He'd lived in Tampa only a year, but he'd made some good friends without realizing it.

They hadn't allowed him to get lonely, but despite their company, he'd missed Gabi as if he'd misplaced a body part. His heart, maybe.

Marcus took a sip of beer and looked at Cullen. "Nothing you can do, thank you, unless you enjoy pounding on FBI agents."

Cullen grinned. "Tempting... Got a reason or are you just bored?"

"Gabrielle isn't in town." Every day that had gone by, he'd expected to hear from her. But she hadn't called. Hadn't left a message. The memory of her eyes when she'd said, "*Good-bye, Marcus,*" haunted him. "She hasn't returned to her job, and I can't find her. Her phone and address are buried well, and neither her Miami office nor Vance will give me her phone number or even relay a message."

"I can see how that would burn your ass." Cullen frowned. "The agents got here a few minutes ago. They stopped by the bar to say thanks." Cullen glanced at his sub. "Sweetheart, did you see where Z and the others went?"

Andrea finished drawing a beer and frowned at Marcus. "You look terrible. You shouldn't be here."

"Irrelevant," Marcus said. "Where's Z?"

Andrea set the drink in front of Olivia and muttered, "Men are such idiots," winning a snort of laughter from the domme.

"Pet," Cullen warned.

She sniffed and set her hands on her hips. Her attitude resembled Gabi's so much that grief slid like a knife between his ribs. "Fine, just die and see if I care. They're way at the back, close to the cages, behind the giant fern planter."

"Thank you, Andrea," Marcus said. "Cullen, please swat her ass for me."

"Be my pleasure to do that little thing, buddy."

As Marcus walked away, he heard a squeak and a thud as a mouthy sub got tossed onto the bar, and then the slap of a hand on bare flesh.

Andrea's voice rose. "*Chíngate*, cabrón."

Marcus shook his head, smiling. That insult would probably get her gagged.

The secluded sitting area held the FBI agents and some of the Shadowlands Masters. In the chorus of greetings, Raoul patted an empty chair. "We waited for you."

"Thank you," Marcus acknowledged.

The only sub present, Jessica, was curled up in Z's lap, looking much like the kitten he called her, and Marcus smiled at her. The misery of not having Gabi in his arms hurt worse than the hole in his shoulder.

Z nodded at the agents, an unspoken gesture that they had the floor.

Vance leaned forward. "First, this information is privileged and not to be shared with anyone, even your subs." He glanced at Jessica. "Anyone, pet."

She nodded.

"You know Jessica and Gabi's kidnapping followed three others in Tampa." Vance scowled. "The man killed on the dock, Maganti, was a private investigator here in Tampa. He received a list of women, investigated them, and chose four who could easily disappear. He did the same thing about two years ago."

"Two years apart?" Nolan straightened. "That's a fucking long setup."

"So it seems." Vance rubbed his neck. "We didn't gain enough information, dammit. The boat escaped clean. Maganti died. The hireling knows very little."

"Were they involved in the Atlanta kidnappings?" Marcus asked.

Vance shook his head. "Only here."

"Two years ago. More than one city. You're dealing with a human trafficking organization," Marcus said.

"And one that's very well concealed," Galen agreed. "We'd still be in the dark if that Atlanta victim hadn't escaped. We've already found two other cities with this pattern of disappearances."

"That's not good," Dan muttered. The cop shot a frown at Z. "Did any Shadowlands submissives disappear two years ago?"

"I checked." Z's jaw tightened. "A young woman—college student. Not a feisty one. A redhead." As if to reassure himself of her safety, he pulled Jessica closer, and she turned her head into his shoulder.

Marcus breathed out slowly. He needed to know for himself Gabrielle was safe.

"I don't understand," Raoul said. "If the student wasn't a brat—"

Vance said, "We examined other Tampa club records. As far as we can tell, four redheaded subs disappeared two years ago."

Nolan grunted. "Specialty items for auction or maybe for filling custom orders."

"Did Maganti or Jang belong to any BDSM clubs?" Marcus asked.

"No," Galen said. "Someone else made up the list of potential victims, and gentlemen, you should assume the spotter is still in place. We will, of course, do our best to root him out, but..."

"We'll watch," Dan said. The other Masters nodded.

Nolan cracked his knuckles. "Be more rewarding if we find him first."

"I didn't hear that," Vance said in a stern voice, obviously trying to suppress a smile. "On a happier note, the agent who'd abandoned Gabi—she did break his nose, by the way—no longer works for the FBI."

Low murmurs around the group, consisting mostly of the designation of "asshole" and "bastard," aside from Nolan, who simply growled.

"That's it." Vance got to his feet, Galen struggled to his, and they shook hands with everyone. Marcus waited patiently.

As Vance talked with Dan, Galen bent down to Jessica. "I'm sorry you got caught up in this, sweetie."

"Not your fault—I was already on the list." Her smile turned to a grin. "Besides, I got to see Master Z kick major ass."

He tugged her hair, grinned at Z. "I like your brat."

Z merely smiled. "As do I. I fear you and Vance will need to find your own."

Galen finally walked over to Marcus. "Thank you for the help. I regret we weren't quick enough to keep you from getting shot."

He pulled an envelope from his suit pocket. "Gabrielle wrote this for you."

His hopes rose, then dropped. A letter meant she didn't want to speak to him. Dammit. "I'd like her phone number."

Galen's eyes held sympathy. "I can't, Marcus. It's not only against the rules, but she requested we not give it to you."

Marcus stepped back, winded as if he'd caught a roundhouse kick to his gut. She didn't want to see him. Not caring how rude it might be, he ripped open the letter and read the few sentences.

Marcus,

Thank you for your care while I was in the Shadowlands. Thank you for saving my life. I'm so very sorry I caused you to get shot.

Galen says you want my number, but I just want to move on and not remember this last month.

His guts felt battered. The last month was one of the finest in his life, and she wanted to forget it?

I'm sure you'll find it a relief not to have a brat among your trainees.

Thank you for everything,

Gabrielle.

Gabrielle, not Gabi. Does that mean we're not even friends either? He saw Galen hadn't moved. "She's sure I'll find it a relief not to have a brat in my trainees. She wants to forget everything—and not speak to me."

"You know, as a law enforcement officer, I recommend you honor the lady's wishes. As a dom..." A corner of Galen's mouth turned up. "Marcus, she was hurting when she wrote the letter, just as much as you are now. I think she's wrong."

Vance had joined them, and he nodded agreement and shook Marcus's hand. "Good luck. You'll need it—but she's worth it."

The two FBI agents walked away, stopping for a minute to observe Sally instruct a dom on the proper way to use a switch.

Marcus sank down into his chair, reading her words again. When he looked up, the others had resumed their seats. "This doesn't make sense. How can she write everything off?"

"Kari did mention... Ah, she's seen you with Gabrielle, and thought you two... Anyway, she asked me... Hell." Dan ran his hands through his hair and scowled. "Okay, it's like this: last Saturday Kari overheard that sub you date—"

"Celine?"

"That's the one. Celine told Gabi that doms don't like bratty subs, and she was surprised you didn't throw her out of the trainees."

Marcus closed his eyes. "Oh wonderful."

"It gets better. Celine apparently said you're her master, and you love her because she never gives you any trouble."

"She's—" Anger flared through him so fast and hot it was a wonder the letter didn't burn. Did Gabi actually believe Celine's bullcrap? That he'd make love with her if he was involved with someone else? "It's bullshit. I've never been her master, never come close to being in love with her. I told her that."

Jessica cleared her throat. "All the subs believe... Um, Celine told everyone you're together."

Marcus sighed. "Well, that explains part of the problem." He noticed Jessica wringing her hands and cleared his throat. "Best you tell me what else I'm missing, sugar."

She hesitated a second. "Did she lie about you hating disobedient subs too? Even though your ex-wife..." She flushed, and her jaw firmed. "Everybody knows you hate brats, Master Marcus. Don't you?"

He might have gotten riled, except the little blonde had tears in her eyes. Why? "No, darlin'. Not anymore." He smiled slightly. "I didn't think I liked sassy behavior until I met Gabi. But I like the challenge. And I like her honesty. When she does submit, it's..." *The sweetest thing in the world.* "I was wrong."

"You really want Gabrielle?"

Marcus sighed. "Yes, Jessica, I do. I intend to do my best to convince her of that." He had enough contacts in law enforcement that he'd locate her eventually.

Jessica studied him, then turned to Z.

"Truth," Z said softly.

Taking a stand in front of Marcus, she crossed her arms over her chest. "If you break her heart, I'm going to hurt you."

Startled, Marcus glanced at Z.

Z gave him a faint smile. "Please recall why the kidnappers targeted our two submissives."

Marcus closed his eyes and shook his head before looking at the diminutive blonde. "I will do my best not to hurt her, Jessica."

"Okay." Jessica smiled. "I'd love to see her face when you show up." When her eyes lit with mischief, Marcus saw how she'd captured Z. "Gabrielle is staying with her parents in Orlando until Monday. Her father is a lawyer at Thompson and Dunn International." She frowned again. "I guess they're really conservative and don't approve of her. When she mentioned them, she sounded...unhappy. Like when she talked about you."

A well-placed stab, especially since she was being honest. But he remembered Gabi had told him much the same thing about her parents. And she'd run away from them as a teenager. "Little Miss Sassy, did your parents have a problem with your behavior?"

"Nah. They always wanted me to stand on my own feet." She grinned. "I was given a fair number of time-outs as a kid, but"—her smile faded—"but my family likes who I am."

Marcus nodded. Gabi thought Marcus didn't approve of her. That he was conservative. Stuffy. He remembered her surprise at seeing him in jeans. When he'd thrown her into the ocean. To top it off, he was a lawyer like her father. Well, he had his work cut out for him, didn't he? "I think I get the picture, Jessica. Thank you."

He could easily track down her father's address, and now he had an idea of what he was up against: *Celine's lies. Thinking he hated brats. Being too much like her parents*. She had a lot to learn. He glanced at the other Masters and smiled slowly. "It's a good thing I've had a lot of practice in instructing little subs, isn't it."

CHAPTER TWENTY-FOUR

After church, Gabi changed into jeans and a green peasant top and stayed in her room, trying to regain her equilibrium. Besides, it gave her a chance to play with her bored cats. Being shut up in the bedroom annoyed the hell out of them. "Soon, guys. Tomorrow we leave." *And I'll be back with my friends. Will have lots to do.*

When she felt poised again, she walked out to the great room. Only ten o'clock and the morning had already got off to a rocky start. Dressed appropriately in a demure dress, heels, and hose despite the heat, she'd attended church service with her parents, hoping to please them. Major mistake.

When they'd introduced her around afterward, their oh-so-polite friends couldn't look away from the ugly marks and yellowing bruises on her face. Since the news had reported only a shoot-out at the Clearwater Docks, Gabi couldn't explain her battered appearance, and everyone plainly assumed she had an abusive boyfriend. Her parents had grown more and more distant. *Oh look, Gabi, you've embarrassed them again.*

One more day and then home.

Finding her parents in the room, discussing the sermon, Gabi stopped in the doorway. "I'm going to make some coffee. Anyone want one?"

"I'd like a latte," her mother said. "Thank you, Gabrielle."

Gabi had just finished making the coffee when the doorbell rang. *Great. More stuffy, parental friends.* Well, she'd hand off the latte and retreat back to her room. She carried the two cups out of the kitchen as her mother entered the great room, followed by Marcus.

Marcus? Here? Not in the club? Here. Her brain shut down as if someone had flipped a switch.

He walked up to her. "Easy, sugar." He carefully took the two cups from her before she spilled them on her mother's white carpet, then set them on the coffee table.

"Do you remember Marcus Atherton, Gabrielle?" her mother asked, giving his dark gray suit an approving look. When Gabi didn't answer, she added, "He says you met on a special assignment in Tampa."

"Um. Yes, I remember him." *What is he doing here?* Her chest hurt as if her heart had shriveled and died. She glanced at the hallway that led to her bedroom and escape, but Mother would be horrified. No hope for it; she had to act politely.

She dropped down on the couch, ignoring her mother's wince at her lack of grace. "What brings you to Orlando, Marcus?" *And how did you find out my location? Didn't you get my letter?*

Walking right past an empty chair, he joined her on the couch, sitting close enough she could feel the warmth of his thigh against hers—close enough to make it obvious they were more than just friends. Her mother's eyebrows rose.

"I came over to take you out for lunch, sugar." He took her hand, then smiled at her parents. "I do apologize for the discourtesy of calling unannounced."

Gabi tried to pull her hand away without her parents noticing, and amusement lit his eyes. She glowered at him. "Didn't you see Vance and Galen?"

His grip flexed in a way that reminded her of how incongruously strong he was. "I did. They gave me your note and told me how much you looked forward to seeing me again."

They did not. They wouldn't. Would they? She remembered Galen's expression when she'd said she didn't want to talk to Marcus. "*He deserves more than that*," he'd said.

This isn't fair.

Marcus watched his little sub's face flush a vivid pink. The big brown eyes had lit with joy when she'd seen him and now shot sparks at him. Smothering a laugh, he turned back to her parents. How had such a cold couple created someone as bright and warm as Gabi? He knew others like the Renards; his old law firm had been filled with their type. He hadn't realized how much he'd enjoyed being away from pompous assholes until now.

He studied Gabi for a moment, having to suppress his rage at the sight of the bruising on her forehead, her cheek, her jaw. Her mangled wrists—he'd have to avoid hurting them. Yet just the sight of her filled him with pleasure.

"Mr. Renard." He stood to shake hands with her father. "I believe someone said you work for Thompson and Dunn? In law?"

The man's chest puffed slightly. "I specialize in corporate law, yes."

"An intriguing field." Marcus smiled and added, "I'm an assistant district attorney in Tampa."

"Why how nice," her mother said. The approving look Gabi got from her parents warmed Marcus's heart and probably shot his chances with her to hell. "Can I get you something to drink, Mr. Atherton?"

"No. But thank you." He smiled. "I didn't mean to disturb your morning." As he watched Gabi's parents, their body language and expressions, Marcus could clearly see their attitude toward their daughter, that of two snooty Siamese cats faced with a bouncy puppy. His heart broke for her. As warm and perceptive as Gabi was... Had they been as disapproving of her when she'd been a child? No wonder she'd run away. He'd have joined her.

After today, if she still considered him anything like her father, Marcus would paddle her ass.

"We'd be pleased to have you join us for lunch here," Mrs. Renard said.

"He can't stay," Gabi announced, her voice deliberately rude. She frowned at him. "I'm afraid I'm occupied today, Marcus. It's a shame you didn't call before you wasted your time."

Her mother gasped, and her father's face turned flat.

Marcus laughed. *There she is, my little brat.* Now to show her that her behavior wouldn't drive him away. "You can spit at me all you want, darlin'," he said, cupping her cheek and forcing her to meet his eyes. "Do bear in mind I deal with drug dealers, murderers—and worst of all, cops, every day. I doubt that you can shock me with your behavior."

"You don't want—"

"I do want." He took her hand, moved his grip to her undamaged forearm to remind her who was in charge, and pulled her to her feet. "I appreciate you letting me interrupt your morning, ma'am, sir." Without releasing Gabi—she'd make a run for it, he knew—he politely shook hands with her stunned father.

Then he simply dragged his insubordinate sub out of her parents' house.

She tried to rebel again when he opened the car door for her. "Listen, this is not—I don't want—"

"Gabrielle." He cupped her cheek and looked down into her velvety brown eyes. "Get. In. The. Car."

Gabi scrubbed her hands on her jeans and tried to show an impassive face as Marcus drove through the city. Didn't he understand this wouldn't work? Was he like some...some predator that gave chase if their prey ran from them?

"If you keep all those thoughts inside, your brain will

explode," he said lazily. He steered the car to the curb and took her hand in his. "We can discuss this right now, or we can wait until after lunch and then have at it. Your only choice is when."

God, why did the determination in his deep voice turn her insides to liquid? She swallowed, wishing she saw a future for them. But look at him. In a suit, as always.

Then again, the way he'd acted at her parents' house... He'd been rude to them. That wasn't like him at all. *I'm so confused.* "Later. Please."

"All right, darlin'." He brushed her lips with a soft kiss, leaving her longing for more. After pulling a cell phone from his suit, he punched a number and a second later said, "We should get there in about thirty minutes." The cell went back into his pocket.

"Who was that?"

"I thought since I've met your family today, you should meet mine. My grandparents will join us."

What? She looked at her jeans and peasant top in horror, then stared at him. "Marcus, I'm not dressed for a nice restaurant." *Dear God, is he insane?*

His lips quirked. "I'm not sure if that's a compliment or insult. You didn't worry about your appearance when you thought it was only me for lunch."

Her mouth dropped open. She hadn't, had she? "Ah..."

"You no longer think I'll judge you by what you wear. We're making progress, I do believe." He tugged at the puffy sleeve of her top, the elastic letting him pull it down to expose her shoulder. He kissed the bare skin and murmured, "As it happens, I rather like this top."

Great, her clothing was not only too casual, but the kind he'd want to play with. She pulled her sleeve up.

He pulled it down.

She was doomed.

He was still smiling ten minutes later when he turned his car into a drive. She frowned at the sign. "We're going to the Animal Kingdom?" Mr. Suit and Disney?

"Are you allowed to live in Florida if you don't like Disney?" He chuckled at the amazed look she gave him. At a guard station, he slowed to give his name and was waved on.

Not long afterward, Gabi stared in wonder as they walked through the African-themed lobby of the Kidani Lodge and down a spiral staircase to the Sanaa Restaurant. Hanging baskets mingled with pottery-jar lamps. Colorful cloth hangings and beaded mosaics decorated the walls. Tree branches seemed to dissolve into the thatched ceiling. She stopped to stare. "This is amazing."

He smiled. "Wait until you see the view from the windows." After slinging his gym bag over his shoulder, Marcus set his hand low on her back, guiding her toward a table where an older couple sat. His grandparents. In tan slacks and a short-sleeved shirt, the silver-haired man had keen eyes with a sunburst of wrinkles at the corners, a Roman nose, and a stern jaw. He rose as they approached.

"Gabrielle, this is my grandfather, Ben Atherton, and my grandmother, Abby." His grandmother had tousled white curls, softly wrinkled skin, and an infectious smile.

Marcus kissed Gabi's fingertips and finished, "And here is my very reluctant girlfriend, Gabi Renard."

Reluctant. She would kill him...somehow...the minute they were alone. "It's nice to meet you both."

"Gramps," Marcus said, "her father is William Renard, a lawyer with Thompson and Dunn International. You might have met him."

Ben's bushy brows drew together. "I've made his acquaintance, although I don't recall having him in front of my bench."

Marcus closed his hand around Gabi's and murmured, "He doesn't always sound like it, but Gramps was a judge before he retired."

I complain about lawyers, so I get to eat lunch with a judge? This so isn't fair.

"Very into rules and regulations. Pretty narrow-minded, I thought." Ben tilted his head at Gabi and gave a considering look. "If what my grandson says about you is true, I bet you had him fit to be tied, young lady."

Her mouth dropped for a second before she recovered. "Yes, I'm afraid I did."

"Please sit, everyone," Abby said.

Marcus seated Gabi and kissed her cheek. "I'll be right back, sugar. I want to change."

And the bastard abandoned her without looking back.

After a quick change of clothing in the restroom, Marcus strode into the restaurant. When he saw Gramps sitting alone, he froze, then spotted Gabi at one of the giant windows with his grandmother. The two appeared mesmerized by the giraffe striding past. He let out a sigh of relief, realizing he'd been worried the little sub would flee.

When Marcus sat down, his grandfather glanced at the two women a few feet away. "She's polite, but she doesn't intimidate worth a damn. I do believe I like her."

Marcus snorted. "You would. Unfortunately, the problem is getting her to stay. She thinks I'm the same type as her parents, and you're right about his personality. Her mother is worse."

Gramps's mouth flattened into a line. "Renard is a pompous bastard and wound up tighter than an eight-day clock. You're nothing alike, son."

"Hopefully I can keep her around long enough to realize it."

"We ordered for you, by the way. Your young lady has an adventurous spirit, at least in foods."

The bread sampler had arrived before the two women returned to the table, laughing and chatting easily. Nana could put anyone at ease, and Marcus smiled. He kept realizing how much Gabi was like her.

His sub's eyes widened when she saw him. *What? Oh, the clothes.* After she sat down beside him, he leaned over to murmur into her ear, "I spend most of my time in jeans, sugar. Sorry to disappoint you."

She grinned. "You're trying to destroy all my illusions, aren't you?" She lowered her voice, "By the way, you have a fine ass. Sir."

He choked. And hardened instantly. He gave her a "you will pay" stare, and she actually giggled.

When he looked up, Nana beamed at him in obvious approval. Well then. Now to win over his grandfather. If his grandparents approved, so would the rest of the Atherton clan. Marcus leaned back in his chair and smiled at Gabi. He'd bet her previous Christmases had been formal, cold affairs. Dignified. When he took her to his parents' home in rural Georgia, she was in for a shock.

"I've been admiring your hair, Gabi," Nana said. "As it happens, I'm thinking of putting a few pink or green streaks in mine just to shock the ladies in my bridge club."

Marcus's mouth dropped open, and Gramps sputtered like a badly tuned engine.

"I think you'd shock more than just the ladies." Snickering at the men, Gabi fingered the blue strand in her hair. "You're braver than I am—I never planned to do something quite so permanent."

He'd thought she'd done it as a show of defiance—although the blue *was* rather odd, considering how she liked coordinating colors. "So why did you?"

"My job has unexpected...benefits." She gave him a rueful look. "I went to see a teenager who'd had a...bad experience, but she refused to talk with me. Wanted me to leave. But then she said she'd planned to dye her hair." Gabi's eyes darkened. "It's a girl thing, trying to change ourselves as if we can change our lives too."

Marcus took her hand. He'd have to ask someday how she'd changed herself as a teenager.

"Anyway, I volunteered to help, and halfway through, I got enthused. When I smeared blue on my hair, well, she started to laugh and..." When Gabi's fingers tightened on his, he knew the girl had talked and shared undoubtedly horrific memories with his compassionate woman. "We had a nice chat, and I discovered I rather like the blue. I went back last month to have her put some more in."

Yeah, he definitely loved this woman. He wanted to pull her into his arms; he settled for running a finger down her cheek.

She gave him a suspicious frown. "What?"

"You please me more than I can say, Gabi," he said softly. A pretty pink colored in her cheeks. That first day he'd seen her, he'd known it would be a delight to watch her flush.

"Um. Thank you."

Smiling, he handed her a piece of the traditional naan bread. She scooped up some hummus and took a bite. When she closed her eyes in pleasure, he remembered she'd had the same expression when sucking his cock, when he kissed her, when he bent her over... He shifted in his chair, needing to drag her to the hotel room he'd rented. Right now.

Across the table, his grandfather exchanged amused smiles with Nana. Totally obvious, was he? He found he didn't care in the least. But he had work to do here, and he might as well start off by killing two birds with one stone. "Gramps, do you remember the woman I introduced y'all to at the beginning of the summer? Celine?"

Beside him, Gabi stiffened, her face turning poker bland as

she sipped her drink. Nana, in contrast, appeared appalled at his rudeness at talking about a previous girlfriend.

"I remember her," Gramps answered. "Sugar wouldn't melt in her mouth. Spineless."

"Good description." Marcus glanced at his little sub. Open shock. The first crack in her believing what Celine had said. Excellent. Now to confront it head-on. "She has a problem with honesty as well. Apparently she's telling people we're in a relationship and that I love her."

Gabi choked on her drink.

"Ah, a witness? What did she tell you, darlin'?"

Her eyes narrowed. "I'm not on the stand, so watch it, Mr. Lawyer."

A snort of appreciation from Gramps.

Marcus put a finger under her chin. "Tell me, Gabrielle."

"She told me you love her because she never gives you any back talk. Whatever you want is what she wants."

"You fancy a biddable woman?" his grandfather said in disbelief.

Nana tsk-tsked at him. "Of course he doesn't, dear. Now hush."

"Do you really think I'd enjoy someone I can walk all over?" Marcus asked, running a finger down her cheek. "Do you realize how boring that would be?"

"But..." From her confused expression, that's exactly what she believed.

"I see. We'll discuss that later then." He let his anger with her show. "Do you think so little of me you believe I would"—the memory of his grandparent's presence made him revise his language—"ah, take you home if I was involved with someone?"

"No." Her gaze dropped. "Not at first. But she said, straight out..."

"She lied, Gabi." Marcus leaned an elbow on the table. "A few dates doesn't make a relationship, and aside from occasional scenes, I'd stopped seeing her well before you. She didn't take the hint, so I told her, rather bluntly, a couple of weeks ago that I had no intention of doing...anything...with her again."

Brown eyes met his, and he saw her temper spark. "She lied to me? Out-and-out lied?"

Marcus smothered his smile. "I'm afraid so, sugar."

Her growl sounded like a higher version of Nolan's.

Gramps slapped his hand on the table. "So what are you going to do about this woman?"

"You have any suggestions, Gabi?"

She thought for a moment, and her lips curved. "Whatever you want is what she wants...so what if you *wanted* her to spend an evening with Ma—" She cut the word off and flushed slightly. "With Sam?"

Marcus stared at her, then roared with laughter. "You possess an evil mind, little brat."

"Is Sam ugly or something?" Nana asked.

"No. Actually Sam's a very nice guy, but he has a rather well-known kinky side." Marcus winked at Gramps. "He's a hard-core sadist, Nana, and he has a fondness for whips."

Gramps barked a laugh.

Nana's eyes widened. "My goodness, how do you meet such interesting people?" She tapped a finger against her lips, then nodded, shocking him—and Gabi—completely. "That would be a fine predicament to put her in, bless her heart, and an appropriate consequence for her lying."

Marcus smiled at Gabi. "Means you'll need to come to Tampa for the show, darlin'."

"I...I..." She averted her eyes. "You know, we should eat while the food is still warm, don't you think?"

Well, he might have won a battle, but obviously the war was not yet won.

The time with Marcus's grandparents had been wonderful, Gabi thought, as Marcus opened the door to his hotel room. Damn, they were fun.

His grandmother volunteered at various Tampa wildlife rescue groups, had tried to draft Gabi into helping, and been disappointed to hear she lived in Miami.

In contrast, his opinionated, pushy grandfather had deliberately prodded Gabi with idiotic statements, rather like poking a stick at a caged monkey. Finally when he'd complained about the money going to health insurance for children, she'd lost her temper and ripped his logic to shreds. He had a roaring laugh almost as wonderful as Marcus's. After he caught his breath, he'd told Marcus, "She'll do."

They liked me. Yes, most people did, but she'd never expected approval from *Marcus's* family.

And Marcus hadn't acted stuffy at all. He'd held his own with his grandfather, bantered with his grandmother, and every time he laughed, heat streaked down her spine.

"C'mon in, sugar," Marcus said, holding the door open for her.

"I can't believe you took a room in a Disney resort." The African decor continued in the room, with warmly golden tones, wood carvings, and bright patterns on the bed—the very big bed. She looked away.

"Since you like the panthers at that cat rescue place so much, I thought you'd enjoy this."

He'd remembered. Warm fuzzies edged aside some of her nerves.

After pouring two glasses of wine, he walked onto the balcony. "Come here, darlin'. Let's talk."

Just like that, she felt as if someone had wrapped a big hand around her throat, cutting off her voice. Her feet wouldn't move until he curled his finger up in a "come here" motion.

Fine. They really did need to get this over with. She joined him on the balcony, sipped the smooth pinot noir, and pretended to watch the animals on the grassland. *Talk*. How could she make him understand? Even if he thought he wanted her, he didn't. He wouldn't. She mustn't let him push her into something he'd regret.

"What are we talking about?" she asked lightly. The low murmur of conversation came from other balconies, a little boy yelled in frustration, someone had their music turned to a loud rock station.

Marcus frowned and shook his head. "This isn't going to work."

Her hopes that should *never* have arisen drained away when he pushed her back into the room and closed the balcony door. "Okay." Her voice didn't shake. Much. "I didn't think it would." She set her glass on the small table in the sitting area.

He tilted his head in puzzlement and then smiled, grabbing her hand as she headed for the door. "No, darlin', I mean we can't talk on the balcony. There are too many people around. And you don't appear capable of rational discussion at this point."

"What?"

"We'll try irrational first." He grasped the bottom of her blouse and pulled it over her head. Before she got past "Marcus!" her bra followed the top onto the floor. "What are you doing?"

He chuckled, ignoring her attempts to keep him from yanking down her jeans zipper. "What do you think?"

"This...this isn't talking."

"Sure it is. Now just stand right there, sugar."

When she stepped back instead, his frown and the stern set of his jaw stopped her cold. She'd learned to obey the trainer far too well. Before she collected her resolve, he'd removed her jeans and thong.

"Marcus..." She forced the words out. How had she let this go so far? "This isn't a good idea."

He stepped closer, touching her cheek lightly with his fingertips. "I missed you, Gabi."

The open emotion in his low voice shook her, the pull toward him as hard to fight as a riptide. "No," she whispered.

"You are appallingly stubborn," he said under his breath. He tugged her hair and stepped back.

She hauled in a breath.

"So let's have a look at you." His gaze ran down her body, leaving a wake of heat in its path; then his eyes darkened. He brushed a finger over the black bruise on her left breast. "How did this happen?"

Her throat constricted, and she swallowed against the nausea accompanying the memory. "Jang got rough."

His mouth tightened, but he only nodded and examined the bruises on her back and hips and shoulders. "How did you get these?"

"Falls." She found a smile for him. "Being dropped into a big box. Knocked onto a dock." She touched the abrasion on her forehead. "This was the dock too."

He traced around the ugly bruise on her right side, and she winced. He frowned. "Are your ribs cracked or broken?"

"Bruised." She sighed when he lifted his eyebrows. "Only a crack or two from when Jang kicked me. Then again, I did kick him in the balls."

A dimple appeared beside his mouth when he smiled. "Good for you, darlin'." With firm hands, he sat her on the edge of the bed. Cupping her cheek, he examined the bruise there and the others along her jawline. "From the dock?"

"Jang."

"I owe Z a drink for taking care of him for me." His words were mild, but she saw the fury in his eyes and the tension in his muscles. Oddly enough, his anger on her behalf drained some pain from her own memories.

She rubbed her cheek against his palm. "Vance said Z did a thorough job. Jang's ribs were definitely broken."

"Knowing every breath he takes will hurt for a long time does help." He tipped her chin up and scrutinized her face. "He put his hands on you... How badly is that still bothering you? I would think it might bring back some ugly memories."

"A few." She closed her eyes, unable to tolerate the piercing gaze. "I was...scared." Trapped, hurt, no way out. She shivered.

He sat down beside her and enclosed her hands in his warm ones. "Go on."

She tried to shrug. "I've had a few panic attacks. It's getting better, maybe because I managed to fight back a little this time. And I chose to play decoy, so everything didn't happen out of the blue, for no reason. I'm more upset about..." She swallowed against the lump in her throat. "My friend. K-Kim. There's not much hope now."

"Ah, darlin', I'm sorry," he said softly. "Come here now." His hard arms closed around her and pulled her against his chest. Her eyes pooled with tears because she had someone to lean on, even if for only a short time. The comfort... No one had held her since the hospital, and God, she'd needed that. As if he could tell, he simply cuddled her for a while, rocking slightly. His chin rested on the top of her head, and she felt enclosed in warmth and safety.

"You know, you scared me spitless, li'l subbie. First when I heard you'd been kidnapped, and then...even worse, seeing your box tip toward the water."

She smiled against his shirt. Other people besides her could be frightened. "Thank you for not letting me drown. Vance said you got hit by a pipe when you swung me back onto the dock." She pulled back and touched the bruised, abraded spot on the edge of his forehead, half covered by hair. He had a bruise on his jaw too. He'd taken a fist in the face. "Thank you for rescuing me."

"My pleasure."

She unbuttoned his shirt. The white gauze bandage on his left shoulder seemed horribly wrong on his golden tan skin. A yellowing, round bruise bloomed over his left ribs, and she gave him the same inquisitive gaze he'd used on her.

"Took a punch."

God, look at him. Bandages, bruises, cuts. All from knowing her. She'd almost gotten him killed. Her eyes filled with tears.

"Now don't you start watering up over a few marks, sugar." He pulled her back against his side. "I get worse in karate classes."

"You almost died," she said. She pushed her head against his arm, shaking inside so hard she might shatter. She'd gotten past most of the aftereffects, but the nightmares of those few minutes hadn't lessened. *Cesar yelling, "Fucking cunt." Her body no longer her own. Freezing. Marcus's yell, "Gabi, down!" The crack of the pistol.* "If I'd dropped like you ordered, you..." *The sound he made, the blood, so horribly red.* "I'm sorry, Marcus. You worked so hard on getting me past freezing up, and still I didn't move and you—I'm so sorry."

"And you've felt guilty ever since." He actually chuckled, and she looked up to see the amusement on his face. "Did you really think one evening would fix you all up? A problem like yours doesn't disappear so easily, Gabi, and if you were thinking straight, you'd know it, Miz Counselor."

She stared at him. "You don't blame me?"

"For something you have no control over? Hardly. And if you'll trouble yourself to remember, one minute before you froze, you kept me from getting shot. That bullet probably would have killed me. We're even, darlin'." He wiped the tears from her cheeks with his thumbs and smiled down at her. "Besides, taking a bullet in a successful FBI operation has made my reputation in the DA's office."

"Oh. Well." Men. Strange, strange creatures.

"Anything else we need to discuss about the fight?"

She shook her head. So that's why he'd wanted her naked—to check her injuries. All her worries about having to tactfully refuse him were silly. Relieved...and disappointed, she reached down and picked up her jeans and thong.

"Nope." He pulled them out of her grip and pointed to the center of the bed. "Put yourself there."

"But—"

"We're not finished yet, darlin'."

CHAPTER TWENTY-FIVE

She opened her mouth to argue, caught his "I've spanked you once and I can do it again" stare, and slid backward on the bed to the designated spot. Pulling her legs up, she wrapped her arms around her knees, feeling very exposed. When she noticed his leather toy bag sitting by the headboard, a quiver shook her. *Sneaky. What was the sneaky lawyer planning?* Her hands started to sweat, and her heart thudded hard enough to do damage to her rib cage.

He shrugged out of his shirt and tossed it over a chair. Joining her on the bed, he leaned against the headboard. "Now we'll discuss you and me. Come here."

Why did he get to keep his jeans on? But it was...a little reassuring. Maybe he didn't plan to make love. Then why couldn't she put her clothes back on? *I'm so confused.* "I think I'd rather stay here. Marcus, can't you understand this won't work? There is no you and me. We're totally incompatible."

He snorted in exasperation, snagged her arm, and pulled her gently onto his lap. At the feeling of his hard arms around her, she felt her eyes blur with tears. *Again. Don't do this to me, Marcus.*

"What we have here is a failure to communicate," he said, his dark, rich drawl thicker than normal. "You best tell me why you ran away from me and sent Galen with a letter."

"I didn't run. I came here to stay with my parents."

"Do not even try to bullshit me, Gabrielle."

The sound of the less than polite term halted her thoughts for a second. His darkened expression and the dangerous look in his eyes warned her his tolerance had reached a limit.

She pushed away her internal "don't do this" voice and gave him the simple truth. "I'm not a sweet submissive, Marcus."

"I do believe I have grasped that fact."

"You don't want a brat. You don't want the problems or the troubles. I know that and..." She stared at her hands. "I thought about pretending to be a sweet, quiet submissive for you, but... after staying with my parents, I know I wouldn't be able to do it for long, and it'd break my heart to put that look in your eyes again."

He put one hand on each side of her face, and his thumbs stroked over her cheekbones. "What look, sugar?"

"Disappointment," she whispered.

"You're going to disappoint me sometimes," Marcus said. Her gaze got caught in the blueness of his. "If I disappointed you, Gabi, would you want me to leave?"

"No. But it's different. I know who you are, and I wouldn't want you to change."

"There we go. Gabrielle, I don't mean for you to change. I love who you are, little brat."

Her breath caught, and joy spiraled up inside her like a whirlwind of glitter. *Love? He loves me? Me?* And then she shook her head. "No. No, you don't."

"Contrary little sub—never accepting anything. Why am I not surprised?" He smoothly reversed positions with her so her back rested against the headboard and he straddled her bare thighs. "Gabrielle, over the last month, you've made every sweet, obedient submissive seem boring."

The spurt of hope faded quickly as logic returned. "You hate when I disobey you. I saw that."

"Sugar, when you were acting and I didn't know it, you drove me crazier than a june bug," he agreed.

Absentmindedly he ran his hands over her breasts, distracting her. Damn him, she craved his touch like a drug, wanted to be in his arms, under him. She closed her hands on his wrists, needing him to hear her. "I wasn't pretending all the time. Don't you understand?" she said. "And—"

"I do understand, Gabi." His lips curved. "I'd guess only about half of your bratty behavior was an act."

She blinked. *He knew*? "Then why are you here?"

"I discovered I like matching wits with you. I like your honesty. I like seeing you struggle to submit, and sometimes winning and sometimes losing." He tugged on her blue lock of hair.

Everything in her body started to turn to mush. But this couldn't be right. He had to be confused. "No."

"Oh yes." He frowned. "But I want you in Tampa. Or me in Miami. And you in my house."

She remembered how Vance had mentioned he could get her transferred to Tampa. *No. Leaving now.*

His lips curved. "If I wake up needing to beat on a little sub in the morning, I want her bottom available."

The glint in his eyes said he was joking—mostly—but not all. She swallowed hard, imagining his hand spanking her butt. The flash of heat bunched her nipples into jutting peaks.

He glanced at her breasts and raised his eyebrows. God, that smile of his. "I reckon you like the idea of a morning beating," he murmured.

"No, I don't." Hope and fear fought, drowning her in churning emotions. *I can't think*. She clung to the one fact—he needed to understand it couldn't work. "I won't cooperate. Not always, and then you won't like me."

"You've set your teeth into that notion, haven't you?" He pulled a huge wrist cuff from his bag and a roll of gauze. "Best we test it, then."

Wait. "No. We're not going to do this."

Ignoring her struggles, he pinned her with his weight, captured one hand, and held it securely. She couldn't fight him and chance hurting his shoulder, but trying to yank her arm out of his grip got her nowhere. After he wrapped gauze over the abrasions on her left wrist, he buckled the cuff on. "Nolan happened to own an extra wide set of cuffs," he commented. He lifted her arm and snapped the cuff to a rope attached to the headboard.

How could she not have spotted the restraints? But nooooo, she'd been too busy staring at him.

He did her other wrist and patted her hand. "These shouldn't rub on your arms where you're still sore." He snapped the right cuff to another rope and sat back.

He'd restrained her wrists against the headboard on each side of her head. She tugged at them and winced when the movement pulled on her ribs. "I can't believe you!"

"Oh, I'm not done yet, sweetheart." The big corner post of the headboard had a rope wound around the wood...and a cuff attached.

"You set everything up. You planned this."

"Darlin', I wasn't just a Boy Scout, I was an *Eagle* Scout." He proceeded to attach the cuff to her ankle. He did the same on the other side. "I do like how flexible you are, but you let me know if this hurts your ribs." He watched her closely as he tightened the ropes, forcing her legs upward toward the corner posts on the headboard.

"After you're all healed up and we're home, I'll have your feet almost to your head," he said. At the thought of being tied up in his bed, desire edged beneath her frustration.

He tied off the restraints. "I reckon this will do for today." She was slouched against the headboard, wrists on each side of her head. Her legs were pulled up and widely separated, and her feet high in the air halfway between her hips and her shoulders. She tugged on her legs, unable to even make the board wiggle—solidly made bed—and realized he was watching her with a faint smile on his face. His pleasure at seeing her bound showed clearly.

And knowing he was aroused by her helplessness heated her blood.

He ran his hands down the insides of her thighs, pausing on either side of her pussy. "I do like seeing you so spread and exposed." He touched her clit, the merest brush of his fingers, sending a burn through her, a growing need for so, so much more. "And havin' your feet waving in the air tilts that pink li'l pussy up so I can play with it." His gaze on her seemed as warm as his fingers as he touched her, teasing between her folds. "Seems you're a tad excited."

"I'm n—"

A gentle swat right on her open pussy sent fire stinging down her nerve endings. She gasped.

"Don't lie to me, Gabrielle." His eyes were firm. "That's not the same as defying me. We will be honest with each other. Am I clear?"

"I'll try. I don't lie, unless sometimes... But I can't talk about..." Her words tangled.

His smile showed his approval, warming her deep inside. "I understand, darlin'. You haven't lied unless you're being a brat. And you have trouble sharing your thoughts. We'll work on that one."

He kept assuming they'd be together...

"However, I will not accept lying even when you're acting sassy. No lies. Anytime. Understood?" His fingers stroked the crease between her hip and thigh. Then he shot her a hard look. "Answer me."

"Yes, Sir."

She was beautiful, Marcus thought. Her big brown eyes were

stormy with emotion, her breasts jiggled with her breathing, and her nipples had peaked tight from her excitement. *I love this woman.*

Too soon, Marcus would usually think, to be so certain, but he'd been involved with enough women to know when one felt exactly right. Seeing her chatting with his grandparents—and teasing Gramps—confirmed his belief. Gabi fit with them and him like a missing piece of the puzzle, snapping into place in a way that other women, even his ex-wife, never had.

"Marcus?"

He smiled down at her. Tied and quivering. So appealing. Her expression showed desire and trust...and worry, a mixture more stimulating to a dom than any aphrodisiac. Having him in control excited her, and although she trusted him not to hurt her, she knew he could and would push her out of her comfort zone. Especially today.

He did enjoy that smidgen of worry in Gabi's wide eyes.

"So sass me *now*, little sub," he said.

She fired right up at his patronizing tone. "I sass when I want to, not at your command."

"That'll work," he murmured and pushed a finger into her. Hot, wet tissues enfolded him, and damn, his cock wanted to be in her sweet little pussy. She arched, giving a shocked squeak. *Talking's over, little sub.*

Lying down, shoulders between her legs, he started to rest on a forearm, winced at the stab of pain in his shoulder, and switched to the other arm. He inhaled. Oh yes. Her aroused female scent had overwhelmed the fragrance of soap. Still watching her face, he gently licked her clit.

The stifled gasp of shock and pleasure she gave made him smile. Did she have any idea of how cute she was?

Then she stiffened, starting to get a glimmer of his intent and how much he planned to take from her. "Marcus," she whispered. "No." She tugged frantically on the restraints and winced.

Her ribs. "Stop, Gabi."

She didn't—in fact pulled harder, her teeth gritted.

Stubborn woman. He slapped her round little butt hard enough to sting, and she froze. Her startled eyes met his.

"Struggling will hurt your ribs. You will not continue."

At his hard command, her pupils dilated. The muscles in her thighs relaxed, then her arms. She sighed.

Such sweet surrender. As he'd suspected, her brattiness was only superficial, her submissiveness went heart-deep. Unable to help himself, he nuzzled the line between her hip and thigh, fragile and soft. "I love you, Gabi, and we are going to remove these doubts of yours. Today."

Her breathing increased when she realized she couldn't stop him. Couldn't even fight back.

And then he got right down to business, moving around to each of the hot spots he'd noted in previous encounters—the high sides of her clit, the firm area on top of the hood. He smiled as he felt the bundle of nerves harden. Pushing her right to the edge didn't take long at all, considering she'd heated up the minute he'd cuffed her wrist.

Quivers ran through her body as he kept her on the pinnacle with teasing, leisurely licks and measured in-out movements of his finger. Soon she was trying to pull her hips up toward his mouth, despite the restraints.

"Say 'I love you, Master.'" His lips curved. She wasn't blind with need yet, and he knew what would happen.

"You're not my master. You're an asshole is what you are. Stop teasing me," she said in a hoarse voice.

"An asshole? Didn't you have an anatomy class in college?" He reached into his toy bag and took out an anal plug, one larger than any he'd used on her before. "Let me show you what an asshole is. Considering I'll be using yours one of these days, we might as well start getting you ready."

"No. No, wait."

With a quick squirt of lube between her cheeks and another onto the plug, Marcus ignored her squirming and pressed it against her back hole.

Oh, God. "You bastard." Burning seared Gabi's anus as the plug stretched the ring of muscle at the opening. Wide...wider. She wiggled uncontrollably. With an unheard plop, it slipped in. The pain eased, leaving her nerves tingling. "Damn you."

"Well now, that looks nice," he said. He licked her clit again, his tongue hot and wet as it traced erratic patterns around her increasingly sensitive nub.

She was going to die; she knew it. Her hips canted upward as the plug in her backside sent odd nerves tap-dancing from her bottom all the way to her spine. Under his slow, determined stroking, her clit swelled until it felt like an overripe melon just waiting to split. She closed her eyes. *Oh God.*

"Please," she whispered. "Dammit, Marcus..."

"Not there yet," he murmured, and his finger circled her entrance. The anal plug pressed against her vagina as he pushed his finger into the compressed space. Too tight. Her insides pulsed around the new intrusion, the feeling incredibly intense.

His finger pressed, rubbed against something inside her vagina, and she felt the pulsing start to expand. Ruthlessly he licked her clit and stroked inside her, pushing her higher and higher until all she could think about was the next touch of his tongue, the next slide of his finger.

He stopped. His finger slid out, leaving her empty and throbbing.

"Say 'I love you, Master.'" he repeated, not lifting his head. His warm breath brushed over her excruciatingly sensitive tissues.

She couldn't think, couldn't feel anything except his lips barely brushing her clit. "Damn you," she moaned. *Bastard, jerk, putz.* "I love you," and she did. But still—master?—*asshole*, only he'd gotten revenge for her calling him that, and now her anus throbbed in time with her pussy—"Master. Oh, pleeeeease..."

He didn't move. She opened her eyes.

His face was still, his clear blue eyes intent. "I believe master sounds just right...when *you* say it," he mused, almost to himself. Then he smiled at her. "Very nice, Gabrielle." His lips closed over her clit even as he thrust two fingers into her—*two*—stretching her.

She gasped at the exquisite blast of sensation.

One tiny pause and then he sucked strongly on her clit, and his fingers pressed deeper.

Everything inside her burst. Fireworks of searing pleasure exploded in her core, rocketing upward, outward until it seemed even her hair and fingernails tingled.

He kept her going, gently but implacably, coaxing the last few shudders from her. Her heart hammered in her ears so loudly she couldn't hear herself gasping for breath.

When he sat back on his knees, satisfaction showed in his smile and eyes.

Dammit, she'd begged. Called him "Master." Wasn't she planning to show him how much of a problem she'd be? Not cave in, for heaven's sake. He was too good at this stuff. Sneaky lawyer. "Let me go now. You got what you wanted," she grumped.

"Oh, not even close, little subbie. You're not even close to convinced yet," he said, and the feeling of his strong hands gripping her thighs made her jerk. His thumbs pulled her labia apart. He looked and smiled at her. "Nice and pink and wet, the way I like it. Now say 'I love you, Master' again."

What was this? "Dream on. I'm not into the master stuff." Why couldn't she think of something nasty to say? Where had her inner brat gone, dammit?

"I see." He unhurriedly unzipped his jeans, and his shaft sprang out. Maybe a little over average thickness, but long—long enough it had given her a few bad moments. With slow movements, he covered himself in a condom, his eyes pinning hers. "I reckon you'll come to see it my way after we ...discuss...this further."

Smiling, he pushed inside her, an infinitely wonderful slide of flesh against flesh, filling her...and filling her... She started to squirm against the overly full feeling as the anal plug and his cock fought for space.

When she whimpered, he slowed but kept advancing, his gaze on her eyes, her mouth, her shoulders. "Easy, sugar. You can take me—and you will." He stopped when he was embedded deep inside her.

So full. Tiny spasms sent sparks zipping over her nerves.

His fingertips grazed over her cheek. "So pink and flushed," he murmured, holding her gaze with the sheer power of his. The world shifted sideways, and she shook at the feeling of being possessed, inside and outside. She stared up at him helplessly.

His gaze gentled, and he rubbed his cheek against hers. "Yes, little sub, today you will give me everything."

He leaned forward, his weight on one arm, and started thrusting in a hard, driving rhythm. He took her mouth, deeply, sweetly, never slackening.

To her surprise, her own arousal started to climb, and she moaned. How did he do this to her? Would she ever get enough of him?

As if he felt her response, he pulled back enough to smile down at her. "I love you, Gabrielle," he murmured, and before she could react, he reached down between them and slid his fingers slickly over and around her clit.

"Oh God." She hadn't been ready, but she exploded anyway, her hips bucking against his. The waves this time were less intense but rolled through her over and over until the air itself thickened and she could only arch and ride the pleasure out.

Eventually her breathing slowed. A fine sweat coated her body, and she tasted salt on her lips. Each beat of her heart pulsed against the plug, against his hard cock.

He was hard?

Keeping his groin pressed against hers, he pushed to a kneeling position. "Say 'I love you, Master' again."

She gave a huff of disgust, feeling as if she'd run a marathon. Her mind had hazed. "I thought we had this discussion."

He chuckled. "I'm yet in the mood to discuss it."

Oh, God, he hadn't gotten off. Her body seemed to be sinking down into the mattress, and he was still hard.

He pulled his toy bag closer and came out with...dammit, nipple clamps.

She jerked, pulling at the restraints uselessly, and only succeeded in shoving his cock against the anal plug inside her. Her vagina spasmed again, the surge of pleasure intense enough to make her gasp. Somehow her body didn't seem like her own anymore.

He stroked over her nipples and sighed. "I fear you're all soft now that you've come. I'll have to fix that first." With a wicked smile, he leaned forward and licked her left nipple, then took it in his mouth and sucked. Gently, and then more powerfully, until she actually felt blood surging into it. Each suck pulled at something in her groin. He let go. "Aren't you pretty now?" He touched a finger to the dark red, firmly bunched peak.

He rubbed it dry and fastened on a clamp, watching her closely as he tightened it, then tightened it more until the slight bite of pain became a throbbing pressure.

"It hurts," she objected, making his cheek crease with a smile. He flicked her nipple. She yelped, and her insides spasmed around his cock.

From his chuckle, he'd enjoyed the sensation. "I'd say it's just right." He teased her other nipple into hardness and applied the second one. Then, to her dismay, he attached a pea-sized weight to the dangling chains. The weights bounced at her sides, a steady painful pulling against the clamps.

Her hands tried to reach her breasts, and she groaned with

frustration. Her nipples hurt and burned...yet she was getting aroused again, maybe because with every movement the thing in her butt reminded her it was there, and his cock...

He dropped forward onto his uninjured arm and eased his cock out. In. She moaned at the long, slick slide of him, how he pressed against the anal plug with every thrust. Tingles danced in feather touches over her skin, and blood started pooling low in her belly.

She stared at the door, at escape—and knew she didn't want to leave. Ever. She had the feeling of being over a cliff, hanging on with just her fingertips.

Callused fingers on her cheek turned her face back to his. He studied her face slowly, making it clear that there was nothing she could hide from him.

"Why are you doing this?" she whispered. "Is this punishment?"

"Sugar, I don't think getting a sub off punishes her." His eyes never lessened in their intensity. "But it can teach her something."

To her shock, he moved faster, and with each slamming thrust, the weights hanging from her nipples swung, pulling painfully. The twinges shot straight to her clit until she desperately needed to come again, and there was no way she possibly could.

Marcus saw the disbelief in her eyes as her body spiked from arousal into clawing need. With each swing of her nipple clamps, her vagina contracted around him, threatening his control. Before his own demand became critical, he reached between them to her tender little clit, already well on its way to hardness again. He found the firmness under the soft, slick tissue, and he rubbed until the nub stood up—and damn, the feel of it almost sent him over. He stroked harder, faster, knowing she'd need more stimulation this time, after she'd already gotten off twice. Her muscles went taut. She panted, her head rolling back and forth as if she could deny her own body's response.

She probably could, he realized. She'd ignore what she needed because the admission would make her feel she was less than perfect. Well, he'd work on that also. For now, he twisted his hand sideways enough to catch her clit between his thumb and fingers and pinched it gently with each thrust. With the rhythm and pressure, her body tightened until she stopped breathing, holding rigidly still.

The pinnacle. He squeezed a tad harder, and she came with such a scream that he was glad he'd shut the balcony door. She shuddered, and the convulsing of her pussy around his cock almost took him with her.

He could spend a lifetime fucking her and count himself happy.

She blinked at him with glazed eyes. "Are you insane?"

He'd pushed himself back on his knees to talk. Now he pinched her clit in response to the rudeness. She squeaked, and her vagina spasmed again, making him smile. "Do you want clamps on your clit?" he asked softly.

Her eyes widened, and if she could have retreated through the wall, she would have. He chuckled and ordered again, "Say 'I love you, Master.'"

She started to automatically sass, and he moved slightly. Still hard. Her mouth fell open. "You..." She shut her mouth quickly, obviously realizing his hand rested on her clit. "Why are you doing this?"

Because you need to know that I'll love you even when you fight me. But telling her wouldn't do anything. She needed to know it, down at gut level. "Say 'I love you, Master.'"

Her mouth shut, her chin in an adorable stubborn set.

"No?" He sighed. "You're proving to be right difficult." Which was why he'd saved this for last. He put his hand between her ass cheeks and flipped the control on the butt plug.

What was he...? The plug in her ass came to life. Gabi already felt stuffed full, and now that thing vibrated inside her, sending every nerve into spasms. "Oh no no no."

"Oh yes, little brat," he said softly. "I do enjoy the challenge, darlin', and I can see we're going to have a lot of fun." His eyes danced with laughter and passion as he leaned forward and took her mouth, hard and possessively.

He started to move. Everything had already heated up inside her; the vibrations in her back hole shimmered to her vagina and now mixed with the unbelievably erotic slide of his cock. Her hands clenched around the ropes as he sped up, really, really hammering into her, and she realized how much he'd held back before. Each thrust sent the weights on the breast clamps spinning. It felt as if someone was tugging on her nipples, each small jolt merging into the strange, disconcerting vibrations. Sensations rushed through her, tumbling her as if she'd been caught in a raging surf.

Her vagina tightened. Her thighs tightened. Her whole body tightened.

He didn't make her wait. He simply angled his cock differently. With each short, hard stroke, he ground his pelvis against her clit. She soared higher. The edges of her vision blurred, leaving only his blue eyes staring into hers, not releasing her, keeping her with him. Against the rushing in her ears, she heard him drawl, "I love you, Gabrielle."

With a low groan, he pushed in so far she felt him slam into her cervix. His cock jerked as he came and somehow merged with the vibrations in her ass and the pressing of his groin against her clit. Her climax blew over her like a hurricane, sweeping her up and destroying any defenses she had remaining. Pleasure battered her, her body completely at its mercy. At his mercy.

When he pulled out of her, he set off more spasms, and more again with the removal of the plug. The sharp pain of the clamps being released sent her into another orgasm.

He had removed the wrist and ankle cuffs before her

breathing slowed. Her mind felt full of gauzy clouds, and if someone had asked her to get off the bed, she'd have cursed them. If she could have found her tongue.

When Marcus lay beside her and took her in his arms, it was the most wonderful feeling she'd ever known. Her body had tumbled away with the surf, but he found her, kept her afloat. "You look a tad lost, sweetheart," he said, his amusement so obvious, she wanted to hit him.

And hold him. And stay there forever.

"I love you," she whispered, and if it sounded a little blurry, he still understood. His arm tightened around her.

"More."

"I love you, Master. You asshole."

With her head on his chest, she heard his laughter rumble upward and burst out, deep and rich, reminding her of the first hint she'd had that he was much, much more than Mr. Perfection. He pressed a kiss to the top of her head, and she gave a sigh of sheer contentment.

A second later, his fingers tilted her chin, forcing her to look into intense blue eyes as he said, "I love you, Gabrielle, and you are mine. We will be together, sugar." His lips curved. "If your brattiness bothers me, I think you know now that I can—and will—simply fuck it right out of you."

His lesson. He'd done all this to push her into defying him—and to show her how much he enjoyed the challenge. The knowledge shook something deep inside her.

Eyes steady on hers, he waited.

Oh, she couldn't hide anything from him, and with the knowledge, she surrendered completely. Her eyes filled with tears.

He caressed her cheek, murmuring, "There we go. My little brat."

"I really do love you." God, she really, really did. And she wanted everything he'd said—to live with him, to play with him.

He loves me – he likes *me*. Heart overflowing, she kissed him as sweetly as any master might want.

With a low laugh, he rolled on top of her and took a kiss that left hers in the dust.

When he pulled back, he rubbed his cheek against hers. *My big cat*. "I think there's a glass of wine calling. And perhaps a balcony with some animals to watch." The sun lines at the corners of his eyes crinkled. "If you can behave yourself, of course. Otherwise we can stay in here."

She glared, then took a breath and said, "I'll behave," so sweetly that his eyes narrowed.

And she would too because if she had another orgasm today, it might just kill her. But tomorrow...

Where did I put that list of insults?

ALSO BY CHERISE SINCLAIR

Masters of the Shadowlands Series

Club Shadowlands

Dark Citadel

Breaking Free

Lean on Me

Make Me, Sir

To Command and Collar

This Is Who I Am

If Only

Show Me, Baby

Servicing the Target

Protecting His Own

Mischief and the Masters

Beneath the Scars

Defiance

The Effing List

Mountain Masters & Dark Haven Series

Master of the Mountain

Simon Says: Mine

Master of the Abyss

Master of the Dark Side

My Liege of Dark Haven

Edge of the Enforcer

Master of Freedom

Master of Solitude

I Will Not Beg

The Wild Hunt Legacy

Hour of the Lion

Winter of the Wolf

Eventide of the Bear

Leap of the Lion

Healing of the Wolf

Heart of the Wolf

Sons of the Survivalist Series

Not a Hero

Lethal Balance

What You See

Soar High

Standalone Books

The Dom's Dungeon

The Starlight Rite

ABOUT THE AUTHOR

Cherise Sinclair is a *New York Times* and *USA Today* bestselling author of emotional, suspenseful romance. She loves to match up devastatingly powerful males with heroines who can hold their own against the subtle—and not-so-subtle—alpha male pressure.

Fledglings having flown the nest, Cherise, her beloved husband, an eighty-pound lap-puppy, and one fussy feline live in the Pacific Northwest where nothing is cozier than a rainy day spent writing.

Printed in Great Britain
by Amazon